By Timothy Zahn

THE
ICARUS HUNT

TIMOTHY ZAHN

BANTAM BOOKS
NEW YORK • TORONTO • LONDON • SYDNEY • AUCKLAND

This edition contains the complete text
of the original hardcover edition.
NOT ONE WORD HAS BEEN OMITTED.

THE ICARUS HUNT

PUBLISHING HISTORY
Bantam Spectra hardcover edition published August 1999
Bantam Spectra paperback edition / July 2000

SPECTRA and the portrayal of a boxed "s" are trademarks of
Bantam Books, a division of Random House, Inc.

ISBN 0-553-57391-8

Published simultaneously in the United States and Canada

Bantam Books are published by Bantam Books, a division of
Random House, Inc. Its trademark, consisting of the words "Bantam
Books" and the portrayal of a rooster, is Registered in U.S. Patent
and Trademark Office and in other countries. Marca Registrada.
Bantam Books, 1540 Broadway, New York, New York 10036.

PRINTED IN THE UNITED STATES OF AMERICA

OPM   10   9   8   7   6   5   4   3   2   1

CHAPTER

1

They were waiting as I stepped through the door into the taverno: three of them, preadult Yavanni, roughly the size of Brahma bulls, looming over me from both sides of the entryway. Big, eager-eyed, and territorial, they were on the prowl and looking for an excuse to squash something soft.

From all indications, it looked like that something was going to be me.

I stopped short just inside the door, and as it swung closed against my back I caught a faint whiff of turpentine from the direction of my would-be assailants. Which meant that along with being young and brash, they were also tanked to the briskets. I was still outside the invisible boundary of the personal territories they'd staked out for themselves in the entryway; and if I had any brains, I'd keep it that way. Yavanni aren't very bright even at the best of times, but when you're outweighed by two to one and outnumbered by three to one, brainpower ratio isn't likely to be the deciding factor. It had been a long day and a longer evening, I was tired and cranky, and the smartest thing I could do right now was get hold of the doorknob digging into my back and get out of there.

I looked past the Yavanni into the main part of the taverno. The place was pretty crowded, with both humans and a representative distribution of other species sitting around the fashionably darkened interior. It was likely to stay well populated, too, at least as long as anyone who tried to leave had to pass the three mobile mountains waiting at the door. A fair percentage of the clientele, I could see, was surreptitiously watching the little drama about to unfold, while the rest were studiously ignoring it. None of either group looked eager to leap to my defense should that become necessary. The two bartenders were watching me more openly, but there would be no help from that direction, either. This section of the spaceport environs lay in Meima's Vyssiluyan enclave, and the Vyssiluyas were notoriously laissez-faire where disputes of this sort were concerned. The local police would gladly and industriously pick up the pieces after it was all over, but that wasn't going to be much comfort if I wound up being one of those pieces.

I looked back at the Yavanni flanking my path, one a little way ahead and to my left, the other two to my right. They still hadn't moved, but I had the mental picture of coiled springs being tightened a couple more turns. I hadn't run, didn't look like I was going to run, and their small minds were simmering in eager anticipation of the moment when I put a foot across that invisible barrier and they got to see how many colors of bruises they could raise on me.

I wasn't armed, at least not seriously. Even if I had been, blasting away from close range at three full-size Yavanni was not a recommended procedure for anyone desiring a long and happy life. But there was a trick I'd heard about a few years ago, a nice little combination of Yavannian psychology and physiology that I'd tucked away for possible future reference. It looked, as the saying went, like the future was now. Gazing at each of the Yavanni in turn, I cleared my throat. "Do your mothers know you boys are here?" I demanded in the deepest voice I could manage.

Three jaws dropped in unison. "It's late," I continued before they could respond. "You should be home. Go home. Now."

They looked at each other, their earlier anticipation floundering in confusion. Talking like a Yavannian dominant male was probably the last response they'd expected from an alien half their size, and the molasses they used for brains was having trouble adjusting to the situation. "Did you hear me?" I snapped, putting some anger into my voice. "Go home."

The one on the left apparently had faster molasses than the other two. "You are not Yavannian," he snarled back at me in typically Yavannian-mangled English. A fresh wave of turpentine smell accompanied the words. "You will not speak to us that way." Paws flexing, he took a step toward me—

And I opened my mouth and let out a warbling, blood-freezing howl.

He froze in place, his alien face abruptly stricken as his glacial brain caught up with his fatal error. I was stationary and he was moving, which meant *he* had now violated *my* territory. I was the injured party, I had given out with the proper Yavannian accusation/indictment/challenge shout, and I was now entitled to the first punch.

By and by, of course, he would remember that I wasn't a Yavanne and therefore not entitled to the courtesy of Yavannian customs. I had no intention of giving that thought time to percolate through. Taking a long step toward him, I tightened my hands into fists and drove both of them hard into his lower torso, into the slight depressions on either side of the central muscle ridge.

He gave a forlorn sort of squeak—a startling sound from a creature his size—and went down with a highly satisfying thud that must have shaken the whole taverno. Curled around himself, he lay still.

The other two were still standing there, staring at me with their jaws hanging loosely. I wasn't fooled—flabbergasted or not, they were still in territorial mode, and the minute I stepped onto either's chosen section of floor I would get mauled. Fortunately, that was no longer a problem. The left side of the entryway was now free territory; stepping over the downed Yavanne, I passed through the entryway and into the taverno.

There was a small ripple of almost-applause, which quickly evaporated as those involved belatedly remembered that there were still two Yavanni left on their feet. I wasn't expecting any more trouble from them myself, but just the same I kept an eye on their reflection in the brass chandelier domes as I made my way through the maze of tables and chairs. There was an empty table in the back, comfortably close to the homey log fireplace that dominated that wall, and I sat down with my back to the crackling flames. As I did so, I was just in time to see the two undamaged Yavanni help their unsteady colleague out into the night.

"Buy you a drink, sir?"

I turned my head. A medium-sized man with dark skin stood in the dim light to the right of my table, a half-full mug in his hand, a thick thatch of white hair shimmering in the firelight. "I'm not interested in company right now," I said, punching up a small vodkaline on the table's menu selector. I wasn't interested in drinking, either, but that little fracas with the Yavanni had drawn enough attention to me as it was, and sitting there without a glass in my hand would only invite more curiosity.

"I appreciate what you did over there," the man commented, pulling out the chair opposite me and sitting down as if he'd been invited to do so. "I've been stuck here half an hour waiting for them to go away. Bit of a risky move, though, wasn't it? At the very least, you could have broken a couple of knuckles."

For a moment I gazed across the table at him, at that dark face beneath that shock of white hair. From the age lines in his skin he clearly had spent a lot of his life out in the sun; from the shape of the musculature beneath his jacket he hadn't spent that time lounging around in beach chairs. "Not all that risky," I told him. "Yavanni don't get that really thick skin of theirs until adulthood. Kids that age are still pretty soft in spots. You just have to know where those spots are."

He nodded, eyes dropping momentarily to the ship patch with its stylized "SB" on the shoulder of my faded black-leather jacket. "You deal a lot with aliens?"

"A fair amount," I said. "My partner's one, if that helps any."

"What do you mean, if it helps any?"

The center of the table opened up and my vodkaline appeared. "If it helps you make up your mind," I amplified, taking the glass off the tray. "About offering me a cargo."

A flicker of surprise crossed his face, but then he smiled. "You're quick," he said. "I like that. I take it you're an independent shipper?"

"That's right." I wasn't all that independent, actually, not anymore. But this wasn't the right time to bring that up. "My name's Jordan McKell. I'm captain of a Capricorn-class freighter called the *Stormy Banks*."

"Specialty certificates?"

"Navigation and close-order piloting," I said. "My partner Ixil is certified in both drive and mechanical systems."

"Actually, I won't be needing your partner." He cocked an eyebrow. "Or your ship, for that matter."

"That makes sense," I said, trying not to sound too

sarcastic. "What exactly *do* you need—a fourth for bridge?"

He leaned a little closer to me across the table. "I already have a ship," he said, his voice dropping to a murmur. "It's sitting at the spaceport, fueled and cargoed and ready to go. All I need is a crew to fly her."

"Interesting trick," I complimented him. "Getting a ship here without a crew, I mean."

His lips compressed. "I had a crew yesterday. They jumped ship this morning after we landed for refueling."

"Why?"

He waved a hand. "Personality conflicts, factional disputes—that sort of thing. Apparently, both factions decided to jump without realizing the other side was going to, too. Anyway, that doesn't matter. What matters is that I'm not going to make my schedule unless I get some help together, and quickly."

I leaned back in my chair and favored him with a sly smile. "So in other words, you're basically stuck here. How very inconvenient for you. What kind of ship are we talking about?"

"It's the equivalent of an Orion-class," he said, looking like a man suddenly noticing a bad taste in his mouth. Revising his earlier estimate of me downward, no doubt, as his estimate of how much money I was going to try to squeeze out of him went the opposite direction. "Not a standard Orion, you understand, but similar in size and—"

"You need a minimum of six crewers, then," I said. "Three each certified competent in bridge and engine-room operations. All eight specialty certificates represented: navigation, piloting, electronics, mechanics, computer, drive, hull/spacewalk, and medical."

"I see you're well versed in the Mercantile Code."

"Part of my job," I said. "As I said, I can cover nav and piloting. How many of the rest are you missing?"

He smiled crookedly. "Why? You have some friends who need work?"

"I might. What do you need?"

"I appreciate the offer." He was still smiling, but the laugh lines had hardened a bit. "But I'd prefer to choose my own crew."

I shrugged. "Fine by me. I was just trying to save you a little running around. What about me personally? Am I in?"

He eyed me another couple of heartbeats. "If you want the job," he said at last, not sounding entirely happy with the decision.

Deliberately, I turned my head a few degrees to the left and looked at a trio of gray-robed Patthaaunutth sitting at the center of the bar, gazing haughtily out at the rest of the patrons like self-proclaimed lords surveying their private demesne. "Were you expecting me to turn you down?" I asked, hearing the edge of bitterness in my voice.

He followed my gaze, lifting his mug for a sip, and even out of the corner of my eye I could see him wince a little behind the rim of the cup. "No," he said quietly. "I suppose not."

I nodded silently. The Talariac Drive had hit the trade routes of the Spiral a little over fifteen years ago, and in that brief time the Patth had gone from being a third-rate race of Machiavellian little connivers to near domination of shipping here in our cozy corner of the galaxy. Hardly a surprise, of course: with the Talariac four times faster and three times cheaper than anyone else's stardrive, it didn't take a corporate genius to figure out which ships were the ones to hire.

Which had left the rest of us between a very big rock and a very hard vacuum. There were still a fair number of smaller routes and some overflow traffic that the Patth hadn't gotten around to yet, but there were too many non-Patth ships chasing too few jobs and the resulting economic chaos had been devastating. A few of the big shipping corporations were still hanging on, but most of the independents had been either starved out of business or reduced to intrasystem shipping, where stardrives weren't necessary.

Or had turned their ships to other, less virtuous lines of work.

One of the Patth at the table turned his head slightly, and from beneath his hood I caught a glint of the electronic implants set into that gaunt, mahogany-red face. The Patth had a good thing going, all right, and they had no intention of losing it. Patth starships were individually keyed to their respective pilots, with small but crucial bits of the Talariac access circuitry and visual display feedback systems implanted into the pilot's body. There'd been some misgivings about that when the system first hit the Spiral—shipping execs had worried that an injury to the Patth pilot en route could strand their valuable cargo out in the middle of nowhere, and there was a lot of nowhere out there to lose something as small as a starship in. The Patth had countered by adding one or two backup pilots to each ship, which had lowered the risk of accident without compromising the shroud of secrecy they were determined to keep around the Talariac. Without the circuitry implanted in its pilot—and with a whole raft of other safeguards built into the hardware of the drive itself—borrowing or stealing a Patth ship would gain you exactly zero information.

Or so the reasoning went. The fact that no bootleg copies of the Talariac had yet appeared anywhere on the market tended to support that theory.

The man across from me set his mug back down on the table with a slightly impatient-sounding clunk. Turning my eyes and thoughts away from the hooded Patth, I got back to business. "What time do you want to leave?"

"As early as possible," he said. "Say, six tomorrow morning."

I thought about that. Meima was an Ihmis colony world, and one of the peculiarities of Ihmisit-run spaceports was that shippers weren't allowed inside the port between sundown and sunup, with the entire port sealed during those hours. Alien-psychology experts usually attributed this to some quirk of Ihmis superstition; I personally put it down to the healthy hotel business the policy generated at the spaceport's periphery. "Sunrise tomorrow's not until five-thirty," I pointed out. "Doesn't leave much time for preflight checks."

"The ship's all ready to go," he reminded me.

"We check it anyway before we fly," I told him. "That's what 'preflight' means. What about clearances?"

"All set," he said, tapping his tunic. "I've got the papers right here."

"Let me see them."

He shook his head. "That's not necessary. I'll be aboard well before—"

"Let me see them."

For a second he had the expression of someone who was seriously considering standing up and going to look for a pilot with a better grasp of the proper servility involved in an owner/employee relationship. But he merely dug into his inside jacket pocket and pulled out a thin stack of cards. Maybe he liked my spirit, or maybe he was just running out of time to find someone to fly his ship for him.

I leafed through them. The papers were for a modified Orion-class freighter called the *Icarus,* Earth registry, mastership listed as one Alexander Borodin. They were also copies, not the originals he'd implied he was carrying. "You Borodin?" I asked.

"That's right," he said. "As you see, everything's in order for a morning lift."

"Certainly looks that way," I agreed. All the required checks had been done: engine room, thrusters and stardrive, computer, cargo customs—

I frowned. "What's this 'sealed cargo section' business?"

"Just what it says," he told me. "The cargo hold is situated in the aft-center section of the ship, and was sealed on Gamm against all entry or inspection. The Gamm port authority license is there."

"Came in from Gamm, did you?" I commented, finding the license on the next card down. "Quiet little place."

"Yes. A bit primitive, though."

"It is that," I agreed, stacking the cards together again. I glanced at the top card again, making careful note of the lift and clearance codes that had been assigned to the *Icarus,* and handed them back across the table. "All right, you've got yourself a captain. What's the up-front pay?"

"One thousand commarks," he said. "Payable on your arrival at the ship in the morning. Another two thousand once we make Earth. It's all I can afford," he added, a bit defensively.

Three thousand in all, for a job that would probably take five or six weeks to complete. I certainly wasn't going to get rich on that kind of pay, but I probably wouldn't starve, either. Provided he picked up the fuel and port duty fees along the way, of course. For a moment I thought about trying to bargain him up, but the look on his face implied it would be a waste of time. "Fine," I said. "You have a tag for me?"

"Right here," he said, rummaging around inside his jacket again, his expression twitching briefly with surprise that I had not, in fact, tried to squeeze him for more money as he'd obviously expected me to do. Briefly, I wondered which direction that had moved his opinion of me, but gave up the exercise as both unprofitable and irrelevant.

His probing hand found what it was looking for, and emerged holding a three-by-seven-centimeter plastic tag covered with colored dots. Another Ihmis quirk, this one their refusal to number or in any other way differentiate the two hundred-odd landing squares at their spaceport. The only way to find a particular ship—or a particular service center or customs office or supply depot, for that matter—was to have one of these handy little tags on you. Slid into the transparent ID slot in a landing jacket collar, the tag's dot code would be read by sensors set up at each intersection, whereupon walk-mounted guidelights would point the befuddled wearer in the proper direction. It made for rather protracted travel sometimes, but the Ihmisits liked it and it wasn't much more than a minor inconvenience for anyone else. My assumption had always been that someone's brother-in-law owned the tagmaking concession. "Anything else you need to know?"

I cocked an eyebrow at him as I slid the tag into my collar slot in front of the one keyed to guide me back to the *Stormy Banks*. "Why? You in a hurry?"

"I have one or two other things yet to do tonight, yes," he said as he set down his cup and stood up. "Good evening, Captain McKell. I'll see you tomorrow morning."

"I'll be there." I nodded.

He nodded back and headed across the taverno, maneuvering through the maze of tables and the occasional wandering customer, and disappeared through the door. I took a sip of my vodkaline, counted to twenty, and headed off after him.

I didn't want to look like I was hurrying, and as a result it took me maybe half a minute longer to get across the taverno than it had taken him. But that was all right. There were a lot of spacers roaming the streets out there, but the overhead lights outside were pretty good, and with all that white hair he should be easy enough to spot and follow. Pushing open the door, I stepped out into the cool night air.

I had forgotten about the Yavanni. They hadn't forgotten about me.

They were waiting near the entrance, partly concealed behind one of the decorative glass entryway windbreaks that stuck a meter outward from the wall on either side of the door itself. Recognizing a particular alien is always a dicey proposition, but obviously this bunch had mastered the technique. Even as I stepped out from the shelter of the windbreaks, they began moving purposefully toward me, the one in front showing a noticeable forward slouch.

I had to do something, and I had to do it fast. They'd abandoned their previous territorial game—that much was obvious from the way they bunched together as they moved confidently toward me. I'd shamed them in front of the whole taverno, and what they undoubtedly had in mind was a complete demonstration as to why that had been a bad decision on my part. I thought about digging inside my jacket for my gun, realized instantly that any such move would be suicide; thought about ducking back into the taverno, realized that would do nothing but postpone the confrontation.

Which left me only one real option. Bracing myself, I took a quick step partway back into the windbreak, turned ninety degrees to my left, and kicked backward as hard as I could with my right foot.

In most other places windbreaks like these were made out of a highly resilient plastic. The Vyssiluyas preferred glass—tough glass, to be sure, but glass nonetheless. With three angry Yavanni lumbering toward me I was understandably in no mood for half measures, and the force of the kick seemed to shoot straight through my spine to the top of my head. But I achieved the desired result: the glass panel blew out, scattering a hundred pieces across the landscape.

I caught my balance and jumped backward through the now mostly empty box frame. A large wedge of jagged glass that was still hanging tentatively onto the side of the frame scraped at my jacket as I went through. Trying to avoid slicing my fingers on the edges, I got a grip on it and broke it free. Brandishing it like a makeshift knife, I jabbed at the Yavanni.

The Yavanne in front stopped short, generating a brief bit of vaguely comedic confusion as the other two bumped into him. For all their bulk and aggressiveness, Yavanni are remarkably sensitive to the sight of their own blood, and the thought of charging into a knife or knifelike instrument can give even the hardiest a moment of pause. But only a moment. Like most other unpleasantries, anticipation is often worse than the actual event, and as soon as their molasses minds remembered that they'd be all over me.

But I wasn't planning to be here when that happened. With the windbreak gone and the Yavanni bunched together, I now had a completely clear exit route at my back. Flipping my shard of glass at the lead Yavanne, I turned and ran for it.

I got only a couple of steps before they set up a startled howl and lurched into gear after me. They'd eventually get me, too—in a long straightaway human legs couldn't outmatch Yavannian ones. But for the first few seconds, until they got all that body mass moving, I had the advantage. All I had to do was find something to do with it.

I knew better than to waste time looking over my shoulder, but I could tell from the sounds of their foot thuds that I still had a reasonably good lead when I reached the corner of the taverno and swung around into the narrow pedestrian alleyway separating it from the next building over. An empty alleyway, unfortunately, without what I'd hoped to find there. The Yavanni hove around the corner; lowering my head, I put all my effort into getting every drop of speed I could out of my legs. They would probably get me, I knew, before I could circle the building completely. If what I was looking for wasn't around back, I was going to be in for some serious pain.

I rounded the next corner with the Yavanni uncomfortably close behind me. And there it was, just as I'd hoped to find it: a pile of half-meter-long logs for the taverno's big fireplace, neatly stacked against the wall and reaching nearly to the eaves of the roof. Without slowing my pace, I headed up.

I nearly didn't make it. The Yavanni were right on my heels and going far too fast to stop, and their big feet slammed into the logs like bowling disks hitting the pins. The whole pile went rippling down behind me, and if I'd been a fraction of a second slower I'd have gone down right along with it. As it was, I came within an ace of missing my flying leap upward at the eaves when my takeoff log bobbled under my feet and robbed me of some hard-earned momentum. But I made it and got the desired grip, and a second later had hauled myself over the edge and onto the roof.

Not any too soon, either. I was just swinging my legs up over the edge when one of the logs came whistling up past the eaves to disappear into the night sky. My playmates below, proving themselves to be sore losers. I didn't know whether Yavanni were good enough jumpers to get to the roof without the aid of the woodpile they'd just demolished, but I had no particular desire to find out the hard way. Keeping my head down—there were plenty more logs where that first one had come from—I got my feet under me and headed across the roof.

All the buildings in this section of the spaceport periphery were reasonably uniform in height, with only those narrow alleys separating them. With a little momentum, a gentle tailwind, and the inspirational mental image of irritated Yavanni behind me I made it across the gap to the next rooftop with half a meter to spare. I angled across that one, did a more marginal leap to the building abutting against its back, and kept going. Along the way I managed to get out of my jacket and turn it inside out, replacing the black leather with an obnoxiously loud paisley lining that I'd had put in for just this sort of circumstance. Aiming for a building with smoke curling out of its chimney, I located its woodpile and made my way down.

The Yavanni were nowhere to be seen when I reentered the main thoroughfare and the wandering groups of spacers, townspeople, come-ons, and pickpockets.

Unfortunately, neither was the white-haired man I'd been hoping to follow.

I poked around the area for another hour, popping in and out of a few more tavernos and dives on the assumption that my new employer might still be trolling for crewers. But I didn't see him anywhere; and the spaceport periphery was far too big for a one-man search. Besides, my leg was aching from that kick to the windbreak, and I needed to be at the spaceport when it opened at five-thirty.

The Vyssiluyas ran a decent autocab service in their part of the periphery, but that thousand commarks I'd been promised weren't due until I showed up at the *Icarus*, and the oversize manager of the slightly seedy hotel where Ixil and I were staying would be very unhappy if we didn't have the necessary cash to pay the bill in the morning. Reluctantly, I decided that two arguments with large aliens in the same twelve-hour period would be pushing it, and headed back on foot.

My leg was hurting all the way up to my skull by the time I finished the last of the four flights of stairs and slid my key into the slot beside the door. With visions of a soft bed, gently pulsating Vyssiluyan relaxation lights, and a glass of Scotch dancing with the ache behind my forehead, I pushed open the door and stepped inside.

The soft bed and Scotch were still a possibility. But the lights apparently weren't. The room was completely dark.

I went the rest of the way into the room in a half fall, half dive that sent me sprawling face first onto the floor as I yanked my plasmic out of its concealed holster under my left armpit. Ixil was supposed to be waiting here; and a darkened room could only mean that someone had taken him out and was lying in wait for me.

"Jordan?" a smooth and very familiar Kalixiri voice called from across the room. "Is that you?"

I felt the sudden surge of adrenaline turn into chagrined embarrassment and drain away through my aching leg where it could hurt some more on its way out. "I thought you'd still be up," I said blackly, resisting the urge to trot out some of the colorful language that had earned me a seat in front of that court-martial board so many years ago.

"I am up," he said. "Come take a look at this."

With an amazingly patient sigh, I clicked the safety back on my plasmic and slid the weapon back into its holster. With Ixil, the object of interest could be anything from a distant nebula he'd spotted through the haze of city lights to an interesting glow-in-the-dark spider crawling across the window. "Be right there," I grunted. Hauling myself to my feet, I kicked the door closed and rounded the half wall into the main part of the room.

For most people, I suppose, Ixil and his ilk would be considered as much a visual nightmare as the charming Yavanni lads I'd left back at the taverno. He was a typical Kalix: squat, broad-shouldered, with a face that had more than once been unflatteringly compared to that of a squashed iguana.

And as he stood in silhouette against the window, I noticed that this particular Kalix was also decidedly asymmetric. One of those broad shoulders—the right one—appeared to be hunched up like a cartoonist's caricature of a muscle-bound throw-boxer, while the other was much flatter. "You're missing someone," I commented, tapping him on the flat shoulder.

"I sent Pix up onto the roof," Ixil said in that cultured Kalixiri voice that fits so badly with the species' rugged exterior. One of the last remaining simple pleasures in my life, in fact, was watching the reactions of people meeting him for the first time who up till then had only spoken with him on vidless starconnects. Some of those reactions were absolutely priceless.

"Did you, now," I said, circling around to his right side. As I did so, the lump on top of that shoulder twitched and uncurled itself, and a whiskered nose probed briefly into my ear. "Hello, Pax," I greeted it, reaching over to scritch the animal behind its mouse-like ear.

The Kalixiri name for the creatures was unpronounceable by human vocal apparatus, so I usually called them ferrets, which they did sort of resemble in their lean, furry way, though in size they weren't much bigger than laboratory rats. In the distant past, they had served as outriders for Kalixiri hunters, running ahead to locate prey and then returning to their masters with the information.

What distinguished them from dogs or grockners or any of a hundred other similar hunting partners was the unique symbiotic relationship between them and their Kalixiri masters. With Pax riding on Ixil's shoulder, his claws dug into the tough outer skin, Pax's nervous system was right now directly linked to Ixil's. Ixil could give him a mental order, which would download into Pax's limited brain capacity; and when he returned and reconnected, the download would go the opposite direction, letting Ixil see, hear, and smell everything the ferret had experienced during their time apart.

For Kalixiri hunters the advantages of the arrangement were obvious. For Ixil, a starship-engine mechanic, the ferrets were invaluable in dealing with wiring or tubing or anything else involving tight spaces or narrow conduits. If more of his people had taken an interest in going into offworld mechanical and electronic work, I'd often thought, the Kalixiri might well have taken over that field the same way the Patth had done with general shipping.

"So what on the roof do you expect to find interesting?" I asked, giving Pax another scritch and wondering for the millionth time whether Ixil got the same scritch through their neural link. He'd never commented about it, but that could just be Ixil.

"Not on the roof," Ixil said, lifting a massive arm. "Off of it. Over there."

I frowned where he was pointing. Off in the distance, beyond the buildings of the spaceport periphery and the more respectable city beyond it, was a gentle glow against the wispy clouds of the nighttime sky. As I watched, three thruster sparks lifted from the area and headed off horizontally in different directions. "Interesting," I said, watching one of the sparks. It was hard to tell, given our distance and perspective, but the craft seemed to be traveling remarkably slowly and zigzagging as it went.

"I noticed it about forty minutes ago," Ixil said. "I thought at first it was the reflected light from a new community that I simply hadn't seen before. But I checked the map, and there's nothing that direction except a row of hills and the wasteland region we flew over on our way in."

"Could it be a fire?" I suggested doubtfully.

"Unlikely," Ixil said. "The glow isn't red enough, and I've seen no evidence of smoke. I was wondering if it might be a search-and-rescue operation."

From the edge of the window came a gentle scrabbling sound; and with a soft rodent sneeze Pix appeared on the sill. A sinuous leap over to Ixil's arm, a quick scamper—with those claws digging for footholds the whole way up—and he was once again crouched in his place on Ixil's shoulder.

There was a tiny scratching sound like a fingernail on leather that always made me wince, and for a moment Ixil stood silently as he ran through the memories he was now pulling from the ferret's small brain. "Interesting," he said. "From the parallax, it appears to be considerably farther out than I first thought. Well beyond the hills, probably ten kilometers into the wilderness."

Which meant the glow was also a lot brighter than I'd thought. What could anyone want out there in the middle of nowhere?

My chest tightened, the ache in my leg suddenly forgotten. "You don't happen to know," I asked with studied casualness, "where exactly that archaeology dig is that the Cameron Group's been funding, do you?"

"Somewhere out in that wilderness," Ixil said. "I don't know the precise location."

"I do," I said. "I'll make you a small wager it's smack-dab in the middle of that glow."

"And why would you think that?"

"Because Arno Cameron himself was in town tonight. Offering me a job."

Ixil's squashed-iguana face turned to look at me. "You *are* joking."

"Afraid not," I assured him. "He was running under a ridiculous alias—Alexander Borodin, no less—and he'd dyed that black hair of his pure white, which made him look a good twenty years older. But it was him." I tapped my jacket collar. "He wants me to fly him out of here tomorrow morning in a ship called the *Icarus*."

"What did you tell him?"

"At three thousand commarks for the trip? I told him yes, of course."

Pix sneezed again. "This is going to be awkward," Ixil said; and then added what had to be the understatement of the week. "Brother John is not going to be pleased."

"No kidding," I agreed sourly. "When was the last time Brother John was pleased about *anything* we did?"

"Those instances have been rare," Ixil conceded. "Still, I doubt we've ever seen him as angry as he can get, either."

Unfortunately, he had a point. Johnston Scotto Ryland—the "Brother" honorific was pure sarcasm on our part—was the oh-so-generous benefactor who had bailed Ixil and me out of looming financial devastation three years ago by adding the *Stormy Banks* to his private collection of smuggling ships. Weapons, illegal body parts, interdicted drugs, stolen art, stolen electronics, every disgusting variety of happyjam imaginable—you name it, we'd probably carried it. In fact, we were on a job for him right now, with yet another of his secretive little cargoes tucked away in the *Stormy Banks*'s hold.

And Ixil was right. Brother John had not clawed his way up to his exalted position among the Spiral's worst scum peddlers by smiling and shrugging off sudden unilateral decisions by his subordinates.

"I'll square it with him," I promised Ixil, though how exactly I was going to do that I couldn't quite imagine at the moment. "It was three grand, after all. How was I supposed to turn that down and still keep up the facade that we're impoverished independent shippers?"

Ixil didn't react, but the ferrets on his shoulders gave simultaneous twitches. Sometimes that two-way neural link could be handy if you knew what to look for. "Anyway, there's no reason why Brother John should get warped out of shape over this," I went on. "You can take the *Stormy Banks* the rest of the way to Xathru by yourself. Then he can have his happyjam and guns and everybody can relax. I'll look at Cameron's flight path in the morning and leave you a message at Xathru as to where the most convenient place will be for you to catch up with us."

"Regulations require a minimum of two crewers for a Capricorn-class ship," he reminded me.

"Fine," I said shortly. It was late, my leg and head were hurting, and I was in no mood to hear the Mercantile Code being quoted at me. Especially not from the one who'd ultimately gotten me in this mess to begin with. "There's you, there's Pix, and there's Pax. That's three of you. The details you can work out with the Port Authority in the morning."

With that I stomped out of the living area—being careful to stomp on my good leg only—and went into the bath/dressing room. By the time I'd finished my bedtime preparations and rejoined Ixil I'd calmed down some. "Anything new?" I asked him.

He was still staring out the window, the two ferrets perched on his shoulders staring out right alongside him. "More aircraft seem to have joined in the activities," he said. "Something out there has definitely piqued someone's curiosity."

"Piqued and a half," I agreed, taking one last look and then heading for my bed. "I wonder what Cameron's people dug up out there."

"And who could be this interested in it," Ixil added, turning reluctantly away from the window himself. "It may be, Jordan, that our discussion of Brother John's cargo will turn out to be moot. You may reach the *Icarus* in the morning to find it already in someone's hands."

"Not a chance," I said, easing my aching leg gingerly under the blankets.

"And why not?"

I lay back onto a lumpy pillow. Yet another lumpy pillow, at yet another lumpy spaceport, in what seemed to be an increasingly lumpy life. "Because," I said with a sigh, "I'm not nearly that lucky."

CHAPTER

2

The sky to sunward was gaudy with splashes of pink and yellow when I arrived at the spaceport at five the next morning. A crowd of spacers, humans and aliens both, was already milling around the gates, most of them impatient to get to their ships and head out on the next leg of their journeys. A few of the more impatient were making the standard disparaging comments about Ihmis customs; the Ihmis door wardens standing watch by the gates as usual ignored them.

There were no Patth in the waiting group, of course. Over the past few years there had been enough of what the diplomats call "unpleasant incidents" around spaceports for most port authorities to assign Patth ships their own gates, service facilities, and waiting areas. Port authorities hate dealing with the paperwork associated with assault and murder, and planetary governments are even less interested in earning the sort of sanctions the Patth routinely dish out for any affront to their people, real or imagined.

Which, come to think about it, made the three Patth

I'd seen mixing with the common folk at the taverno last night something of an anomaly. Either they'd been young and brash, old and confident of local protection, or simply very thirsty. Distantly, I wondered if they'd run into any accidents on their way home.

At 5:31 the edge of the sun appeared over the horizon; and at that moment the gates unlocked and swung open. I joined the mass of beings flowing through, checking my collar once to make sure the tag Cameron had given me was still there. I hadn't spotted Cameron himself in the crowd, which either meant he was waiting at a different gate or that whoever had been searching his archaeological dig last night had already picked him up. Either way, I still planned to check out the *Icarus*, if only to see which species was standing guard over it.

A heavy, aromatic hand fell on my shoulder. "Captain Jordan McKell?"

I turned. Two of the Ihmis wardens had come unglued from their posts and were standing behind me, impressive and intimidating in their ceremonial helmets. "I'm McKell," I confirmed cautiously.

"Come with us, please," the Ihmisit with his hand still on my shoulder said. "Port Director Aymi-Mastr would like to speak to you."

"Sure," I said as casually as I could manage with a suddenly pounding heart as they gestured to the side and we worked our way across the pedestrian stream toward the Meima Port Authority building just inside the fence twenty meters away. Our papers were in order, our cargo cleared, our fees paid. Had someone finally backtracked one of Brother John's cargoes to the *Stormy Banks*? If so, we were going to have some very awkward explaining to do.

I'd never been in this particular Port Authority before, but I'd logged enough hours in Ihmis hotels and tavernos to have a pretty good idea what to expect. And I was mostly right. The friendly lighting, ex-

tremely casual furniture, and smiling faces were hall-
marks of the Ihmis style, all designed to put visitors at
their ease.

From what I'd heard, all those same friendly touches
remained cheerfully in place right up to the point when
they strapped you to the rack and started cranking.

"Ah—Captain McKell," a deep voice called as I was
led across the bustling main room to a large and clut-
tered desk in the corner. Director Aymi-Mastr was typical of the species, with bulging, froglike eyes, four
short insectoid antennae coming up from just above
those eyes, and costal ridges around the sides of the
face and neck. A female, of course; with Ihmisits the
females were generally the ones with the organizational
skills necessary to run a zoo like this. "Good of you to
drop by. Please sit down."

"My pleasure, Director," I said, sitting down in the
chair at the side of the desk, deciding to pass over the
fact that I hadn't had much choice in the matter. One
of the other Ihmisits set my bag on the desk and started
rifling through it; I thought about complaining, decided
against it. "What's this about?"

"To be perfectly honest, Captain, I'm not entirely
certain myself," she said, selecting a photo from the
top of a stack of report files and handing it to me. "A
message has come down from my superiors to ask you
about this person."

It was a picture of Arno Cameron.

"Well, he's a human," I offered helpfully. So it
wasn't Brother John's cargo they wanted after all. At
the moment I couldn't decide whether that was good or
bad. "Aside from that, I don't think I've ever seen him
before."

"Really," Aymi-Mastr said, dropping the pitch of
her voice melodramatically. She leaned back in her
chair and steepled her fingers in front of her—like the
melodramatic tone, an annoying habit many Ihmisits
had picked up from the old Earth movies they con-

sumed by the truckload. "That's very interesting. Particularly given that we heard from a witness not fifteen minutes ago who claims you were talking to him last night in a Vyssiluyan taverno."

A family of Kalixiri ferrets with very cold feet began running up and down my spine. "I hate to impugn the integrity of your witness," I said flatly, tossing the photo back onto the desk. "But he's wrong."

The frog eyes narrowed. "The witness was very specific about your name."

"Your witness was either drunk or a troublemaker," I said, standing up. That taverno had been crowded, and after my grandstand play against the three Yavanni there would be a dozen beings who would remember me, at least half of whom would probably also remember me talking with Cameron. I had to bluff my way out of here, and fast, before they started digging deeper.

"Sit down, Captain," Aymi-Mastr said sternly. "Are you telling me you weren't out last night?"

"Of course I was out," I said, putting some huffiness into my voice as I reluctantly sat down again. "You don't expect anyone to spend any more time than they have to in one of those Vyssiluyan hotel bug-traps, do you?"

She gave me the Ihmis equivalent of a wry smile, which just made her face that much more froglike. "A point," she conceded. "Did you visit any tavernos?"

I shrugged. "Sure, I hit some of them. What else is there for a spacer to do around here? But I didn't talk to anyone."

She sighed theatrically. "So you say. And therein lies the trouble." She picked up a report file and opened it. "Your word, against that of an unidentified and unknown informant. Which of you should we believe?"

"Wait a minute—you don't even know who he is?" I demanded, feeling sweat starting to gather under my collar. I wasn't particularly good with Ihmis lettering, but I'd made it a point to learn what my name looked like in most of the major scripts in the Spiral. That was my Commonwealth Mercantile Authority file she was holding; and nothing in there was likely to make my word compare favorably against anyone else's. "What kind of scam *is* this, anyway?"

"That is what we're trying to find out," Aymi-Mastr said, frowning at the file and then up at me. "This photo doesn't do you justice at all. When was it taken?"

"About seven years ago," I told her. "Back when I started doing independent shipping."

"No, no justice at all," she repeated, peering closely at me. "You should arrange to have a new one taken."

"I'll do that," I promised, though offhand I couldn't think of anything that was lower on my priority list at the moment. For someone on Brother John's payroll, it could be a distinct advantage to not look like your official photos. "I've been through a lot since then."

"Indeed you have," she agreed, leafing through the pages. "To be honest, Captain, your record hardly encourages us to take your word for this. Or for anything else, for that matter."

"There's no need to be insulting," I growled. "Anyway, all that happened a long time ago."

"Five years in the EarthGuard Auxiliary," Aymi-Mastr went on. "Apparently a reasonably promising career that went steeply downhill during the last of those years. Court-martialed and summarily drummed out for severe insubordination."

"He was an idiot," I muttered. "Everyone else knew it, too. I was just the only one who had the guts to tell him that to his face."

"In most colorful detail, I see," Aymi-Mastr said, flipping over another page. "Even knowing only a fraction of these Earth words, it's an impressive list." She flipped over another two pages—highlights of the court-martial, no doubt—and again paused. "After that was a four-year stint with the Earth Customs Service. Another potential career ended with another sudden dismissal. This one for taking bribes."

"I was framed," I insisted. Even to my own ears the protest sounded flat.

"Protests of that sort begin to sound weaker after the first one," Aymi-Mastr said. "I see you managed to avoid jail time. The note here suggests the Customs Service decided you were too embarrassing for a proper trial."

"That was their excuse," I said. "It also conveniently robbed me of any chance to clear my name."

"Then there were six months with the small firm of Rolvaag Brothers Shipping," she continued, flipping more pages. "This time you actually struck someone. The younger Mr. Rolvaag, I see—"

"Look, I don't need a complete quarterly review of my life," I cut her off brusquely. "I was there, remember? If there's a point to this, get to it."

The Ihmisit who'd been quietly searching my bag sealed it and straightened up. He exchanged a couple of words with Aymi-Mastr, then walked away, leaving the bag behind. I wasn't surprised; there was nothing in there that could possibly be construed as improper. I hoped Aymi-Mastr wasn't too disappointed. "The point is that you hardly qualify as an upstanding, law-abiding citizen," Aymi-Mastr said, returning her attention to me. "Not to file too sharp a point onto it, but you are the sort of person who might indeed give aid and assistance to a murderer."

The word was so completely unexpected that it took a couple of turns around my brain before finally coming to a stop. *Murderer?* "Murderer?" I asked carefully. "This guy *killed* someone?"

"So says the report," Aymi-Mastr said, watching me closely. "Do you find that so difficult to believe?"

"Well, frankly, yes," I said, feigning confusion. I didn't have to feign too hard. "He looks like such a solid citizen in that picture. What happened? Who did he kill?"

"The director of an archaeological dig out in the Great Wasteland," Aymi-Mastr said, setting my file aside and steepling her fingers again. "There was a massive explosion out there early yesterday morning—you didn't hear about that?"

I shook my head. "We didn't make landfall until a little after local noon. I *did* ask what the slowdown was, but no one would give me a straight answer."

"The blast sent large gales of mineral dust into the atmosphere," Aymi-Mastr explained. "Our sensors and guide beacons were disrupted for over an hour, which is what caused the backup in traffic. At any rate, when investigators went to look, they located the severely burned body of a Dr. Ramond Chou hidden in one of the underground grottoes the group had been exploring. The order was immediately given to round up all those associated with the dig for questioning."

She picked up Cameron's photo from the desk and handed it to me again. "This man is the only one still at large. Others of the group have identified him as the murderer."

Which explained the big search out in the wasteland last night. "Well, best of luck in finding him," I said, eyeing the photo again. "But if you ask me, he's long gone by now. Probably took off under cover of that sensor scramble you mentioned."

"That may indeed be the case," Aymi-Mastr conceded. "There was an unconfirmed report that something may have lifted out through the cloud of debris." She waved a pair of antennae at the photo. "But on the other palm is the statement that you were seen with him last night. Look closely, Captain. Are you certain you didn't exchange even a few words?"

She was making it so easy for me. All I had to do was say, yes, he'd hired me for a job, but that that was before I knew he was a murderer. Aymi-Mastr would ask what I knew, I would hand over the tag Cameron had given me, they would pick him up at the *Icarus*'s landing ramp, and I could walk away free and clear.

And best of all, I wouldn't have to face Brother John about this disruption in his precious schedule.

With a sigh, I shook my head. "I'm sorry, Director Aymi-Mastr," I said, laying the photo back on the desk. "I wish I could help. I really do—I don't much care for murderers myself. But I didn't talk to him, and I don't even remember seeing him go by on the street. Whoever your anonymous witness thinks he saw, it wasn't me."

For a four-pack of heartbeats she just gazed at me. Then, with a shrug as human and as ridiculous-looking on her as the finger-steepling thing, she nodded. "Very well, Captain, if that's your final word."

"It is," I said, deciding to ignore the sarcasm of that last comment as I stood up. "May I go now? I *do* have a schedule to keep."

"I understand," she said, standing up to face me. "Unfortunately, before you leave Meima we will have to perform a complete search of your ship." She held out a hand. "Your guidance tag, please."

I frowned, suddenly acutely conscious of the *Icarus* tag sitting there in plain sight in my collar slot. "Excuse me?"

"Your guidance tag, please," Aymi-Mastr said; and though all the genial trappings were still in place, I could sense the sudden hardening of her tone. "Please don't require me to use force. I know you humans consider Ihmisits to be laughable creatures, but I assure you we are stronger than we look."

For a long second I continued the face-off. Then, muttering under my breath, I reached up and slid both tags from the slot. "Fine," I growled, palming Cameron's tag and slapping the *Stormy Banks*'s onto the desk. Brother John's cargo, I knew, would be well enough disguised to weather even a serious Ihmisit customs search. "Help yourselves. Just don't leave a mess."

"We shall be quick and neat," she promised. "In the meantime, if you'd like, you can wait in the guest room behind the striped door."

"I'd rather wait in the hospitality center," I said stiffly, snagging the handle of my bag and pulling it over to me. "If you're going to waste my time this way, you can at least let me get some breakfast."

"As you wish," Aymi-Mastr said, giving me the Ihmis gesture of farewell. Her phone warbled, and she reached over to pick it up. "We should be finished within the hour," she added as she held the handset to her neck slits.

I spun on my heel and stalked across the room toward the door, trying to put as much righteous indignation into my posture as I could. They were letting me go, and they hadn't taken my phone. Either they didn't seriously suspect me, Aymi-Mastr's accusations to the contrary, or they *did* seriously suspect me and were hoping to follow me to wherever I was hiding Cameron.

"Captain McKell?" Aymi-Mastr called from behind me.

For a flickering half second, I considered making a run for it. But the door was too far away, and there were too many Ihmisits between me and it. Bracing myself, I turned back around. "What?" I demanded.

Aymi-Mastr was still on the phone, beckoning me back. I thought again about running, decided it made no more sense now than it had five seconds ago, and headed back.

By the time I reached the desk she had finished the conversation. "My apologies, Captain," she said, putting down the phone and holding out the tag she'd taken from me. "You may go."

I frowned suspiciously at the tag like it was some

sort of kid's practical joke that would snap a spring against my finger if I took it. "Just like that?"

"Just like that," Aymi-Mastr said, sounding midway between embarrassed and disgusted. "My superiors just informed me they've heard from our mysterious informant again. It seems the charge has now changed: that you were seen instead in the company of the notorious armed robber Belgai Romss. He attacked a storage depot over in Tropstick three days ago."

I frowned. What the hell sort of game were they playing? "And, what, you want me to take a look at *his* photo now?"

"That won't be necessary," Aymi-Mastr said, her disgust deepening. "Apparently, our friend missed the follow-up story of Romss's capture early yesterday morning, before your ship arrived."

She pushed the tag toward me. "Obviously merely a troublemaker, as you suggested. Again, my apologies."

"That's all right," I said, cautiously taking the tag. No spring snapped out to sting my fingers. "Maybe next time you won't be so quick to jump on something like this without proof."

"With a murder investigation, we must always investigate every lead," she said, drumming her fingers thoughtfully on the top of my file. "A safe journey to you, Captain."

I turned again and headed for the door, sliding the *Stormy Banks* tag back into my collar slot but continuing to palm the *Icarus* one. No one tried to stop me, no one called me back, and two minutes later I was once again out in the open air. It was all over, and I was free to go.

I didn't believe it for a minute. It was all too pat, too convenient. The Ihmisits were still looking for Cameron, and they still thought I was the one who was going to lead them to him. And they'd turned me loose hoping I'd do exactly that.

And unless they planned to tail me all the way to the

Icarus—which was, I supposed, an option—that meant they'd planted a tracker on me.

The question was how. Molecular-chain echo transponders were useless in the radio cacophony inside a major port, so it had to be one of the larger, needle-sized trackers. But I'd watched Aymi-Mastr's flunky as he searched my bag, and would have been willing to swear in court that he hadn't planted anything.

Which meant it had to have been planted after the search. And then, of course, it was obvious.

Carefully, I eased the tag out of my collar and took a good look; and there it was, slid neatly and nearly invisibly lengthwise through the bottom edge of the tag. Getting hold of the end with finger and thumbnail, I managed to pull it free of the plastic.

Now came the problem of how to get rid of it without the telltale motionlessness that would occur if I simply tossed it in the nearest trash bin. Fortunately, the opportunity was already close at hand. Coming rapidly through the crowd, three seconds away from intersecting my path, was a short Bunkre with one of those glittering, high-collared landing jackets that always remind me of something you'd see at an Elvis revival. Adjusting my step slightly, I turned my head partially away to make it look accidental, and slammed full tilt into him.

"Sorry," I apologized, grabbing his shoulders to help him regain his balance. I straightened his collar where the impact of my shoulder had bent it, at the same time pulling a five-commark piece out of my pocket. "My personal fault entirely," I gave the proper Bunkrel apology as I offered him the coin. "In partial compensation, please have a meal or drink on the labor of my arms."

He snatched the coin, grunted the proper Bunkrel wheeze of acceptance and forgiveness, and immediately changed course toward the hospitality building. Five commarks was about ten times the compensation the accident warranted, and he was clearly bent on spending the money before the clumsy human realized his mistake and came looking for change.

With luck, he'd also be so busy spending it he wouldn't notice that while I was straightening his collar I'd left him a small present. I let him get a ten-meter head start, then followed.

The hospitality center straddling the main pathway thirty meters inward from the entrance gate wasn't much more than your basic Ihmis taverno, just built on a larger scale and with correspondingly higher prices. I walked straight across the crowded dining area, past the line of small private dining chambers, and through the NO ADMITTANCE door into one of the storage rooms.

As I'd expected, the room was empty, the entire staff out serving the rush of opening-hour customers. I crossed to the service door on the far side, shucking off my jacket and again turning it inside out. There was no ID slot on this side, but I could wedge the *Icarus* tag between the zipper and covering flap where the scanners could read it. Unlocking the door, I stepped out into the spaceport proper again and got onto the nearest of the guidelighted slideways meandering between the various landing pads. We would see now just how alert the Ihmisits were, and how badly they wanted to follow me.

To my mild surprise, they apparently didn't want it very badly at all. Serious interest on their part would have meant an actual, physical tail on hand to augment the signal from the tracker; but I kept a close watch as I shifted between slideways at the prompting of the guidelights, and saw no indication of anyone performing a similar dance. Either my jaunt through the hospitality building and jacket switch had caught them completely by surprise, or the tracker had just been a token reaction to a possible lead who might still be of interest but probably wasn't. Or else they had no particular reason to follow me because they had no idea the *Icarus* even existed.

Or else they knew all about the *Icarus* and were already waiting for me there, and all of this was simply their helpful way of offering me the rope I would need to hang myself. A wonderfully cheery thought to be having at six in the morning.

I'd been riding along the slideways in what seemed like circles for about fifteen minutes, and was starting to quietly curse the entire Ihmis species, when the yellow guidelights running ahead of me finally turned the pink that indicated I was there. Taking one last surreptitious look around, I hopped off my current slideway, circled the stern of a Trinkian freighter, and came face-to-face with the *Icarus*.

To say that the first sight was a letdown would be to vastly understate the case. The ship looked like nothing I'd ever seen before; like nothing I'd ever imagined before. Like nothing, for that matter, that had any business flying.

The bow section was built along standard lines, with the necessary splay-finger hyperspace cutter array melding into the equally standard sensor/capacitor nose-cone arrangement. But from that point on, anything resembling normal starship design went straight out the window. Behind the bow the ship swelled abruptly into a large sphere, a good forty meters across, covered with the same dark gray hull plates as the nose cone. The usual assortment of maneuvering vents were scattered around its surface, connecting aft to the ship's main thrusters via a series of conduits running through the narrow space between the inner and outer hulls.

Behind the large sphere was a smaller, twenty-meter-diameter sphere squashed up into the aft section of the larger one, with a saddle-surface cowling covering the intersection between them. Behind the second sphere, looking almost like it had been slapped on as an afterthought, was a full-size engine section that looked like it had come off a Kronks ore scutter, and one of the more disreputable ones at that. Hugging the surface of the small sphere here on the ship's port side, running from the aft part of the large sphere to the forward part of the engine section, was a hard-shell wraparound space tunnel. Near the center of the wraparound was the entryway, currently sealed, with a pair of floodlights stuck to the wraparound just above the top two corners. A collapsible stairway extended the ten meters from the red-rimmed hatch down to the ground, with an entry-code keypad on the handrail near the bottom. There was a landing skid/cushion arrangement propping up the engine section somewhat, but the bulge of the larger sphere still forced the bow cone to point up into the sky at about a ten-degree angle.

The overall visual effect was either that of an old-style rocket that had suddenly lost hull integrity in vacuum and bulged outward in two places, or else some strange metallic creature that had become pregnant with twins, one of them a definite runt. I hadn't been expecting something sleek and impressive, but this was just ridiculous.

"Looks like something a group of semitrained chimps put together out of a box, doesn't it?" a cheerful voice commented at my side.

I turned. A medium-sized man in his early thirties with wavy blue-streaked hair and a muscular build had come up beside me, gazing up at the *Icarus* with a mixture of amusement and disbelief. "Succinctly put," I agreed, lowering my bag to the ground. "With one of the chimps having first spilled his coffee on the instructions."

He grinned, setting his bag down next to mine. "I believe that between us we have indeed captured the essence of the situation. You flying with us?"

"So I was told," I said. "Jordan McKell, pilot and navigator."

"Jaeger Jones, mechanic," he identified himself, sticking out his hand. "Boscor Mechanics Guild."

"Good outfit," I said, shaking his hand. He had a good solid grip, the sort you'd expect of a starship mechanic. "Been waiting long?"

"No, just a couple of minutes," he said. "Kind of surprised to be the first one here, actually. From the way Borodin talked last night, I figured he'd be in as soon as the gates opened. But the entry's locked, and no one answered when I buzzed."

I stepped over to the base of the stairway and touched the OPEN command on the keypad. There was a soft beep, but nothing happened. "You check to see if there were any other ways inside?" I asked, looking up at the ship again.

"Not yet," Jones said. "I went around that Trink's bow first to see if I could see Borodin coming, but there's no sign of him that direction. You want me to circle the ship and see what's on the other side?"

"No, I'll do it," I said. "You wait here in case he shows up."

I headed aft along the side, circling the rest of the small sphere, then walking alongside the engine section. Seen up close, some of the hull plates did indeed look like they'd been fastened on by Jones's semi-trained chimps. But for all the cosmetic sloppiness, they seemed solid enough. I rounded the thruster nozzles—which looked more professionally installed than the hull plates—and continued forward along the starboard side.

I was halfway to the smaller sphere when a pair of indentations in the engine section caught my eye. Thirty centimeters apart, they were about a centimeter wide each, and an exploring finger showed they were about two centimeters deep and five more down, running to an apparent point. Basically like the latch grooves for a snap-fit lifeline, except that I'd never seen two of them set this close together before. Peering up along the side of the hull, squinting in the glare of the rising sun, I could see what looked like four more pairs of the slots rising in a vertical line to the top of the engine section.

I mulled at it for a moment, but I couldn't come up with any good reason to have a group of latch grooves here. Still, considering how unorthodox the rest of the *Icarus*'s design was, I wasn't inclined to waste too much brainpower on the question right now. The ship's specs should be in the computer; once we were off the ground, I could look them up and see what they were for.

On impulse, I pulled out the now useless guidance tag and tore it in half. Loosely wadding up the pieces, I carefully stuck one into each of the lower two latch grooves, making sure they were out of view. The thin plastic wouldn't block or impede any connector that might be put into the slot, but the act of insertion would squash the plastic down to the bottom of the groove, leaving proof that something had been there.

I finished the rest of my inspection tour without finding anything else of particular interest. The wrap-around tunnel/airlock we'd seen on the port side had no match on the starboard, as I'd thought it might be, and there were no other entrances into the ship that I could see. By the time I returned to the stairway, there were four others and their luggage waiting with Jones: two men, a Craean male, and—surprisingly enough, at least to me—a young woman.

"Ah—there you are," Jones called as I came around the curve of the smaller sphere to join them. "Gentlefolk, this is our pilot and navigator, Captain Jordan McKell."

"Pleased to meet you," I said, giving them a quick once-over as I joined the group. "I sure hope one of you knows what's going on here."

"What do you mean, what's going on?" one of the newcomers demanded in a scratchy voice. He was in his early twenties, thin to the point of being scrawny, with pale blond hair and an air of nervousness that hung off his shoulders like a rain cloak. "You're the pilot, aren't you? I thought you pilots always knew everything."

"Ah—you've been reading our propaganda sheets," I said approvingly. "Very good."

He frowned. "Propaganda sheets?"

"A joke," I said, sorry I'd even tried it. Apparently, humor wasn't his strong point. "I was hired off the street, just like all the rest of you were."

I sent a casual glance around the group as I spoke, watching for a reaction. But if any of them had had a different sort of invitation to this party, he was keeping it to himself. "I'm sure we'll all have our questions answered as soon as our employer arrives," I added.

"*If* he shows up," the other man murmured. He was tall, probably around thirty years old, with prematurely gray hair and quietly probing eyes. His musculature was somewhat leaner than Jones's, but just as impressive in its own way.

"He'll be here," I said, trying to put more confidence into my tone than I felt. Having a murder charge hanging over Cameron's head was going to severely cramp his mobility. "While we're waiting, how about you starting off the introductions?"

"Sure," the gray-haired man said. "I'm Almont Nicabar—call me Revs. Engine certification, though I'm cleared to handle mechanics, too."

"Really," Jones said, sounding interested. "Where'd you journeyman on your mechanics training?"

"I didn't go through an actual program," Nicabar said. "Mostly I just picked it up while I was in the service."

"No kidding," Jones said. Apparently our mechanic was the terminally sociable type. "Which branch?"

"Look, can't we save the social-club chat till later?" the nervous kid growled, his head bobbing restlessly as he checked out every spacer that came into sight along the walkways.

"I'm open to other suggestions," I said mildly. "Unfortunately, as long as the entryway's locked—"

"So why don't we open it?" he cut me off impatiently, peering up at the wraparound. "A cheeseball hatch like that—I could pop it in half a minute."

"Not a good idea," Jones warned. "You can break the airlock seal that way."

"And that would leave our hull/EVA specialist with nothing to do," I said, turning to the Craea. "And you are, sir?"

"I am Chort," the alien said, his voice carrying the typical whistly overtones of his species, a vaguely ethereal sound most other beings either found fascinating or else drove them completely up a wall. "How did you know I was the spacewalker?"

"You're far too modest," I told him, bowing respectfully. "The reputation of the Crooea among spacewalkers far precedes you. We are honored to have you with us."

Chort returned the bow, his feathery blue-green scales shimmering where they caught the sunlight. Like most of his species, he was short and slender, with pure white eyes, a short Mohawk-style feathery crest topping his head, and a toothed bird's bill for a mouth. His age was impossible to read, but I tentatively put it somewhere between fifteen and eighty. "You're far too generous," he replied.

"Not at all," I assured him, putting all the sincere flattery into my voice that I figured I could get away with. The entire Craean species loved zero gee, whether working in it or playing in it, with the lithe bodies and compact musculature that were perfect for climbing around outside ships. On top of that, they seemed to have a sixth sense when it came to the depressingly regular hull problems created by hyperspace pressure, plus the ability to evaluate the condition of a plate through touch alone.

All of which meant they were highly in demand for hull/EVA positions aboard starships, to the point where ship owners frequently tried to cajole, bribe, or otherwise steal them away from rivals in port. I wasn't sure how Cameron had managed to get him to sign on with us, but a little ego-massage here and there wouldn't hurt our chances of keeping him here.

Unfortunately, our nervous type either didn't understand such subtleties or just didn't care. "Oh, give it a rest," he growled. "He saw your luggage, Chort—you can tell there's a vac suit in there."

The blue-green scales edged with the pale red of surprise. "Oh," Chort said. "Of course. There's certainly that, too."

"Don't mind him," I told the Craea, controlling my annoyance with a supreme effort. "He's our certified diplomacy expert."

Jones chuckled, and the kid scowled. "I am not," he insisted. "I'm electronics."

"Do you have a name?" Nicabar asked. "Or are we going to have to call you Twitchy for the rest of the trip?"

"Har, har," he said, glowering at Nicabar. "I'm Shawn. Geoff Shawn."

"Which just leaves you," I said, turning to the woman. She was slim, with black hair and hazel eyes, probably no older than her mid-twenties, with the sort of lightly tanned skin of someone who played a lot outdoors. Like Shawn, she seemed more interested in the passing pedestrian traffic than she was in our little get-acquainted session. "Do you cover both the computer and medical specialties?"

"Just computers," she said briefly, her eyes flicking to me once in quick evaluation, then turning away again. "My name's Tera."

"Tera what?" Jones asked.

"Just Tera," she repeated, giving him a coolly evaluating look.

"Yes, but—"

"Just Tera," I cut Jones off, warning him with my eyes to drop it. She might just be the shy type; but there were also several religious sects I knew of who made it a policy to never give their full names to outsiders. Either way, pressing her about it would be pointless and only add more friction to a crew that, by the looks of things, was already rapidly reaching its quota.

"Means we're missing our medic," Nicabar put in, smoothly stepping in and filling the conversational awkwardness. "I wonder where he is."

"Maybe he's having a drink with Borodin," Shawn said acidly. "Look, this is stupid. Are you *sure* that entryway's sealed?"

"You're welcome to try it yourself," I told him, waving at the keypad and wishing I knew what our next move should be. I certainly didn't want to leave Cameron behind, particularly not with a murder charge outstanding against him. But if the Ihmisits had already picked him up, there wasn't much point in our hanging around, either. Maybe I should give Ixil a call over at the *Stormy Banks* and have him do a quiet search.

From above me came the ka-thunk of released seals and the hissing of hydraulics, and I spun around to see the entryway door swinging ponderously open. "What did you do?" I demanded, looking at Shawn.

"What do you mean, what did I do?" he shot back. "I pushed the damn OPEN button, that's what I did. It was unlocked the whole time, you morons."

"Borodin must have had it on a time lock," Jones said, frowning. "I wonder why."

"Maybe he's not coming," Tera suggested. "Maybe he never intended to in the first place."

"Well, I'm not going *anywhere* without the advance he promised," Shawn said flatly.

"Besides which, we don't know exactly where we're

supposed to go," I reminded them, stepping past him and peering up the stairway. It canted to the right at a slight angle, one more example of slightly shoddy workmanship to add to my growing list. I could see a glowing ceiling light over the hatch inside the wrap-around, but nothing else was visible from this angle.

"He told me we were going to Earth," Chort offered.

"Right, but Earth's a big place," I reminded him. "With lots of different parking spaces. Still, we might as well go in." I picked up my bag and started toward the stairway—

"Hang on a second, Jordan," Jones cut me off. "Someone's coming."

I turned around. From around the stern of one of the nearby ships a large, bulky man was jogging toward us like a trotting hippo, a pair of travel bags bouncing in his grip. "Hold on!" he called. "Don't leave yet. I'm here."

"And who are you?" I called back.

"Hayden Everett," he said, coasting to a stop beside Tera and taking a deep breath. "Medic certificate. Whew! Had some trouble at the gate—didn't think I was going to make it."

"Don't worry, you're not the last," Jones said. "Our employer hasn't shown up yet, either."

"Really?" Everett said, frowning. He had short black hair and blue eyes, and the slightly squashed features I usually associated with professional high-contact sports types. Up close, I could see now that, unlike Jones and Nicabar, most of his impressive body mass ran to fat, though there were indications there'd been a fair amount of muscle there once upon a time. He was also crowding fifty, considerably older than the rest of our group, with an impressive network of wrinkles around his eyes and mouth.

I could also see that despite the implication that he'd jogged along the slideways all the way from the gate, there was no sheen of sweat on his face, nor was he even breathing all that hard. Despite his age and surface fat, his cardiovascular system was apparently in pretty decent shape.

"Really," Jones assured him. "So what do we do now, McKell?"

"Like I said, we go inside," I told him, starting up the steps. "Revs, you get to the engine room and start your preflight; I'll find the bridge and get things started from that end. The rest of you, bring your luggage and find your stations."

Given the *Icarus*'s iconoclastic design I knew that that last order was going to be a challenge. To my mild surprise, someone had anticipated me. The wraparound tunnel curved around the smaller sphere to a pressure door at the surface of the larger sphere—apparently, the whole wraparound served as the ship's airlock—and attached to the wall of the corridor on the far side of the pressure door was a basic layout of the ship.

"Well, that's handy," Tera commented as the six of us crowded around it, Nicabar having already disappeared in the other direction along the wraparound to the engine room. "Where's the computer room?—oh, there it is. Odd placement."

There was a murmur of general agreement. The interior layout was fully as odd as the exterior design, with the three levels of the sphere laid out in possibly the most arbitrary fashion I'd ever seen. The bridge was in its standard place, nestled just behind the nose cone on the mid deck; but the computer room, instead of being connected to the bridge as usual, was at the opposite end of the sphere, pressed up against the wall of the smaller sphere on the starboard side of the centerline, directly behind the wall we were currently looking at. The machine shop, electronics shop, and EVA prep area were slapped together on the port side, where vibrations and electronic noise from one would inevitably slop over into the other, with the sick bay and galley/dayroom across the corridor from them just forward of the computer room.

The top deck consisted of six cracker-box-sized sleeping cabins and an only slightly larger head, plus two main storage rooms; the lower deck was two more sleeping cabins, another head, the main bulk of the ship's stores, and the air- and water-scrubbing and reclamation equipment. There were other, smaller storage cabinets scattered around everywhere, apparently wherever and however the designer's mood had struck. The three decks were linked together by a pair of ladders, one just behind the bridge, the other aft near the wraparound.

I also noticed that while the wraparound and engine section were drawn with a certain minimal detail, the smaller sphere was drawn as a solid silhouette, labeled simply CARGO, with no access panels or hatches shown. When Cameron had said the cargo was sealed, he'd meant it.

"This has got to be the dumbest ship I've ever been on," Shawn declared in obvious disgust. "Who built this thing, anyway?"

"It'll be listed on the schematics," I told him. "Tera, that'll be your first job after you get the computer up and running: Pull up the plans so we can see what exactly we've got to work with. Everyone else, go get settled. I'll be on the bridge if you need me."

I headed up the corridor—literally *up* it; the *Icarus*'s floors were sloped at the same ten-degree angle as the ship itself—and touched the release pad set into the center of the door.

Considering all the extra space the *Icarus* had over the *Stormy Banks,* I might have expected the bridge to be correspondingly larger, too. It wasn't. If anything, it was a little smaller. But whatever other corners Cameron and his cronies had cut with this ship, at least they hadn't scrimped on vital equipment. The piloting setup, to my right as I stood in the doorway, consisted of a full Wurlitz command console wrapped around a military-style full-active restraint chair, a half-dozen Valerian monitor displays to link me to the rest of the ship, and a rather impressive Hompson RealiTeev main display already activated and showing the view out the bow of the ship. To my left, the other half of the room was dominated by a Gorsham plotting table connected to a Kemberly nav database records system.

And sitting in the center of the plotting table were an envelope and a large metal cash box.

I stepped over to the table and crouched down, giving the box a long, careful look. There were no wires that I could see; no discolorations, no passive triggers, nothing that struck me as an obvious booby trap. Holding my breath, I picked it up and eased it open a crack.

Nothing snapped, flashed, hissed, or blew up in my face. Perhaps I was getting paranoid in my old age. Exhaling quietly, I opened it the rest of the way.

Inside was money. Crisp one-hundred-commark bills. Lots of them.

I looked at the cash for another moment, then set the box back on the plotting table and opened the envelope. Inside were a set of cards, the originals of the registration and clearance papers Cameron had showed me in the taverno last night, plus a single sheet of paper with a hand-printed message on it:

To the captain:

Due to circumstances beyond my control, I will not be able to accompany you and the Icarus *after all. I must therefore trust in your honor to take the ship and its cargo to Earth without me.*

When you reach Earth orbit, please contact Stann Avery at the vid number listed at the bottom of the page. He will give you specific delivery instructions for your cargo and arrange your final payment. The settlement will include a substantial bonus for you and the others of the crew, over and above what we've already agreed to, provided the ship and cargo are delivered intact.

In the meantime, the initial payments for all of you are in the box, as well as the money for fuel and docking fees you'll need along the way.

Again, my apologies for any inconvenience this sudden change of plan may cause you. I would not be exaggerating when I say that delivering the Icarus *and its cargo safely will be the most significant accomplishment any of you will ever do in your lives. It may in fact be the most significant deed any human being will perform during the remainder of this century.*

Good luck, and do not fail me. The future of the human race could well lie within your hands.

It was signed "Alexander Borodin."

My first thought was that Cameron really needed to cut back on those melodramas and star-thrillers he was watching in the evenings after work. My second was that this was one hell of a hot potato for him to have dropped into my lap on no notice whatsoever.

"McKell?" a female voice called from behind me.

I turned to see Tera making her way uphill into the bridge. "Yes, what is it?"

"I wanted to check out the bridge," she said, glancing around the room. "I was kind of hoping the main computer might be stashed in here."

I frowned. "What are you talking about? Isn't it back in the computer room?"

"Yes, I guess it is," she said with a grimace. "I was hoping that piece of junk was the backup."

Those cold ferret feet started their wind sprints up my back again. The computer was very literally the nerve center of the entire ship. "Just how bad a piece of junk *is* it?" I asked carefully.

THE ICARUS HUNT 47

"Noah had a better one on the ark," she said flatly. "It's an old Worthram T-66. No decision-assist capabilities, no vocal interface, no nanosecond monitoring. Programming like I haven't seen since high school, no autonomic functions or emergency command capabilities—shall I go on?"

"No, I get the picture," I said heavily. Compared to normal starship operation, we were starting out half-blind, half-deaf, and slightly muddled—rather like a stroke victim, actually. No wonder Cameron had decided to jump ship. "Can you handle it?"

She lifted her hands. "Like I said, it's an echo from a distant past, but I should be able to work it okay. It may take me a while to remember all the tricks." She nodded toward the letter in my hand. "What's that?"

"A note from the camp counselor," I told her, handing it over. "You were right; it seems we're going on this hike by ourselves."

She read it, her frown turning to a scowl as she did so. "Well, this is awkward, I must say," she said, handing it back. "He must have left this last night, before the spaceport closed."

"Unless he managed to get in and out this morning," I suggested.

"Well, if he did, he must have been really traveling," she growled. "I know *I* got here about as fast as I could. So what do we do now?"

"We take the *Icarus* to Earth, of course," I told her. "That's what we agreed to. Unless you have a date or something."

"Don't be cute," she growled. "What about our advance pay? He promised me a thousand commarks up front."

"It's all here," I assured her, patting the cash box. "As soon as I get the preflight started I'll go pass it out and let the rest know about the change in plans."

Her eyes lingered momentarily on the box, then shifted back to me. "You think they'll all stay?"

"I don't see why not," I said. "As far as I'm concerned, as long as I get paid, a job's a job. I'm not expecting any of the others to feel differently."

"Does that mean you're officially taking command of the ship and crew?"

I shrugged. "That's how the Mercantile Code lays it out. Command succession goes owner, employer, master, pilot. I'm the pilot."

"Yes, I know," she said. "I was just making sure. For the record."

"For the record, I hereby assume command of the *Icarus*," I said in my most official voice. "Satisfied?"

"Ecstatic," she said with just a trace of sarcasm.

"Good," I said. "Go on back to your station and start beating that T-66 into submission. I'll be along in a few minutes with your money."

She glanced at the cash box one last time, then nodded and left the bridge.

I set the box and papers on my lap and got to work on the preflight, trying to ignore the hard knot that had settled into my stomach. Cameron's note might have been overly dramatic, but it merely confirmed what I'd suspected ever since he'd invited himself over to my taverno table and offered me a job.

Somewhere out in the Meima wasteland, that archaeological team had stumbled onto something. Something big; something—if Cameron's rhetoric was even halfway to be believed—of serious importance.

And that same something was sitting forty meters behind me, sealed up inside the *Icarus*'s cargo hold.

I just wished I knew what the hell it was.

CHAPTER

3

Even with the clearance codes and papers Cameron had left with his note, I was fully expecting there to be trouble getting the *Icarus* off the ground. To my mild and cautiously disbelieving surprise, there wasn't. The tower gave us permission to lift, the landing-pad repulsor boost got us up off the ground and into range of the perimeter grav beams, and a few minutes later we were hauling for space under our own power.

After Tera's revelation about the archaic computer system we'd been saddled with, I had been wondering just what kind of shape the drive would be in. But there, too, my pessimism turned out to be unnecessary, or at least premature. The thrusters roared solidly away, driving us steadily through the atmosphere toward the edge of Meima's gravity well, and with each of my periodic calls back to the engine room Nicabar assured me all was going just fine.

It wouldn't last, though. I knew it wouldn't last; and as the capacitors in the nose cone discharged into the cutter array and sliced us a link hole into hyperspace, I warned myself that things were unlikely to continue running this smoothly. Somewhere along the way, we were going to run into some serious trouble.

Six hours out from Meima, we hit our first batch of it.

My first warning was a sudden, distant-sounding screech sifting into the bridge, sounding rather like a banshee a couple of towns over. I slapped the big red KILL button, throwing a quick look at the monitors as I did so, and with another crack from the capacitors we were back in space-normal.

"McKell?" Nicabar's voice came from the intercom. "You just drop us out?"

"Yes," I confirmed. "I think we've got a pressure crack. You reading any atmosphere loss?"

"Nothing showing on my board," he said. "Inner hull must still be solid. I didn't hear the screech, either—must be somewhere at your end of the ship."

"Probably," I agreed. "I'll roust Chort and have him take a look."

I called the EVA room, found that Chort was already suiting up, and headed aft. One of the most annoying problems of hyperspace travel was what the experts called *parasynbaric force,* what we nonexperts called simply *hyperspace pressure.* Ships traveling through hyperspace were squeezed the whole way, the pressure level related through a complicated formula to the ship's mass, speed, and overall surface area. The earliest experimental hyperspace craft had usually wound up flattened, and even now chances were good that a ship of any decent size would have to drop out at least once a trip to have its hull specialist take a look and possibly do some running repairs.

Considering what I'd seen of the *Icarus*'s hull back on the ground, I was frankly surprised we'd made it as far as we had.

Tera and Everett were standing in the corridor outside the EVA room when I arrived, watching Jones help a vacsuited Chort run a final check on his equipment. "Well, that didn't take long," Tera commented. "Any idea where the problem is?"

"Probably somewhere here on the larger sphere," I said. "The computer didn't have any ideas?"

She shook her head. "Like I said, it's old and feeble. Nothing but macro sensors, and no predictive capability at all."

"Don't worry," Chort assured us, his whistly voice oddly muted by his helmet. "That screech didn't sound bad. Regardless, I will find and fix it."

"Someone's going to have to go into the wraparound with him, too," Jones put in. "I checked earlier, and there aren't any of the connections or lifeline-feeds of a standard airlock."

I'd noticed that, too. "You volunteering?" I asked him.

"Of course," he said, sounding surprised that it was even a question. "EVA assist *is* traditionally mechanic's privilege, you know."

"I'm not concerned with tradition nearly as much as I am whether we've got a suit aboard that'll fit you," I countered. "Tera, pull the computer inventory and see what we've got."

"I already checked," she said. "There are three suit/rebreather combos in Locker Fifteen. It didn't list sizes, though."

"I'll go look," Jones volunteered, checking one last seal on Chort's suit and squeezing past him. "That's lower level, Tera?"

"Right," she said. "Just forward of Cabin Seven."

"Got it." Jones eased past me and headed for the aft ladder.

"So how will he handle it?" Everett asked. "Go into the wraparound and feed Chort the lifeline from there?"

"Basically," I nodded. "There's a slot just outside the entryway where the secondary line can connect, but he'll want Jones feeding him the primary line as he goes along. Otherwise, it can get kinked or snarled on the maneuvering vents, and that eats up time."

"I've heard of snarled lines giving false readings on sensors, too," Tera put in. "He might wind up fixing a hull plate that didn't need it."

"That won't happen," Chort assured her. "I will know the damage when I reach it."

"I'm sure you will," Everett said, lumbering down the corridor toward the aft ladder. "I'll see if Jones can use a hand."

There were indeed three vac suits in the locker, one of which fit Jones just fine, and with Everett's help he was suited up in fifteen minutes. Five minutes after that he and Chort were in the wraparound, the airlock doors at both ends were sealed, and I was on the bridge with the hull monitor cameras extended on their pylons.

And we were set. "Ready here," I called into the intercom. "Revs, go ahead and shut down the gravity."

"Right," Nicabar acknowledged from the engine room, and I felt the sudden stomach-twisting disorientation as the *Icarus*'s grav generator went off-line. I double-checked the airlock status and keyed for the suit radios. "It's all yours, Chort. Let him out easy, Jones."

Given that Jones had a Craea at the other end of his line, my automatic warning was probably both unnecessary and even a bit ridiculous. Before the outer hatch was even all the way open Chort was out on the hull, pausing briefly to snap his secondary line into the connector slot and heading nimbly across the wraparound, using his hull-hooks and stickypads as if he'd been born in zero gee.

"Mind if I watch?" a voice asked from the doorway behind me.

I turned my head. Shawn was floating just outside the door, gazing past me at the monitors, an intense

THE ICARUS HUNT 53

but oddly calm look on his face. "No, come on in," I invited.

"Thanks," he said, maneuvering his way into the room and coming to a stop hovering beside my chair. "There aren't any monitors in the electronics shop, and I've never seen a Craea spacewalk before."

"It's definitely a sight to behold," I agreed, trying not to frown as I studied his profile. The twitchy, nervous, sarcastic kid who'd been such a pain in the neck while we were waiting outside the *Icarus* had apparently been kidnapped sometime in the last six hours and replaced by this near-perfect copy. "How are you doing?"

He smiled, a little shamefacedly. "You mean how come I'm not acting like a jerk?"

"Not exactly the way I would have put it," I said. "But as long as you bring it up . . . ?"

"Yeah, I know," he said, his lip twisting. "That's another reason I wanted to talk to you, to apologize for all that. I was . . . well, nervous, I guess. You have to admit this is a really strange situation, and I don't do well with strange situations. Especially early in the morning."

"I have trouble with mornings sometimes myself," I said, turning back to the monitors. "Don't worry about it."

"Thanks. He's really good, isn't he?"

I nodded. Chort was moving slowly along the edge of the cowling that covered the intersection of the two spheres, his faceplate bare centimeters above the hull as he glided over the surface. Here and there he would stop for a moment, touching something with his long fingers and occasionally selecting one of the squeeze tubes from the collection clamped to his forearms. I thought about getting on the radio and asking what he was doing, but decided against it. He clearly knew his business, and there didn't seem any point in distracting him with a lot of questions. I made a mental note to pick up a set of zoomable hull cameras at our next stop.

The whistle from the radio speaker was so unexpected that Shawn and I both jumped, a movement that the zero gee magnified embarrassingly. "There it is," Chort said as I grabbed my restraint straps and pulled myself firmly down into the chair again. "A small pressure ridge only. Easily repaired."

He set to work with his squeeze tubes again. "I'll never understand about that stuff," Shawn commented. "If it's so good at fixing hull cracks and ridges, why not coat the whole hull with it?"

"Good question," I agreed, throwing him another surreptitious glance. Calm, friendly, and now even making intelligent conversation. I made another mental note, this one to restrict all my future interactions with him until after he'd had his morning coffee or whatever.

If Chort was a representative example of Craean spacewalking ability, it was no wonder they were so much in demand. In less than ten minutes he'd sealed the ridge, tracked two jaglines radiating from that spot, and fixed them as well. "All secure," he announced. "I will check the rest of the sphere, but I believe this is the only problem."

"Sounds good," I said. "Before you go any farther forward, you might as well go aft and run a quick check on the cargo and engine sections."

"Acknowledged," Chort said, turning around and heading back over the side of the cargo sphere. He paused once, moved down the side toward the wrap-around—

And suddenly, with another stomach-wrenching disorientation, I fell down hard into my chair.

Shawn yelped in surprise and pain as he dropped like a rock to the deck beside me. But I hardly noticed. Incredibly, impossibly, the *Icarus*'s gravity field had gone back on.

And as I watched in helpless horror, Chort slammed against the side of the cargo sphere, caromed off the wraparound, and disappeared off the monitor screen.

"Revs!" I barked toward the intercom, twisting the camera control hard over. "Turn it off!"

"I didn't turn it on," he protested.

"I don't give a damn who turned it on!" I snarled. I had Chort on the screen now, hanging limply like a puppet on a string at the end of his secondary line at the bottom of the artificial "down" the *Icarus*'s gravity generator had imposed on this small bubble of space. "Just shut it *down*."

"I can't," he bit back. "The control's not responding."

I ground my teeth viciously. "Tera?"

"I'm trying, too," her voice joined in. "The computer's frozen up."

"Then cut all power to that whole section," I snapped. "You can do *that*, can't you? One of you?"

"Working on it," Nicabar grunted.

"Computer's still frozen," Tera added tautly. "I can't see him—is he all right?"

"I don't know," I told her harshly. "And we *won't* know until we get him back—"

I broke off suddenly, my breath catching horribly in my throat. Concentrating first on Chort's fall, and then on getting the gravity shut down, it hadn't even occurred to me to wonder why Chort had fallen that far in the first place. Why Jones hadn't had the slack in the primary line properly taken up, or for that matter why he hadn't already begun reeling the Craea back into the wraparound.

But now, looking at the outside of the entryway for the first time since the accident, I could see why. Hanging limply over the sill of the hatchway beside the equally limp primary line was a vacsuited hand. Jones's hand.

Not moving.

"Revs, do you have a suit back there?" I called, cursing under my breath, trying to key the camera for a better look inside the entryway. No good; Jones had turned the overhead light off and the shadow was too intense for the camera to penetrate.

"No," he called back. "What's the—oh, *damn*."

"Yeah," I bit out, my mind racing uselessly. With the entryway open to space, the wraparound was totally isolated from the rest of the ship by the pressure doors at either end. I could close the hatch from the bridge; but the way Jones was lying, his hand would prevent it from sealing.

The only other way to get to him would be to depressurize one side of the ship so we could open the door. But we couldn't depressurize the sphere—there were only two vac suits left for the four of us still in here, and I wasn't about to trust the room or cabin doors to hold up against hard vacuum. And without a suit for Nicabar, we couldn't depressurize the engine room, either. My eyes flicked uselessly over the monitors, searching for inspiration—

"He's moving," Nicabar called suddenly. "Mc-Kell—Chort's moving."

I felt my hands tighten into fists. The Craea's body was starting to twitch, his limbs making small random movements like someone having a violent dream. "Chort?" I called toward the microphone. "Chort, this is McKell. Snap out of it—we need you."

"I am here," Chort's voice came, sounding vague and tentative. "What happened?"

"Ship's gravity came on," I told him. "Never mind that now. Something's happened to Jones—he's not responding, and I think he's unconscious. Can you climb up your line and get to him?"

For a long moment he didn't reply. I was gazing at the monitor, wondering if he'd slipped back into unconsciousness, when suddenly he twitched again; and a second later he was pulling himself up the line with spiderlike agility.

Thirty seconds later he was in the wraparound, pulling Jones out of the way of the door. I was ready, keying for entryway seal and repressurization of the wraparound.

Two minutes later, we had them back in the ship.

The effort, as it turned out, was for nothing.

"I'm sorry, McKell," Everett said with a tired sigh, pulling a thin blanket carefully over Jones's face. "Your man's been gone at least ten minutes. There's nothing I can do."

I looked over at the body lying on the treatment table. The terminally sociable type, I'd dubbed him back at the spaceport. He'd been terminal, all right. "It was the rebreather, then?"

"Definitely." Everett picked up the scrubber unit and peeled back the covering. "Somewhere in here the system stopped scrubbing carbon dioxide out of the air and started putting carbon monoxide in. Slowly, certainly—he probably didn't even notice it was happening. Just drifted to sleep and slipped quietly away."

I gazed at the hardware cradled in those large hands. "Was it an accident?"

He gave me an odd look. "You work with air scrubbers all the time. Could something like this have happened by accident?"

"I suppose it's possible," I said, the image of that massive search Ixil and I had spotted out in the Meima wilderness vivid in my memory. No, it hadn't been any accident. Not a chance in the world of that. But there was no sense panicking Everett, either.

"Hm," Everett said. For another moment he looked at the scrubber, then smoothed back the covering and put it aside. "I know you're not in the mood right now to count your blessings, but bear in mind that if Chort had died or broken his neck in that fall, we'd have lost both of them."

"Blessings like this I can do without," I said bitterly. "Have you looked at Chort yet?"

He grunted. "Chort says he's fine and unhurt and refuses to be looked at. If you want me to run a check on him, you'll have to make it an order."

"No, that's all right," I told him. I'd never heard anything about the Craean culture being a particularly stoic one. If Chort said he was all right, he probably was.

But whether he would stay that way was now open to serious question. With that phony murder charge someone had apparently succeeded in scaring Cameron off the *Icarus*, and the guilt-by-association bit had nearly bounced me, as well. Now, Jones had been rather more permanently removed from the crew list, and Chort had come within a hair of joining him.

And all this less than eight hours into the trip. The universe was spending the *Icarus*'s quota of bad luck with a lavish hand.

"A pity, too," Everett commented into my musings. "Jones being the mechanic, I mean. He might have been the only one on board who could have tracked down what went wrong with the grav generator. Now we may never know what happened."

"Probably," I agreed, putting the heaviness of true conviction into my voice. If Everett—or anyone else, for that matter—thought I was just going to chalk any of this up to mysterious accident and let it go at that, I had no intention of disillusioning them. "That's usually how it goes with this sort of thing," I added. "You never really find out what went wrong."

He nodded in commiseration. "So what happens now?"

I looked over at Jones's body again. "We take him to port and turn him over to the authorities," I said. "Then we keep going."

"Without a mechanic?" Everett frowned. "A ship this size needs all eight certificates, you know."

"That's okay," I assured him, backing out the door. "Nicabar can cover for the few hours it'll take to get to port. After that, I know where we can pick up another mechanic. Cheap."

He made some puzzled-sounding reply, but I was already in the corridor and didn't stop to hear it. Cameron's course plan had put our first fueling stop at Trottsen, seventy-two more hours away. But a relatively minor vector change would take us instead to Xathru, only nine hours from here, where Ixil and the *Stormy Banks* were due to deliver Brother John's illegal cargo. We needed a replacement mechanic, after all, and Ixil would fit the bill perfectly.

Besides which, I suddenly very much wanted to have Ixil at my side. Or perhaps more precisely, to have him watching my back.

CHAPTER

4

The parquet dockyard on Xathru was like a thousand other medium-sized spaceports scattered across the Spiral: primitive compared to Qattara Axial or one of the other InterSpiral-class ports, but still two steps above small regional hubs like the one we'd taken off from Meima. The Parquet's landing pits were cradle-shaped instead of simply flat, smoothly contoured to accommodate a variety of standard ship designs.

Of course, no one in his right mind would have anticipated the *Icarus*'s lopsided shape, so even with half its bulk below ground level the floors still sloped upward. But at least here the entryway ladder could be reconfigured as a short ramp with a rise of maybe two meters instead of the ten-meter climb we had had without it. Progress.

Nicabar volunteered to help Everett take Jones's body to the Port Authority, where the various death forms would have to be filled out. I ran through the basic landing procedure, promised the tower that I would file my own set of accident report forms before we left, then grabbed one of the little runaround cars scattered randomly between the docking rectangles and headed out to the StarrComm building looming like a giant mushroom at the southern boundary of the port.

Like most StarrComm facilities, this one was reasonably crowded. But also as usual, the high costs involved with interstellar communication led to generally short conversations, with the result that it was only about five minutes before my name was called and I was directed down one of the corridors to my designated booth. I closed the door behind me, made sure it was privacy-sealed, and after only a slight hesitation keyed for a full vid connect. It was ten times as expensive as vidless, but I had Cameron's thousand-commark advance money and was feeling extravagant.

Besides, reactions were so much more interesting when face and body language were there in addition to words and tone. And unless I missed my guess, the coming reaction was going to be one for the books. Feeding one of Cameron's hundred-commark bills into the slot, I keyed in Brother John's private number.

Somewhere on Xathru, StarrComm's fifty-kilometer-square starconnect array spat a signal across the light-years toward an identical array on whichever world it was where Brother John sat in the middle of his noxious little spiderweb. I didn't know which world it was, or even whether it was the same world each time or if he continually moved around like a touring road show.

Neither did InterSpiral Law Enforcement or any of the other more regional agencies working their various jurisdictions within the Spiral. They didn't know where he was, or where the records of his transactions were, or how to get hold of either him or them. Most every one of the beings working those agencies would give his-upper right appendage to know those things. Brother John's influence stretched a long way across the stars, and he had ruined a lot of lives and angered a lot of people along the way.

Considering my current relationship with the man and his organization, I could only hope that none of those eager badgemen found him anytime soon.

The screen cleared, and a broken-nosed thug with perpetual scowl lines around his eyes and mouth peered out at me. "Yeah?" he grunted.

"This is Jordan McKell," I identified myself, as if anyone Brother John had answering the phone for him wouldn't know all of us indentured slaves by sight. "I'd like to speak with Mr. Ryland, please."

The beetle brows seemed to twitch. "Yeah," he grunted again. "Hang on."

The screen went black. I made a small private wager with myself that Brother John would leave me hanging and sweating for at least a minute before he deigned to come on, despite the fact that fielding calls from people like me was one of his primary jobs, and also despite what this vid connect was costing me per quarter second.

I thought I'd lost my wager when the screen came back on after only twenty seconds. But no, he'd simply added an extra layer to the procedure. "Well, if it isn't Jordan McKell," a moon-faced man said in a playfully sarcastic voice, looking even more like a refugee from a mobster movie than the call screener had, his elegantly proper butler's outfit notwithstanding. "How nice of you to grace our vid screen with your presence."

"I'm amazingly delighted to see you, too," I said mildly. "Would Mr. Ryland like to hear some interesting news, or are we just taking this opportunity to help you brush up on your badinage?"

The housethug's eyes narrowed, no doubt trying to figure out what "badinage" was and whether or not he'd just been insulted. "Mr. Ryland doesn't appreciate getting interesting news from employees on the fly," he bit out. The playful part had evaporated, but the sarcasm was still there. "In case you've forgotten, you have a cargo to deliver."

"Done and done," I told him. "Or it will be soon, if it isn't already."

He frowned again; but before he could speak, his face vanished from the screen as a different extension cut in.

And there, smiling cherubically at me, was Brother John. "Hello, Jordan," he said smoothly. "And how are you?"

"Hello, Mr. Ryland," I said. "I'm just fine. I'm pleased everyone over there is so cheerful today, too."

He smiled even more genially. To look at Johnston Scotto Ryland, you would think you were in the presence of a philanthropist or a priest or at the very least a former choirboy—hence, our private "Brother John" nickname for him. And I suspected that there were still people in the Spiral who were being taken in by that winning smile and clear-conscienced face and utterly sincere voice.

Especially the voice. "Why shouldn't we be happy?" he said, nothing in his manner giving the slightest hint of what was going on behind those dark and soulless eyes. "Business is booming, profits are up, and all my valued employees are working so wonderfully together."

The smile didn't change, but suddenly there was a chill in the air. "Except for you, Jordan, my lad. For some unknown reason you seem to have suddenly grown weary of our company."

"I don't know what could have given you that impression, Mr. Ryland," I protested, trying my own version of the innocent act.

"Don't you," he said, the temperature dropping a few more degrees. Apparently, innocence wasn't playing well today. "I'm told the *Stormy Banks* docked on Xathru not thirty minutes ago. And that you weren't on it."

"That's right, I wasn't," I agreed. "But Ixil was, and

so was your merchandise. That's the important part, isn't it?"

"All aspects of my arrangements are important," he countered. "When I instruct you to deliver a cargo, I expect *you* to deliver it. *And* I expect you to take it directly to its proper destination, without unscheduled and unnecessary stops along the way. That *was* our agreement; or do I have to bring up—again—the five hundred thousand in debts I bailed you and your partner out of?"

"No, sir," I sighed. Not that I was ever likely to forget his largesse in that matter, what with him reminding me about it every other assignment. "But if I may be so bold, I'd like to point out that another of your standing instructions is that we should maintain our facade of poor but honest cargo haulers."

"And how does that apply here?"

"I was offered a position as pilot on another ship for a one-time transport job," I explained. "A thousand commarks up front, with another two on delivery. How could I turn that down and still pretend to be poor?"

That line of reasoning hadn't impressed Ixil very much back on Meima. It impressed Brother John even less. "You don't seriously expect me to buy that, do you?" he demanded, the cultured facade cracking just a bit.

"I hope so, sir, yes," I said. "Because that *is* why I did it."

For a long moment he studied my face, and I found myself holding my breath. Brother John's tentacles stretched everywhere, even to backwater worlds like Xathru. A touch of a button, a few pointed words, and I would probably not even make it out of the StarrComm building alive. A flurry of contingency plans, none of them very promising, began to chase each other through my mind.

And then, suddenly, he smiled again, the chill that

had been frosting the screen vanishing into warm sunshine. "You're a sly one, Jordan—you really are," he said, his tone implying that all sins had graciously been forgiven. "All right; since you've gotten my cargo delivered on time, you may go ahead and take this other ship and cargo home. Consider it a vacation of sorts for all your service these past three years, eh?"

Considering what I'd already been through on the *Icarus,* this trip was not exactly turning out to be my idea of a good time. But compared to facing Brother John's vengeance, I decided I couldn't complain. "Thank you, Mr. Ryland," I said, giving him my best humble gratitude look. "I'll let you know when I'll be available again."

"Of course you will," he said; and suddenly the warm sunshine vanished again into an icy winter's night. "Because you still owe us a considerable debt. And you know how Mr. Antoniewicz feels about employees who try to leave without paying off their debts."

Involuntarily, I shivered. Mr. Antoniewicz was the head of the whole organization, with a shadowy identity that was even more carefully guarded than Brother John's. Rumor had it that there were already over a thousand warrants for his arrest across the Spiral, ranging from happyjam manufacture to mass murder to deliberately starting brush wars so that he could sell arms to both sides. The badgemen would probably give any *two* appendages to smoke him out of his lair. "Yes, sir," I told Brother John. "I wouldn't want to disappoint either of you."

"Good," he said. His smile shifted to somewhere in early April, glowing with springtime warmth but with the threat of winter chill still lurking in the wings. "Then I'll let you get back to your new ship. Good-bye, Jordan."

"Good-bye, Mr. Ryland," I said. He glanced up over the camera and nodded, and the vid went dead.

I sat there scowling at the blank screen for nearly a minute, trying to sort through the nuances of the conversation. Something here didn't feel quite right, but for the life of me I couldn't figure out what it was.

And I was painfully aware that that *life of me* phrasing could well turn out to be literally the case. If Brother John—or Mr. Antoniewicz above him—decided that I had outlived my usefulness or otherwise needed to be made an example of, he would hardly telegraph that decision by threatening me on an open vid connect. No, he would smile kindly, just as he had there at the end, and then he would touch that button and say those few pointed words, and I would quietly vanish.

A soft rustling of bills startled me out of my reverie: what was left of my hundred commarks feeding down into the change bin. I collected the bills and coins together, wondering if I should just go ahead and feed them back in. I could give Uncle Arthur a call . . .

With a sigh, I slid the bills loosely into my ID folder and dropped the coins into a side pocket. Uncle Arthur had been the conniving benefactor who'd worked so hard to get Ixil and me connected with Brother John in the first place, back when our soaring debts were threatening to land us in fraud court, and I just knew what he would say if I even suggested I might be in trouble with the organization.

Besides, it was unlikely that he would lift a finger to try to help me even if I did call him. In his own way, he was as much a reclusive figure as Mr. Antoniewicz, and he had made it abundantly clear that he liked it that way. It would serve him right if he had to read about my death on the newsnets.

Overhead, the lights flickered twice, a gentle reminder that my call was finished and others were waiting their turn for the booth. Standing up, I pulled my plasmic from its holster nestled beneath my left armpit, checked the power pack and safety, then returned the weapon to concealment, making sure it was loose enough for a quick draw if necessary. Then, taking a deep breath, I unsealed the door and stepped out into the corridor.

None of the dozen or so people present shouted in triumph or whipped out a weapon. In fact, none of them gave me so much as a second glance as I made my way back down the corridor to the main lobby. Aiming for an unoccupied corner where I could have at least a modicum of privacy, I pulled out my phone and punched Ixil's number.

He answered on the third vibe. "Yes?"

"It's Jordan," I told him. "What's your status?"

"I've landed and finished the entry forms," he said. I had to hand it to him; not a single cue anywhere in words or tone to indicate the surprise he was undoubtedly feeling at hearing from me here on Xathru. I could imagine Pix and Pax were doing some serious twitching, though. "I've also made contact with the local representative and started off-loading the cargo."

"Good." So we were almost rid of Brother John's happyjam. Best news I'd heard all day. "When you're finished, upgrade to a long-term docking permit, lock down the ship, and get yourself over to Dock Rec Three-Two-Seven."

There was just the briefest pause. "Trouble?"

"You could say that, yes," I told him. "Our mechanic was killed during the flight, and I need a replacement. You're it."

"An accident?"

I grimaced. "At this point I'm not really sure. Better come prepared."

Once again, he took it all in stride. "I'll be there in forty minutes," he said calmly.

"I'll be there in thirty," I said, hoping fervently that I wasn't being overly optimistic. "See you soon."

I keyed off and, squaring my shoulders, crossed the lobby and headed out into the sunlight, tension and uncertainty mixing together to make the skin on my back crawl. Just because nothing had happened to me in the StarrComm building didn't mean it wasn't going to happen somewhere else between here and the *Icarus*.

"Hey, Hummer," a crackly voice came from my left.

I jumped, hand twitching automatically toward my hidden gun. But it was only a Grifser, his tiny eyes peering up at me from leprous-looking skin, his spindly paws held out pleadingly. Brother John might use aliens from time to time when they suited his purposes, but he would never use them to discipline one of his own people, even a lowly smuggler in his final disgrace. Like most of the Spiral's criminal organizations—human and alien both—the Antoniewicz organization was oddly but vehemently ethnocentric. "What?" I asked.

"You got any caff?" the alien asked plaintively. "I pay. You got any caff?"

"Sorry," I said, brushing past. Grifsers were absolutely nuts for Earth-style caffeinated beverages or snacks—it actually qualified as a drug for them, putting it on the controlled substance list anyplace they had a decent-sized enclave. Elsewhere in the Spiral, they created nuisances of themselves around spaceport entrances and tavernos, but most of them knew how to more or less graciously take no for an answer. Those who weren't feeling all that gracious were usually at least smart enough not to press the point with beings half again their size and twice their weight.

This particular Grifser was apparently on the trailing edge of both those bell curves. "No!" he insisted, darting around behind me and coming up again on my right. "Caff caff—now now! Will *pay* for it."

"I said *no*," I snapped, reaching out to push him away. I didn't have time for this nonsense.

"Caff!" he insisted, grabbing my arm and hanging on to it like a mottled-skin leech. "Give me caff!"

Swearing under my breath, I grabbed one of his

paws and pried it off. I was working on prying the other away when a long arm snaked its way around my back from my left to an overly familiar resting place just beneath the right side of my rib cage. "Hello, old Hummer chum," a voice crooned into my left ear.

I turned my head to find myself gazing at close range into an alien face that looked like a topographical map of the Pyrenees. "If you don't mind, friend—"

"Ah—but I do mind," he said. His hand shifted slightly, dipping expertly under the edge of my jacket and then burrowing upward to rest against my rib cage again.

And suddenly the hard knot of his fist was joined by something else. Something that felt cold through my shirt and very, very sharp. "It's a wrist knife," my assailant confirmed in a low voice. "Don't make me use it."

"Not a problem," I assured him, feeling chagrined, scared, and stupid all at the same time. Brother John had totally blindsided me on this one, catching me like some fool fresh off the cabbage truck.

From my right another of his species appeared, tossing a four-pack of cola to the Grifser with one hand as he reached under my jacket and relieved me of my plasmic with the other. "Now," the first said as their decoy ran off gurgling with delight over his prize. "Let's go have ourselves a nice little chat."

Flanking me on either side like a couple of long-lost friends, they guided me through the usual crowd of spaceport traffic, along a couple of narrow and increasingly depopulated service streets, and eventually into a blind alley blocked off at the far end by a warehouse loading dock. It was a long way to go, I thought, for what was going to be only tentative privacy.

But more importantly, from my point of view anyway, the trip itself was already a major blunder on their part. The ten-minute walk had given me enough time to recover from the shock and start thinking again, and that thinking had persuaded me that my original assessment had indeed been the correct one. Whoever these thugs were, they weren't Brother John's enforcers. Not just because he didn't like aliens, but because his boys would have dropped me right there in front of the StarrComm building instead of engaging in all this unnecessary exercise.

All of which boiled down to the fact that, whatever I wound up having to do to them, no one was likely to care very much. At least, that's what I hoped it boiled down to.

They settled me with my back against the loading dock and took a prudent couple of steps away. The first was now holding his wrist knife openly: a kind of push knife sticking out from his palm at right angles to his arm, the weapon strapped to his hand and wrist so that it couldn't be snatched or kicked out of his hand. The other was holding my plasmic loosely at his side, not crassly pointed but ready if it was needed. Both aliens were roughly human in height and build, I could see now, except with simian-length arms and foreshortened torsos. The relief-map look of their faces was repeated over their entire bodies, or at least the parts that were visible sticking out of the long brown neo-Greek tunics they were wearing.

"If this is a shakedown, I'm already broke," I warned, getting in the first word just to irritate them as I gave their outfits a casual once-over. There were no bulges or asymmetric bagginess that I could see. Either they didn't have any backup weapons at all—which would be pretty careless on their part—or else they were holstered behind their backs.

"It's not a shakedown," Lumpy One said, waving his wrist knife back toward the main docking area. "We want your cargo."

I blinked in surprise. "You want to steal fifty cases of combine machine parts?" I asked incredulously.

They exchanged furtively startled glances. "That's not what you're carrying," Lumpy Two growled.

I shrugged. "That's what it says on the manifest and the crates. If there's anything else in there, the Barnswell Depot is going to have a lot of explaining to do."

For a long second Lumpy One seemed at a loss for words. Then his crack of a mouth cracked a little wider in what I decided was probably his version of a sly smile. "Clever," he said. "But not clever enough. You are Jordan McKell, you came here from Meima, and you have a highly valuable cargo aboard your ship. We want it."

"Jordan who?" I asked. "Sorry, boys, but you missed completely on this one. My name's Ivo Khachnin, I'm flying a ship called the *Singing Buffalo,* and I'm carrying fifty cases of farm-equipment parts. Here—I can prove it." I reached a hand into my jacket—

"Stop!" Lumpy One barked, leaping forward with knife held ready. "I'll get it."

"Sure, pal," I said, managing to sound both startled and bewildered by his violent reaction. In point of fact, I'd been counting on it. "Fine. Help yourself."

He approached at a cautious angle, staying out of his partner's line of fire, which at least proved he hadn't picked up his street-mugging technique solely from watching Grade-B star-thrillers. Carefully, he set the point of his wrist knife against my throat and reached into my inside jacket pocket. The probing fingers located my ID folder and pulled it out, holding it cautiously by a corner as if expecting it to be boobytrapped.

And as it came free from my jacket, the bills I'd slipped carelessly inside in the StarrComm booth slid out and fluttered colorfully to the ground.

It was a small distraction, but it was all I needed. As their eyes flicked involuntarily to the floating commarks, I jerked my head back and around, moving it out of contact with Lumpy One's knife, simultaneously snapping up my left hand to catch his wrist behind the knife strap. Pushing his arm high, I ducked under it and spun 180 degrees around, ending up standing behind him with his knife arm between us, bent upward toward his neck at what I very much hoped was a painful angle.

"Release him!" Lumpy Two spat. He was holding my plasmic straight out at me now, clutched in a two-handed grip, his whole body trembling.

"Make me," I grunted, looping my right arm around Lumpy One's throat and pulling him hard back against me. If I'd guessed wrong about this—if he did not in fact have a backup weapon—I was now officially in serious trouble.

But he did. There it was, a hard flat object pressing against my abdomen as I held him to me. Cranking his arm up another couple of centimeters, eliciting a gasped phrase that was probably an unfavorable comment on my parentage, I twisted the knife tip down and jabbed it into the fabric of his tunic. With the jammed knife preventing him from lowering his arm, and the limits of his own tendon structure preventing him from raising it, the limb was effectively self-immobilized, freeing my left hand. Reaching up the back of his tunic, I grabbed his weapon.

Lumpy One shouted something, probably a warning, to his companion. But by then it was already too late. Almost too late, anyway. Lumpy Two got off a shot that nearly scorched the side of my face as the superheated plasma ball made a near miss, and fired another that would have seared my right arm and possibly killed Lumpy One outright if I hadn't bent my knees suddenly, driving my kneecaps into the backs of Lumpy One's legs and dropping us both halfway to the ground. The jolt of the sudden movement sent the embedded knife tip tearing a couple of centimeters farther into the cloth and, judging from Lumpy One's gasp, into the skin beneath it as well.

And then I had his weapon out and pointed over his shoulder. The gun wasn't remotely like anything I was familiar with, but I didn't have time to do anything except hope like hell it had some stopping power behind it. Flicking a thumb key that I hoped was the safety, I squeezed the trigger.

From the size and shape of the weapon, I would have guessed it to be a fléchette thrower or maybe a two-shot scattergun. It wasn't. My hair and skin tingled with electrical discharge; and suddenly Lumpy Two was writhing in agony in the middle of a sheathing of blue-white coronal fire.

The electrical firestorm lasted about two seconds. From the looks of things, Lumpy Two himself didn't last nearly that long.

Under other circumstances I would probably have taken a few seconds to gape at the unexpected display of firepower I'd just unleashed. But I wasn't given that chance. Mouthing obvious obscenities, Lumpy One broke out of my grasp with a sudden lurch and spun around to face me, the sound of tearing cloth warning that he was half a second away from freeing his knife hand. I jumped to the side, swinging the alien weapon around; and as he got his arm free and lunged toward me, I fired again.

With the same result. Three seconds later, I was standing alone over two alien bodies, both of them charred literally beyond recognition.

I had seen a lot of repulsive things in my years of knocking around the Spiral, but this one definitely took the cake. Glancing around for any sign of witnesses— our little confrontation seemed to have gone unnoticed—I squatted down beside the corpses, trying to breathe through my mouth as I forced myself to sift through what was left of their clothing.

But there was nothing. No ID folders, no cash wallets, not even any bank cards. Or at least, I amended to myself, nothing that had survived the attack.

Lumpy Two was wearing a duplicate of the alien handgun in a half-melted holster at the small of his back. I managed to pry it loose and pocketed both weapons for future study. I retrieved my ID folder and cash from the ground—Lumpy One had dropped all of it when I jumped him—and returned my now scorched but still functional-looking plasmic to its holster. Taking one final look around, I headed away at a brisk walk.

Ixil was waiting for me at the *Icarus*'s entryway. "I thought you were going to be here in thirty minutes," he greeted me as I came up.

"I ran into a little trouble," I told him. "Why didn't you go inside?"

"I thought it would be better if you were here to introduce me," he said. "Besides, the entryway appears to be double-locked."

"Great," I scowled, punching the new code I'd set up after leaving Meima into the keypad. A double-locked entryway in port either meant the rest of the crew had sacked out for a couple of hours' sleep or, more likely, they'd scattered to the four winds the minute my back was turned.

"Had you told them to stay with the ship?" Ixil asked as the hatch swung open.

"No, I was too busy making arrangements to get Jones's body to the Port Authority and worrying about what I was going to say to Brother John," I said. "Under the circumstances, I wish I had, though."

"I thought you smelled a bit singed," he said. "Why don't we go inside and you can tell me all about it."

"Let's talk here instead," I said, sitting down inside the wraparound where I could look out into the docking area. "If people with guns start wandering casually toward the ship, I'd like to see them before they get here."

"Reasonable," Ixil agreed, sitting down a couple of meters away from me where he could cover a different field of view from mine. As he settled down, Pix and Pax hopped off his shoulders and skittered down the ramp, vanishing in opposite directions around the ship. "Now," Ixil said, "why don't you start at the beginning."

So I started at the beginning, with my near arrest on Meima, and gave him the whole story, finishing with my near death on Xathru half an hour earlier. The two ferrets came in twice while I was talking, dumping their scouting information on Ixil and presumably getting new instructions before scampering off again. Given that Ixil didn't know anyone involved in any of this, I wondered what exactly he was having the outriders look for. Maybe it was just pure Kalix hunters' instinct.

"I seem to have missed all the excitement," he said when I finished. "A pity."

"I wouldn't worry about it if I were you," I warned. "It's still a long way to Earth."

"It is that," he conceded. "You said you took the aliens' weapons?"

I passed them over to him. He looked at the charred one for a moment, his nose wrinkling at the smell, then exchanged it for the other. "Interesting," he said, studying it closely. "Coronal-discharge weapons aren't exactly new—I presume from your description that that's what these are—but I've never heard of such compact ones before."

"I've never seen one of any size," I said. "I can tell you one thing, though: These things really mess up victim identification."

"I can imagine," he said soberly. "Face, retinas, and prints, plus any IDs or datadisks the victim happens to be carrying, all destroyed or badly damaged. A convenient little side effect of the killing shot."

"You have such a way with words," I growled. "I just hope these things don't catch on with the taverno brawling crowd."

"I think that highly unlikely," Ixil assured me. "Aside from the tremendous manufacturing costs involved and the relative ease of detection, corona weapons by their nature have a very short range. Three meters, I'd guess; four at the outside."

I shivered. In an uncomfortably large number of situations, a four-meter range would be perfectly adequate for the purpose. "Remind me to practice up on my distance shots."

"Good idea." He dropped the guns into his hip pouch. "I'll try taking one apart later and see if I can figure out where it was made. Right now, I'm more curious about this deadly accident of yours."

"I'll admit right up front that it's got *me* stumped," I said, feeling disgusted with myself. Strange and unpleasant things were happening all around me, and so far I didn't have a handle on any of it. "I ran a diagnostic across the whole system, and I can't figure how the grav generator kicked in when it did."

"You are, of course, hardly an expert in such things," Ixil pointed out, not unkindly. "There are three main locations where the generator can be turned on: the bridge, engineering, and computer."

"Right," I said. *That* much I knew. "I was on the bridge—and *I* didn't do it—Revs Nicabar was in engineering, and Tera was handling the computer."

"Both of them alone, I take it?"

"Nicabar definitely was," I said. "The only way back there is through the wraparound, which was serving as airlock at the time."

"Odd design," Ixil murmured, glancing around.

"Tell me about it," I said dryly. "I don't know if

Tera was alone, but the only person who could have been with her was Hayden Everett, our medic."

"Who you also said helped Jones on with his suit before the incident," Ixil said thoughtfully.

"You think there's a connection?"

He shrugged, a human gesture he'd picked up from me. "Not necessarily; I merely note the fact. I also note the fact that if Everett *wasn't* with Tera, that means all the rest of the crew were alone."

"Actually, no," I corrected him. "Geoff Shawn, the electronics man, had come to the bridge to watch Chort's spacewalk on my monitors."

"Really," he said. "Interesting."

I cocked an eyebrow. "In what way?"

"I said there were three main places where the grav generator could be turned on," he said, stroking his cheek thoughtfully with stubby fingertips. "But there are probably several other places where someone could jump power into the system."

"I was afraid of that," I said heavily. "I suppose it would be too much to ask that there would be no way to set that sort of thing up with a timer."

"You mean so that Shawn's appearance on the bridge might have been solely to establish an alibi for himself?"

"Something like that."

He shrugged again. "If he could tap into the system, I see no reason he couldn't set it up on a timer, too." He paused. "Of course, for that matter, the same thing goes for Chort and Jones."

I frowned. "You must be kidding."

"Must I?" he countered. "Look at the facts. Chort wasn't injured in the fall, at least not very seriously. And if Jones set it up, he may have planned to catch him before he fell too far."

"And his motive?"

"Whose, Jones's or Chort's?"

"Either one."

Ixil shrugged. "What motive does anyone here have? That's the main reason I hesitate to ascribe any of this to malice."

I sighed; but he was right. Considering the *Icarus*'s haphazard design, glitches could easily turn out to be the rule rather than the exception. "What about Jones's rebreather?"

Ixil hissed softly between his teeth. "That one I don't like at all," he said. "I don't suppose you still have it."

I shook my head. "We had to turn over the suit and rebreather both with Jones's body."

"I was afraid of that," he said. "I would have liked to have looked it over. Frankly, I don't know if it's even theoretically possible for a rebreather to malfunction that way on its own."

"Then you're thinking sabotage?"

"That would be my guess; but again, for what purpose? Why would anyone aboard want to kill Jones?"

"How should I know?" I asked irritably. "These people are total strangers to me."

"Exactly my point," he said. "From your description of how Cameron was hiring his crewers, all these people are supposedly also total strangers to each other."

I frowned. That part hadn't occurred to me. "You're right," I said slowly, thinking back to that first meeting back at the base of the *Icarus*'s stairway. "No one gave any indication of knowing any of the others. At least not when I was watching."

"Which implies that if any of this is deliberate there must be some other motivation," Ixil concluded. "The general sabotage of the ship, perhaps, or the systematic disabling of the crew."

"Tied in with Cameron's failure to show up at the ship, maybe?" I suggested.

"Could be," Ixil agreed. "The massive manhunt we saw near the archaeology dig would support that theory, not to mention your playmates with the high-tech weaponry."

I drummed my fingers on the deck. "So where does that leave us?"

"With quite a few unknowns," Ixil said. "The key one, in my mind, being this mysterious cargo you're carrying. Have you any idea what's in there?"

"None whatsoever," I said. "There's nothing listed in the computer that I could find, and there are no access panels listed on the schematics where we could even go to take a look. When Cameron said it'd been sealed, he meant it."

"We may have to find some way to unseal it before we're done with this," Ixil said.

There was a scrabbling sound at the hatchway, and Pix and Pax appeared. "Okay, I give up," I asked, finally tired of wondering about it. "What exactly have they been doing out there? Neither you nor they know what any of the crew looks like."

"Given your brush with the Lumpy Brothers, as you call them, it occurred to me that someone might have the *Icarus* under surveillance," Ixil said as the ferrets climbed his torso to his shoulders again. "I'm watching for anyone who seems to be loitering around the area without a legitimate reason to do so."

"Ah. And?"

"If he's there, he's very good at his job," Ixil concluded. "By the way, is one of your crewers about one-point-nine meters tall and bulking out at a good hundred ten kilograms, with short black hair and a face like a throw-boxer with a bad win/loss record?"

"Sounds like our medic, Everett," I said, scooting across the floor to his side. Sure enough, there he was, heading toward us with an air of brisk determination about him. "Yes, that's him," I confirmed, getting to my feet. "Be nice, now—he's probably never seen a Kalix before."

Apparently lost in his own thoughts, Everett didn't

even notice us standing in the shadow of the wrap-around until he was halfway up the ramp. Judging from how high he jumped, he had indeed never seen a Kalix before. "It's all right—don't worry," I said quickly, before he could turn tail and run for the hills. "This is Ixil. He's with us."

"Ah," Everett said, regaining his balance and most of his composure and peering oddly at Ixil. "So *this* is your partner. Ixil, was it?"

"Yes," Ixil said. "How did you know I was Jordan's partner?"

Everett blinked. "He said he would be bringing his partner in to take Jones's place," he said, looking at me uncertainly. "Just before we set down. Didn't you say that?"

"Yes, I did," I confirmed. "Any problems with the drop-off?"

"Not really," he said. "It was your basic fifteen-minute inquest. They did want to keep the suit and rebreather, though."

"I figured they would," I said. "Where's Nicabar?"

"He headed off somewhere after the inquest," Everett said. "Why, is that a problem?"

"It could become one," I said. "Did you happen to see any of the others on your way back?"

"I passed Shawn at one of the vendor stalls a few minutes ago," he said. "I haven't seen anyone else."

"Perhaps it's time we called them," Ixil suggested. "I presume you have their phone numbers, Jordan?"

"Yes, they're programmed into list two," I said, handing him my phone. "Give them a call, will you, and tell them to get back as soon as they can. I'll make sure the refueling's been finished and get the rest of the paperwork out of the way."

"What can I do?" Everett asked.

You can tell me who out there has it in for this ship and its crew, the suggestion ran through my mind. But there was no point springing something like that on him. Odds were he hadn't the faintest idea anyway. "Go make sure your gear's ready for liftoff," I told him instead. "As soon as the rest get back, we're out of here."

CHAPTER

5

They straggled in over the next hour, Shawn and Nicabar clearly glad we were getting under way, Tera just as clearly annoyed that we'd cut short what had apparently been a successful shopping spree, at least judging from the number of bags she hauled aboard. Chort didn't show any particular preference one way or the other.

With the ever-looming threat of hue and cry from the Port Authority over the deaths of my two assailants—and the associated threat that the port might be summarily shut down at any minute—I spent the entire time sweating as I fought upstream against bureaucratic inertia, trying to finish Jones's death report and all the procedural preflight paperwork before the bodies were discovered.

To my surprise, we got cleared and headed out into space without any sign of official outrage or panic over the charred remains I'd left at the loading dock. Perhaps the spot the Lumpy Brothers had picked for my interrogation had been more private than it had looked. Either that, or someone had done a very efficient job of sweeping the whole incident under the rug.

I'd had short conversations with each of the crewers on the trip from Meima, but most of them had either concerned basic ship's business or were just casual chat. But now, with everything that had happened since then, I decided it was time to skip past the surface and find out what exactly these people were made of. If someone was out to get us, I needed to know which ones I could trust not to buckle under pressure.

And so, as soon as we'd made our slice into hyperspace and were on our way, I left Ixil watching the bridge and headed aft.

The *Icarus*'s engine room was just like the rest of the ship, only more so. The same odd arrangement of equipment and control systems was repeated back there, as if Salvador Dali had been in charge of the layout. In addition, though, the general attempt elsewhere to keep the various cables and fluid conduits tucked out of the way in the gap between the inner and outer hulls had seemingly been abandoned here. They were everywhere: a bewildering, multicolored spaghetti tangle that brushed against sleeves and shins and occasionally threatened to clothesline the unwary traveler.

And buried away at his control console near the middle of the sculpted chaos was Revs Nicabar.

"Ah—McKell," he greeted me as I successfully negotiated past a final pair of thick conduits leading to the large, shimmery Möbius strip that was the heart of the *Icarus*'s stardrive. "Welcome to Medusa's Lair. Watch your head."

"And arms, legs, and throat," I added, pulling out a swivel stool from the side of his console and sitting down. "How's it flying?"

"Amazingly well, actually," he said. "Rather surprising, I know, considering that it looks like a refugee from a Doolian scrap heap. But whoever the designer was, at least the builder had the sense to install some decent equipment."

"It's like that on the bridge, too," I said. "Good equipment, odd placement. I'll make you a small wager that it was a working spacer who designed it, not some so-called expert. Tell me, did you have any problems out in the port back there?"

His eyes narrowed, just a bit, and I saw his gaze flick to the side of my head where the plasmic near miss had slightly singed my hair. I didn't think the marks showed; possibly I was wrong. "None at all," he said. "Of course, I was only outside a half hour or so—up till then I was sitting on the fuelers making sure they did their job properly. I take it there was some trouble I missed out on?"

"You might say that," I allowed. "Tell me about yourself, Revs."

I'd been hoping my sudden change of topic would spark a telling reaction. What I got was equally informative: no reaction at all. "What do you want to know?" he countered calmly.

"Let's start with your background," I said. "Where you picked up your drive certification, how long you've been flying, why you were at loose ends on Meima, and how you were hired for this trip."

"I learned drive-jocking in the service," he said. "EarthGuard Marines, stationed mostly out among the settlements in the Kappa Vega Sector. I was in for ten years, left six years ago to try my hand in the private sector."

"Odd timing," I said. "Considering that by then the Patth had already swallowed up the lion's share of the Spiral's shipping."

"It was a gamble, but I'd had enough of military life by then and thought I could make a go of it. Mostly, I was right." He shrugged. "As to the *Icarus*, I got signed up more or less simultaneously with my resignation from my previous ship."

"Oh?"

"Yes." His face hardened. "I'd just found out my freighter was actually mask-shilling for the Patth."

I frowned. "That's a new one on me."

"It's the latest Patth twist to get around local protection ordinances," he said. "On some of these worlds twenty to forty percent of cargo tonnage has to be carried by local shippers. So the Patth hire a ship on the sly, load it to the gills with as much stuff as it can carry, and send it on in. It skews the numbers, the Patth pocket the profits, and it pulls business away from the people the ordinances are supposed to protect." He shrugged. "Typical Patth connivery."

"I take it you resigned in something of a huff?"

He grinned suddenly. "I don't know if 'huff' quite covers it, but I made damn sure I was loud enough for everyone in the taverno to hear what was happening. Anyway, Borodin was there at the bar talking to someone else, and when I stomped out he followed and offered me this job."

He glanced around. "Though if I'd known what I was getting into, I might have looked a little harder for something else."

He looked at me, his eyes suddenly cool. "My turn for a question. Do you always carry a gun on board your own ship?"

I cocked an eyebrow. "I'm impressed. I didn't realize it was so obvious."

"Ten years in EarthGuard," he reminded me. "Do I get an answer?"

"Sure," I said. "Number one: It's not exactly my ship. Number two: I was kidnapped in port by a couple of alien lads who wanted our cargo."

"Interesting," he murmured. "And you suspect someone aboard of complicity with them?"

"I can't imagine why anyone would be," I said. It was a perfectly true statement, even if it wasn't precisely an answer to his question.

"No, of course not," he agreed in a tone that implied he'd heard both the words I'd said and the words I hadn't said and would be mulling them over later on his own. "In which case, I presume this visit is for the purpose of judging whether or not I'll be helping you circle the wagons if and when the shooting starts?"

I had to hand it to him, the man was sharp. "Very good," I said approvingly. "I hereby withdraw all the unkind thoughts I've had toward EarthGuard Marines over the years. Most of them, anyway."

"Thanks," Nicabar said dryly. "The answer's a qualified yes. I've dealt with my share of pirates and hijackers, and I don't like them much. You can count on me to help fight them off. *But.*"

He leveled a finger at my chest. "My support *and* my presence are conditional on the cargo being totally legit. If I find out we're running drugs or guns or that we're mask-shilling for the Patth, I'm out at the next port. Clear?"

"Clear," I said firmly, hoping I sounded heartily on his side on this one. If he ever found out about my connection with Brother John, I was going to have some fancy verbal dancing to do. "But I don't think you have anything to worry about on any of those scores. Borodin told me the cargo had been cleared through customs on Gamm, and one would assume they were reasonably thorough."

"Borodin told me that, too," Nicabar said darkly. "But then, Borodin's not here, is he?"

"No, he's not," I conceded. "And before you ask, I don't know why."

"I didn't think you did." He peered at me thoughtfully. "If you ever find out, I presume you'll tell me."

"Of course," I said, as if it went without saying, as I stood up. "I've got to get back to the bridge. See you later."

I made my way back through the wiring undergrowth, wishing irreverently for a machete, and ducked through the aft airlock hatch into the wraparound. Nicabar was sharp, all right. Maybe a little too sharp. Perhaps his lack of reaction to my story about being jumped was because he already knew all about it.

In which case, unfortunately, I ran immediately and solidly into the question of why he hadn't then done something to keep the *Icarus* from leaving Xathru. Unless the Lumpy Brothers were just hunting cargoes at random, maybe working strictly on their own.

But that one didn't wash at all. They'd known me by sight and name, and they'd known I'd come in from Meima. And they sure as hell hadn't bought those corona weapons off a gun-shop rack.

I was halfway through the wraparound, still turning all the questions over in my mind, when I heard a dull, metallic thud.

I stopped dead in my tracks, listening hard. My first thought was that we had another pressure ridge or crack; but that wasn't at all what the noise had sounded like. It had been more like two pieces of metal clanking hollowly against each other.

And near as I could tell, it had come from someplace immediately ahead of me.

I unglued myself from the deck and hurried ahead, ducking through the forward airlock and into the main sphere, all my senses alert for trouble. No one was visible in the corridor, and aside from the galley/dayroom three rooms ahead on my right all the doors were closed. I paused again, listening hard, but there was nothing but the normal hum of shipboard activity.

The first door ahead on my right was the computer room. I stepped up to it and tapped the release pad with my left hand, my right poised ready to grab for my plasmic if necessary. The door slid open—

Tera was seated at the computer, holding a hand pressed against the side of her head. "What?" she snapped crossly, glaring at me.

"Just checking on you," I said, glancing around the

room. No one else was there, and nothing seemed out of place. "I thought I heard a noise."

"That was my head banging against the bulkhead," she growled. "I dropped a datadisk and ran into the wall when I leaned over to get it. Is that all right with you?"

"No problem," I said hastily, backing out rapidly and letting the door close on her scowl. This was twice now, counting my spectacularly unnecessary floor dive back in that Meima hotel room, where I'd overreacted and made something of a fool of myself.

The difference was that Ixil was already used to that sort of thing from me. Tera wasn't, and my face was hot as I glowered my way forward.

Ixil was seated in the restraint chair when I reached the bridge, Pix and Pax nosing curiously around the bases of the various consoles in their rodent way. "How was Nicabar?" he asked.

"Smart, competent, and apparently on our side," I told him. "Tera, unfortunately, probably now thinks I'm an idiot. Did you hear a metallic clunking noise a couple of minutes ago?"

"Not from here, no," he said, snapping his fingers twice. The two ferrets abandoned their exploration in response to the signal, scampering up his legs and onto his shoulders. "They didn't hear anything, either," he added. "Could it have been a pressure ridge forming?"

"No, it wasn't anything like that," I said. "Tera told me she'd bumped her head on the bulkhead. But that's not what it sounded like to me."

"Perhaps it was Shawn across the corridor from her in the electronics workshop," Ixil suggested as the ferrets headed down his legs to the deck again. "He said he was going to be tearing apart and cleaning one of the spare trim regulators."

"He came here? Or did he use the intercom?"

"He came here," Ixil said. "He wanted to ask you to run a decision/diagnostic on the regulators already on-line, not wanting to have one of the spares torn apart if there was any chance we might need it."

"Unfortunately, this ship has all the decision-making capabilities of a politician up for reelection," I said. "Tera's computer back there is just this side of utterly useless."

"Yes, he mentioned that," Ixil agreed. "I did what I could in the way of a diagnostic, then told him to go ahead."

"Fine," I said, pulling out the console's swivel stool. I sat down facing Ixil, keeping the door visible at the corner of my eye. "I presume you took the opportunity to find out a little about him?"

"Of course," he said, as if there would be any doubt. "An interesting young man, though he strikes me as something of the rebellious type. He's quite well traveled—he went on several survey-match trips while in tech school, including one that followed Captain Dak'ario's famous journey across the Spiral three hundred years ago."

"Sounds like a flimsy excuse to get out of real classes." I sniffed. "Which school was it?"

"Amdrigal Technical Institute on New Rome," he said. "Graduated fifth in his class, or so he says."

"Impressive, if true," I admitted grudgingly. "What was he doing on Meima?"

"He was out of work," Ixil said. "Why, he wouldn't say—he went rather evasive every time I tried to move us back to that topic. He *did* say that he was sitting in a taverno wearing his class jacket and being picked on by some kids from a rival school when he caught Cameron's eye."

"Borodin, please, at least in public," I cautioned him. "That's the name everyone else aboard knows him by."

"Right. Sorry." He paused, an odd expression flitting across his face. "There's one other thing that may or may not mean anything. Have you noticed Shawn seems to have a rather peculiar odor about him?"

I frowned. My first reaction was to think that that was possibly the strangest comment Ixil had ever made, certainly in recent memory. But Ixil was a nonhuman, with access to a pair of even more nonhuman outriders, and all of them had different sensory ranges from mine. "No, I hadn't," I said.

"It's quite subtle," he said. "But it's definitely there. My initial thought was that it might be related to a possible medical problem, the odor coming either from the illness itself or induced by medication."

I felt my throat tighten. "Or it could be coming from some other kind of drug. The illegal type, maybe?"

"Could be," Ixil said. "Not standard happyjam, I don't think, but there are any number of variations I'm not familiar with." He shrugged. "Then again, it could also be a result of something exotic he had for lunch in the port."

"Nice to have it narrowed down." Still, in all the years I'd known Ixil his instincts had never steered him wrong in this sort of thing. And there *had* been the attitude change I'd noticed myself in Shawn earlier in the trip, a change that could well have had something to do with drugs. "All right, we'll keep an eye on him. See if he smells the same tomorrow after a day of shipboard food."

"I will," he promised. "Speaking of tomorrow, I notice you've scheduled our next fueling stop on Dorscind's World. I thought I might remind you that Dorscind's World is not exactly a highlight of the average five-star tourist cruise."

"Which is precisely why I picked it," I told him. Pix and Pax had finished their deck-level tour of the bridge now and had scampered out the door into the corridor. I sent up a silent prayer that they wouldn't run across Everett; with his bulk, the big medic might step on them before he even noticed they were underfoot. "Paperwork accuracy has never been exactly a high priority with the Port Authority there, particularly if you're a few commarks heavy on the docking fees. I figure that the eighty-two hours it'll take to get there should be long enough for us to create a new identity for the *Icarus* that'll be good enough to pass muster."

"I'm sure we can put something together," he rumbled, eyeing me speculatively. "Did your tangle with the Lumpy Brothers bother you that much?"

"More than you know," I assured him grimly. "You see, according to the schedule Cameron left me—the schedule he presumably filed with the Meima Port Authority—the *Icarus*'s first stop was going to be Trottsen. We weren't supposed to be on Xathru at all."

His squashed-iguana face hardened. "Yet the Lumpy Brothers knew you were there."

"*And* called me by name," I nodded. "Granted, they may have tagged me when my turn was called at the StarrComm building—I had no reason at the time not to give my right name there. But why pick on me at all?"

Ixil nodded thoughtfully. "Can't be one of the crew," he murmured, half to himself. "If someone here wanted the cargo, he would have simply stolen it himself after everyone else left the ship."

"Depending on whether he could get through Cameron's security sealing," I said. "But at the very least he would have made sure the *Icarus* didn't lift. And all he needed to do to accomplish that was to phone the Port Authority with an anonymous report about a pair of crisped bodies lying next to a cul-de-sac loading dock."

Ixil cocked his head to the side. "In other words, he could have used the same technique that got you detained on Meima."

"Yes," I agreed. "And the fact that it *didn't* happen on Xathru implies to me that it wasn't someone aboard who pulled that stunt on Meima. But it *does* suggest a reason why the Lumpy Brothers latched on to me but not on to anyone else aboard."

Ixil nodded. "The Meima Port Authority report had your name."

"Not only my name, but my name linked with Cameron's," I said. "Someone got hold of that near-arrest report and disseminated it to assorted associates across the Spiral with instructions to be on the lookout for me. The Lumpy Brothers just happened to get lucky."

"Or else backtracked your name to the *Stormy Banks* and looked up my flight schedule," Ixil suggested. "That might explain how they happened to be hanging around the StarrComm building."

"I hadn't thought of that part," I acknowledged. "You're probably right."

"It also indicates our employer is probably still at large," Ixil continued, stroking his cheek thoughtfully. "I imagine he remembers all the rest of the names of the people he hired on Meima, in which case the private alert ought to have included their names as well."

"Good point," I said, grimacing. What had become of Cameron was still high on my list of annoying loose ends. "Though that's not definitive—I doubt any of the others had their names called over a loudspeaker in the market."

"Which leaves us only the question of who's behind all this," Ixil concluded. "And how we smoke him or them out into the open."

"Maybe that's *your* only unanswered question," I said. "Personally, I'm already on page two of that list. And as to who's pulling the strings in the background, I'm not at all sure we even want to go poking that direction. It seems to me that our job right now is to get the *Icarus* and its cargo to Earth, preferably with it and us in one piece. Well, one piece each, anyway."

"You may be right." He hesitated. "You said you called Brother John to discuss this sudden change in plans. You didn't say whether or not you'd also spoken with Uncle Arthur."

I grimaced. "No," I said. "I was hoping we could—oh, I don't know. Surprise him, maybe?"

Even without the ferrets on his shoulders to do their twitching thing, I had no trouble reading Ixil's reaction to that one. "I won't waste time by asking if you seriously believe that to be a good idea," he said. "I'll make you a small wager: that he won't be any happier at your accepting this job than Brother John was."

"If you're expecting me to cover that bet, you can forget it," I said sourly, the proverbial admonition against trying to serve two masters running through my mind. No, Uncle Arthur would definitely not be happy with me over this one. And the longer I put off calling him, the unhappier he was likely to get. "Oh, all right," I sighed. "I'll call him as soon as we hit Dorscind's World."

"That's the spirit," he said, with all the cheerful enthusiasm of someone who would probably find himself unavoidably busy tightening bolts on the *Icarus* while I was sweating it out under Uncle Arthur's basilisk glare in a StarrComm booth. "What's our plan until then?"

"To create a new identity for the *Icarus,* and to keep an eye on our backs," I said. Across at the bridge door, the two ferrets reappeared and headed straight up Ixil's legs. "As far as I'm concerned, we still don't have a satisfactory explanation of what happened to Jones and Chort—"

The ferrets reached Ixil's shoulders; and abruptly, he made a quick double slashing motion across his throat with his fingertips. "—makes the best apple brandy anywhere in the Spiral," I said, shifting verbal gears as smoothly as I could manage. The voice of someone speaking, I knew, could be heard well before the actual words could be made out, as could the sharp break of that voice being suddenly cut off. "In fact, I'd put it up against anything made on Taurus *or* even Earth—"

I caught a movement from the corner of my eye; at the same time Ixil turned his head in that direction and nodded courteously. "Good evening, Tera," he said, breaking into my improvised babbling. "What can we do for you?"

I turned to face the door. Tera was standing in the doorway, a slight frown on her face as she took in Ixil seated in the restraint chair with me on the swivel stool. "You can get yourself out of that chair, that's what," she said. "The clock on the wall—and Mercantile regs—say it's time for a shift change. It's my turn for the bridge."

I frowned at my watch. Preoccupied with everything else that was happening, I hadn't even thought about that. "You're right," I acknowledged. "Sorry—I'm not used to flying a ship where there are real shift changes and everything."

"Which I presume also explains why your mechanic's in the control chair instead of you," she countered. "You, Ixil, need to take over for Nicabar in the engine room; and you, McKell, need to hit the sack."

"I'm fine," I insisted, getting to my feet. In that moment, though, I realized that she was right. Overall lack of sleep plus general tension level had combined with the Lumpy Brothers incident and my still-sore leg to suddenly throw a haze of wooziness over the universe. "On the other hand, maybe it would be a good idea to go under for a couple of hours," I amended.

"Make it eight of them and you've got a deal," she said, jerking a thumb back down the corridor. "Go on—I'll let you know if there's any trouble. You're in one of the cabins on the lower level, right?"

"Right," I said. "Number Eight."

"Fine," she said, settling herself into the chair Ixil had just vacated. "Pleasant dreams."

I stepped out the door and clanked my way down the bare-metal rungs of the ladder to the lower deck. The central corridor—as with the mid deck, there was only one—was deserted. No big surprise, since aside from storage and recycling equipment there were only two sleeping cabins down here, mine and the one Ixil had moved into. A quiet part of the ship, where the rhythmic humming of the various machines would be quite conducive to lulling a weary traveler to sleep.

But I wasn't going to sleep. Not yet. Instead, I walked the length of the corridor to the aft ladder and headed back up to the mid deck, treading as quietly on the rungs as I could.

Ixil was nowhere in sight, having apparently already disappeared into the wraparound to relieve Nicabar in the engine room. At the forward end of the corridor, I saw that Tera had rather pointedly closed the bridge door behind her. A girl who liked her privacy, I decided, though there might not be anything more to it than the natural reticence of a lone woman locked in a flying tin can with four unfamiliar men and two alien males. But whatever the reason, it was going to make my current project that much safer.

The computer-room door was closed, too, but that was all right; near as I could tell, none of the *Icarus*'s doors locked. Taking one last look around to make sure I wasn't being observed, I opened the door and went inside, closing it behind me.

The room looked exactly the way it had when I'd last seen it, except of course that Tera wasn't there. The Worthram T-66 computer dominated the space, pressing up against the aft bulkhead and covering much of the starboard wall as well. Fastened to the forward bulkhead was a two-sectioned metal cabinet with the hard-copy printer on one side and a set of shelves crammed with reference material and datadisks on the other. Squeezed in between the two was the computer control desk where Tera fought to beat the archaic machine into submission.

And where, allegedly, she'd been sitting when she hit

her head hard enough for me to hear from the wraparound.

I went over and sat down in the chair. It wasn't
nearly as fancy as the one on the bridge; but then, in
emergency maneuvers it was far more important for
the pilot to stay in his seat than the computer jock.
Taking a deep breath, I leaned forward and banged my
head experimentally against the edge of the control
panel.

Even granted that I was hearing it from a more personal angle, the thud didn't sound anything like what
I'd heard earlier. That one had definitely been metallic;
this one sounded exactly like a skull whacked against a
control board.

Rubbing thoughtfully at my forehead and the dull
ache that had joined the chorus throughout my body, I
looked slowly around the room. So there were two
possibilities. Either Tera had coincidentally hit her head
against something at about the same time I'd heard
that metal-on-metal sound, or else she was lying. If the
former, then I needed to look elsewhere; if the latter,
there was something else in here that had in fact made
the noise.

The problem was, what? Unlike Ixil's machine shop,
there weren't any tools lying around or hanging on
racks that might fall and clatter against the deck. There
were plenty of cables and connectors, but they were for
the most part light and rubber-coated. The cabinet was
plain metal, but it was bolted to the bulkhead. Besides,
if it had tipped over, it would have left a mess of manuals and datadisks scattered on the deck which she
wouldn't have had time to pick up. The manuals themselves, it went without saying, couldn't possibly make
such a sound.

Unless, it suddenly occurred to me, one of the manuals wasn't what it seemed.

It took me the better part of ten minutes to pull each
of the manuals off the shelf, examine it carefully, and

put it back in its place. Ten wasted minutes. None of them was anything other than it appeared, and none of them could have made that noise.

Which left only one possibility. Whatever Tera had dropped, she was carrying it with her. A wrench, possibly, though what she would need a wrench for I couldn't imagine.

Or a gun.

The mid-deck corridor was still deserted as I left the computer room and made my way down the aft stairway. I was tired, my head was now competing with my leg to see which could ache the most, and I had the annoying sense that I was chasing my own tail. Even if Tera did have a weapon, that didn't necessarily mean she was up to anything. Besides, it was still entirely possible that the noise had come from somewhere else. I didn't really believe it, but it *was* possible.

The Number Eight sleeping cabin was like the other seven aboard the *Icarus*: small and cramped, with a triple bunk against the inner hull and a triple locker facing it from the corridor-side wall. An intercom was set into the inner hull beside the triple bunk, with a meter of empty hull space on its other side where a lounge seat or computer desk would have gone on a properly furnished ship. Clearly the ship had been designed to carry a lot more passengers than were currently aboard; as it was, we all conveniently got a cabin to ourselves, with one on the upper deck as a spare. The privacy was useful in that it gave me a fair amount of freedom of movement; not so useful in that it offered that same freedom to everyone else, too.

The light switch was by the door. I punched it to nighttime dim, then crossed the room and lay down on the bottom bunk. Unrolling the blanket over me, I slid my plasmic under the pillow, where it would be available if needed, and closed my eyes. With unpleasant images of a frowning Uncle Arthur flickering behind my eyelids, I fell asleep.

•   •   •

I awoke slowly, in slightly disoriented stages, vaguely aware that something was wrong but not exactly sure what. The light was still at the dim level I'd set, the door was still closed, and I was still alone in the cabin. The rhythmic drone of the environmental system was still vibrating gently through the air and hull around me. The deeper hum of the stardrive—

The deeper hum of the stardrive wasn't there.

The *Icarus* had stopped.

I had my boots and jacket on in fifteen seconds flat, almost forgetting to grab my plasmic in my rush to get out of the room. I hurried out into the corridor, went up the forward ladder like a cork out of a bottle, and charged into the bridge.

Seated in the restraint chair, Tera turned a mildly questioning eye in my direction. "I thought you were asleep," she said.

"Why have we stopped?" I demanded.

Her eyebrows lifted a bit higher. "We've got another hull ridge," she said calmly. "Chort's getting ready to go out and fix it."

I scowled past her at the displays. Sure enough, the new camera I'd had Ixil and Shawn install in the wraparound showed two space-suited figures just sealing the pressure door behind them. One was obviously Chort; the other was just as obviously Ixil. "You should have called me," I growled.

"Why?" she countered. "There's nothing to this operation that the pilot needs to have a hand in. Besides, you're off-duty, remember? Go back to bed."

The radio speaker clicked. "We're ready, Tera," Ixil's voice said. "You can shut down the grav generator."

"Acknowledged," Tera said, flipping back the safety cover and turning the switch ninety degrees. "Shutting off gravity generator now."

She pushed the switch, and I went through the usual momentary disorientation before my stomach settled down. "Go back to bed," Tera repeated, her eyes on the monitors. "I'll call you if there's a problem."

"I'm sure you would," I said shortly. Once again, it seemed, I had managed to embarrass myself in front of this woman. This was getting to be a very bad habit. "I'll stay a bit."

"I don't need you," she said flatly, flicking a single glowering glance at me and then turning her attention back to the monitors. "More to the point, I don't want you. Go away."

"Do we know where the ridge is?" I asked, ignoring the order.

"Big sphere; starboard side," she said. "Chort thinks it's a small one."

"Let's hope he's right."

She didn't answer. For a few minutes we watched the monitors together in silence, anxious silence on my part, frosty silence on hers. I presumed that Ixil had made it his business to make sure the grav generator couldn't impulsively go on-line again; but I didn't know for sure, and I didn't want to ask him about it on an open radio channel. I tried to figure out how I would lock down the generator if it was up to me, but I didn't know enough about the intricacies of the system.

"You two been flying together long?" Tera broke into my thoughts.

I blinked at her in mild surprise. Casual conversation from Tera was something new in my admittedly brief acquaintance with her. "Six years," I told her. "I took him on about a year after I bought the *Stormy Banks*. I figured having a partner would help me run cargoes faster and more efficiently and bring in more money."

"I take it it didn't work?"

"What makes you say that?" I countered, long experience with that question putting automatic defensiveness into my voice.

"You're here, aren't you?" she said. "Sorry—I didn't mean that the way it sounded. With the Patth handling almost everything worth shipping these days, it's a wonder *everyone* else hasn't been driven out of business."

"Give them a few more years," I said sourly. "The way they're going, it won't be long before they have it all."

"At least everything legitimate," she said, giving me a sideways look. "You *do* run legitimate cargoes, don't you, McKell?"

"Every single chance I get," I said, trying to put a touch of levity into my tone as I gazed at her profile, wishing I could read what was going on behind those hazel eyes of hers. Had she talked to someone while we were on Xathru? Heard something, perhaps, about my forced affiliation with Brother John and the Antoniewicz organization? "What about you?" I asked, hoping to change the subject. "How long have you been flying?"

"Not long," she said. "What do you do when you can't get legitimate work?"

So much for changing the subject. "Sometimes we're able to pick up intrasystem cargoes," I told her. "Occasionally we have to find temp jobs in whatever port we're stuck in until something comes along. Mostly, we eat real light."

"You're not a big fan of the Patth, then, I take it?"

"No one who hauls cargo for a living is a fan of the Patth," I said darkly, my conversation with Nicabar flashing to mind. "Is this your subtle way of suggesting we might be carrying a Patth cargo?"

There were a lot of things, I knew, that a competent actress could do with her body, voice, and expression. But the last time I checked, the red flush that rose to briefly color Tera's cheeks wasn't one of them. "We'd better not be," she said, the studied casualness in her voice a sharp contrast to the emotion implicit in that reddened skin. "Though I doubt we'll find out for sure anywhere this side of Earth."

"If even then," I pointed out. "Whoever Borodin's got working that end isn't under any obligation to let us watch while he cuts the cargo bay open."

"No, of course not," she murmured, almost as if talking to herself. "I wonder why he lied to us about coming along."

"Who, Borodin? What makes you think he *did* lie?"

She shrugged. "You saw that note he left. He had to have written it before the Ihmisits closed the port down for the night."

I thought about Director Aymi-Mastr of the Meima Port Authority and that murder charge she'd talked about. "Unless he just had it here as a precaution," I suggested. "Maybe he fully intended to join us, but circumstances prevented him."

She snorted. "Right. A full bottle, or a warm bed. Circumstances."

"Or a small matter of murder," I said.

She looked at me, her eyes narrowing. "Murder?"

"That's right," I said. "I was told there was a warrant out for his arrest on a possible murder charge."

She shook her head. "Hard to believe," she said. "He seemed like such a normal, upstanding man."

"That's exactly what *I* said when they asked me about it," I said approvingly. "Nice to know there's at least one thing we agree on."

"Well, now, wait a minute," she warned cautiously. "I never said I thought he didn't do it, I just said it was hard to believe. I don't know anything about the man."

"Sure, I understand," I assured her. In fact, I understood far more than she probably realized. Just as her involuntary blush when talking about the Patth had given me a glimpse into her emotional state, so, too, had the complete lack of any such coloring when I told her about Cameron's murder charge. And that despite her alleged total surprise at hearing such shocking news.

Maybe she'd already used up all of her emotional reactions for one day. Or maybe she hadn't been surprised by the murder charge for the simple reason that she'd already known all about it.

"Computer Specialist Tera?" Chort's whistly voice came over the speaker. "I believe I'm finished here. Shall I check the rest of the hull?"

I was still watching Tera closely, which was why I caught the slight but unmistakable tightening of her facial muscles. Perhaps she was thinking along the same line that had suddenly occurred to me: that it had been just as Chort had set off on a similar check of the cargo and engine hulls his last time out that the accident with the grav generator had occurred.

If it was, in fact, an accident. Perhaps someone aboard didn't want anyone taking a close look at the outside of the cargo sphere.

For a moment I was tempted to tell him to go ahead, just to see if our theoretical spoilsport still had his same access to switches or junction boxes or whatever. But only for a moment. Ixil was sharing the hot spot with Chort, and the spoilsport might decide he didn't like Ixil any more than he'd liked Jones. I had no interest in risking Ixil's life or health, at least not then. Certainly not over a theory that hadn't even occurred to me until five seconds ago.

"This is McKell," I said toward the speaker before Tera could answer. "Don't bother, Chort—we don't have time for it. You and Ixil just get back in and button up."

"Acknowledged," he whistled.

"That was my job," Tera reminded me, throwing a brief glare in my direction. But to my hypersensitive eye, the glare didn't seem to have the kind of fire behind it that I would have expected. Maybe she and I had indeed been thinking along the same lines, or maybe her chip-shoulder act was starting to wear a little thin. "You're off-duty, remember?"

"Right," I said. "I keep forgetting. You can handle things here?"

She didn't even bother to answer that one, just gave me a look that said volumes all by itself and turned back to the monitors. Properly chastened, I floated out of the bridge, maneuvered down the ladder well, and returned to my cabin. I was once again stripping off my jacket when the warning tone sounded and gravity came back on.

For a long time after that I just lay in my bunk, staring at the closed door in the dim light, as I ran that last conversation through endless repeats in my mind. Tera was an enigma, and in general I hated enigmas. In my experience, they nearly always spelled trouble.

Unless I had been reading her words and her reactions all wrong. Or, worse, had somehow imagined them entirely. It certainly wouldn't be the first time I had oh-so-cleverly Sherlocked myself straight down a blind alley.

But I hadn't imagined the mishap with the grav generator or Jones's death. I hadn't imagined my brief detention on Meima, or the Lumpy Brothers, or their unreasonably advanced hand weaponry.

And I certainly hadn't imagined Arno Cameron, amateur archaeologist and head of one of the largest and most influential industrial combines in the Spiral, sitting in a grimy Vyssiluyan taverno and all but begging me to fly the *Icarus* to Earth for him.

No, the facts were there, at least some of them. What they meant, though, I didn't have the foggiest idea.

But a small group of unclearly related facts can chase each other around a single overtired brain for only so long. Eventually, I fell asleep.

CHAPTER

6

The port facilities on Xathru had been a couple of steps above those on Meima. The single commercial port on Dorscind's World, in contrast, was at least five steps back down again.

Not that the equipment itself was a problem. On the contrary, the landing cradle was the best the *Icarus* had seen yet, with the kind of peripheral and support equipment that a place like Meima could only dream of. It was, rather, the port's clientele that put Dorscind's World well below the standards set by the Spiral's tour cruise directors. Planned by its developers as a high-class gambling resort, things hadn't quite worked out that way for the colony. It had been slipping since roughly day two, with the big money and high-spinners fading equally rapidly into the sunset.

The only thing that had kept the place from vanishing from the map altogether was its gradual and reluctant transformation into the sort of place where questionable papers and shady cargoes were generally winked at. With the Patth shipping domination, the shady-cargo slice of the pie chart had been steadily growing among non-Patth carriers.

And as a result, business at the Dorscind's World port was booming.

There was of course no record of a freighter named the *Second Banana* having filed a flight plan for Dorscind's World. But as I'd expected, minor technicalities of that sort didn't even raise an eyebrow here. The usual docking fee, plus a few more of Cameron's hundred-commark bills, and we had our landing cradle. I paid off the port official who came to the ramp to collect, made arrangements for refueling, and ordered delivery of replacement foodstuffs and some more of Chort's magic hull-repair goo.

And after that, it was time for me to venture out into the dubious charm of the port city. Leaving the rest of the *Icarus*'s crew behind.

The rest of the crew wasn't happy about that. Not one bit. "This is insane," Shawn snarled as I faced down the pack of them at the forward wraparound pressure door, a task made all that harder psychologically by the upward tilt of the *Icarus*'s decks that had them all looming over me. "I've been to a dozen places like this—it's no more dangerous than downtown Tokyo as long as you mind your own business."

"It *would* be nice to get out into the open air," Everett seconded. "Medically speaking, recycled air starts wearing on a person after a while. Besides, the exercise would do us good."

"The exercise could also get you killed," I told him bluntly, charitably passing up the obvious comment about how his bulk hardly indicated that exercise would be his top priority out there. "Or weren't any of you listening to what I said about what happened to me on Xathru?"

"We were all listening, McKell," Tera said. "As far as I'm concerned, that's a reason for *you* to stay out of sight, not us."

"Believe me, I wish I could," I said with one hundred percent honesty. The last thing I wanted to do was face down more of the Lumpy Clan and their coronal-discharge weapons. Though to be honest, without having a flight schedule to guide them, the chances they could have tracked me here were vanishingly small. "Unfortunately, I have an errand to take care of out there. One which I have to do personally."

Which wasn't quite as hundred-percent honest as the first part had been. Ixil could make the long-over-due call to Uncle Arthur as well as I could. But Ixil had made it abundantly clear that he really didn't want to field that one; more to the point, I wanted him and the ferrets here to watch over the *Icarus*. "But none of that matters," I went on. "What matters is that as pilot, I'm also the captain. And I say you're staying here."

"So that's where the pig stick goes, huh?" Shawn snarled, his face working as he glared at me with blazing eyes. Once again, as it had when we'd first met, Shawn's veneer of civility had cracked badly, revealing the callously rude young brat underneath. "You little tin-plate dictator—you love this, don't you? Well, forget it—just forget it. I'm not sitting here staring at the walls while you're out having fun. Neither is anyone else."

"That's enough, Shawn," Nicabar said quietly. Quietly, but with the full weight of all those years as an EarthGuard Marine in his voice.

Shawn either didn't notice or didn't care. "Well, runny muck to you, too," he bit out at Nicabar. His whole body was trembling now, his fists opening and closing like relays in an unstable feedback loop, and out of the corner of my eye I saw Ixil ease a little closer beside him. "I'm not staying cooped up in here—I'm *not*."

"Look, son, I understand how you feel," Everett said, laying a hand on Shawn's shoulder. "But he *is* our captain—"

"I don't care," Shawn snapped, shrugging off the hand. "I'm going out. Now!"

And with that, he bunched his hands into fists and dived straight toward me.

He didn't get very far. Ixil was ready on his right and Nicabar on his left, and each of them grabbed an arm right in mid-leap. For a moment Shawn struggled in their grip, mouthing obscenities and threats mixed liberally with snarls in an alien language I didn't understand. But he might as well have tried to walk away with the *Icarus* resting on his foot. Ixil and Nicabar held on; and without warning, Shawn suddenly collapsed in their grip, whimpering softly under his breath.

"Bring him back here," Everett said quietly, gesturing as he backed down the corridor toward the sick bay. "I'll give him something."

Ixil caught Nicabar's eye; the tall man nodded understanding and shifted around behind Shawn, taking his other arm from Ixil and half guiding, half carrying the moaning kid down the corridor behind Everett. They all disappeared inside, the door closed behind them, and Ixil looked back at me. "That was interesting," he said.

"Is he ill?" Chort asked, his alien face as usual impossible to read. "Perhaps we should take him to a full-service medical center."

"Let's see what Everett can do with him first," I said, throwing a glance at Tera. Her face, too, was unreadable. "Look, I've got to go. I'll be back as soon as I can."

"Go ahead," Ixil said. "We'll handle things here."

I headed down the ramp—as on Xathru, the landing cradle here was concave, putting part of the *Icarus*'s bulk beneath ground level and making a long climb unnecessary—and crossed to the edge of our landing square. A high-speed slideway ran past two landing squares over, with two short layers of lower-speed transfer slideway beside it, and in a minute I was being carried briskly westward toward the edge of the spaceport where the map had said the StarrComm building was located.

The port was busy today, I noticed with some concern as I studied my fellow slideway travelers with the same casual and nonintrusive glances they were using back on me. The extra anonymity provided by a crowd was always useful, but crowded slideways also often meant crowded StarrComm booths. Even before we'd landed I had wanted to make this stop as brief as possible. Now, after Shawn's performance back there, I wanted it even more.

It took me nearly fifteen minutes to reach the StarrComm building, only to find my fears had been realized. The entire place was in use, with estimated waiting times for a booth hovering around half an hour.

I tried to talk my way higher on the waiting list, but on a place like Dorscind's World the operators were used to much more serious threats and bullying than I was willing to try and wouldn't budge. Conceding defeat, I accepted the numbered card they handed me— no one asked for or gave out names here—and retreated across the lobby to the waiting-room taverno. Not surprisingly, it, too, was doing a brisk business, but I was lucky enough to arrive just as a pair of Mastanni were leaving a small table near the entrance and was able to grab it. I glanced at the menu, punched up the cheapest drink they had, and sat back to glower at the large display over the bar indicating which customers were currently next in line for the booths.

It wasn't an encouraging sight. At the leisurely rate the numbers were crawling upward, I decided darkly, the operator's estimation of thirty minutes was entirely too optimistic. I hadn't wanted to make this call to Uncle Arthur, but being forced to sit here and wait for the chance to have myself verbally flensed was just adding insult to injury. I tried to come up with a clever way to circumvent the system, but it was really only mental steam-venting. On Dorscind's World, the people I'd be cutting in line in front of would not be the sort to greet such attempts with genial smiles. I had enough trouble in my life already without going out and finding more.

A shadow passed over me; and to my annoyance a thin, wiry man with dark hair and a scraggly beard plopped himself down in the chair across from me. "Hey, old buddy," he greeted me expansively. "How's it going?"

"It's going just fine," I told him automatically, frowning. His tone and expression implied we knew each other, and he did indeed look vaguely familiar, but for the life of me I couldn't place him.

He apparently picked up on my uncertainty. "Aw, come on, Jordie old buddy," he said, sounding hurt. "Don't tell me you don't remember your old drinking pal."

And in that moment, it all came disgustingly back. James Fulbright, small-time gunrunner and smuggler, the only person I'd ever met who was either too stupid or too stubborn for me to break of using the hated nickname *Jordie*. I'd been trying to negotiate a deal with his group when Uncle Arthur had fixed me up with Brother John instead. The drinking bouts that had been a centerpiece of Fulbright's negotiations had been one of the definite low points in my life. "Hello, James," I sighed. "Small Spiral, isn't it?"

"Small as you'd ever want," he agreed, grinning with a mouthful of uneven teeth. Rumor had it they'd started out perfectly straight, but that every time one was knocked out during a brawl he'd had it put back crooked just to make himself look meaner. "Waiting to make a call, huh?"

"Yes," I said, bowing to the inevitable. "Can I get you a drink?"

"Oh, I think you can do better than one measly drink," he said. "How much cash you got on you?"

I stared at him, warning bells belatedly going off in the back of my mind. Fulbright was still smiling, but I could now see the hard edge beneath the grin. He was definitely not here just to cadge drinks. "What are you talking about?" I demanded quietly.

"I'm talking about a shakedown," he said, lowering his voice to match mine. "What'd you think? All for your own good, of course. So. You got ten grand on you? That's what it's gonna take, you know. At least ten grand."

For a good three seconds I just stared at him, wondering what in hell was going on. There he sat, alone, both hands on the table, his right casually holding a folded piece of paper, his left open and empty. His sleeves were too tight to be concealing a quick-throw gun or knife, and there was no way he could beat me to a standard draw with his jacket zipped and mine half-open. It was possible he had a backup somewhere in the room already targeting me; but even drawing a weapon in here would be begging for trouble, and starting a firefight would be even worse. And why pick on me in the first place? "Maybe you don't know I'm not running independent anymore," I said at last. "I'm connected with a pretty big organization. They wouldn't think much of this."

His smile went a bit more brittle. "Yeah, well, whoever they are, I can guarantee they won't lift a finger to help you on this one," he said. "Believe it or not, Jordie, I'm your only friend in this room right now." With a smooth motion, he flipped open the paper in his hand and swiveled it around to face me.

I glanced down. And found myself looking at my own Mercantile Authority file photo.

I looked up at Fulbright, startled. "Go ahead," he said encouragingly. "Read it."

I looked back down at the flyer. It was an urgent

request for information about the current location of one Jordan McKell, pilot/captain of the Orion-class freighter *Icarus,* registry and configuration unknown. It didn't say why McKell was being sought, but included two contact numbers, a local Dorscind's World phone number and a StarrComm vid connect—the latter, like Brother John's number, one of the anonymous types that gave no indication of which world it was connected to.

It also promised a reward to the one who fingered me. A straight five thousand commarks.

"I don't know what you've done now, Jordie," Fulbright said softly, "but you're in one hell of a lot of trouble. Everyone in this place probably has one of these things by now—the guy was passing them out like free fruit sticks. The only reason you're still walking around is that that's such a lousy picture."

He grinned. "That, plus no one figured you'd come to a sleazepit like this. I'd guess that's what's tying up the StarrComm lines—everyone's calling their buddies to pass the word."

"Probably," I murmured. But *someone* thought I might come to a sleazepit like this; whoever was at the other end of that phone number, at the very least. Someone was very intent here about covering all the bases, and from all indications he was covering them very well. And unlike the Lumpy Brothers, that same someone knew the name of the ship I was flying. "Tell me, was this walking fruit-stick tray a bipedal alien with long arms and lumpy skin?"

Fulbright's forehead creased slightly. "Naw, he was a human. Short and kind of wimpish—your basic accountant type."

"Doesn't sound like he really belongs in a place like this," I suggested. "You sure it's not a scam of some sort?"

"At a hundred commarks a crack?" Fulbright scoffed. "Who cares?"

I frowned. "A hundred? The flyer says five thousand."

"That's the finder's fee," Fulbright said. "The guy's been handing out a hundred with each flyer. Just to make sure it gets read, I guess."

I felt cold all over. Five thousand commarks to find me—that could be anything, from anywhere. But for the hunter to be passing out additional thousands of commarks in cash just to generate interest meant something very big indeed was going on.

And the only thing that had saved me so far was that abominably poor photo in my Mercantile file. That, and the fact that the one person here who *did* recognize me was angling for a higher bounty. "Okay," I said to Fulbright. "Ten thousand it is. But I don't have it on me. We'll have to go back to the ship."

His eyes narrowed, and in the twitching of his eyebrows and lips I could practically read his line of reasoning: that if he was able to get a good look at the *Icarus,* he might be able to peddle the description for another few thousand from the unidentified accountant type. "Okay," he said, unzipping his jacket and stuffing the flyer into an inside pocket. He stood up, giving me a glimpse of a gray handgun holstered at the left side of his belt, and nodded toward the door. "Sure. Let's go."

We headed out of the taverno, crossed the lobby, and out the StarrComm-building door. Halfway across the lobby he surreptitiously pulled his gun from its holster and stuffed it and his right hand into his side jacket pocket. Former drinking buddies or not, he obviously didn't trust me very far. "Which landing cradle are you in?" he asked as I headed toward the nearest slideway, which happened to be headed north.

"You can read the number for yourself when we get there," I grunted, looking surreptitiously around for inspiration. This particular slideway didn't seem well populated, and it didn't take a genius to see why: instead of being taken to the main bulk of the docking squares, we were headed toward what appeared to be a maintenance area.

A fact which wasn't lost on Fulbright. "I hope you're not trying to pull something on your old pal, Jordie," he warned, stepping up close behind me and pressing the muzzle of his gun into my back. Even through the concealing jacket material I imagined it felt very cold. "Because I wouldn't like that. I wouldn't like that at all."

"You don't think I'd put a hot ship down in one of the regular cradles, do you?" I countered, looking down at my feet. The slideway was mainly solid, but just ahead on our right was one of a number of holes where small patches of the material had worn off or torn away at the edge of the moving belt. This particular tear was roughly triangular, leaving a gap about ten centimeters long and five wide through which I could see the grillwork of the underlying support and drive system zipping past. Every half second or so a bright blue light winked past, probably a glow that helped mark the edge of the slideway at night.

"So where is it?" Fulbright demanded.

"Patience, James, patience," I said, gazing down at the triangular tear and the grillwork underneath and doing a quick mental calculation. It would be tight, not to mention destructive, but it should work.

I half turned my head and gestured toward my jacket. "My phone's vibing," I told him. "Okay if I answer it?"

Out of the corner of my eye I caught his frown. "Leave it," he ordered.

"Not recommended," I told him mildly. "My partner will come looking for me if I don't answer. You don't want to mess with him. Certainly not for a measly five thousand commarks."

Once again, I could almost watch the gears turning in his head. He'd never actually met Ixil—we'd always been careful to keep Ixil in a low-profile position when dealing with gangs and their antialien biases—but I'd planted enough hints with Fulbright that he had a pretty good idea of my partner's capabilities. I waited patiently, letting him work it out for himself, not in any particular hurry. We were starting to get into the maintenance and supply areas now, where the only people around were generally working inside the various buildings. Working, moreover, with the kind of heavy machinery that would effectively drown out the sounds of trouble, up to and including gunshots. The deeper we got into this area, the better I liked it.

"All right," he said suddenly, stepping close behind me and getting a grip on my jacket collar as he again jammed his gun warningly into my kidney. "Take it out slow—two fingers, left hand."

Carefully, I eased my jacket open and just as carefully pulled out my phone. "Okay?" I asked, holding it up for his approval. Without waiting for an answer, I shifted my grip on the phone and brought it to my ear.

Or rather, tried to do so. Somewhere along the way my fingers suddenly fumbled and the phone squirted out of my hand to clatter onto the slideway in front of me.

"Damn!" I muttered, taking a long step forward.

If I'd given Fulbright half a second to think, he probably wouldn't have fallen for it. But I didn't; and he did. Just as it was perfectly natural for me to try to retrieve my phone, so, too, was it perfectly natural for him to courteously let go of my jacket to enable me to do so. I dropped to one knee and snagged the phone just as it was about to skitter off the edge of the slideway; and with a quick jerk I jammed the lower end through the hole in the belt and into the gridwork beneath.

For a split second the slideway faltered, just a brief instant before the sheer inertia of the system overcame the slender piece of plastic and metal and tore the phone to shreds. But it was enough. Caught completely flatfooted, Fulbright lost his balance and stumbled forward, his knees coming up short against my side, the impact sending him tumbling helplessly over my back to sprawl on the slideway.

I was on him in an instant, locking his right wrist in place with one hand and trying to get a clear shot at his neck or stomach with the other. He struggled furiously, mouthing curses that would have frosted glass, but he didn't have a chance and he knew it. He was lying on his free left arm, and with me keeping his right hand trapped in his pocket he couldn't even bring his gun to bear on me. Besides all of which, I was bigger than he was.

I got an opening and slammed my fist into his neck just behind his ear. He twitched and gave a weak roar that was more than half whimper. I hit him again, and he collapsed and lay still.

I took a few seconds to catch my breath and take a quick look around. No one was visible. Keeping a cautious hold on his gun hand, I worked the weapon out of his grip and pulled it out of the pocket. It was a Kochran-Uzi compact three-millimeter semiautomatic, a nasty enough weapon in a taverno fight but an extremely stupid thing to carry aboard a starship, where a bullet can go through machinery and hulls with all sorts of unpleasant consequences. Dropping the gun into my pocket, I hauled the unconscious man half to his feet and half leaped, half fell off the slideway.

About ten meters to my right was a stack of empty forklift pallets piled up against the corner of one of the buildings. Getting a grip under Fulbright's arms, I dragged him over and laid him down on the ground facing them. His jacket, like mine, was leather, but his shirt was made of a thick but more pliable cloth. I pulled his right arm out of the jacket sleeve, carefully sliced off the exposed shirtsleeve with my pocketknife, put the jacket back on him, and cut the sleeve into thick strips.

Two minutes later, his hands were tied securely behind him and he had a gag in his mouth. Another three minutes' work and I had manhandled one of the pallets down off the top of the stack and had the edge of it resting more or less comfortably across his legs, with most of the weight being supported by the stiff soles of his boots.

Fulbright wasn't going anywhere for a while, and for a long moment I was tempted to leave it at that and get out while I could. But that five-thousand-commark reward meant that someone out there had upped the ante on this game, and I still didn't have the foggiest idea what the stakes were or even what the game was.

But with a little luck, maybe I could at least find out who some of the other players were.

Fulbright's phone was in the same pocket as the flyer. I pulled out both, consulted the flyer, then punched in the local number it listed.

A voice answered on the second vibe; a voice, I decided, that definitely fit with the wimpish accountant description. "Thompson," he said briskly.

"My name's James," I said, imitating Fulbright's voice as best I could. Odds were Thompson wouldn't even remember James Fulbright, let alone his voice, but I'd already taken more chances than I cared to for one day. "That guy you're looking for—Jordan McKell? You said five thousand for finding him. How much for delivering him all trussed up?"

He didn't hesitate. "Ten thousand," he said. "Do you have him there now?"

I felt my throat tighten, my somewhat snide preconception of the man vanishing in a puff of unpleasant smoke. No accountant I'd ever met was anywhere near that quick and free with the money they handled. Whoever Thompson was, he was no simple flunky. "Yeah, I got him," I said. "I'll be waiting for you off the north spaceport slideway, next to the Number Twelve machine shop. Bring the money."

THE ICARUS HUNT   117

"We'll be there in fifteen minutes," he promised, and hung up.

I put the phone away, scowling to myself. *We*. That meant he was bringing friends, almost certainly friends with muscle. I would have liked to have told him to come alone, but that would have looked suspicious—a man who passes out hundred-commark bills as a come-on would hardly try to stiff a customer, certainly not over ten grand. Once again, I considered that the better part of valor would be to run for it; once again, I made myself stay put. I set the stage as best I could, then settled down to wait.

He was there well within his promised fifteen minutes, and he did indeed have muscle with him. Unpleasantly familiar muscle: two more members of the Lumpy Clan. Apparently these things liked to travel in pairs.

"Mr. James?" Thompson called toward me as he and the Lumpies hopped off the slideway.

"Right here," I called back, half turning to look vaguely over my shoulder at them as I waved a hand in invitation. I was squatting down facing the now conscious Fulbright with my back to them, a position I hoped would disguise any of the height-and-build cues that might give away my identity. "Come on, hurry," I added. "I think he's coming to."

Lying on his left side with his back also to them, Fulbright had his head twisted around and was glaring daggers up at me. But with his gag still in place, and his hands and feet still immobilized, there wasn't a lot he could do about the situation. Even without the gag he probably wouldn't have had much to say, not with my plasmic half-concealed inside my jacket digging into his side. If we both made it off Dorscind's World intact, I suspected, he wasn't going to be smiling cheerfully the next time we ran into each other.

But at the moment I couldn't be bothered about

such vague and uncertain futures. Right now my sole concern was whether or not I could survive the next ten seconds.

I needn't have worried. Thompson might be more than a flunky, and the Lumpies were professional enough in their own right, but it apparently never occurred to any of them that their quarry might pull something this insane. They hurried incautiously forward, the Lumpies pulling a pace or two ahead of Thompson; and then, as they got within three steps of me, I snapped my head left as if I'd suddenly seen something and jabbed a finger toward a gap between two of the maintenance buildings. "Watch out!" I barked.

The Lumpies were professionals, all right. Braking to an instant halt, they jumped backward in unison, putting themselves between Thompson and the unknown danger. I jumped back, too, landing upright beside Thompson; and as the Lumpies yanked their guns out of their back holsters, I slid around behind Thompson, got an arm around his neck, and pressed my plasmic into his right ear. "Don't turn around," I said conversationally. "But do set your weapons on the ground."

Again in unison, and flagrantly ignoring my orders, they started to swivel around. I shifted my aim and sent a plasma blast directly between them to spatter off the ground ahead. "I said not to turn around," I reminded them, returning my plasmic to its previous resting place against Thompson's sideburn. He flinched away from the residual muzzle heat, but I pressed it hard against the skin. It wouldn't damage him, and I'd always found that a little mild pain did wonders for cooperation. Especially with people who weren't used to it.

Thompson was apparently very unused to pain. "Don't move," he seconded hastily, his voice breaking slightly at the top. "Do what he says—he means it."

"I do indeed," I agreed. "Anyway, heroics would be

wasted. I'm not going to hurt anyone unless I have to—don't forget I could have shot both of you in the back just now. So be smart and put your guns on the ground in front of you—slowly, of course—and then take two steps past them."

They obeyed quickly and without argument, raising my estimation of Thompson's status another couple of notches. He might look like an accountant with no stomach for even potential conflict; but when he talked, even in a squeaky voice, people listened.

More importantly, they obeyed. The Lumpies became models of cooperation, dutifully stepping past their weapons and lying facedown as I ordered with their hands visible. I retrieved their guns—between them and Fulbright and the first set of Lumpies, I was starting to make a nice little weapons collection here—and had Thompson relieve them of the restraints I knew they would have brought with them.

He came up with two sets, which seemed to be one set too many unless they either *had* planned to stiff Fulbright or else intended to shackle me hand and foot and carry me away draped over someone's shoulder like a bag of cement. But whatever the reason, it was certainly a convenient number for my purposes. A minute later I had the Lumpies cuffed together through one of the slots in the bottom pallet with Thompson cuffed on the other side of the stack. With the weight of the rest of the stack on top, and the utter lack of leverage any of them had to work with, I was pretty sure they would stay put until someone happened by, which from the evidence would probably not be until the next shift change at the maintenance buildings. Hopefully, that wouldn't be for at least another couple of hours.

"You won't get away with this," Thompson warned as I went quickly through his pockets. "Not a chance in the universe. If you release me now, I promise nothing will happen to you because of this incident."

"Nothing over and above what you planned to do to

me anyway?" I suggested. "Thanks, but I'll take my chances."

"Your chances don't exist, McKell," he said flatly. "And we don't want you, anyway. All we want is the *Icarus*. All of you are free to go." He cocked his head to the side as he looked up at me, a gesture that somehow made him look even more like an accountant. "I'll do better, in fact. I can promise you that if you'll turn the *Icarus* over to me, you'll profit quite handsomely on the deal."

"Thanks, but this will do," I said, withdrawing a neat stack of hundred-commark bills from one of his inside pockets. "I know it's not nice to steal," I added, slipping the stack into my pocket, "but we're likely to have some unexpected expenses along the way. If you'll give me your name and address, I'll make sure you're properly reimbursed."

"Fifty thousand, McKell," he said, staring unblinkingly into my eyes. "Fifty thousand commarks to take me to the *Icarus* and walk away."

I gazed down at him, a hard lump forming in my throat. What in hell's name were we carrying, anyway? "I appreciate the offer," I said, checking the other inside pocket. This one yielded a phone and a slim documents folder. "But I'm already under contract."

"A hundred thousand," he said. "Five hundred thousand. Name your price."

I patted his shoulder and stood up. "You might be surprised sometime to find out what money can't buy," I said, tossing his phone onto the stack of pallets where none of them could reach it and pocketing the documents folder. "See you around."

"You're making a big mistake, McKell," he said. His voice was quiet, but it held an absolute conviction that sent a chill up my back. "You have no idea who you're dealing with."

"Maybe this will tell me," I countered, tapping the pocket where I'd put his folder.

I passed around to the other side of the pallets, where Fulbright was still lying trussed up glaring at me. "Sorry about this, James," I apologized. "I'll make it up to you next time, all right?"

The look in his eyes made it abundantly clear what his plans were for the next time. But again, that was a future too distant to worry about right now.

I hopped on the southbound slideway and headed back toward the spaceport center, keeping an eye on the Lumpies and Thompson as long as they were in sight. The minute they were lost to view I got off the slideway and headed east toward the *Icarus*'s landing cradle, walking quickly along until I reached a properly directed slideway and getting on it.

And there, with finally a moment of breathing space, I opened Thompson's folder and started going through his papers. I was only halfway through when I put them back into my pocket and pulled out Fulbright's phone.

"Yes?" Ixil's melodic voice answered.

"It's me," I said. "How's the fueling going?"

"Probably no more than a quarter finished," he said. "They only got here fifteen minutes ago."

"Tell them to quit and seal the ship back up," I told him. "And get the bridge and drive preflights started. We're out of here as soon as I get back."

There was just the briefest pause. "What did Uncle Arthur *say*?"

"I never got to talk to Uncle Arthur," I told him. "And I'll explain as much as I can when I get there. Just get us ready to fly, all right?"

"Got it," he said. "We'll be ready when you are."

The *Icarus* was buttoned down, with no fuelers in sight, by the time I retracted the ramp and sealed the hatchway. Tera and Everett tried to collar me in the corridor, demanding to know what the rush was; I ordered them back to their stations in no uncertain terms and headed to the bridge.

Ixil was waiting for me there. "All set," he said, standing up and relinquishing the control chair to me. "Nicabar is ready with the drive, the fuelers are paid off, and I've got lift permission from the tower."

"Good," I said, sliding into the chair and sounding the lift alert. "Let's get out of here."

We were off the ground, nearly out of Dorscind's World's atmosphere, and driving for the blackness of space when he finally broke the silence. "Well?"

I leaned back in my seat. "Someone out there wants to get hold of the *Icarus*," I said. "They want it very badly."

He frowned. "Why?"

"I don't know why," I said, pulling Thompson's documents out of my pocket and handing them over. "But I do know who."

He leafed through the papers, and stopped at the same place I had. Staring at the plain ID card with its operative number and ornate governmental seal and nothing else, the ferrets on his shoulders twitching with his astonishment. "I don't believe it," he said mechanically, looking up at me.

"I don't believe it either," I agreed grimly. "But it's true. We, my friend, are being chased by the Patth."

CHAPTER

7

"But it doesn't make sense," Ixil protested.

"On the contrary, it makes perfect sense," I countered. "It has to. We just don't know what that sense is yet, that's all."

Ixil muttered something in his own language, rubbing a fingertip along the corner of my locker. We had retired to my cabin as the most private place on the ship to talk after I'd gotten us into hyperspace and turned the bridge over to Tera. Technically, it was Shawn's shift, with Chort on watch in the engine room, but given the shape Shawn had been in when I left earlier I wouldn't have trusted him to butter bread for me, let alone watch over a ship I was on.

And between then and now, I'd had time to do some serious thinking. "Look, it's very simple," I went on. "At least, the basics of it are. The archaeological dig on Meima found something big—that much is clear from the fact that Cameron himself came out there to take a look. They brought in the *Icarus*—"

"Wait a minute," Ixil put in. "How did they bring it in without the Port Authority having a record of it?"

"Probably in pieces," I said. "You've seen what this thing looks like—odds are Cameron flew it in in sections, along with some of his tech people to put it together, and maybe with the archaeological team helping with some of the gruntwork. They probably built it underground, which would explain why none of the normal incoming traffic noticed it on the surface."

"Then that massive explosion Director Aymi-Mastr told you about was to blow the roof off one of those underground caverns and let the ship out."

"Right," I nodded. "Along with conveniently scrambling the spaceport sensors so that its departure wouldn't be noticed. I'd give a lot to know what they added to the explosive or the dirt strata to pull that off—again, it was probably Cameron's techs who handled that one."

"So why didn't they just leave then?"

I shook my head. "I don't know. Either they didn't have a crew put together yet, or else they wanted an official spaceport stamp to add legitimacy to things."

"Or perhaps were planning to bring the entire archaeological group out together," Ixil suggested. "There's certainly plenty of extra carrying capacity aboard."

"Good point," I agreed, glancing over at the three-bunk tier. "And they couldn't all get on board and leave right then because they knew the authorities would come to investigate the explosion. Finding the site deserted would raise red flags from here to Thursday, which was exactly what they didn't want.

"Anyway, so the *Icarus* lifted up under cover of the cloud, maybe circled the planet once, and joined the line of incoming ships waiting clearance to land. They put down, showed their forged Gamm Port Authority sealed-cargo license, and were in. The crew left the ship, planning to take off again in the morning with the whole crowd aboard and a genuine lift document that would get them back to Earth with no raised eyebrows from anyone."

"Except that something went wrong," Ixil said heavily. "The question is, what?"

"Somebody tumbled to the scheme, obviously," I said. "Not the Patth themselves, I don't think. Or if it was, they didn't realize right away the full significance of what Cameron's people had dug up—if they had, they'd have pushed the Ihmisits into locking down the port completely."

"The Lumpy Brothers or their friends, perhaps?"

"Possibly," I agreed, "though I'm still not sure how they fit into this. But whoever it was, and however they tumbled to it, they were interested enough to raid the dig, grab everyone in sight, and send the Ihmisits hunting for anyone who may have slipped through the net."

"Like Cameron?"

"Like Cameron," I nodded. "And so there he was, alone on Meima, with the authorities on his tail, a hot ship locked away behind a fence where he couldn't get at it, and no one to fly it even if he could."

Ixil shook his head. "Not a situation I'd want to find myself in."

"The way things are going, you may get your chance at it yet," I warned. "Still, Arno Cameron didn't build a multitrillion-commark industrial empire by lying down and giving up when things got tough. He started going through the periphery tavernos, probably very systematically, looking for enough spacers at loose ends to put together a new crew."

"And to all appearances he succeeded," Ixil said. "Which leads immediately to the question of why he didn't fly out with you."

"That one's got me stumped, too," I conceded. "Clearly, they hadn't caught him yet—Director Aymi-Mastr and her frog-eyed heavies grabbing me on the way into the port proved that much. He may have decided that trying to walk through a relatively narrow port gate under the gaze of a pair of Ihmis door wardens would be pushing his luck too far."

"Even if staying behind meant they would eventually run him down?"

"He might have decided that giving the *Icarus* a head start was worth that risk." I grimaced. "Which he may now have lost. Unlike the Lumpy Brothers, our generous Patth agent with the stack of hundreds knew the *Icarus*'s name."

"Possibly," Ixil said. "On the other hand, we presume they had the rest of the group already in custody. Perhaps one of them finally talked." He paused, his eyes narrowing in thought. "There is, of course, another possible explanation for Cameron's absence, given the accidents that have happened on board. Perhaps one of the spacers he hired was not the innocent out-of-work drifter he seemed. Particularly now that we know that the Patth *do* have non-Patth agents on retainer."

"That thought has spent a lot of time twirling around my brain, too," I acknowledged. "The problem is, why hasn't he done anything recently? If he's trying to damage the crew or slow down the ship, why haven't there been more such accidents?"

"Be careful what you wish for," Ixil warned.

"I'm not wishing for it," I assured him fervently. "I'm just trying to understand it. Okay, he killed Jones and shook up Chort a little, but that was about it. He certainly wasn't busy throwing wrenches in the gears while we were on Xathru and Dorscind's World."

"He didn't call in the authorities at either place, either," Ixil agreed. "As I see it, there are two other possibilities we haven't yet addressed. First, that the attack on Jones was personal to Jones. Once he was dead, the perpetrator stopped perpetrating because his job was finished."

"But why pick on Jones?" I countered. "No one aboard knew anyone else prior to boarding."

"So we assume," Ixil said. "That may turn out not to be the case. Second, and possibly more intriguing, the attack on Jones may have been staged by Jones himself."

I frowned. "To what end?"

"To the end of allowing him to jump ship without any attached suspicion," Ixil said. "Think about it. If the carbon monoxide hadn't killed him, you would certainly have put him off the ship on Xathru for a complete medical check. That would have left him with names and complete descriptions of you and the rest of the crew, details of the *Icarus* itself, and very possibly the itinerary Cameron had planned for the trip to Earth. *And* he would have had complete freedom of movement."

"The itinerary wouldn't have done him any good," I said mechanically. This angle had never even occurred to me. "We're already way off Cameron's plan, and will be staying that way as long as the docking-fee bribe money holds out. You're suggesting he just miscalculated, then?"

"I don't know." Ixil paused. "There is, of course, one other possibility we haven't touched on. Did you think to search Jones's body before it was taken off the ship?"

A tight knot formed in the center of my stomach. "No, I didn't," I said. "It never even occurred to me."

"It's possible whoever killed him did so in order to use his body as a receptacle for passing information," Ixil suggested. "Hard data, perhaps, such as photos or schematics that couldn't easily be sent via phone."

"But why bother?" I asked. "They all had complete freedom of movement on Xathru. Why not just deliver it in person?"

"Perhaps the murderer didn't want to risk being seen in the company of the wrong people."

I mulled that one over. "Which would imply we were dealing with a genuine professional here."

Ixil nodded. "Yes. It would."

I hissed thoughtfully between my teeth. There were indeed people out there, I knew, who would go to such lengths to complete a mission. But to have one of them just happen to be aboard the *Icarus* was pushing the bounds of credibility way beyond even their normal elasticity range. "Again, though, if someone wanted the *Icarus* badly enough to slip that kind of professional aboard, why haven't we been stopped already?"

"That is indeed a key question," Ixil conceded. "I'm afraid, Jordan, that there are still too many missing pieces to this puzzle."

"The biggest of which is sitting back there in our cargo hold," I agreed grimly. "I'm starting to think it's about time we had ourselves a close look at it."

Ixil rubbed his cheek. "I don't know," he said doubtfully. "I've looked over the schematics Tera pulled from the computer. There aren't any access panels shown at all."

"You've got a cutting torch in the mechanics shop, don't you?" I pointed out. "An access hole is basically wherever we want to make one."

"I wasn't thinking so much about getting in as I was of covering up afterward the fact that we'd done so," Ixil said mildly. "If Jones didn't engineer his own accident—and to be honest, I really don't think he did—then whoever did is still aboard. We may not want to set up a situation where he would be able to get a look of his own into the hold."

Unfortunately, he was right. "All right," I said reluctantly. "We'll play along while longer. But you might want to get your cutting equipment ready just the same. At some point I don't think we're going to be able to afford to continue flying blind."

"Perhaps," Ixil said. "How much of this are you planning to tell the others?"

"As little as possible," I said. "I've already told Tera I ran afoul of someone back there who had decided to make it his business to hijack the *Icarus*."

"Which is more or less true."

"Eminently true," I agreed. "I also mentioned the murder charge against Cameron to her, just to see what kind of reaction I'd get."

"And that was?"

"Protests of surprise, but no visible evidence of it," I told him. "Though I'm not sure where exactly that leaves us. I think that the rest of the details, including the fact that the Patth are involved, should be left out of the story for the moment. We've got enough trouble as it is explaining why we're running under fake IDs and why no one should mention the name '*Icarus*' in groundside conversations. There's no need to scare them, too."

"I agree," Ixil said, looking around and snapping his fingers twice. Pix and Pax scampered out from under my bunk and whatever they'd found to explore there and climbed up his legs and torso back to his shoulders. "I'll go up and . . ."

He trailed off, an odd look on his face. "What is it?" I asked.

"I don't know," he said slowly, the look still there. "Something's not quite right. I can't put my finger on it."

I was on my knees now, plasmic in hand, my full attention on the deck where the ferrets had emerged from beneath the bunk. Carefully, one hand on the edge of the bunk to steady myself, I leaned over and looked underneath.

Nothing. No one scrunched up in hiding, no mysterious packages ready to go boom in the quiet watches of the night, no indication of hidden bugs or bottles of poisonous spiders, no evidence of tampering at all. Just a plain metal deck with a plain metal hull beyond it.

I got back to my feet. "Nothing there," I reported, brushing off my knees with my free hand.

"Of course not," Ixil said, his face wrinkling in a different way. "We would certainly have seen and recognized anything obvious."

I knew that, of course. On the other hand, it wasn't his bunk in his cabin. "So how unobvious is it?" I asked.

"Very," he said, shaking his head. "It's rather like one of those ideas or memories that floats around the edge of your mind, but which you can't quite tease out into the open."

"Keep trying," I told him.

"I will," he promised, throwing one last frown at the bunk and turning toward the door. He was reaching for the release pad when, beside the middle bunk, the intercom crackled. "Captain McKell, this is Chort," the Craea's familiar voice whistled through the speaker, the rhythmic thuds and hums of the engine room in the background. "Is Mechanic Ixil there with you?"

I stepped around the bunks to the intercom and tapped the key. "Yes, he is," I told him. "Trouble?"

"Nothing serious, I don't think," Chort assured me. "But I am in need of his assistance. The readings indicate an intermittent fault in the Darryen modulator relay, with possible location in the power-feed couplings."

"Probably the connectors," Ixil rumbled from behind me. "Those go out all the time."

"So I understand," Chort agreed. "I thought perhaps you and your outriders could either confirm or deny that possibility before I wake Drive Specialist Nicabar and ask him to open the conduit."

"No problem," Ixil said, tapping the door-release pad. "I'll be right there."

He stepped into the corridor and headed for the aft

ladder. "Thank you," Chort said as the door closed again. The intercom clicked off, and I was alone.

For a few minutes I stood there, listening to the various hums and clanks and throbbings, staring at my bunk and the wall behind it. I've never had any particular problems with the loneliness or unpleasant self-evaluation that for some people make solitude something to be avoided. For that matter, given that much of my human interaction lately had been with people like Brother John, solitude was in fact something to be actively sought out. I was tired, I'd been running low on sleep since even before that taverno run-in with Cameron, and under normal circumstances I would have been on my bunk and asleep in three minutes flat.

But if there was one thing certain about the *Icarus*, it was that nothing here ever approached what one might consider normal circumstances. And at this point, the latest express delivery of abnormal circumstances seemed to be whatever the nameless oddity was that existed around, under, or inside my bunk.

Plasmic still in hand, I eased carefully onto my stomach on the deck again and just as carefully wiggled my way under the bunk. It was a tight squeeze—a three-tier bunk hasn't got a lot of space underneath it—but I was able to get my head and most of my upper body under without triggering any bouts of latent claustrophobia. I wished I'd thought to snag the flashlight from my jacket, but enough of the cabin's overhead light was diffusing in to give me a fairly reasonable view.

The problem was, as I'd already noted, there was nothing there to see. I was surrounded by a bare metal deck, a bare metal wall, and a wire-mesh-and-mattress bunk of the type that had been around for centuries for the simple reason that no one yet had come up with a better compromise between marginal comfort and minimal manufacturing cost.

I wiggled my way back out, got to my feet, and spent a few more minutes going over the entire room millimeter by millimeter. Like the area under the bunk, there wasn't anything to see.

Nothing obvious, at least. But I knew Ixil, and if he said his outriders had found something odd, then they'd found something odd; and suddenly I decided I didn't much care for the silence and solitude of my cabin. Replacing my plasmic in its holster, I pulled my jacket on over it and left.

I didn't expect there to be much happening aboard the *Icarus* at that hour, and as I climbed the aft ladder to the mid deck I discovered I was right. Tera was on bridge-monitor duty—with, typically for her, the door closed—Chort and Ixil were back in the engine room, and Everett, Nicabar, and Shawn were presumably in their cabins on the upper deck. I thought I might find someone in the dayroom, either eating or watching a vid, but the place was as deserted as the corridor outside it. Either everyone had felt more in need of sleep than food, or else the camaraderie temperature reading aboard the *Icarus* was still hovering down around the liquid-nitrogen mark. Somewhere in the same vicinity, I decided sourly, as my progress at figuring out what was going on.

Just aft of the dayroom was the sick bay. On impulse, wondering perhaps if Everett might still be up, I touched the release pad and opened the door.

There was indeed someone there, dimly visible in the low night-light setting. But it wasn't Everett. "Hello?" Shawn called, lifting his head from the examination table to peer across the room at me. "Who is it?"

"McKell," I told him, turning up the light a bit and letting the door slide shut behind me. "Sorry to disturb you—I was looking for Everett."

"He's on the bridge," Shawn said, nodding toward the intercom beside the table. "Said it was his turn to earn his keep around here and told Tera to go to bed. You can call him if you want."

"No, that's all right," I said, suppressing a flicker of

annoyance. Strictly speaking, Tera should have cleared any such shift changes with me, but she and Everett had probably thought I was trying to catch up on my own sleep and hadn't wanted to disturb me. And the ship's medic *was* supposed to be available for swing shifts if any of the regular crewers were unable to cover theirs. "How come you're still here?" I asked, crossing the room toward him.

He smiled wanly. "Everett thought it would be best if I stayed put for a while."

"Ah," I said intelligently, belatedly spotting the answer to my question. With the dim light and the way the folds in his clothing lay, I hadn't seen until now the straps pinning his arms and legs gently but firmly to the table. "Well . . ."

My discomfort must have been obvious. "Don't worry," he hastened to assure me. "Actually, the straps were my suggestion. It's safer for everyone this way. In case the stuff he gave me wears off too quickly. I guess you didn't know."

"No, I didn't," I admitted, feeling annoyed with myself. With the unexpected entry of the Patth into this game dominating my thoughts, I'd totally forgotten about Shawn's performance at the airlock. "I guess I just assumed Everett had given you a sedative and sent you off to bed in your own cabin."

"Yes, well, sedatives don't work all that well with my condition," Shawn said. "Unfortunately."

"You *did* say he'd given you something, though, right?" I asked, swinging out one of the swivel stools and sitting down beside him. Now, close up, I could see that beneath the restraints his arms and legs were trembling.

"Something more potent at quieting nerves," he told me. "I'm not sure exactly what it was."

"And why do your nerves need quieting?" I asked.

A quick series of emotions chased themselves across his face. I held his gaze, letting him come to the decision at his own speed. Eventually, he did. "Because of a small problem I've got," he said with an almost-sigh. "Sort of qualifies as a drug dependency."

"Which one?" I asked, mentally running through the various drug symptoms I knew and trying without success to match them to Shawn's behavior patterns. Ixil had suggested earlier that the kid's emotional swings might be drug-related, but as far as I knew he hadn't been able to nail down a specific type, either.

And Shawn's answer did indeed come as a complete surprise. "Borandis," he said. "Also sometimes called jackalspit. I doubt you've ever heard of it."

"Actually, I think I have," I said carefully, the hairs rising unpleasantly on the back of my neck even as I tried to put some innocent uncertainty into my voice. I knew about borandis, all right. Knew it and its various charming cousins all too well. "It's one of those semilegit drugs, as I recall. Seriously controlled but not flat-out prohibited."

"Oh, it's flat-out prohibited most places," he said, frowning slightly as he studied me. Maybe my uncertainty act hadn't been enough; maybe he didn't think a simple cargo hauler should even be aware of such sinful things, let alone know any of the details. "But in most human areas it's available by prescription. If you have one of the relevant diseases, that is."

"And?" I invited.

His lips tightened briefly. "I've got the disease. Just not the prescription."

"And why don't you have the prescription?"

He smiled tightly. "Because I had the misfortune to pick up the disease in a slightly illegal way. I—well, some friends and I went on a little private trip to Ephis a few years ago."

"Really," I said. That word wasn't the first thing that popped into my mind; the phrase *criminal stupidity* held that honor. "*That* one I've definitely heard of. Interdicted world, right?"

His smile went from tight to bitter. "That's the place," he said. "And I can tell you right now that not a single thing you've heard about that hellhole is hyperbole." His mouth twitched. "But of course, sophisticated college kids like us were too smart to be taken in by infantile governmental scare tactics. And we naturally didn't believe bureaucrats had any right to tell us where we could or couldn't go—"

He broke off, a violent shiver running through him once before his body settled back down to its low-level trembling. "It's called Cole's disease," he said, his voice sounding suddenly very tired. "It's not much fun."

"I don't know many diseases that are," I said. "Are the rules for interdicted planets really that strict? That you can't even get a prescription for your medicine, I mean?"

He snorted softly, and for a moment a flicker of the old Shawn pierced the fatigue and trembling, the arrogant kid who knew it all and looked down with contempt on mere mortals like me who weren't smart or educated or enlightened enough. "Strict enough that even admitting I'd been to Ephis would earn me an automatic ten-year prison sentence," he bit out. "I don't think a guaranteed supply of borandis is quite worth that, do you?"

"I guess not," I said, making sure to sound properly chastened. People like Shawn, I knew, could often be persuaded to offer up deep, dark secrets for no better reason than to prove they had them. "So how do you get by?"

He shrugged, a somewhat abbreviated gesture given the strictures of the restraints. "There are always dealers around—you just have to know how to find them. Most of the time it's not too hard. Or too expensive."

"And what happens if you don't get it?" I asked. Drugs I knew, interdicted worlds I knew; but exotic diseases weren't part of my standard repertoire.

"It's a degenerative neurological disease," he said,

his lip twitching slightly. "You can see the muscular trembling has already started."

"That's not just the borandis withdrawal?"

"The withdrawal is part of it," he said. "It's hard to tell—the symptoms kind of mix together. That's followed by irritability, severe mood swings, short-term memory failure, and a generally high annoyance factor." Again, that bitter smile. "You may have noticed that last one when I first got to the ship on Meima. I'd just taken a dose, but I'd pushed the timing a little and it hadn't kicked in yet."

I nodded, remembering how much calmer, even friendly, he'd been a few hours later during Chort's ill-fated spacewalk. "Remind me never to go into a spaceport taverno with you before your pill," I said. "You'd get both our necks broken within the first three minutes."

He shivered. "Sometimes I think that would be a better way to go," he said quietly. "Anyway, if I still don't get a dose, I get louder and more irrational and sometimes even violent."

"Is that still a mixture of withdrawal and disease?"

"That one's mostly withdrawal," he said. "After that, the disease takes over and we start edging into neural damage. First the reversible kind, later the non-reversible. Eventually, I die. From all reports, not especially pleasantly."

Offhand, I couldn't think of many pleasant ways to die, except possibly in your sleep of old age, which given my early choices in life wasn't an option I was likely to face. If Shawn persisted in pulling stunts like sneaking onto interdicted worlds, it wasn't likely to remain one of his options, either.

Still, there was no sense in letting the old man with the scythe get at any of us too easily. "How long before the neural damage starts?" I asked.

He gave another of his abbreviated shrugs. "We've

got a little time yet," he said. "Nine or ten hours at least. Maybe twelve."

"From right now?"

"Yes." He smiled. "Of course, you probably won't want to be anywhere around me well before that. I'm not going to be very good company." The smile faded. "We *can* get to a supplier before then, can't we? I thought I heard Tera say it was only about six hours away to wherever the hell we're headed."

"Mintarius," I said, making a show of consulting my watch. In reality, I was thinking hard. I'd originally picked Mintarius precisely because it was close, small, quiet, and unlikely to have the equipment to distinguish our latest ship's ID from a genuine one. A perfect place to slip in, get the fuel our unexpectedly quick exit from Dorscind's World had lost us, and slip out again.

Unfortunately, Mintarius's backwater status also meant that illegal drug suppliers would be few and far between. And those who *were* there were likely to concentrate on the lowest common denominators like happyjam, not the more esoteric, semimedicinal ones.

I thought about that, and about the increasingly serious Patth search for us, and about the fact that Shawn's decision to go to Ephis had been a voluntary signing of his own death certificate anyway. But no matter how I sorted them out in the balance, there really wasn't any choice.

"It's actually a little farther than that," I told Shawn, getting to my feet. "Don't worry, though, we should make it in plenty of time. Assuming things go as planned—"

I broke off suddenly, turning my head and stretching out with all my ears. Barely heard over my own voice had been a faint dull metallic thud. The same unexplained sound, as near as I could tell, that I'd heard in the wraparound just after we'd left Xathru.

"What?" Shawn demanded, making no attempt to keep his voice down. "What's the problem?"

"I thought I heard something," I told him, suppressing the exceptionally impolite word I wanted to say. There might have been a follow-up sound, or even a lingering echo that could have given me a chance of figuring out its approximate direction. But both those chances were gone now, buried under Shawn's inopportune and overly loudmouthed question.

"What, you mean that thunking sound?" he scoffed. "It's nothing. You hear it every once in a while."

I frowned, my annoyance with his bad timing vanishing into sudden new interest. "You've heard it before?"

"Sure," he said, some of that old Shawn arrogance creeping into his tone. "Couple of times just while I've been lying here today. You want my opinion, it's probably something in the flush equipment in the head."

"Could be," I said noncommittally. He could have whatever opinion he wanted, but I'd been flying for half my life and there was absolutely nothing in a ship's plumbing that could make that kind of noise. "You said Tera went back to her cabin?"

"All I said was that Everett relieved her," he corrected me, his tone suddenly testy. "She could have gone outside for a walk for all I know." He waved a hand impatiently around the strap. "Look, what does any of this have to do with my medicine? Nothing, that's what. You *are* going to be able to get it, right?"

"I'll do what I can," I said, reaching down and swinging the swivel stool back into storage again. Clearly, the obnoxious stage of Shawn's withdrawal was starting, and I'd already had as much of that as I needed for one trip. "I'll see you later. Try to get some rest."

"Yeah," he muttered as I made my way to the door. "Sure—easy for *you* to say. What a bunch of—"

The sliding door cut off the noun. Just as well. I started to turn toward the bridge; but as I did so I caught the soft sound and faint vibration of a heavy footstep from behind me. I turned to see Ixil come into the corridor from the wraparound, a toolbox in his hand. "Trouble?" he murmured.

"No more than usual around here," I told him, not wanting to get into Shawn's problems just now. "I thought I might as well go and relieve Everett on the bridge."

Pix and Pax twitched at that, Ixil no doubt wondering what our medic was doing on bridge watch when Tera was supposed to be holding the fort there. But he clearly wasn't any more interested in holding serious conversations in open corridors than I was, and merely nodded. "We found the problem with the modulator relay," he said, continuing on down the corridor toward me. "All fixed."

"Good," I said, lifting my eyebrows and nodding fractionally behind me and to my right, toward the door to the mechanics shop. He nodded back, just as fractionally. Now, when everyone seemed to have taken themselves elsewhere, would be an excellent time for him to see what kind of cutting equipment Cameron had left us.

We went the rest of the way forward together in silence, Ixil breaking off to the left to the mechanics-room door aft of the bridge, me continuing the rest of the way past the forward access ladder to the bridge door. I tapped the release pad, and the door slid open.

For a moment I just stood there, staring in disbelief at the sight before me. Everett, his bulk nearly filling the small space between the command console and nav table, was half-turned to face me, his arms and right leg lifted in what looked like a grotesque parody of some kind of ballet step.

For a moment we stared at each other, and behind those blue eyes I watched his self-conscious embarrassment change almost reluctantly to a sort of stubborn pride. Then, very deliberately, he looked away and lowered his right foot back to the deck, his hands and arms tracing out a complicated design in the air as he did so. Just as deliberately, he moved his left foot around behind his right, his hands shifting again through the air.

And suddenly, belatedly, I realized what he was doing. Not ballet, not some odd playacting posturing, but a martial-arts kata.

I waited where I was, not moving or speaking, until he'd finished the form. "Sorry about that," he said, breaking the silence at last as he straightened up from his final crouch and squeezed back into the restraint chair. "I was feeling a little dozy, and a bit of exercise always perks me up."

"No apology or explanation needed," I assured him, stepping into the bridge but leaving the door locked open behind me. Back when we'd first met, I remembered thinking his face had that slightly battered look of someone who'd done time with high-contact sports. Apparently, that snap judgment had been correct. "What form was that? I don't think I've ever seen it before."

"It's not one usually put on display," he said, rubbing a sleeve across his forehead. Not that there'd been any sweat there that I could see. Maybe he kept it all inside the wrinkles. "Are you a practitioner or connoisseur of the martial arts?"

"Neither," I said. "I got a smattering of self-defense training when I was in EarthGuard, but there was no particular style involved and I was never all that good at it. But my college roommate was a certified nut on the subject, watching everything he could find, and I picked up some of it by sheer osmosis." I nodded toward the empty section of deck where he'd been performing. "Actually, what that reminded me of most was throw-boxing."

Everett lifted his eyebrows. "Very good. Yes, that was indeed a throw-boxing training kata. I did a bit of the professional circuit when I was younger." He snorted gently. "And in better shape, of course."

"Very impressive," I said, and meant it. I'd dealt with professional throw-boxers once or twice in my life, and knew the kind of tough breed those men and women were. "How long ago was that?"

"Oh, a good twenty years now," he said. "And you wouldn't be nearly so impressed if you knew my win/loss record." He frowned at me. "What are you doing here, by the way? I thought you were asleep."

"I came up to check on things and happened on your patient still strapped to the examination table," I told him. "You know what's wrong with him?"

"He told me it was a borandis-dependency problem," he said. "Coupled with a chronic case of Cole's disease."

"You believe him?"

He shrugged. "The diagnostic confirmed the withdrawal aspects," he said. "The medical database isn't complete enough to either confirm or refute the Cole's disease."

"Close enough," I told him, my last lingering suspicion that Shawn might have been faking the whole thing fading away. Muscle tremors and obnoxiousness were one thing, but a med diagnostic computer wasn't nearly so easily fooled.

"Unfortunately, that leaves us with a problem," Everett went on. "According to the database, borandis is a controlled drug. It's going to take more than just a ship's medic's certificate to get some for him on Mintarius."

"I know," I said. "Don't worry, we'll figure something out."

"I hope so," he said. "The prognosis for untreated Cole's disease is apparently not a very positive one."

"So he told me," I nodded. "Small wonder, I suppose, that he was at loose ends on Meima." I lifted my eyebrows slightly. "Speaking of which, I've been meaning to ask how you wound up in that same position. At loose ends, I mean."

He made a wry face. "Caught in the middle of a jurisdictional dispute, I'm afraid. One of the crewers on my previous ship pushed the captain one time too many and wound up rather badly injured. A trouble-maker—I'm sure you know the sort. At any rate, I helped him get to the med facility at the Meima space-port for treatment; and while we were out, the captain apparently decided he could do without both of us and took off."

"Yet another Samaritan winds up with the splin-tered end of the stick," I murmured.

He shrugged. "Perhaps. Frankly, I was just as happy to see their thrusters fading into the sunset. When Bo-rodin came into the restaurant where I was eating look-ing for someone with a med certificate, I jumped at the chance."

"Well, we're certainly glad to have you here," I said, glancing around the bridge. "Look, we're not more than a few hours from landing, and I can't sleep any-way. Why don't I take over and let you go hit the sack."

"Oh," he said, sounding and looking surprised. "Well . . . if you're sure."

"I'm sure," I told him. "There's nothing you can do for Shawn at the moment, and you might as well be rested when we hit ground."

"I suppose," Everett conceded, heaving himself out of the chair. I stepped forward out of his way as he moved to the doorway. "Do call me if you change your mind and want to at least catch a catnap."

"I will," I promised.

He left the bridge, turning right at the ladder and plodding his way up to the top deck. I waited until his feet were out of sight, gave him another ten count, then closed the bridge door behind me and stepped over to the nav table.

Given the set of parameters I was stuck with on this, I wasn't expecting the task ahead to be an easy one. I needed a world that was large enough and decadent enough to have an illicit drug-distribution network in place, with the kind of laissez-faire attitude toward paperwork that would let us slip in under our false ID, and yet wasn't a haven for the kind of career criminals who would be sporting crisp new hundred-commark bills and keeping their eyes peeled for anyone resembling my Mercantile Authority file photo. And it had to be somewhere within, say, nine hours of our present position.

It took only five minutes to conclude that there was exactly one place on the charts that even came close to fitting my requirements: the Najiki colony world of Potosi, currently seven hours distant. It had the kind of cosmopolitan populace that promised that vices of all sorts would be in evidence, and it was run by beings with such keen eyesight—and such a stratospheric self-confidence—that they seldom used scanners to check ships' papers.

There was, in fact, just one small factor that kept Potosi from being absolutely ideal. It was also a major hub for the Patth shipping industry.

I stared at the listing for a while, perhaps hoping that in my tiredness I was imagining things and that if I looked long enough it would go away. But no such luck. Certain parts of Potosi, including the sky above it, were going to be crawling with Patth, and that was just the way it was.

But there was nothing for it. Not unless we wanted to sit around and watch Shawn die.

It was a matter of two minutes to cancel the Mintarius course and recalculate a vector to take us to Potosi instead. Listening carefully, I was just able to hear the subtle shift in thrust tone from the drive as we swung over the twenty-three degrees necessary to make the course change.

And I'm convinced that it was precisely because I was listening so carefully that even through two closed doors I heard the muted pop and the equally faint and choked-off scream.

I was in the corridor half a second later, heading for the mechanics-room door five meters away. I crossed the distance in two seconds more, hearing a soft but ominous hissing sound that grew steadily louder as I neared it. I slapped the pad, and the door slid open.

And with a roar like a rabid dragon a wall of flame blew out of the doorway toward me.

An instant later I was rolling to my feet from three meters farther down the corridor with no clear memory of how I'd gotten there. I spun back to the open doorway, the terrifying image of Ixil trapped in the midst of that inferno paralyzing my entire thought process. I clawed my way back to the doorway, the smell of burning acetylene filling my nose and mouth, a small and still functional part of my mind noting with some confusion that there was now no trace of the wall of flame that had sent me diving instinctively away. I reached the doorway, bracing myself for the worst, and looked inside.

It was bad enough, but not nearly as bad as I'd feared. Off to the left, the twin tanks of the *Icarus*'s oxyacetylene cutting torch were sitting upright beside the main workbench, the pressure of the compressed gases sending their connected hoses writhing together along the deck like a pair of demented Siamese-twin snakes. From the open ends of the coupled hoses was spewing an awesome spray of yellow flame. Even as I took it all in I was forced to once again duck back as the skittering hoses swung past the doorway and sent another burst my direction—clearly, that was what I'd mistaken earlier for an all-encompassing wall of flame. The blast swept past and I looked back inside.

And it was only then, in the back of the room beyond the flopping hoses, that I spotted Ixil.

He was lying against the line of equipment-storage lockers that made up the back wall, his torso half–propped up against the lockers, his eyes closed. There was no sign of Pix and Pax; odds were they were cowering in a nook or corner somewhere. If they were even alive. Ixil's right pant leg was smoldering above his low boot, but otherwise the fire didn't seem to have marked him.

But that bit of grace wasn't going to last much longer. Even just since I'd started watching I could see that the hoses' gyrations were swinging wider with each oscillation, and within a minute or less they would be twisting around to the point where the fire stream would be washing directly over my unconscious partner.

"God and hellfire," a voice breathed in my ear.

I twisted my head around to find Nicabar standing just behind me, staring wide-eyed into the room. "I heard the commotion and smelled the fire," he said. "Where's the damn suppression system?"

"There isn't one," I bit out, jabbing my finger toward the bridge door. "There's an extinguisher just inside the bridge to the left."

He was off before I'd even finished the sentence. I turned back to the mechanics room, dodging back just in time as the semirandom fire spray once again did its best to take my eyebrows off. There was another extinguisher, I knew, just inside the door to my right; the question was whether I could slip into the room and get to it without incinerating myself.

Unfortunately, at that point came an even bigger question: What could I do with the thing if and when I got to it? Shipboard fire extinguishers used a two-prong approach, the foam smothering the air away from the flames while simultaneously pulling out as much of the heat as possible. But that acetylene fire had a lot of heat built up already, possibly more than a small extinguisher canister could handle; and given that the blaze had its own built-in oxygen supply, the question of smothering was even more problematic.

There was a breath of sudden movement beside me. "Got it," Nicabar said, holding the half-meter-long orange canister ready in the doorway. "Straight in?"

"Straight in," I told him. He squeezed the handle, and a stream of yellowish fluid sprayed toward the writhing hoses, its loud hissing joining the crackle of the flames. Joining, but not eliminating. For a few seconds the blaze faltered as the droplets sucked heat away from it, but then seemed to gather its strength again in defiance. The hoses twisted around in their unpredictable way, sending the tip skittering off the edge of Nicabar's spray, and with an almost-triumphant roar the fire blazed fully back to life.

But those few seconds were enough. I jumped into the room and ducked to my right, grabbing at the bright orange object at the edge of my peripheral vision as I kept my main attention on the fire and Nicabar's attack on it. The quick-releases holding the extinguisher to the bulkhead worked exactly as they were supposed to, though in the mood I was in I would have had the canister off the wall no matter how it was fastened there. I continued to my right, twisting the canister around into position in my hands as I moved. I got it lined up just as the hoses started to shift toward me, and squeezed the handle.

My spray joined Nicabar's, and the tanks and hoses all but vanished into a roiling cloud of mist. But the fire itself was still clearly visible, diminished but a long way yet from being quenched. And with the gas pressure driving its erratic movements completely unaffected by the foam, it was still just as dangerous as it had been before.

There was only one chance, and I had to take it before the extinguishers ran dry and the flame roared back to full strength again. Squeezing the handle hard, keeping my stream of foam aimed as best I could, I charged straight in toward our adversary. Nicabar shouted something from the doorway, but I couldn't make out what he was saying over the noise. The hoses finished their oscillation the other direction and started swinging back, and in about half a second the flame would get its chance to incinerate me on its way to doing the same to Ixil.

And at the last moment, with my best effort at the long jump since failing to make my college track team, I leaped over the flame and landed squarely on the end of the hoses, pinning them in place on the deck.

I heard Nicabar give an encouraging whoop, and suddenly the billowing mist from his extinguisher was flowing coldly around my legs, a sharp contrast to the backwash of heat that already seemed to be trying to cook my feet inside my boots. But for that final two seconds I didn't care about either the fire or Nicabar's efforts to put it out. Dropping my own canister onto the deck, I grabbed the valve handle on the acetylene tank and twisted for all I was worth.

And with one final indignant gasping wheeze from the hoses, the fire went out.

CHAPTER

8

"All I can say is that you were very lucky," Everett said, shaking his head as he finished sealing the last burn pad around Ixil's leg and picked up the medical scanner again. "Very lucky indeed. I know *my* hearing's not up to picking up sounds that subtle, especially through two doors. If I'd still been on the bridge instead of McKell, I'd be pulling a blanket over your face about now."

"Yes, I know," Ixil said, his voice and manner the subdued humility of someone who knows he's done something stupid that has put himself in danger and made trouble for everyone else. Glancing over at the med-room doorway, where Nicabar, Tera, and Chort were silently watching the procedure, I could see traces of sympathetic embarrassment in their faces, the normal reaction of polite people having to witness another person's private shame.

I didn't feel any such embarrassment myself. But then, I knew full well that this humility bit was completely out of character for Ixil, that it was all merely for show in the hopes of allaying any suspicions anyone might have about the sort of person he really was.

Vaguely, I wondered if one of the observers standing in the doorway was putting on a similar performance.

"Next time I suggest checking *all* the equipment before you start it up," Everett went on sternly, running the scanner slowly along Ixil's burned leg as he frowned at the readings. Not surprisingly, Cameron's people had failed to include a Kalixiri module with their med computer, and I could almost guarantee the readings were like nothing Everett had ever seen before. Fortunately, Ixil had another, uninjured leg to use for comparison.

"I'll second that," I put in, throwing a glance at the other end of the room. Still strapped to the examination table, Shawn's face—for that matter, his entire body—was practically dripping with impatience and a near-total contempt for Ixil and his injuries, a marked contrast to the solicitude everyone else was showing. Still, aside from a single sour question about what the hell was going on as we'd hustled Ixil inside, he'd kept his mouth shut. Maybe his borandis-withdrawal sarcasm was under better control than he'd implied, or maybe he was in the calm side of one of the mood swings he'd mentioned. Or maybe he'd seen Ixil's expression and was possessed of a finer-tuned survival instinct than I'd thought. "The shape this whole ship is in," I added diplomatically, turning back to Ixil, "it's a wonder more of the equipment hasn't fallen apart."

"I know," Ixil said again. "I heartily promise to be more careful next time."

"We can all consider ourselves lucky the lesson wasn't learned more painfully," Everett said, shifting the scanner from Ixil's leg to the impressively swelling bruise on his forehead where the torch head had slammed into him when it sheared apart, the impact throwing him back against the lockers and knocking him out cold.

He didn't remember that last part himself, of course, having been unconscious at the time. But the ferrets hadn't been injured in the accident, and once I'd coaxed them out from behind the row of lockers where they'd gone to ground Ixil had been able to sample their memories and confirm the entire sequence of events.

"At any rate, that's all I can do for now," Everett concluded, putting the scanner aside and smoothing the burn pads one last time. "Except for a painkiller or sedative, of course. Either would help you sleep."

"Don't worry, I'll sleep just fine," Ixil assured him. "There really isn't all that much pain."

Everett looked doubtful, but he nodded and headed for the sonic scrubber. "As you wish," he said as he started cleaning his hands. "If you change your mind just let me know. I'm sure there's *something* aboard that will work on a Kalix."

"I'll keep that in mind," Ixil promised, easing off the stool where Everett had been working on him and standing up.

Or more accurately, trying to stand up. His leg wobbled beneath him, and he grabbed at the wall for balance.

As cues went, it was one of the more obvious ones I'd ever been tossed. "Hang on, I'll give you a hand," I said quickly, stepping to his side as I juggled Pix and Pax around to free up one of my hands. The furry little beasts were less than cooperative—they'd gone back to Ixil's shoulders long enough for him to get their version of the accident, but he was still in pain and they weren't at all interested in sharing in it. But with a little creative shuffling I got them settled in on shoulder and forearm and was able to assist a limping Ixil out past the group at the doorway. "Excitement's over for the night," I told them as we made our slow way down the corridor. "Tera, I'd appreciate it if you'd take over on the bridge."

"Consider it done," she said.

Ixil had a lot of qualities that I admired, but a sylph-like body frame wasn't one of them. Fortunately, the wounded-warrior act lasted only as long as it took us to get down the ladder and out of sight of any of the gallery that might have lingered behind after the show. Once on the lower deck, he made it the rest of the way to his cabin under his own steam.

"An interesting experiment," he commented as he maneuvered his way onto the center bunk. "Not that it's one I would have chosen on my own. Thank you for your help, by the way. I owe you one."

"We'll add it to your side of the ledger," I said briefly, resisting the urge to bring up all the times he'd hauled me bodily out of similar predicaments. The Kalixiri way of handling injuries was to go into a deep, comalike sleep while healing, and from the looks of Ixil's drooping eyelids he was three-quarters of the way there already. The fact that he hadn't dropped off the second he hit the bunk implied there was something he wanted or needed to say to me before he went under, and it certainly wasn't to go over our personal win/loss score sheet.

"I believe we can safely cross Jones off our suspect list," he murmured, his eyelids closing completely and then opening partway again, like sliding doors with a bad feedback loop. "I didn't just turn that torch on tonight without doing a complete equipment check, Jordan. I looked it over two days ago, just after I came aboard at Xathru. The sabotage has to have been done since then."

I stared at him, something large and invisible taking me by the throat and gently squeezing. A cutting torch was a totally innocuous tool to have aboard a starship, and there was no reason whatsoever for anyone to sabotage it that way. Unless, of course, someone really, *really* didn't want us cutting our way into the sealed cargo hold.

The only catch was that no one else should have known we were even considering such an action. That conversation had taken place less than an hour ago, with only Ixil and me present, in the privacy of my cabin.

Apparently, someone had taken it upon himself to listen in.

I opened my mouth to ask Ixil how this bit of auditory legerdemain might have been accomplished, closed it again with the question unvoiced. Ixil's eyes were squeezed shut, his breathing slow and even. He'd delivered his message, was down for the count, and barring an extremely urgent and probably extremely loud catastrophe he was going to stay that way for however many hours it took to heal his leg and head.

And for that same number of hours, I was going to be on my own.

Ixil had made up the lower bunk for Pix and Pax, bunching the blanket up for them to snuggle into and putting their food and water containers where they could easily get to them. I spent a few minutes getting them settled there, then pulled the blanket off the top bunk and tucked it under Ixil's mattress, wedging its center under the lower bunk beside the ferrets' nest and letting the rest drape down from there onto the floor. Assured that they could get to the floor if they wanted exercise or to Ixil if they wanted company, I turned off the light and left the cabin.

There were no locks on any of the *Icarus*'s interior doors. Up till now I hadn't really worried much about that; but up till now my partner hadn't been lying comatose and reasonably helpless after what might or might not have been an effort to kill him. Pulling out my multitool, checking both ways down the corridor to make sure I was unobserved, I removed the cover of the release pad from the center of the door and pulled out the control chip. On the underside, snugged inconspicuously between two of the connector feet, was what I was looking for: the timing dial, which told the door how many seconds it was to stay open unless you overrode it by locking the door in place. Using the narrowest screwdriver from the multitool, I eased the dial from its preset position all the way to zero, then returned the chip to its socket.

Experimentally, I touched the release pad. Not only did the door open barely ten centimeters before slamming shut again, it did so with a startlingly loud clunk as the buffer mechanism that normally provided for a smoother closing failed to engage. For a moment I flashed back to the metal-on-metal sound I'd heard at least twice now aboard the *Icarus*, wondering if there could simply be a bad buffer in one of the doors. But even allowing for the sound to be filtered by distance, I knew this wasn't it.

I put the cover back on the pad and went down the corridor to my own cabin. It was far from a perfect solution—anyone bent on unscrupulous deeds, after all, could presumably open the release pad himself and ungimmick it as easily as I had, assuming he knew about the adjustment dial, which most people didn't. But for the moment it was the best I could do. At least this way any attempt to get to Ixil would generate a noise and vibration that I ought to be able to hear from my own cabin. Ixil himself, of course, with a completely separate touch-pad mechanism on his side of the door, could come out anytime he wanted. I reached my cabin, dithered momentarily about whether I should gimmick my own door as I had Ixil's, decided against it, and went in.

The room was still as small and as unadorned as it had always been, but as I put my back against the door I found myself looking at it with new eyes. Somehow, someone had overheard our last conversation in here, and had overheard it clearly enough to nip up to the mechanics room and sabotage the cutting torch.

The question was how.

The wall separating the cabin from the corridor was solid metal, a good five centimeters thick. The bulkheads were even thicker, probably nine or ten centimeters, and on the side away from the corridor was the *Icarus*'s inner hull, with no more than another twenty centimeters between it and the outer hull. Outside the outer hull, of course, was the vacuum of space. There were, I knew, ways to hear through solid metal walls, but all of them involved fairly sophisticated equipment and even then success was not at all guaranteed aboard a starship where the whole frame was continually vibrating with everything from engine drone to voices and footsteps two decks away. The bunks were too simple and flimsy to conceal a hidden transmitter strong enough to punch a radio signal through that much metal; ditto for the lockers. After that tracker incident on Meima, I'd made it a point to regularly signal-scan both myself and Ixil for such unwanted hitchhikers, and had just as regularly found nothing. And finally, there was nothing on any of the walls that could camouflage any such listening device.

Except the intercom.

I unfastened the cover of the intercom with my multitool, swearing silently at myself the whole time. It was the oldest trick in the book: Sometime when I was out, probably during our stop on Dorscind's World, someone had slipped in here and rearranged a few wires so that the intercom was continually on, at least as far as one other specific intercom was concerned. Someone who'd known what he was doing could have done it in three minutes. Still swearing, still feeling like a fool, I pulled the cover off the intercom and peered inside.

It was an intercom, all right. A simple, standard, bottom-of-the-line ship's intercom. The kind you could buy for five commarks in any outfitter's shop anywhere across the Spiral.

And it hadn't been tampered with.

I stared at it for a good three minutes of my own, prodding wires aside with my screwdriver as I visually traced every one of them from start to finish at least five times. Nothing. No gimmicking, no crossed wires, no questionable components, nothing that shouldn't be there. Nothing even left the box except two power wires and a slender coax cable—exactly the right number—which disappeared through a tiny hole in the inner hull to join the rest of the maze of wiring and plumbing laid out in the narrow gap between inner and outer hulls.

Slowly, I replaced the intercom cover, now thoroughly confused. Had we been wrong about an eavesdropper? Had the accident with the cutting torch been just that? Or if not an accident, then sabotage simply on general principles by someone who didn't want the *Icarus*'s cargo examined, and not a reaction to our conversation at all?

I didn't believe it for a minute. I'd had only a brief look at the torch head that had done its best to take off the top of Ixil's skull, but that one look had been enough. The screw connector holding the head onto the connected hoses had had its threads badly crimped, probably with compression pliers, so that when the pressure built up enough it had come loose in that explosive fashion. As sabotage methods went it had been effective enough; but it had also been fairly clumsy and, more to the point, extremely quick and simple. Not the sort of job one would expect even an amateur to pull, at least not an amateur with the time to do the job more subtly.

Which implied our saboteur had been rushed in his task. Which meant it had, in fact, been a response to our conversation.

Which meant I was back to square one. How had he overheard us?

I spent the next fifteen minutes going over the lockers and bunks, and found exactly what I'd expected, namely, nothing. Then, stretching out on my bunk, I stared at the bottom of the bunk above me and tried to think.

When you have eliminated the impossible, Sherlock Holmes was fond of saying, whatever remains, however improbable, must be the truth. It wasn't an aphorism I particularly subscribed to, mainly because in real life eliminating all the various impossibles was usually a lot trickier than in Holmes's fictional setting. However, in this particular case, the list of directions the answer could be hiding in was definitely and distressingly short. In fact, as I turned the problem over in my mind, I found there was exactly one of Sherlock's improbables left.

Ixil had mentioned earlier that he'd looked over the full schematics for the *Icarus*. It was a fair assumption that he'd gone ahead and kept a copy, so I went back to his cabin, ungimmicked the door, and went inside. The room looked exactly the way I'd left it except that Pix and Pax were now up on the middle bunk with Ixil, nosing around the hip pouch where he habitually kept some of the little treats they especially liked. I put them back on their bunk where they wouldn't get rolled over on if Ixil shifted in his sleep, raided the pouch and gave them two of the treats each, then checked his locker. The schematics were there, a sheaf of papers rolled tightly together. I tucked the roll under my arm, regimmicked the door on my way out, and returned to my cabin.

I looked first at the main overview, noting in particular the diameter of the main sphere that made up the forward section of the ship. The number listed was forty-one-point-three-six meters—a strangely uneven number, I thought, but one I trusted implicitly. Ship dimensions were critically important when landing-pit assignments were being doled out, and no one ever got them wrong. Not more than once, anyway.

Two sheets down was the one I was most interested

in: the schematic for the mid deck. Digging a pen out of my inside jacket pocket, I turned the first sheet over for some clean space and started jotting down numbers.

Even given the inherent problem of fitting mainly rectangular spaces into a giant sphere, the *Icarus*'s various rooms were quite oddly shaped, and the semirandom placement of storage lockers, equipment modules, and pump and air-quality substations only added to the layout mess. But I was in no mood to be balked by a set of numbers, even messy ones, and I set to work.

And in the end, they all matched.

It was not the answer I'd been expecting, and for several minutes after rechecking my math I sat in silence scowling at the schematics. I'd been so sure that Sherlock and I had finally been on the brink of figuring this one out. But the numbers added up perfectly, and numbers don't lie.

Or do they?

One page farther down was the lower-deck schematic, the deck I was currently on. A few more minutes' work confirmed that these numbers, too, matched just fine.

But that was just the theoretical part of this project. Now it was time to move on to the experimental work.

A laser measure would have been the most convenient, but after what had happened to Ixil I was a bit leery about scrounging tools out of the *Icarus*'s mechanics room. Fortunately, I didn't have to. I'd seen the printer up in Tera's computer room, and I knew the size paper it used. Laying the schematics out on the floor, I set about using them to measure my cabin. It took just over two minutes, and when I was done I took a couple of the sheets out into the corridor and measured that, too.

And when I was finished, the numbers had stopped matching.

Each of the inner-hull plates was about a meter

square and held in place by sixteen connectors. The average spacer's multitool isn't really the proper gadget to use for removing hull plates, but mine was a somewhat better model than the average and had a couple of additional blades those missed out on. By the time I was down to the final four—the ones in the corners—I was getting pretty adept at the procedure. I paused long enough at that point to dig out my flashlight and set it on the deck where it would be handy; after a moment's thought I drew my plasmic and put it down beside the light. Then I removed the last four connectors and eased the plate out of place.

And there, dimly seen by the reflected overhead light from my cabin, was the gray metal of the outer hull. Not twenty centimeters beyond the inner hull like it was supposed to be, but a solid meter and a half away.

Plasmic in one hand and flashlight in the other, I leaned my head cautiously into the opening and looked around. The pipes and cables and conduits that normally ran through the 'tweenhull area were all in evidence, fastened securely to the inner hull just the way they were supposed to be. The rest of the space was completely empty except for the series of struts that fastened the two hulls together. Struts, I decided, that would provide a strenuous but workable jungle-gym walkway for anyone who wanted to move unseen about the ship.

As well as a convenient work platform for, say, someone desiring to tap into the coax cable from an intercom. Specifically, *my* intercom. I turned my light on the spot off to the left where the relevant wires emerged, but it was too far away and my angle too shallow to see with certainty whether or not anything had been tampered with.

The nearest support strut in that direction was nearly half a meter away. Laying my gun and light on the deck beside me, I gathered my feet under me, gauged the distance, and leaped carefully toward it.

And with a sudden stomach-twisting disorientation, I jerked sideways and slammed hard onto my right shoulder and leg against the outer deck.

It says a lot for the shock involved that my first stunned thought was that the *Icarus*'s grav generator had malfunctioned again, shutting off at the precise moment I jumped—this despite the fact that I was now lying flat on my side against the outer hull. It took another several seconds before my brain caught up with the fact that I *was,* in fact, lying against the outer hull, the term "lying" automatically implying a gravitational field.

Except that this gravitational field was roughly at right angles to the one I'd just left in my cabin. The only one that the *Icarus*'s generator could create. The only one, in fact, that had any business existing here at all.

Slowly, carefully, I turned my head to what was now "up" from my new frame of reference. There was my cabin, a meter above my head, with my plasmic and light clinging unconcernedly to what was from my perspective a sheer wall. Even more carefully, I leaned my torso up away from the hull, half expecting that this magic grip would suddenly cease if I let go of the hull and send me sliding down to the underside of the *Icarus*.

I needn't have worried. Except for the total impossibility of its vector, this field behaved more or less like the one created by a normal ship's grav generator. I reached up toward my cabin, and because I was paying close attention I was able to feel where the two gravity vectors began to conflict with each other a few millimeters my side of the inner hull. At least now I knew what the anomaly was that Pix and Pax had detected while scampering beneath my bunk, and why neither they nor Ixil had been able to interpret it.

It also explained how our mysterious eavesdropper/saboteur had been able to move around so easily. No dangerous or athletic strut-leaping required; all he had to do was crawl around like a spider on a wall. I snagged my light and gun and brought them to me, nearly dropping the plasmic when its weight suddenly shifted in my grip. It might not take great athletic ability to move around in here, I amended, but it did take some getting used to. Holstering the weapon, I shifted myself cautiously toward my intercom, still not entirely trusting this phenomenon.

I was easing up to get a closer look at the wires when I heard a small scraping sound in the distance.

For a moment I thought I'd imagined it, or else that it had merely been some normal ship's noise distorted by the echo chamber I was lying in. But then the sound came again, and I knew I'd been right the first time.

There was someone else in here with me.

Silently, I shut off my light and put it in my pocket, at the same time drawing my plasmic. Then, not nearly as silently, but as silently as I could manage, I set off down the curving hull.

It was, in retrospect, probably not the most brilliant thing I'd ever done in my life. However it was he'd discovered this cozy little back stairway, our saboteur surely had a better idea of the lay of the land in here than I did, including knowing where all the best hiding places and ambush sites were. He was furthermore presumably already acclimated to the place, whereas I was still distracted by the nagging feeling that at any minute the hull's peculiar gravity would fail and I would become the cue ball in a giant spherical game of bumper billiards. But at the moment all that I could think of was that I had a chance to nail him dead to rights, and I was going to take it.

I started off by scooting along the hull on my backside, but quickly gave that up as not nearly quiet enough, not to mention being a posture that tended to leave me with my back to the direction I was going. I tried switching to a standard hands-and-knees crawl, but after a couple of meters decided that that was no good either, leaving my gun hand as it did too far out of line to get off a quick shot if necessary. The only other option I could think of was the one I finally adopted, a crouching sort of duck waddle that was hard on the knees and undignified in the extreme, but at least had the advantage of leaving my gun and me pointed in the same direction.

The sound had seemed to come from above me, the term "above" referring to the direction toward the *Icarus*'s top deck, so that was the direction I headed. It was slower going than I'd expected, partly because of the awkwardness of my stance and the need for silence, but also because of the unpleasant vertigo effect of having my head bobbing along just about where the two competing gravity fields mixed at roughly equal strength. The effect became steadily more pronounced as I passed the mid deck and continued around toward the top of the ship, with the angle between the gravity vectors gradually veering from ninety degrees toward an even more disconcerting 180.

I don't know how long the slow-motion chase went on. Not long, I think, not more than fifteen or twenty minutes' total. Between my aching knees and swimming head and the fact that I was alone in a dark space with a man who had already killed once, my time sense wasn't at its best that night. Every thirty seconds or so I paused to listen, stretching out with all my senses over the rumbling background noise and vibration of the ship, trying for a new estimate of where he was.

It was on the fifth or sixth such halt that I realized that what had up till now been occasional incautious scraping sounds had suddenly become something far more steady. Steady scraping noises, yet paradoxically quieter than they had been up till then.

My quarry knew I was here.

Earlier, I had come up with the image of being a spider on a wall. Now, suddenly, the image changed from a spider to a fly. A fly pinned by a light against a very white wall. For a dozen heartbeats I squatted there motionlessly, sweating in the darkness as I strained to listen, trying to determine whether the sounds were moving toward or away from me. The latter would mean he was trying to escape, the former that he had yet another violent accident on his mind. And if there was one thing certain here, it was that I couldn't afford to guess wrong.

For those dozen heartbeats I listened; and then I knew. The sounds were definitely moving away, probably downward to my right, though the echo effect made it difficult to tell for sure.

All the reasons why I shouldn't have come in here after him in the first place once again flashed through my mind. Once again, I shoved them aside. I'd already lost several rounds to this man, and I was getting damned tired of it. Picking a vector that would theoretically intersect his, I set off after him.

To this point it had been a slow-motion chase. Now, it became an equally slow-motion game of hounds and hares. I was stopping ever more frequently to listen; but my quarry was doing the same, and as often as not I would pause only to find he had changed direction again. Doggedly, I kept at it, my earlier thought about the possibility of ambush spots never straying too far from my mind. So far our saboteur had shown no indication of being armed, but everyone else I'd run into on this trip had been and there was no reason to expect that whoever had been handing out the guns with such generosity would have neglected his friend here aboard the *Icarus*.

More than once I also considered banging the butt of my plasmic against the inner hull and trying to rouse the rest of the crew to help in the search. But by then I was so thoroughly lost that I had no idea whether I was even near enough to any of the others scattered around the ship for my pounding to do any good. And whether any of them heard me or not, my playmate in here certainly would, and at the first sign of an attempted alarm he might well postpone his escape plan in favor of shutting me up first.

And then, in the distance ahead of me, I saw a faint glow appear, so faint that I wasn't sure at first whether I was simply imagining it. My first thought was that our convoluted intertwined wanderings had brought us back to the vicinity of my cabin and the open inner-hull plate. But even as I realized that the combined gravity vector was wrong for that, the distant glow vanished, accompanied by a dull, metallic thud. A sound like two pieces of metal clanking hollowly against each other.

The same sound I'd heard from the wraparound after my talk with Nicabar, and had been trying to track down for nearly two days.

I kept going, but there was clearly no point in hurrying. My quarry had led me around the barn a couple of times and had now popped back through his rabbit hole to the safe anonymity of the *Icarus* proper. By the time I reached the spot where the glow had been, assuming I could pinpoint it at all, he would have the connectors back in place and it would be just one more of seventeen thousand other inner-hull plates.

A couple of minutes later I reached the vicinity where I estimated the glow had been. As expected, every one of the hull plates in the area looked exactly alike, and I still had no idea where exactly I was. Briefly, I thought about trying to dig my way through, but a single glance was all it took to see that the hull-plate connectors couldn't be removed from this side.

But maybe there was another way to mark my place here.

I played my light across the inner-hull plates over my head, searching among the haphazard arrangement of piping and wires until I found what I was looking for: the telltale power wires and coax cable of an intercom, their ends disappearing through the inner hull half a meter to the side of my estimated position for my quarry's escape hatch.

I'd left my multitool back on my cabin floor, but the contact edge of my plasmic's power pack was rough enough for my purposes, and it took only a few minutes of work for me to abrade the insulation on the power wires enough to leave a small section of bare wire on each of them. Putting the plasmic aside, I touched the two bare spots together.

There was no spark—the power level was far too low for that—but what the operation lacked in pyrotechnic dramatics it more than made up in personal satisfaction. Somewhere in the bowels of the *Icarus,* I knew, a circuit breaker had just popped in response to the short circuit I'd created. All I had to do was find which one, and I'd have my suspect intercom identified. And with it, the saboteur's rabbit hole.

Making sure the bare spots stayed together, I wrapped the wires as best I could to hold them that way. On most starships the main computer's nursemaid program would pick this up in a flash and send a maintenance flag to both the bridge and engine-room status boards. With the *Icarus's* archaic system, though, I doubted that it had such a program. Even if it did, there would be no way to reset the circuit breaker until the wires were unjinxed.

Which left only the problem of finding my way back to my cabin and hunting up the appropriate breaker box before my adversary tumbled to what I'd done and fixed the short circuit.

Now that I was no longer engaged in a chase, the navigational task was straightforward if a bit tedious. Holding my light loosely by finger and thumb, I held it near the edge of the inner hull and watched which way it tried to turn. That gave me the direction of ship's down, and I headed that way until further measurements with my impromptu pendulum showed I was at the sphere's South Pole. Picking a direction at random,

I moved along it for a few meters, then began circling at that latitude until I spotted the glow of my cabin light filtering through the opening. Three minutes after that, I was back.

With everything else that had happened, I almost forgot to check my own intercom's coax cable for tampering, which had, after all, been the original purpose of this exercise. Not that I was expecting to find anything else, but for completeness it seemed the proper thing to do. A cursory examination was all it took to discover that it had indeed been tapped into.

I climbed back into my cabin, noting as I did so the curious fact that the hull's gravitational field seemed to hold on to me more strongly now that I'd been all the way into it than it had before I'd first landed on the outer hull. Possibly it was just my imagination; but on the other hand this field was so unlike anything I'd ever experienced anyway, I was perfectly willing to grant it one more bit of inexplicable magic. Between this and the Lumpy Brothers' exotic weaponry, the strange technology was starting to get a little too thick on the ground for my taste.

Putting hull-plate connectors back in with a multitool was a different skill entirely from taking them out, but it wasn't that hard and I wasn't going to bother with more than the four corners for now anyway. A few minutes of leafing through Ixil's sheaf of schematics and I had the proper breaker box identified: up on the top deck with the rest of the crew cabins.

The general stir that had accompanied Ixil's injuries had long since faded away, and the *Icarus* was again quiet. I climbed the aft ladder to the top deck and moved silently down the corridor, half expecting one of the cabin doors to open and someone to take a potshot at me. But no one did, and I reached the breaker box without incident. It was recessed into the bulkhead at the forward end of the corridor with five other breaker boxes, just beyond the forward ladder. It was also quite small, though given that it apparently only contained the ship's twenty-six intercom breakers I shouldn't have expected anything very big.

Not surprisingly, given the *Icarus*'s designer's overly optimistic faith in the goodness of his fellow men, none of the breaker boxes was locked. The hinges squeaked slightly as I pulled the proper one open, but not loudly enough to wake up any of the sleepers nearby. With a tingling sense of anticipation, I shined my light inside.

According to Ixil's schematic, the box held twenty-six low-voltage circuit breakers. At the moment, however, all it held was twenty-six circuit-breaker sockets.

I gazed at the empty box for a few more seconds, twenty-twenty hindsight turning my anticipation into a sour taste in my mouth. With the wires still touching behind the intercom, the saboteur had, of course, been unable to reset the telltale breaker. So he'd simply taken them all out.

Score one more round to him. This was getting to be a very bad habit.

With the same faint squeak of the hinges I closed the cabinet door again. There might be some spare breakers aboard, but since virtually nothing ever went wrong with the things there very well might not be. Besides, anyone smart enough to have anticipated my actions in the 'tweenhull space was probably already ahead of me there, too. By the time I found the spares—or found and cannibalized another set of same-sized ones from a different box—he would undoubtedly have the intercom wires fixed again.

The walk back down to my cabin seemed longer somehow than the upward trip had been a few minutes earlier. I retrieved a connector tool from the mechanics room on my way and finished sealing the hull plate back into position, then lay back down on my bunk and tried to think. I thought for a while, but it didn't seem to be getting me anywhere, so I went back up to the mid deck to check on the bridge.

Tera was still faithfully on duty, or was once again faithfully on duty if she'd been the one scooting around between the *Icarus*'s hulls. I volunteered to take over for her while she grabbed something to eat from the dayroom, and as she passed by me I tried to see if I could spot any oil stains on her clothing or smell any lingering aromas. There was nothing out of the ordinary that I could detect.

But then, I didn't seem to have picked up any stains or smells while I was between decks, either. Inconclusive, either way.

As soon as she was out of sight I did a complete check of the bridge, equipment and course heading both. Tera was still reasonably high on my list of suspects; and even if she wasn't the one sporting the brand-new collector's set of circuit breakers, there was no reason a saboteur who liked fiddling with intercoms couldn't extend his hobby to more vital equipment.

But everything checked out perfectly. Sinking wearily into the command chair, I propped my elbows on the armrests and my chin on my hands and stared at the hypnotic flickering of the lights on the status display until Tera returned. We exchanged good-nights, and I went back to my cabin. Giving up my efforts at thinking as at least temporarily unproductive, I lay down on my bunk and went to sleep.

CHAPTER
9

Potosi was the most populous world we'd hit yet, big enough that it was no longer a colony but a full-fledged member of the Najiki Archipelago, a series of thirty or so Najiki worlds scattered across several hundred light-years and winding its way through at least three other species' claimed regions or spheres of influence. That the other species tolerated what might otherwise have been seen as an unacceptable intrusion on their sovereign territories was a tribute to Najiki diplomacy and bargaining skill.

That, plus their unique gift for creating wealth and their willingness to share that wealth with governments who were generous enough in turn to grant them right-of-way corridors through their space. The cynics, of course, would put it rather more strongly.

There were five major InterSpiral-class spaceports on the Potosi surface, the largest and most modern of which was heavily dominated by the Patth mercantile fleet. As soon as we were in range, I contacted the controller and asked for a landing bay in the port farthest away from it. Under some circumstances, I knew, a request that specific might have raised eyebrows, or whatever the Najik used for eyebrows. But the Patth near monopoly on shipping had hit this area particularly hard, leaving an almost-universal hatred for them in its wake, and I knew that the controllers would take it in stride.

Unfortunately, that same universal hatred also meant that every other incoming non-Patth ship was also making the same demand; and most of *them* were regular visitors here. In the end, in a result that fit all too well with the depressing pattern of the entire trip so far, not only were we not granted a slot half a continent away as requested, but were instead put down square in the middle of the Patth hub.

Once again, I told the rest of the crew to stay aboard while I went out shopping. Once again, they weren't at all happy about it.

"I don't think you understand the situation," Everett rumbled, staring disapprovingly down at me from his raised position on the slanted deck. "It seems to me that if we could simply take Shawn to the port med center and show them his symptoms—"

"We could then all sit around a quiet room somewhere," I finished for him. "Explaining to the nice Najik from the Drug Enforcement Division just how it was he got a borandis addiction in the first place. Remember the hijacking threat—this would not be a good place to make ourselves conspicuous."

He snorted. "No one would try a hijacking here in the middle of a major spaceport."

"You must be kidding," I growled. "With strangers wandering around all over the place, and no one knowing anyone else, either spacers or ground personnel? It's a perfect spot for it."

His lips compressed briefly. "What about you?" Tera spoke up, gesturing at my newly recolored hair and eyes and the set of false scars I'd applied to my cheek. "You think that disguise is going to get you past the people looking for you?"

"Someone has to go hunt up a drug dealer," I reminded her patiently. "Would you rather do it yourself?"

"I just don't want you to get caught," she shot back angrily. "If you do, that ends it for all of us."

"I won't get caught," I assured her. "I won't even be noticed. The picture they've got of me is old, and I know the sort of people the Patth are recruiting. They won't be able to get past the hair and eyes, believe me."

"Interesting," Nicabar murmured. "I wonder how one gets to be an expert on how people like that think."

"Don't ask questions you don't want the answers to," I warned him acidly. Maybe a little too acidly; but time was getting tight. And besides, I really didn't want to go out there, either.

There were apparently no more questions that anyone wanted answers to. "That's settled, then," I said into the chilly silence. "Revs, call and get someone out here to fuel up the ship—hopefully, we can get the tanks properly topped off this time. Don't forget that we're the *Sleeping Beauty* now. Everett, keep an eye on Shawn. Keep him quiet until I get back."

Everett's lips compressed again. "I'll do what I can."

"What about Mechanic Ixil?" Chort asked. "Is he all right?"

"He's resting in his cabin," I told them, deliberately bending the truth a bit. If our saboteur didn't already know about Kalixiri healing comas, I had no intention of enlightening him. "Don't worry, he'll come out when he's ready. I'll be back in two hours."

They were still standing together in the wraparound as I headed down the ramp, looking for all the world like hapless waifs watching the last bus leaving for the orphanage. I hoped they wouldn't still be standing there like that when the fuelers came by to start filling the tanks. It would look a little odd.

The slideways here were similar to the ones on Dorscind's World, only better maintained, as well as being equipped with transparent half-cylinder shields overhead to ward off the elements. At the moment the protection wasn't necessary, but judging by the dark clouds beginning to gather on the horizon it likely would be soon.

The port itself was neat, efficient, and as clean as a port could be, not a great surprise with the Patth directly running three-quarters of it and having a strong say in the operation of the rest. The civilian area just outside the port, though, wasn't under even their nominal control and was likely to be just as dark, sinister, and vice-ridden as any other spaceport environs in the Spiral. There I would find the dealers in happyjam and other forms of misery, at least one of whom—I hoped—would have borandis in stock.

The problem, of course, was finding the right needle in the correct haystack. Under normal circumstances that would take a great deal of time, time neither Shawn nor I nor the *Icarus* had to spare at the moment. I had to cut through the danger and tedium of the search process and go straight to the source.

Fortunately, or maybe unfortunately, I had the source's phone number.

The screen lit up to show the same broken-nosed thug who had answered Brother John's line the last time I'd called. "Yeah?"

"It's Jordan McKell," I said. "I need some information."

The scowl lines around his eyes deepened as he frowned at me. "McKell?"

"Yes; McKell," I said, striving mightily for patience. I'd already lost twenty minutes of my promised two hours, ten in getting to the StarrComm building and ten more waiting for a free booth, and I wasn't inter-

ested in playing Greek chorus to one of Brother John's
housethugs. "I'm disguised, all right? I need some information—"

"Hang on," he interrupted me. "Just hang on."

The screen went black. I glared at my watch, suddenly very tired of Brother John and his vicious yet
stupid people. The next one on the line would probably
be that moon-faced thug in the butler's outfit, who by
now had probably figured out what badinage was and
would waste more of my time trying to come up with
some.

The screen cleared; but to my surprise it wasn't the
butler. "Hello, Jordan," Brother John said. The voice
was as smooth as ever, but the usual cherubic smile
was nowhere to be seen. "Do you have any idea what
kind of stir you've been creating out at that end of the
Spiral?"

"Have I, sir?" I asked.

The chill visibly surrounding him abruptly dropped
into the subzero range. "Don't play innocent with me,
McKell," he snarled, his veneer of civility cracking like
a cheap packing crate. "A ship from Meima, they're all
saying—a rogue freighter the Patth are panting like sick
dogs to get their callused little hands on. Are you going
to sit there and tell me that's not you?"

"Yes, sir, it's me," I said hastily. It was impossible to
grovel properly in a StarrComm booth, but insofar as
vocal groveling was possible I was groveling for all I
was worth. "I'm sorry, I didn't mean it that way. I just
didn't realize how much of a stir we were actually causing."

The temperature stayed where it was. "I don't like
commotions, McKell," he warned. "I don't like them
at all. Commotions draw attention, and I don't like
attention. You don't like attention, either."

"I know, sir," I agreed humbly. "Believe me, I'm
trying as hard as I can to get out of the spotlight."

"Trying how?" he demanded. "It's not your ship or

your problem—just walk away from it. Where are you? I'll have you picked up."

He had a point, all right. Half of one, anyway. It wasn't my ship; but it *was* my problem. "I can't do that, sir," I said, bracing myself for another burst of his anger. "I accepted a contract to fly the ship out. A poor but honest independent shipper can't just break contracts that way. Not and continue to look like a poor but honest shipper."

"Who would know?" he countered. His voice was still hard and cold, but at least he hadn't started screaming at me. Maybe I'd gotten him to start thinking it through.

"Too many people," I told him. "A lot of people—some of them spaceport officials—have seen my ID in connection with it. People who might start wondering how an independent shipper could afford to break a contract that way. People who might start wondering if that independent shipper had another source of operating funds." I shrugged, a brief twitching of my shoulders. "And if they did, I wouldn't be very effective as an employee anymore."

For a long minute he just stared at me, breathing heavily, his face unreadable. I gazed back, visually groveling now, wondering uneasily if I'd pushed my hand too far with that last one. Cutting me loose from our agreement would lose him most of the five hundred thousand in debt I still owed him, but the Antoniewicz organization probably blew that much a month just on paper clips. If, on the other hand, he decided that I had become too much of a liability to be trusted on my own, I would be summarily snuffed out like an atmosphere-test candle.

And it would be the height of irony if it turned out I was the one who had talked him into doing it.

"You keep trying to force these decisions on me, Jordan," he said at last. His voice was still cold, but I thought I could detect a slight thawing of the chill factor. "These faits accomplis. There are to be no more of them."

"Yes, sir," I said. "I'm really not trying to do that. It's just that things keep happening too fast, and I keep having to improvise."

"No more of them, Jordan," he repeated in the same tone. "I make myself clear?"

"Yes, sir," I said. "Perfectly."

"Good. Now, why did you call?"

I took a careful breath. "I need to find a dealer, sir."

He blinked at that, the blink turning into an even deeper frown. "A dealer?" he repeated, the chill factor diving into arctic territory again. For all the misery he caused with his happyjam, Brother John was almost puritanical when it came to his own people using the stuff.

"One who carries borandis," I said hastily. "One of my crew is ill with Cole's disease, and borandis is the treatment for it. It's also called jackalspit."

"Yes, I know." For a few more seconds those soulless eyes gazed into mine, his face still unreadable but almost certainly wondering if I was telling the truth or simply spinning a line. I held my breath, trying to look as simple and honest as I possibly could.

And then, to my relief, he shrugged. "Why not? Where are you?"

I got my lungs working again. "Potosi," I said. "Kacclint Spaceport."

He grunted. "A Najiki world. Decent enough bug-eaters."

"Yes, sir," I agreed, mildly surprised that a xeno-phobe like Brother John would be even that compli-mentary toward a nonhuman race. Either he genuinely had some grudging respect for the Najik, or else he had business interests in the Archipelago and the Najik were doing a good job of making money for him. If I had to guess, I'd pick the latter. "I need to know if the organization has a dealer here who can help us. And if so, how to find him."

"Yes." Brother John's eyes flicked to his right. "Just a moment."

The screen blanked. I took another deep breath, suddenly aware of the weight of my plasmic against my side under my jacket. So far, it was all looking hopeful. But I knew better than to risk relaxing, even for a moment. Brother John's moods were notoriously mercurial, and with his already stated displeasure at my being aboard the *Icarus* he might suddenly decide that letting a sick crew member die would be all to the good, either as an object lesson to me or as an extra push to get me to walk away from the whole situation. If he looked like he was going that direction I would have to remind him that Shawn's death would only serve to raise the *Icarus*'s profile that much higher.

He was gone a long time. Long enough that I began to wonder if perhaps he'd decided that this had become more trouble than it was worth, that both Shawn and I were expendable, and he was off making the appropriate arrangements. I was just thinking about pulling out my phone and seeing if Ixil had come out of his coma when the screen abruptly cleared.

"All right," he said briskly. "He's a Drilie named Emendo Torsk, and he runs his business from a street music stand at Gystr'n Corner. I presume your sick crewman can pay?"

"We should have enough, yes," I assured him. "Thank you, sir."

"Don't call here again, Jordan," he said quietly. "Not until this is all over. Is that clear?"

"Yes, sir, perfectly clear," I said. If the *Icarus* was going to go down, and if I was going to be stupid enough to go down with it, he had no intention of being tied in with either of us. "Thank you, sir."

"I'll talk to you when this is all over." He reached to the side, and the connection was broken.

I swallowed, noticing only then how dry my mouth had become. Dealing with Brother John was becoming increasingly hard on me, both because of him personally and because of what he represented. To say I'd ever been genuinely happy about our arrangement would have been far too generous a statement; but lately my quiet distaste seemed to have fermented into a galloping revulsion.

And that was dangerous. Not only because of what it was doing to my own heart and soul, not to mention my stomach, but because men like Brother John have a finely honed sense of people, particularly the people closest to them. I was hardly close to him, just one small employee among thousands, but the Antoniewicz organization hadn't gotten where it was by letting even small employees become disaffected to the point where they dribbled away money or merchandise or secrets. Especially secrets.

Brother John was presumably under no illusions about what it was that kept me working for him; I'd already seen how adept he was at making sure that half-million-commark debt would be hanging over my head for a long time to come. But if he was ever able to penetrate my mask and see the emotion swirling beneath it, he might very well decide I was a walking time bomb that needed to be dealt with.

But there was nothing for it now but to continue on. I'd made my bed, as the saying went, and now all I could do was make myself as comfortable in it as I could.

Unfortunately, for the moment comfort of any sort was out of the question. I'd suffered through yet another conversation with Brother John; and now I had to do what I'd been postponing for at least three worlds now.

It was time for a nice long chat with Uncle Arthur.

The call screener on Uncle Arthur's vid was female, cheerful, and if not actually beautiful, definitely edging in that direction. Following on the heels of Brother John's surly male screener with the plastic-surgeon-baiting face, it was a contrast that seemed all the vaster for the comparison.

Until, that is, you looked closely into her eyes. For all her attractiveness, for all her easy smile and aura of friendliness, there was something cool and measuring and even ruthless that could be seen in those eyes. Given the proper circumstances, I had long suspected, she would be able to kill as quickly and efficiently as any of the ice-hearted thugs in Brother John's household.

But then, that was to be expected. She did, after all, work for Uncle Arthur.

"It's Jordan, Shannon," I greeted her, pushing such thoughts out of my mind as best I could. I had to prepare to talk to Uncle Arthur; and anyway, despite the eyes, she *was* really quite good-looking. "Is he available?"

"Hello, Jordan," she said, her smile tightening just a bit. Unlike Brother John's screener, she took my altered face in stride without blinking an eye. "I'll see."

A superfluous comment, of course; she would have signaled Uncle Arthur as soon as she recognized me. And if the tightening smile was any indication, I suspected Uncle Arthur was either sufficiently interested or sufficiently annoyed with me to take the call immediately.

I was right. Even as she turned toward her control board her face abruptly vanished from the screen and was replaced by one considerably less photogenic. An age-lined face, framed by a thatch of elegant gray hair and an equally elegant gray goatee with an unexpected streak of black down the middle, and topped off with a pair of pale blue eyes peering unwinkingly at me across the top of a set of reading glasses.

It was Uncle Arthur.

Judging from past experience, I fully expected him

to get in the first word. I wasn't disappointed. "I presume, Jordan," he said in a rumbling voice that somehow went perfectly with the beard and glasses, "that you have some good explanation for all this."

"I have an explanation, sir," I said. "I don't know whether you'll think it good or not."

For a moment he glared at me, and I could see his face tilting fractionally back and forth. The glasses, I'd long since decided, were about two-thirds necessity for an inoperable eye condition and one-third affectation, with the added benefit of giving him something he could use to subtly throw distracting flickers of light into people's eyes while he was talking to them. That was what he was doing now, though through a vid screen it was a complete waste of his time. Probably pure subconscious habit.

He finished his glaring and leaned back a bit in his chair. "I'm listening," he invited.

"I ran into Arno Cameron in a taverno on Meima," I told him. He would be wanting details—Uncle Arthur always wanted details—but there was no time for me to go into them now. "He was in a jam, with a ship to fly to Earth and no crew. He asked if I would pilot it, and I agreed."

"You just happened to run into him, did you?" Uncle Arthur rumbled ominously. "Did I somehow forget to mention that you weren't supposed to do anything but watch him?"

"He was the one who accosted me, not the other way around," I said. "I didn't think challenging him to a duel for such an impertinence would be a proper response."

He turned the shrivel power of his glare up a couple of notches, but I'd just faced down Brother John, and Uncle Arthur's glares didn't seem nearly as potent in comparison. "We'll leave that aside for the moment," he said. "Have you any idea of the furor you and that ship are causing at the moment?"

Almost the same question, and in very nearly the same tone, that Brother John had asked. "Not really," I said. "All I know for sure is that there are agents of the Patth spreading hundred-commark bills through the Spiral's sewers, with an extra five thousand for the one who fingers me for them."

"Five thousand commarks, did you say?" Uncle Arthur asked, cocking an eyebrow.

"That's what I was told a few hours ago on Dorscind's World," I said carefully. Uncle Arthur had a latent dramatic streak in him, which generally surfaced at the worst times. The fact that he had now slipped into that mode was a bad sign. "Have they upped the ante since then?"

"Considerably." He picked up a sheet of paper, holding it up to the camera as if to prove he wasn't just making it all up. "The Patth Director General has personally been in contact with at least fifteen different governments along your projected route in the past twelve hours," he read from it in the precise, clipped tone he always used when delivering bad news. "They have been informed that a ship called the *Icarus,* with a human male named Jordan McKell in command, is to be detained immediately upon identification. It is then to be held until a representative of the Director General arrives, at which point it is to be turned over to him."

I felt a shiver run up my back. "Or else?"

"Or else," he added, in that same clipped tone, "the Patth will impose mercantile sanctions on the offending governments, the severity of the sanctions to be determined by the offending government's perceived complicity in the *Icarus*'s escape. Up to and including a complete embargo against that species' cargoes."

He laid the paper back down again. "As you say, the ante has been upped," he said quietly. "What in God's name did Cameron's people dig up out there, Jordan?"

"I don't know, sir," I said, just as quietly. "But whatever it is, it's sitting in the *Icarus*'s cargo hold."

Dramatically, it was the moment for a long, heavy silence. But Uncle Arthur's dramatic impulses didn't extend to wasting time. "Then you'd best find a way to learn what it is, hadn't you?" he said.

"Actually, I think I already have," I said. "Found a way, that is. Can you get hold of a personnel list from that archaeological dig?"

"I have it right here," he said. "Why?"

"Because I suspect one of them is aboard the *Icarus*," I told him. "Masquerading as a member of the crew."

The beard twitched slightly. "I think that very unlikely," he said, "since all of them are currently in custody on Meima."

I felt like the floor had just been pulled out from under me. "*All* of them? You're sure?"

"Quite sure," he said, holding up another sheet. "Everyone involved was picked up in that one single night, even the crew of the private ship Cameron flew in on a few days before this all started. Cameron himself is the only one still at large, and the Meima authorities say it's only a matter of time before they run him to ground. They think they spotted him at a Vyssiluyan taverno last night, in fact, but he gave them the slip."

"Wait a minute," I said, frowning. "If they've already got the whole team, why don't they know what the cargo is? For that matter, why don't they have an accurate description of the ship? And they don't, because otherwise the fake IDs Ixil and I keep churning out sure wouldn't fool them."

"Good—you're using fake IDs," Uncle Arthur said. "I'd hoped you were being at least that clever."

"Yes, but why are they working?" I persisted, passing over the question of whether or not there was an insult buried in there. "I trust you're not going to tell me that a bunch of plunder artists like the Patth are squeamish about the classic forms of information gathering, are you?"

"In point of fact, the archaeologists are still in Ihmis hands," Uncle Arthur said. "The Patth are trying to get them, but so far the Ihmisits are resisting the pressure." He grimaced. "But at this point it hardly matters who has them. Cameron took the precaution of having hypnotic blocks put on everyone's memory of certain aspects of the operation. Including, naturally, the *Icarus*'s description and details of its cargo."

I nodded. Obvious, of course, once it was pointed out. Not especially ethical, and probably illegal on Meima to boot, but it was exactly the sort of thing Cameron would have done. "And without the release key, all they can do is batter at the blocks and hope they crack."

"Which I'm sure they're already doing," Uncle Arthur said darkly. "Not a pleasant thing to dwell on; but the point is that the maneuver has bought you some time."

"Yes, sir." So much for my embryonic theory that it was one of Cameron's people who had been trying so hard to keep us out of the *Icarus*'s cargo hold. "Unfortunately, it's also bought someone else some time, too."

"Explain."

I gave him a quick summary of the jinx that had been dogging us ever since leaving Meima. Or since before our exit, actually, if you counted Cameron's failure to make it to the ship. "The incident with Chort and Jones might conceivably have been an accident," I concluded. "But not the cutting torch or the lad skulking between hulls with the handy eavesdroppers' kit. Having the Patth on our tail would have been plenty; but having this added in is way too much of a good thing."

"Indeed," Uncle Arthur said thoughtfully. "You have a theory, of course?"

"I have one," I said. "But I don't think you're going to like it. You said the Ihmisits thought they spotted

Cameron on Meima yesterday. How certain are they of that?"

"As certain as any of these things ever are," he said, his eyes narrowing. "Which is to say, not very. Why, do you think you know where Cameron is?"

"Yes, sir," I said. "I think there's a good chance he's dead."

There was another twitch of the beard. I was right; he didn't like it at all. "Explain."

"It's clear that someone doesn't want us getting a look at the cargo," I said. "I thought that that someone must be one of the archaeologists, but you've now told me that's impossible. So it's someone else. Someone who *does* know what's in there, and who furthermore has decided that having sole proprietorship of that knowledge will be valuable to him."

"It couldn't be Cameron himself?"

"I don't see how," I said, shaking my head. "When I first arrived at the *Icarus* there was a time lock on the hatch, which didn't release until after most of the crew had already assembled. I examined the lock later, and it had definitely been set the previous afternoon, well before the Ihmisits threw everyone out of the spaceport and locked it down for the night. There was no way for Cameron to have gotten aboard before the gates opened again, and he certainly didn't get on after we were there."

"And you think that was because he was already dead?"

"Yes," I said. "One of the people he hired to crew the *Icarus* either knew something about it already or was sufficiently intrigued to take Cameron into a dark alley somewhere and find out exactly what was aboard."

"That would have taken some severe persuasion," Uncle Arthur murmured.

"Which is why I suspect he's dead," I said. "An interrogation that would have gotten him to talk would have left him either dead or incapacitated or drug-comatose. In either of the latter two cases, the Ihmisits or Patth would certainly have found him by now. In the first case . . ." I didn't bother to finish.

"You may be right," Uncle Arthur said heavily. "You will identify this person, of course."

"I certainly intend to try," I said. "It would help if I had some more information on this crew I've been saddled with."

"Undoubtedly. Their names?"

"Almont Nicabar, drive specialist, onetime EarthGuard Marine. Geoff Shawn, electronics. Has Cole's disease and a resulting borandis addiction. Any chance you can get some borandis to me, by the way?"

"Possibly. Next?"

"Hayden Everett, medic. Former professional throw-boxer twenty-odd years ago, though I don't know if it was under his own name or not. Chort, Craea, spacewalker. Nothing else known."

"With a Craea almost nothing else needs to be known," Uncle Arthur put in.

"Possibly," I said. "I'd like him checked out anyway. And finally Tera, last name unknown. She may be a member of one of those religious sects who don't give their full names to strangers, but I haven't yet seen her do anything particularly religious."

"The practice of one's beliefs is not always blatant and obvious," Uncle Arthur reminded me. "A quiet look into her cabin for religious paraphernalia at some point might be enlightening."

"I intend to take a quiet look into all their cabins when I get the chance," I assured him. "Now: descriptions . . ."

I ran through everyone's physical description as quickly as I could, knowing that it was all being recorded. "How fast can you get this to me?" I asked when I was finished.

"It will take a few hours," he said. "Where are you now?"

"Potosi, but I have no intention of staying here any longer than I have to," I told him. "I don't know where we'll be heading next. Someplace quiet and peaceful and anonymous would be a nice change of pace."

"You may have to settle for anonymous," he said, his eyes shifting to the side and his shoulders shifting with the subtle movements of someone typing on a keyboard. "Is there anything else?"

"Actually, yes," I said. "We also seem to have a new group of players in the game." I described the incident with the Lumpy Brothers on Xathru, and the coronal-discharge weapons they'd been carrying. "Have you heard of either this species or the weapons?" I asked when I finished.

"A qualified yes to both," he said, his eyes still busy off camera. "You may recall hearing rumors about a failed covert operation a few years ago in which an elite EarthGuard task force tried to steal data on the Talariac Drive. Weapons very similar to those you describe were used against them, by guards who also match your description."

I sighed. "Which makes the Lumpy Clan some kind of Patth client race."

"Very likely," he agreed. "Don't sound so surprised. Certainly their first efforts to find the *Icarus* would be made quietly, through their own people and agents. It was only after that failed that they began to approach first the Spiral's criminals and now legitimate governments."

I thought about the three Patth Cameron and I had seen in that Meima taverno. So that was why they'd ventured out of their usual restricted hideouts. "Still, it strikes me that they gave up on the quiet approach rather quickly," I pointed out. "Could my smoking the Lumpy Brothers really have rattled them that badly?"

"I doubt it," he said soberly. "More likely it was a

THE ICARUS HUNT   185

matter of new information as to what exactly the prize was they were chasing."

And that knowledge had instantly pushed them into an open and increasingly public hunt. Terrific. "This place you're finding for us better be *real* anonymous," I told him.

"I believe I can make it so," he said. "Can you make Morsh Pon from there in one jump?"

I felt my eyes narrow. "Assuming we can get off Potosi, yes," I said cautiously, wondering if he was really going where I thought he was on this.

He was. "Good," he said briskly. "The Blue District on Morsh Pon, then, at the Baker's Dozen taverno. I'll have the information delivered to you there."

"Ah . . . yes, sir," I said. Morsh Pon was an Ulko colony world, and the Ulkomaals, like the Najik, had a reputation for great talent at creating wealth. Unlike the Najik, however, the Ulkomaals relied heavily on the hospitality industry to make their money, specifically hospitality toward the less virtuous members of civilized society at large. Morsh Pon was a quiet refuge for smugglers and other criminal types, far worse than even Dorscind's World, with the Blue District the worst area on the planet.

Which under normal circumstances, given my connection with Brother John and the Antoniewicz organization, would have made it an ideal place to go to ground. Unfortunately, the current circumstances were far from normal. "I trust you remember, sir," I said diplomatically, "that the Patth have invited the entire Spiral underworld out for a drink?"

"I remember quite well," he said calmly. "It will be taken care of. Now, I suspect time is growing short. You'd best get moving."

It was, clearly, a dismissal. I didn't particularly feel like being dismissed yet—there were still several aspects of this whole arrangement I felt like arguing some more. But when Uncle Arthur said good-bye, he meant good-bye. Besides, he was right; time was indeed growing short. "Yes, sir," I said, suppressing a sigh. "I'll be in touch."

"Do that," he said. The screen blanked, and he was gone.

I collected my change and left the booth. Once again, I half expected one of Brother John's assassins to jump me in the corridor; once again, it didn't happen. I snagged a city map from a rack by the main exit doors, located the street intersection called Gystr'n Corner, and headed outside.

The rain that had been threatening earlier was starting to come down now, a scattering of large fat drops that almost seemed to bounce as they hit the ground. I had already decided that Gystr'n Corner was too far to walk, and now with the rain beginning I further decided not to wait for the public rail system. Brother John wouldn't like that; his standard orders were for us to take public transportation whenever possible, the better to avoid official backtracks. But then, Brother John wasn't here getting wet. Hailing a cab, I gave the driver my destination, told him there would be an extra hundred commarks for him if he got me there fast, and all but fell back into the spring-bare seat as he took off like an attack shuttle on wheels.

With the way I'd been spending money like water lately, first with full-vid starconnects and now on cabs, it was just as well I'd relieved that Patth agent on Dorscind's World of all those hundred-commark bills that had been weighing him down. Now, watching the city, startled vehicle drivers, and outraged pedestrians blurring along past my windows, it occurred to me that perhaps some extra travel-health insurance might have been a good idea, too. My map's key estimated it to be twenty-three minutes from the StarrComm building to Gystr'n Corner. My driver made it in just over fifteen, probably a new land-speed record for the city, possibly for the entire planet.

Emendo Torsk was there as promised, standing in front of a short cabanalike shelter, his squat Drilie shape almost hidden behind the complex multimusic box he was playing with both his hands and the set of short prehensile eating tentacles ringing the base of his neck. A crowd of perhaps twenty admirers were standing in the rain in front of him listening to the music.

I let the driver take the cab out of sight along the street and had him pull to the curb. I paid him, told him to wait, and walked back through the now pouring rain to join the crowd. I wouldn't have guessed there were that many beings on the whole planet who liked Drilie di-choral anthems, even when they were properly performed, which this one emphatically was not. But then, I doubted any of those in attendance were there for the music, anyway.

Fortunately, the piece Torsk had chosen was a short one, and I silently thanked the downpour for whatever part it had played in that decision. Amid the smattering of totally fraudulent applause he passed a large hat around for contributions. I'd made the necessary preparations while careening about in the cab, and as he waved the hat in front of me I dropped in a small package consisting of three tightly folded hundred-commark bills wrapped around a piece of paper with the word "borandis" written on it. Most of the rest of the audience, I saw, had similar donations for him. He finished taking up his collection and gave out with a set of guttural barks that were probably a traditional Drilie thank-you or farewell, then disappeared through the flap into his cabana. At that, the audience faded away, splashing away in all directions to disappear down the streets and alleyways or into the dark and anonymous doorways fronting on the streets.

All of them, that is, except me. Instead of moving back, I moved forward until I was standing directly in front of the long-suffering multimusic box. There I planted myself, facing the flap Torsk had disappeared through, and waited, doing my best to ignore the cold drips finding their way beneath my collar and dribbling down my back. I had no doubt he could see me perfectly well through his cabana; there were several different one-way opaque materials to choose from, and a person in Torsk's profession couldn't afford not to know what was going on around him at all times. I just hoped he'd be curious enough or irritated enough to find out what I wanted before I was soaked completely through.

He was either more curious or irritable than I'd expected. I'd been standing there less than a minute when the flap twitched aside and I found myself looking down into a pair of big black Drilie eyes. "What want?" he demanded in passable English.

"Want borandis," I told him. "Have paid."

"Wait turn," he snapped, waggling a finger horizontally to indicate the now vanished audience.

"Not wait," I told him calmly. Pushing him this way was risky, but I didn't have much choice. The standard pattern seemed to be that you placed your order and came back for it later, probably at Torsk's next performance, and there was no way I could afford to hang around that long. Particularly not if it required sitting through a second concert. "Want borandis. Have paid."

"Wait turn," he repeated, even more snappishly this time. "Or get mad."

"I get mad, too," I said.

Apparently I'd been wrong about the whole crowd having vanished. I was just about to repeat my request when a large hand snaked over my shoulder, grabbed a fistful of my coat, and turned me around. I blinked the rainwater out of my eyes, and found myself looking fifteen centimeters up into one of the ugliest human faces it had ever been my misfortune to see. "Hey—trog—you deaf?" he growled. His breath was a perfect match for his face. "He said to wait your turn."

There was undoubtedly more to the usual speech, probably something along the lines of what would happen to me if I didn't go away immediately. But as I'd long since learned for myself, it was hard to speak when all your wind has been suddenly knocked out of you by a short punch to the solar plexus. I ducked slightly to the side to avoid his forehead as he doubled over without a sound, wincing at the extra dose of bad breath that blew into my face; and as his head dipped out of my line of sight I saw that three more men stamped from his same mold were marching purposefully across the street toward me.

I hit the first man in the same spot again, folding him over a little farther, and half a second later had my plasmic pointed over his shoulder toward the three newcomers. They stopped dead in their tracks. I kept my eyes and the weapon steady on them while I kept hitting the halitosis specialist in selected pressure points with my free hand, trying to make sure that when he went down he would stay there.

He finally did, but it took several more punches than I'd expected. I definitely didn't want to be around when this lad felt like his old self again. I gazed at the reinforcements for another couple of seconds; then, leaving my plasmic pointed their direction, I deliberately turned my head around to face Torsk again. "Want borandis," I said mildly. "Have paid."

"Yes," he said, his face an ashen shade of purple as he stared down at the lump at my feet. Apparently he'd never seen anyone beaten up with one hand before. "Wait short."

He disappeared back into the cabana, but not before I got a glimpse of reflected movement in those big Drilie eyes. I turned my head around, to find the Three Musketeers had tried advancing while I wasn't looking. They stopped even more abruptly than they had the first time, and we eyed each other over the barrel of my plasmic until there was another rustling of wet fabric behind me. "Take," Torsk hissed, jabbing something solid against my shoulder. I turned, half-expecting to see a gun; but it was only a music cassette prominently displaying Torsk's face and name on the front. *The Best of Emendo Torsk,* apparently, with the borandis concealed inside. "Go," he insisted. "Not come back."

"Not come back," I agreed, taking the cassette and tucking it away in an inside pocket. "Unless borandis not good. Then make small wager you hurt plenty."

"Borandis good," he ground out, glaring daggers at me.

I believed him. The last thing a corner drug dealer wanted was to have attention drawn his direction, and my performance here had already disrupted his cozy schedule more than he was happy with. The last thing he would want would be for me to come back in a bad mood.

He had no way of knowing that I couldn't come back even if I wanted to, or that I was even more allergic to official scrutiny at the moment than he was. He was rid of me, and that was what mattered to him. Perhaps he'd even learned not to hire his protection muscle off park benches.

My cab and driver were still patiently waiting where I'd left them. I got in and gave my destination as Gate 2 of the spaceport, the closest one to where the *Icarus* was docked. With visions of another absurdly large tip undoubtedly dancing trippingly through his mind, he took off like a scalded foxbat. Once again I hung on for dear life, my own mind dancing with unpleasant visions of a premature obituary. During the straightaways I managed to break open the cassette and confirm that there were fifteen capsules inside filled with a blue powder that looked like it had come from grinding up the normal tablets that the *Icarus*'s med listing said borandis came in. Closing the cassette and putting it away again, I pulled out my phone and punched in Everett's number.

That all-too-familiar feeling that something was wrong began to tingle through me as the fifth vibe came and went with no answer. By the time he did answer, on the eighth vibe, and I heard his voice, the feeling solidified into a cold certainty. " 'Lo?" he muttered, his voice heavy and slightly slurred, as if I'd just awakened him.

"It's McKell," I identified myself. "What's wrong?"

There was a faint hiss, like someone exhaling heavily into the mouthpiece. "It's Shawn," he said. "He got away."

I gripped the phone tighter, the driver's maniacal slalom technique abruptly forgotten. "Which direction did he go?"

"I don't know how it happened," Everett said plaintively. "He must have slipped the straps somehow—"

"Never mind how he did it," I cut him off. "The recriminations can wait. Which direction did he go?"

"I don't know," Everett said. "I didn't see him leave. We're all out looking for him."

"*All* of you?"

"All but Ixil—we pounded on his door, but he didn't answer, and the door wasn't working right. It's okay—we locked the hatch—"

There was a quiet sputtering click as another phone joined the circuit. "Everett, this is Tera," her voice came excitedly. "I've found him."

"Where?" I snapped, pulling my city map out and trying to shake it open with my free hand.

"McKell?" she asked, sounding both surprised and wary.

"Yes," I said. "Where is he?"

"Outside an outfitter's store at Ude'n Corner," she said. "He's accosting people as they go in."

"That's a good way to get all his troubles ended permanently," I growled, locating the spot on my map. It was only a short block away from Gate 2, where I was headed anyway. "Keep him in sight, but try not to let him see you," I told her. "I'll be there in a couple of minutes and we'll bring him back together. Everett, call Nicabar and Chort and the three of you head back to the ship. Get it ready to fly."

"Now?" Everett asked, sounding surprised. "What about the borandis?"

"Done and done," I told him. "Make sure—"

"You've got it?" Everett asked. "Already?"

"I'm very good at what I do," I told him, trying hard to be patient. "Make sure we've been fueled and are ready to lift as soon as Tera and I get back with Shawn."

Another faint hiss. "All right. We'll see you back at the ship."

There was a click as he disconnected. "Tera?" I called.

"Still here," she confirmed tightly. "And I think people are starting to get irritated by Shawn's ravings. You'd better hurry."

"Trust me," I assured her, wincing as I turned part of my attention back to the automotive drama taking place around me. "He must have made good time to be out of the spaceport already. How long since he jumped ship?"

"About an hour ago," she said. "Just after you left to—"

"An *hour*?" I cut her off in disbelief, a white-hot flash of anger slicing through me. "An *hour*? And you didn't think it worth mentioning to me?"

"We didn't want to bother you," she protested, clearly startled by my sudden anger. "You already had the medicine to find—"

"I don't care if I've got the crown jewels to steal," I snarled. "Something like this happens, you get on the phone and tell me about it. Let *me* worry about what it does to my schedule. Is that clear?"

"Clear," she said, more subdued than I'd ever heard her. For a moment I considered taking another verbal slice of flesh out of her, decided regretfully that it probably wasn't her fault, and kept my mouth shut. Possibly it wasn't any of their faults. Ixil would have known what to do; but Ixil was in his cabin in a coma, and it was painfully obvious that none of the others had anywhere near our experience with this sort of thing.

Instead, I vented my frustration on the map lying open beside me, folding it back up with far more force than was necessary and shoving it into my jacket's left side pocket.

"McKell?" Tera said, her voice suddenly tight. "I think I see a police car heading this way. Red and blue, with a flashing blue light on top, moving very fast."

"Don't worry," I told her. "It's a cab, and I'm in it. Flag me in, will you?"

A block ahead, I saw her step to the curb and raise her hand, a vision of loveliness standing there in the downpour in her stylish drowned-rat look. I directed the driver over to her, dropped two hundred-commark bills on the seat beside him as I got out, and pulled Tera quickly away from the curb as he shot off again in a foaming wave. Maybe I'd wasted all that tip money; maybe that was the way he always drove anyway.

"There," Tera said, pointing across the street.

"I see him," I said. Considering the way Shawn was bouncing around the store entrance waving his arms at everyone in sight, he would have been hard to miss. Taking Tera's arm again, I steered us through the traffic flow toward him.

After everything else that had happened, the capture itself was rather anticlimactic. Pleading and screeching and cursing at the passersby, his wet hair plastered half across his face, Shawn was in no shape to see anything happening around him. Tera and I could have driven up to him in an armored personnel carrier without him noticing. As it was, we simply moved in from opposite sides and grabbed his arms. He gave a single terrific lurch, but there wasn't much strength left in him, and after that one attempt to break free he just stood there shaking in our grip.

We led him away from the door and the pedestrian traffic to the narrow passageway between the outfitter's store and the next building over, Tera murmuring soothingly in his ear the whole way. When we were as far out of the public eye as we were likely to get, I dug out the cassette and fed him one of the borandis capsules. He seemed to be having trouble getting it down until Tera filled her cupped hands with rainwater and gave him a drink.

The effects were quite amazing. Almost immediately his trembling began to subside, and within a couple of minutes he seemed almost back to normal.

At least physically. "You sure took your sweet time about it," he growled, breathing heavily as he brushed his wet hair impatiently out of his face. "Where the hell are we, anyway? You said we were going to Mintarius. This isn't Mintarius. I know—I've been there."

"Change of plans," I told him shortly, peering closely at his eyes. His pupils, strongly dilated when we'd first grabbed him, seemed to be shrinking back to normal size.

"Yeah, well, that change of plans might have killed me," he snapped. "Did you ever think of that? This place must be at least three hours farther than Mintarius was."

"No, just two," I said. He was well enough to travel, I decided; and even if he wasn't, we were going. The sooner he was aboard the *Icarus* and shut away where I didn't have to listen to him, the better. Taking his arm, I pulled him back out toward the main thoroughfare.

"Wait a minute, what's the rush?" he growled, leaning back against my pull. His strength was also making a remarkable comeback. "We just got here. How about just for once sticking around some planet more than five minutes, huh?"

"Shut up and come on," Tera snapped, grabbing his other arm. From the look of surprise that flicked across his face, I guessed she was digging her nails into his skin more than was necessary to maintain the grip. Certainly more than I was; but then, I'd only been irritated by his disappearing act for the past five minutes. Tera had had a whole hour of slogging through the rain in which to work up resentment.

Between her voice, her grip, and whatever he saw in her face, Shawn apparently realized that, too. He shut up as ordered, and docilely followed us down the street and through the spaceport gate. We caught the slideway and headed in.

I kept a careful eye behind us, as well as on the slideways that passed or intersected ours, but I saw no sign of anyone tailing us. I had thought Torsk might have second thoughts about letting me leave so easily, but apparently he'd decided that discretion was the better part of continued employment and had decided to leave well enough alone.

We reached the last freighter parked between us and the *Icarus;* and finally, it seemed, we were out of the woods. We had the borandis, we had Shawn, and no one had pointed toward me and yelled for the Patth. Now, if the *Icarus* had just been fueled properly, we would be in business. Hoping distantly that we wouldn't find the fuelers still trying to figure out how to get the hose into the *Icarus*'s intake, we came around the side of the freighter.

The fuelers weren't there. What was there was a group of ten Najik wearing the black-and-red tunics of customs officers. Standing by the entry ramp.

Waiting for us.

CHAPTER

10

Beside me, Shawn made a strangled sort of sound deep in his throat. "Oh, God," he breathed. "We're dead."

"Quiet," I muttered back, taking a second, closer look at the scene, hoping it wasn't as bad as I'd first thought.

It was. The ten Najik were still there, tall and spindly, with those hairy arms and legs that always made me think of giant four-limbed tarantulas. They were still wearing the customs uniforms, and there was an impatient look in their multiple eyes as they glanced over our direction through the pouring rain.

On the other hand, it could also have been worse. Locks or no locks, customs officers on the prowl normally didn't bother to wait for the captain before going inside a target ship, but simply popped the hatch and apologized later for the damage if apologies were called for. Now, with my second look, I saw why they were still out here getting rained on.

Standing square in the center of the ramp, looking for all the world like a feathery-scaled Horatius holding the bridge, was Chort. From the water running steadily off his fingertips it was clear he'd been there for a while; from the settled look of his stance, it was equally clear he was prepared to stay as long as necessary.

Normally, the presence of such an obstacle wouldn't have slowed down a customs officer any more than a locked hatch would. But Chort was hardly your normal obstacle. He was a Craea; and with Crooea and their spacewalker skills so highly in demand around the Spiral, I could understand why the Najik were reluctant to offend him by shoving their way past into the ship. Especially a locked and apparently unoccupied ship.

Except that it wasn't strictly unoccupied, and for a brief, time-stretched second I tried to think of how to turn that to our advantage. If Tera, Shawn, and I could walk casually past the *Icarus* as if we weren't connected with it at all; and if I could get Ixil on the phone—

We hadn't gotten two steps before any such decisions were taken out of my hands. "There," Chort called out, pointing to me. "There is the captain. You may address your questions to him."

I sighed. "You two stay back," I murmured to Tera and Shawn. There was a rustle as Tera took Shawn's left arm, pulling him subtly to a halt as I continued on toward the ramp. The Najik in the center of the group took a step toward me in response, and now that he was facing me I could see the insignia of a *gokra*—the equivalent of a senior lieutenant—on his collar. Apparently, Customs HQ was taking this very seriously.

"Good day, *Gokra*," I greeted him as we sloshed through the puddles to within a few steps of each other. "Is there a problem?"

"You are the captain of the *Sleeping Beauty*?" he asked. His tone was decidedly neutral.

"I am," I said, wondering fleetingly if Chort might

have slipped up and given them my real name, realized immediately that he hadn't. If he had—if the Najik knew beyond a doubt what they had here—they wouldn't be bothering with a few measly customs officers. They'd have an army battalion here, plus the local Patth ambassador and his staff, plus probably a military marching band thrown in for color. "Is there a problem?"

"You will unseal the hatch," he said, waving back toward the *Icarus*. "You will tell your crewer to move aside, and you will allow us to go in."

"Of course," I said, not moving. "May I ask what the problem is?"

For a moment he seemed disinclined to tell me, but apparently decided there was no harm in playing by the proper Mercantile Code rules. "We have received a report that this ship is engaged in illegal smuggling activities," he said.

The rest of me was soaking wet. My mouth, however, was suddenly dry. "Smuggling activities?" I managed, hoping I sounded more bewildered than guilty.

"Yes," the *gokra* said. "Specifically, that you have unregistered gemstones hidden aboard."

I stared at him, not needing to feign any bewilderment this time. "*Gem*stones?" I echoed. "That's crazy. We're not carrying any gemstones."

"You will please tell your Craea to stand aside," the Najik said, not even bothering to acknowledge my protest. I couldn't blame him; he'd probably heard variants of it twice a day throughout his entire career. "Then you will unseal the hatch and allow us inside. I will need to see your personal identification, as well."

"Of course," I said, brushing some of the water out of my eyes and trying to figure out what the hell was going on. The gemstone story was utter nonsense, of course—you could fill fifty ships the size of the *Icarus* from deck to ceiling with Dritar opals without so much as lifting a Patth eyebrow. But if they suspected the ship in front of us might be the *Icarus,* why bother with this subterfuge?

Answer: they wouldn't. Which meant that they *didn't* know it was the *Icarus.*

Which further meant the Patth weren't involved in this; that it was a purely Najiki affair, with the whole gemstone thing being either a ridiculous bureaucratic error or else a horrifying coincidence. I'd chosen the name *Sleeping Beauty* for our current ship's ID on the assumption that few people in the Spiral were going to name their ships after obscure nineteenth-century Russian ballets. It would be the height of irony if I'd not only guessed wrong, but had managed to pick the name of a bona fide smuggling ship in the bargain.

Unfortunately, in about five minutes the how and why of it weren't going to matter anymore. There were a dozen different numbers etched on engines and consoles all over the ship, numbers that were on various lists all across the Spiral. If Cameron had done a proper job of creating a history for his phantom freighter, those numbers would be in a Mercantile file labeled *Icarus,* and the minute the Najik started checking them we would be finished. If Cameron hadn't filed the numbers, it would simply take a little longer for the soap bubble to burst.

The Najik were still waiting. "Of course," I said again, turning back and stepping to where Tera was still clinging to Shawn's left arm. There was one very tenuous hope here, a hope based on Brother John's offhanded comment earlier about the Najik, and my own hopefully not-too-cynical interpretation of it. "Let me get the hatch unlocked first and get us in out of the rain. Especially Geoff here—he's not well."

Someone in the group gave a deep-bass rumble, the Najiki equivalent of a guffaw, as I took Shawn's right upper arm. Not an unreasonable response, given that Shawn looked more drunk than he did sick, and I took it as a good sign. Customs HQ might be taking this seriously, but apparently not all the officers themselves were. Together Tera and I led Shawn through the Najiki cordon to the near end of the ramp. I keyed in the combination on the pad and, behind Chort, the hatch swung open. Without waiting for permission from the Najik, I moved us forward onto the ramp.

"Keep going," I murmured to Tera, letting go my grip on Shawn's arm and sliding my left arm through his, freeing up that hand while still giving the appearance that I was holding on to him. Extending my reach as much as I could, I dipped into my side jacket pocket for the folded city map I'd stuffed in there earlier. My other hand had already slipped inside my jacket for my pen; and as we passed out of the rain into the shelter of the wraparound I scribbled briefly on the front of the map.

"An interesting ship design," the *gokra* commented from right behind me. He might be courteous enough to let me precede him into my own ship, but that didn't mean he was going to let me get too much of a lead on him. "Ylpea-built, I presume?"

"I really don't know," I said. Now that he mentioned it, I could see an echo of the Ylpean love of French curves in the *Icarus*'s double-sphere shape. Had that been what Cameron had been going for? Regardless, something worth remembering. "I'm just the pilot, not the owner. I don't know anything about its history."

"Ah."

We had moved along the wraparound, and were now coming up on the main sphere. Behind the *gokra* the rest of the Najik had filed in, with a silent Chort bringing up the rear. "But you're not here for a history lesson anyway," I added, pulling my ID folder from inside my jacket and surreptitiously sliding the map inside it. "Here's my ID."

I handed it to him, mentally crossing my fingers. If I'd guessed wrong, it wasn't even going to take until the Najik started calling in console numbers for me to be in big trouble.

He took the folder and opened it. The multiple eyes twitched in unison as he saw the map nestled inside; twitched again as he spotted the note I'd written on it. For a long minute he just stared at it. Once again I was suddenly conscious of the weight of my plasmic against my ribs, knowing full well that opening fire in such a confined space against ten armed opponents would be a quick way of committing suicide. Beside me, Shawn seemed to have stopped breathing, and I could sense a similar tension in Tera on his other side.

Then, almost delicately, the *gokra* closed the folder without even looking behind the map at my actual ID and handed it back to me. "Thank you," he said, almost primly. "We won't be long."

And they weren't. They wandered up and down the various corridors, glanced around the engine room and bridge, casually examined the curving metal of the cargo compartment and confirmed there was no entry hatch, and made a copy of Cameron's fake Gamm sealed-cargo license to take for their files. Nicabar returned while they were poking around; I told him to get dried off and then get the thrusters ready to go. At one point, almost as an afterthought, the *gokra* also presented me with the bill for our fueling, explaining that he'd taken it from the ground crew when he arrived and found them waiting for my return. He didn't seem surprised that I paid the bill in cash, or that there were five extra hundred-commark bills in the stack I gave him.

And that was it. Ten minutes after they'd come in out of the rain, they were out in it again, striding briskly toward the slideways and headed home.

"All right, I give up," Tera murmured from my side as she and I stood in the wraparound and watched them go. "Who is Mr. Antoniewicz, and why won't he be happy if they find anything?"

I grimaced. I hadn't thought she would be able to read the note from her angle as I'd scribbled it on the map. "He's just someone I know," I said evasively. "He has a certain amount of influence around the Spiral."

"I'd say he has a great deal of influence," she said, eyeing me in a way I didn't much care for. "You know him personally or professionally?"

"I've done some business with his people," I said. A movement outside caught my eye: Everett, our last crewman still unaccounted for, had appeared around the bow of one of the nearby ships and was plodding our way, his big feet kicking up impressive splashes with each step. He looked tired; he must have worn himself out looking for Shawn. Not surprising, really, given that he probably considered it his fault the kid had gotten away in the first place. "Here comes Everett," I added to Tera, hoping to forestall any further questions, as I dug out the fake cassette. "Tell him to check Shawn and see if he needs another dose yet— here's the borandis. As soon as he's aboard, seal the hatch and get to the computer room."

I left her there and headed to the bridge, feeling both cautiously relieved and cautiously pleased with myself. I'd been right: Brother John's grudging admiration for the Najik had indeed been based on the fact that the Antoniewicz organization was able to do business with them. Clearly, our customs *gokra* was in on the deal, and dropping Antoniewicz's name had been enough to wave him off us. I still didn't know why the *Icarus* had been fingered for a search, but as soon as we were out of Potosi space that wouldn't matter.

Assuming we *did* get out of Potosi space, of course. If the *gokra* had merely taken the extra cash in order to add attempted bribery to the charges against me, he should be rounding the corner any minute with that army battalion I'd been expecting earlier.

But for once, my pessimism proved unfounded. We

got clearance to lift, the port's grav beams lifted us smoothly out and up, and within a few minutes we were once again in space. I had cut us into hyperspace and was doing a quick check of the systems when the door opened and Everett came in. "We safely away?" he asked.

"Unless the hull decides to collapse, we are," I told him.

He made a face. "Considering the way things have been going, that's not very funny."

"I suppose not," I conceded. "Sorry. How's Shawn doing?"

"Seems to be recovering," he said. "Fortunately, the reversible Cole's disease symptoms begin long before the irreversible damage kicks in. And the borandis dependence itself is more or less reversible at any point. Rather like scurvy in that respect."

"That's handy," I said. "How much of his current trouble is related to the dependence and how much to the disease?"

He shook his head, peering at the displays. "I don't know. The two problems intermix so tightly it takes a specialist to disentangle them. We're going to Morsh Pon next?"

"Yes," I said. "After that little run-in back there, I thought it might be nice to refuel someplace where they don't bother at all with customs formalities."

"If you live to get back out," he said dubiously. "I've heard stories about that world—bands of pirates and smugglers roaming the streets looking for trouble."

"We'll be all right," I told him with a confidence I didn't much feel myself. "I'll make you a small wager that it won't be as bad as you think."

"Um," Everett said noncommittally, still looking doubtful. "Still, you're the captain; power of life and death over your crew, and all that. Speaking of which—the crew, I mean—I haven't seen Ixil since before we landed on Potosi."

"Neither have I," I said. "But I'm sure he's all right."

"Yes," he said hesitantly. "The reason I asked, you see, was that I tried checking on him and his cabin door wouldn't open."

"That's okay—I set it that way to make sure he had some privacy," I assured him. "I just hope it didn't slam on your fingers."

"What do you mean?" Everett asked, looking puzzled. "It didn't slam. It didn't open at all."

I stared at him, a sudden chill running through me. "It didn't open a few centimeters and then shut again?"

"I told you: it didn't even budge," he insisted. "I thought maybe it had gotten jammed—"

I didn't wait to hear any more, jumping out of my seat and dodging past him to the ladder out in the corridor. I slid down it without touching any of the rungs, my heart pounding suddenly in my throat. I reached Ixil's door and tried the release pad.

Everett was right. It didn't budge at all.

I had my multitool out and was unfastening the pad's cover by the time Everett caught up. "You think something's wrong?" he puffed as he came up beside me.

"There's something wrong with the door, anyway," I said, fighting hard to speak calmly, to keep my fear and rage out of my voice. If the saboteur had been here while Ixil was lying helpless . . . but maybe the control chip had simply burned out. With my fingers fumbling slightly in their hurry, I got the cover off.

The control chip hadn't simply burned out. The control chip wasn't there at all. What *was* there looked like it had been attacked by a gorilla with a small sledgehammer.

Beside me, Everett gasped. "What in hell's name—?"

"Our friend who wrecks cutting torches does doors, too," I snarled, dropping the cover on the deck and hurrying to the door to my own cabin. One glance was all I'd needed to know Ixil's release pad was going to need some major work, and I could replace it with the one from my door in a fraction of the time. "Go to the computer room and tell Tera to take the bridge," I called back over my shoulder as I set to work on the fasteners.

I had my release pad off and was starting on Ixil's when Everett returned, a first-aid kit clutched in his hand. "I thought we might need this," he said grimly, setting it down out of my way. "What can I do?"

"Hold this," I said, thrusting the damaged pad into his hands. A first-aid kit wasn't going to do a damned bit of good. Not now. Our saboteur had had plenty of time to make this one a leisurely killing. "What exactly happened after Shawn got loose?"

"He ran out of the ship," Everett said, rubbing at the side of his neck. "I'm afraid he got past me—"

"What about the others?" I cut him off. "Where were they when all this was happening?"

"Well . . ." He fumbled slightly. "I'm not exactly sure. The intercom still isn't working, so I had to go find them one by one. Chort was in his cabin, Nicabar was in the engine room, and I found Tera in the mechanics shop."

"And then?"

"We went outside to see if he was still in the area of the ship. He wasn't, or if he was we didn't see him, so we split up and went looking for him."

"You all left together?"

"Except Nicabar," he said. "The fuelers had arrived, and he stayed behind for a few minutes to get them started."

One of the door's control wires was too tangled to connect properly. I cut off the end, stripped it, and started wrapping it around its contact. "Whose brilliant idea was it not to tell me?"

"Mine, I'm afraid," he said, his voice wincing. "I thought it would just distract you, and you had enough to do at the time already."

I grunted. "Did you see any of the others while you were out hunting?"

"Of course not—we all went off in different directions," he said. "We kept in touch by phone, of course."

Which meant that any of them could easily have doubled back to the *Icarus* with murder on his mind and no one would have been the wiser for it. He wouldn't even have had to dodge the fuelers, who would have been busy on the opposite side of the ship.

The last contact dropped into place, and I heard the faint transient hum as the system integrated. I touched the pad, and the door slid open.

The room was dark. Bracing myself for the worst, I reached inside and turned on the light.

Ixil was lying on the bunk just as I'd left him, Pix and Pax rousing themselves sleepily from beside him in response to the light. Cautiously, I moved forward, studying Ixil as I approached. There were no marks of violence on him, at least none that I could see from my angle.

And then, without warning, he inhaled sharply, like a sigh going in reverse, and his eyes fluttered open. "Hello," he said, blinking up at me.

I stopped short. "You're not dead," I said stupidly.

Ixil's face registered mild surprise. "Were you expecting me to be?" he asked. His eyes flicked around the room, paused briefly on Everett standing in the doorway behind me, then shifted down toward the deck. "What are those?" he added, extending a finger.

I followed the direction he was pointing. Sitting on the deck just inside the edge of the door were three objects. One was the missing control chip from the door release pad; the other two were small glass bottles the size and shape of those in the *Icarus*'s limited pharmacopoeia.

I stepped over and picked them up. One of the bottles held a brown liquid, I noted, the other a fine whitish powder. Both bottles had safety-seal lids; both lids were still securely fastened. "What are they?" I asked Everett, handing them to him.

He frowned at the labels. "Well, this one is prindeclorian," he said, lifting the brown liquid. "It's a broad-spectrum viral inhibitor. The other one's qohumet, a parasite-control dust for feathered or scaled beings like our friend Chort. What they're doing here together I can't imagine."

"I can," Ixil said, his voice suddenly very thoughtful as he rose from the bunk and crossed over to Everett. "If you mix the two of them together and then set fire to the resulting mixture, you get something quite interesting."

The cold chill was starting up again. I knew that tone Ixil was using. Knew it far too well. "And that is?" I prompted.

He took the bottles from Everett and gazed at the labels. "Cyanide gas."

"All right, then, try this," I suggested, scowling at the bridge displays. There wasn't anything there worth scowling at—they were looking just fine—but I was feeling the need to scowl at something. "They were put there as a warning to us."

"To us?" Ixil asked pointedly from the swivel stool across from me, the words mangled by the enormous sandwich he seemed to be trying to line-feed into his mouth. Kalixiri healing comas were unarguably useful things, but they did come with a certain physical cost. That was already Ixil's second such sandwich, and he would probably demolish a third before his hunger even started to abate.

"All right, fine: it was a warning to *you*," I said, scowling some more. "The question is, why bother? What did our saboteur have to gain by slapping a red flag across our noses? Sorry—across *your* nose?"

"If it *was* the saboteur," he said, breaking off a small piece of the sandwich and leaning over to give it to Pax. Both ferrets were on the floor: Pax crouching where he could see the corridor outside the open bridge door, Pix circling the room by the inner hull listening for any eavesdroppers who might wander in from that direction. Ixil and I had already made sure that the intercom system, conveniently reactivated sometime during or immediately after my borandis search, couldn't be used against us again. "Maybe it was someone trying to warn us there's a saboteur aboard."

"If it was, he should learn how to compose letters," I said sourly. "Let's try it from a different angle. Who else aboard might know about that trick with the qohumet and whatever?"

"Prindeclorian," he said around another bite of sandwich. "Hard to tell, unfortunately. It was a favorite of armchair revolutionaries twenty years ago, along with a host of other common-chemical concoctions, and it received a fair amount of word-of-mouth publicity. But it never really caught on, mainly because you either need a small area to contaminate or a large supply of the necessary chemicals."

"And because the fact that you have to set it on fire limits its subterfuge value?"

"Definitely," he agreed. "Most people seeing a bright yellow flame spewing a cloud of greenish smoke won't stick around to see what the smoke might do to them."

"Unless the person in question is in a Kalixiri coma in a cabin the size of a large shoe box," I concluded with a grimace. "You suppose there are other equally handy chemicals aboard?"

Ixil paused to chew. "I imagine almost anything in sick bay would be lethal in a high enough dose," he said when he got his mouth clear again. "Unless you want to throw all of it overboard, there's not much we can do about it."

"That might not be such a bad idea," I growled. "I'm starting to wonder if the only reason you're alive is that Shawn's escape interrupted our would-be killer in his work."

Ixil paused in the act of taking another bite. "Excuse me? I thought your current theory was that the saboteur released Shawn so that he could chase everyone else out of the ship while he came back and did his dirty work."

"That was the old theory," I told him. "This is the new theory. He'd gotten your door open, but then heard the commotion on the mid deck and decided he'd better be found someplace else when they came looking for him. Not wanting to be caught with his pockets full of chemicals, he stashed them inside the room for safekeeping, hied himself off to someplace innocent, and just never got a chance to come back."

"And also put the control chip inside the room so that he wouldn't be able to open the door again himself?"

I glared at him. "That's right, let yourself get mired down in facts. Never mind the simple elegance of the theory."

"My apologies," Ixil said, an odd look on his face as he set the remains of his sandwich on the nav table. "An idea. I'll be right back."

He left. I started another systems check, just for something to do, and did some more glaring at the various instruments. Unfortunately, he was right: If the saboteur planned to come back later, why take out the control chip? Not to mention the rest of the damage he'd done to the release pad.

Unless that had happened since we'd returned. Maybe he'd tried to come back early and found the ship surrounded by Najik customs officers. He wouldn't have had a chance to act after that until the Najik had come and gone, while the rest of us were busy getting the *Icarus* ready to fly.

But why smash the pad at that point? What did it gain him?

Unless he'd already gotten into the cabin and wanted to make sure no one was able to get in to interrupt him. With the inside release pad intact, he would have had no trouble leaving whenever he wanted to.

So what had he done in there?

There was a clumping of heavy footsteps, and Ixil reappeared, carrying a large object wrapped in a folded cloth in his hand. "Have you checked with Pix and Pax since you woke up?" I asked. "I'm wondering if they might have seen someone else in there with you."

"Yes, I have; and no, they didn't," he said, sitting down again. He set the object in his lap and started to unwrap it. "Except for seeing you come in for the ship's schematics, of course. On the other hand, they were both asleep much of the time, so I can't absolutely state that no one else got in."

Dead end. "You need to train them to sleep one at a time."

"If I'd been more alert before I went under I would have tried," he said. "Though it might not have worked. Instructions like that often get lost when I don't have any neural contact with them for a few hours and can't reinforce the orders."

I gestured toward the object in his hand. "What's that?"

"Exhibit A." He pulled back the last fold of cloth, and I found myself looking at what had to be the biggest universal wrench on the ship, the kind used for unbolting thruster casings.

"Ah," I said. "And the significance of it is . . . ?"

"Look closely, right here," he said, pointing at a spot about midway along the rectangular cross-sectioned handle. "See the black streak?"

I leaned forward. It was there, all right: a faint black vertical mark, with a wider and fainter echo beside it as if a charcoal line had been smeared. "Let me guess," I said, leaning back again. "A mark from the rubber edge of your cabin door?"

"Very good," he said, lifting the wrench up by the cloth for a closer look of his own. "Those doors hit pretty hard when the buffer doesn't engage. My assumption is he hit the release pad, then shoved this into the gap when it opened."

And it was still moving as the door hit it; hence, the smeared streak. "That would have left enough of an opening for the bottles, but not enough to get his arm through," I pointed out. "Probably why they weren't farther from the door. Unless he was hoping someone would kick them on the way in or out."

"That wouldn't have done him any good," Ixil reminded me. "You have to ignite the mixture, remember?"

"None of this does him any good," I growled, mentally giving the whole thing up as hopeless. There was some vital information we didn't yet have—I was sure of it. And until we found out what it was all we were going to accomplish by chasing our meager data around was to make ourselves dizzy.

Apparently, Ixil had figured that out, too. "As you suggested in an earlier conversation, it all makes perfect sense," he said, starting to wrap up the wrench again. "We just don't yet know what that sense is."

I nodded to the wrench. "You planning to check it for fingerprints?"

"I was thinking of it," he agreed. "Knowing the *Ica-*

rus, though, I suspect we'll need to use it before we ever get within hailing distance of a proper fingerprinting expert."

"Knowing the *Icarus,* I'd say you were right," I agreed. "So what now?"

"I thought I'd see about fixing my door," he said, tucking the wrench under one arm and snapping his fingers as he reached for the remains of his sandwich. The two ferrets came at his call, scampering up his body to his shoulders. "Your door, rather, since your outer pad's on my cabin now. I can take the pad off the empty Number Two cabin on the top deck and replace the whole thing."

"What if we want to get in there?" I asked.

"What for?" he asked reasonably. "Anyway, we can always move a pad from one of the other cabins temporarily if we need to."

"Point," I conceded. "Okay, go ahead."

"Right. I'll see you later." Stuffing another large corner of his sandwich into his mouth, he headed out.

For a couple of minutes, ignoring my own resolve not to waste time and effort doing so, I chased our meager data around in a couple more circles. It didn't get me anywhere.

And then, behind me out in the corridor, I heard the steady tread of approaching footsteps. Two pairs, from the sound of it, neither of them Ixil's.

It was probably something totally innocent, of course. But I'd had enough unpleasant surprises for one day, and I wasn't interested in having any more of them. Folding my arms across my chest, I slid my right hand out of sight beneath my jacket and got a grip on my plasmic, then swiveled my seat around to face the open doorway.

The first in line was Tera, stalking onto the bridge like she owned it. "McKell," she said in terse greeting. There was nothing the slightest bit friendly about her expression. "We need to talk to you."

Before I could reply, the other half of the "we" stepped into sight behind her: Nicabar, looking even less friendly than she did. Not a good sign. "Come in," I said mildly, ignoring the fact that they were already in. "Revs, aren't you supposed to be on duty in the engine room?"

"Yes," he said, his eyes flicking once to my folded arms. If he suspected I was holding my gun, he didn't comment on it. "I asked Chort to watch things for a few minutes."

Strictly speaking, that was a violation of the Mercantile Code, me being the captain and not being informed and all. But so far this trip I'd been fairly casual about the duty roster, and there didn't seem much point in complaining about it now. "Fine. What can I do for you?"

Tera glanced at Nicabar, who glanced in turn out into the corridor and then unlocked the release, letting the door slide shut beside him. "You can start with some honesty," Tera said as they both looked back at me. "This Mr. Antoniewicz whose name scares off customs inspectors. Who exactly is he?"

It was a trap, of course. And with someone else, it might have worked. But Tera didn't have the facial control or sheer chutzpah to pull it off. "You already know the answer," I said. I shifted my gaze to Nicabar. "Or rather, *you* know it. I see you've already given Tera your version; how about doing the same for me?"

"He's a dealer in death and misery," Nicabar said, his voice as dark as his expression. "He buys and sells drugs, guns, customs officials, governments, and people's lives."

His eyes bored into mine. "And we want to know what exactly your relationship is to his organization."

"Nice speech," I complimented him, stalling for time. I'd known from the start that the relative ease with which I'd obtained Shawn's borandis would inevitably generate speculation among the others as to how

I'd pulled it off. But I hadn't expected that speculation to turn into full-blown suspicion so quickly or so bluntly. This could be very awkward indeed. "Did you work it up specially for this occasion? Or is it left over from the last ship you worked that had ties to Antoniewicz? Or the one before that, or the one before that?"

"What exactly are you implying?" Nicabar asked, his tone the unpleasant stillness of the air when there's a thunderstorm brewing in the distance.

"I'm saying that you and everyone else aboard the *Icarus* has worked for Antoniewicz at one time or another," I told him. "You had no choice. Antoniewicz's fingers stretch into so many nooks and crannies across the Spiral it's practically impossible to engage in any business that *doesn't* touch something he's involved with."

"That's not the same," Tera protested.

"What, if you don't know what you're doing it doesn't count?" I scoffed. "There's a very slippery slope beneath that kind of moral position."

"Speaking of slippery, you still haven't answered our question," Nicabar put in.

"I'm getting to it," I said. "I just wanted to make sure the answer was in the proper context. One of the ways Antoniewicz got a slice of so many pies was by buying up legitimate businesses, especially those in serious financial trouble. I was a legitimate business. Thanks to the Patth shipping monopoly, I got into serious financial trouble. Antoniewicz bought me up. End of story."

"*Not* end of story," Nicabar said. "He didn't just buy your business. He bought *you*."

"Of course he did," I said, putting an edge of bitterness into my tone. "Ixil and I *are* the business."

"So you sold your soul," Nicabar said contemptuously. "For money."

"I prefer to think of it as having traded my pride for

THE ICARUS HUNT 215

a little bottom-line integrity," I shot back. "Or do you think it would have been more honorable to have declared bankruptcy and left my creditors holding an empty bag. Well?"

"How much debt are we talking about here?" Tera asked.

"Five hundred thousand commarks," I told her. "And let me also say that I tried every single legitimate way to get the money before I finally gave up and let Antoniewicz's people bail us out." Which wasn't strictly true, of course. But there was no need to muddy the water here.

"What about now?" she asked.

"What about now?" I countered. "You think I wouldn't love to pay off the debt and be out from under his thumb? Antoniewicz has done this before, you know, and he's quite good at it. The way he's got things structured, we're going to be in servitude to him till about midway into the next century."

"There must be another way," she insisted.

I felt my forehead creasing. For someone who'd come in here ready to accuse me of being the scum of the Spiral, she seemed awfully concerned about my personal ensnarement in this web. Maybe even suspiciously concerned. "Such as?" I asked.

"You could turn him in," she said. "Go to one of the police or drug-enforcement agencies. Or even EarthGuard Military Intelligence—if he deals in weapons they're surely interested in him, too. You could offer to testify against him."

I sighed. "You still don't get it. Look, Tera, every police force in the Spiral has been trying to get their hands on Antoniewicz for at least twenty years. EarthGuard, too, for all I know. The problem isn't evidence or even persuading suicidal fools to testify; the problem is *finding* him. No one knows where he is, and at the rate things are going, no one's going to figure it out anytime soon, either."

"But—"

"And furthermore, blowing the horn on him would end it for me permanently," I cut her off. "He's got my debt held with a bank on Onikki, under their charming debtors' prison laws. All he has to do is call it in, and I'll spend the next thirty years working it off at fifty commarks a day. Sorry, but I have other plans."

"Like spending the same thirty years working for Antoniewicz?" Nicabar said pointedly.

"The choices stink," I agreed. "But at least this way I'm not doing hard labor, and I still get to fly."

"As Antoniewicz's wholly owned drink-fetcher."

I shrugged. "Like I said, the choices stink. If you've got any others, I'm listening."

"What if you could find someone to pay off the debt?" Tera asked.

"Like who?" I demanded. "If the banks wouldn't look at me before, they sure aren't going to start now. Unless one of you has half a million in spare change, it's not going to happen."

The corner of her mouth twitched. "It sounds like you've already given up."

"What I've done is accepted reality." I cocked an eyebrow. "The question is, are you two prepared to do the same?"

Both of them frowned. "What do you mean?" Tera asked.

"I mean you have to decide whether you're going to rise above your finicky scruples and continue to fly with me," I said. I was taking a risk, I knew, bringing up the subject that way. But only a slight one—that was, after all, what they'd come here planning to confront me with in the first place. Besides, if they could be blunt, so could I.

And Tera, at least, could certainly be blunt. "I would think it's a matter of whether *you* will be allowed to continue flying with *us*," she retorted.

"Afraid it doesn't work that way," I said, shaking

my head. "I'm the pilot, hired for the job by Borodin. None of you has the position or rank to replace me."

"Under the circumstances, I doubt you'd have the gall to file a complaint," Nicabar pointed out.

"Oh, I might have the gall," I said. "But I wouldn't, mainly because there wouldn't be anything to gain. You and the *Icarus* would already be gone, taken by the hijackers I've already told you about."

"Assuming there was any truth to that story," Tera scoffed.

"Why would I make something like that up?"

"Maybe you're hoping to scare us all into jumping ship," she said. "Maybe you've got another crew lined up ready to move in when that happens, like you had Ixil ready when Jones got killed. Maybe *you're* the real hijacker."

"Then why didn't I move my crew in on Dorscind's World while you were all out sampling the sights?" I countered. "Why bother with any story at all?"

"And you don't know who these hijackers are?" Nicabar asked.

"All I know is that they're very well organized," I said. "And that for whatever reason, they think they want the *Icarus*."

"They 'think' they want it?"

"Well, *I* sure can't see any good reason for chasing us this way," I told him. "Any cargo that would pass muster well enough on Gamm to earn a sealed-cargo license can't be all that exciting to anyone. Maybe it's the ship itself they want, though personally I find that even less plausible."

I looked back at Tera. "But whatever the reason, it boils down to the fact that you're stuck with me. You try finding a replacement pilot from this point on, and you'll never know whether it's someone the hijackers deliberately dangled in front of you, either one of their own or someone they've hired for the occasion. Not until it's too late, anyway. Have you noticed that none of your cabin doors have locks?"

They exchanged glances. Unhappy glances; trapped-and-not-liking-it-at-all glances. But they were stuck, and they knew it. At the moment the only people they had even a hope of trusting were already aboard the *Icarus*. And it was for sure that none of *them* could fly this front-heavy fitter's nightmare.

"If this is supposed to make us feel better about trusting you, it isn't," Nicabar said. "How do we know you aren't just sticking around hoping to get a better deal?"

"How do I know *you* won't sell out?" I countered. "Or that Tera won't, or any of the others? Answer: I don't. If there were better odds to be had anywhere else, I'd grab them. But there aren't. Not here, not now."

"So why should you care what happens to the *Icarus*?" Nicabar persisted. "Or to any of the rest of us?"

I looked him straight in the eye. "Because I took a contract to fly this ship to Earth. And that's what I intend to do."

"And we can believe that or not?"

I sighed, suddenly weary of this whole stupid game. "Believe whatever you want," I told him. "But if and when we make it to Earth I'll want a full apology."

It would be overly generous to say that he smiled. But some of the implied threat did seem to drain out of his face. I reflected briefly on his former career with the EarthGuard Marines, a career that wouldn't really have trained him how to read people. "I'll remember that," he promised.

"I may even expect a little groveling," I warned, shifting my attention back to Tera. "How about you? Willing to rub shoulders with the drink-fetchers a little longer, or are you going to jump ship at the next port?"

I'd thought the words, or at least the tone, might get

another facial reaction out of her. But she simply studied me, those hazel eyes holding more pity than loathing. "I'll stay," she said. "I took the contract, too."

"Good," I said briskly. "Then we're all one big happy family again. How nice. Revs, I believe you're still on duty?"

"I'll stay with the ship for now, McKell," he said quietly. "But remember what I told you earlier. If I find out we're carrying drugs or guns, I'm out."

I nodded. "I'll remember," I promised.

He regarded me another moment, then nodded back and tapped the door-release pad. It opened, and he disappeared back out into the corridor.

Tera started to follow, but then paused in the doorway. "You're not trapped, Jordan," she said, her voice quiet. Quiet, earnest, and idealistic as all get-out. Generally, it was a combination I hated. On her, oddly enough, it seemed to fit rather naturally. "There's a way out somewhere. You just have to want to find it badly enough."

"I once thought that way," I told her. "Thought there was a quick and simple solution to every problem."

"I didn't say the solution would be quick *or* simple," she said impatiently, the idealism level dropping but the earnestness increasing to more than make up the difference. "I just said that it was there if you really wanted it."

"I'll keep that in mind," I said. "And while I'm doing that, perhaps *you'll* try to remember that job security of any sort is a damn sight better than the starvation diet everyone but the Patth is on these days. It's easy for a computer jock like you—you don't *have* to fly on starships; there are computers everywhere. But I can't very well fly an accounting firm's desk, now can I?"

"I suppose the question is how much security is worth to you," she said. "Compared with, say, self-respect." Turning back to the door, she started to stride out of the room.

"By the way, Tera?" I said.

Almost reluctantly, probably annoyed at my ruining her dramatic exit, she stopped. "Yes?"

"Everett told me you were in the mechanics shop when he came to alert everyone about Shawn's escape," I said. "What were you doing in there?"

She regarded me coolly. "I was looking for a jeweler's screwdriver set," she said. "One of my displays was going funny and I thought it might need some adjustment."

"Ah," I said. "Thank you."

She gazed at me another heartbeat. "You're welcome," she said, turning again and making her exit.

I watched the door slide closed behind her, gave her and Nicabar a minute to get out of the corridor, then went over and locked the door open again. I like my privacy as much as the next man, but if anyone was planning to go for a stroll around the mid deck, I wanted to hear them doing it.

Returning to my chair, I resumed my regimen of scowling at the displays. Tera and Nicabar had at least been up front about their suspicions about me. How many of the others, I wondered, were having the same thoughts, only weren't interested in a confrontation?

I didn't care about being popular. Well, I did, actually, as much as anyone else, but I'd long since resigned myself to the knowledge that people who liked me were going to be few and far between. The vital question right now, though, was not popularity but trust and obedience. If there was any chance at all of making it through the ever-tightening Patth noose, it was going to require all of us working together.

All of us. Including our mysterious saboteur.

It would help enormously if I could figure out what exactly he was going for. But while I could hammer any three or four of the incidents into a workable theory, trying to put all of them together simply refused to work. If someone knew what was in the *Icarus*'s cargo hold, and if it was as valuable as we all thought, why hadn't he turned us in to the Patth on Potosi and claimed the reward? Or had the gem-smuggling tip to Najiki Customs been an abortive attempt to do just that? And how did the attacks on Jones and Ixil fit in?

Abruptly, I sat up straighter in my chair, my mind flashing back to what I myself had said not ten minutes earlier to Nicabar about the hijackers possibly hiring a pilot for the occasion. The Patth might very well be doing just that—they certainly had enough money to spread around, and I was the one person they knew was aboard. A single well-placed shot could take me out of the picture permanently, and make it vital for the rest to find a new pilot.

And if the Patth were dangling high-denomination bills in front of ships' pilots, why not ships' mechanics as well? Our resident saboteur, no matter what his secret talents and certificates, probably couldn't fly a ship this size and shape by himself. But two such talented and certified men just might be able to pull it off.

And if this second man was also a mechanic, then the simplest way to get him aboard was to create an opening in that slot. Our saboteur had succeeded in eliminating Jones; but I'd already had Ixil standing in line to fill the vacancy. Was the implied threat of cyanide poisoning a heavy-handed attempt to scare Ixil off?

If so, he was going to be sorely disappointed. Kalix-iri in general didn't scare very well, and Ixil was even worse at it than the average.

Which unfortunately still left the question of why the *Icarus* wasn't already in Patth hands; and maybe I'd now come up with an answer to that one, too. Uncle Arthur had said the Patth Director General was personally calling the various governments along our route; but what if he was not, in fact, speaking for the entire Patth government? I'd always assumed the Patth were fairly monolithic, at least insofar as their relations with other species were concerned. But what if that wasn't the case?

In that event our saboteur might not have turned us in to the Patth simply because he hadn't yet run across the right Patth to turn us in to. Maybe the customs flap on Potosi had indeed been an attempt to alert someone, only they hadn't gotten the message in time. Or else my maneuver with Antoniewicz's name had gotten us out of trouble and off the planet faster than anyone had anticipated.

The politics of the situation, I knew, I didn't have a hope of unraveling without more detailed information about the Patth, which I didn't expect to be getting anytime soon. However, with this assumption came an unexpected opportunity. Unless our saboteur had been recruited on the spot at the Meima spaceport—which seemed unlikely—it meant that he must have had previous ties to the Patth. Ties that, if I was lucky, would show up in the background reports Uncle Arthur had promised to deliver to me at our next stop.

I looked over my instruments and displays again, and despite the extra fuel cost involved edged our speed up a little. Suddenly, I was very anxious to get to Morsh Pon.

CHAPTER

11

It was an eighty-four-hour flight from Potosi to Morsh Pon, eighty-four hours that went both smoother and more annoyingly than I'd expected them to. We had to make only two stops along the way for Chort to repair more hull ridges, which considering the *Icarus*'s haphazard construction was not a bad showing at all. Perhaps the main hull's spherical design, unlovely though it was, actually stood up better against hyperspace pressure than the lean, graceful lines that I was more used to with starships. Or maybe it was just that all of our good luck was being unidirectionally expended on our hull.

There were no more attempts at sabotage, at least none that came to light, but we had plenty of other trouble. Successive doses of borandis were able to bring Shawn back from the edge and ensure that he wouldn't have any permanent neural damage, at least this time around. Unfortunately, he'd apparently been far enough along that it took more of the medicine than normal to get him properly stabilized. Everett thought we would be okay to Morsh Pon and probably the stop after that, but we were going to have to get hold of a new supply sooner than I'd hoped.

Our archaic computer was another problem that reared its ugly head shortly into the flight. The glitch Tera had mentioned with her display turned out to be nothing as simple as an adjustment problem. Once she opened the computer casing the trouble was instantly obvious: thin layers of almost microscopic dust inside, dust that apparently had just enough electrical conductivity to create flickers of random havoc as the cooling fans blew it across the various boards and components.

It was equally obvious, at least to Ixil and me, how it had happened. Shoved off to the side somewhere in one of the underground chambers on Meima while Cameron's techs put the *Icarus* together, it had had plenty of opportunity to collect dust through its various apertures. But of course none of the rest of our crew knew the ship's history, and dodging the constant stream of questions and complaints—most of the latter from Shawn, despite the alleged civilizing effects of his medicine—wore pretty thin after a while. Ixil bore the brunt of that one as he spent the better part of seventy hours helping Tera and Shawn disassemble the system, clean it thoroughly, and put it back together again.

That all by itself scored as both a plus and a minus on my mental tally sheet. A plus because Ixil closeted with Shawn and Tera meant neither of those two would be skulking around crimping torch nozzles or tapping into intercoms; a minus because it meant that for those same seventy hours I was robbed of Ixil's assistance in anything I might want to do.

Which meant that by the time we had a chance to send Pix and Pax into the open area between the two hulls for a thorough exploration, there was no longer anything in there for them to find. No footprints in whatever dust might have been present before the multitude of vibrations redistributed it; no leftover tool lying behind one of the supports where its owner might have missed it; no trace of the short-circuited intercom power lines, which had apparently been carefully and unobtrusively fixed. About all the ferrets could come up with was the odd fact that the outer hull didn't feel, smell, or taste like anything else they'd ever come across. It certainly wasn't any standard hull metal. At one point I actually wondered if perhaps the Potosi customs people hadn't been as far off the mark as I'd thought, that all Cameron was doing was smuggling gold or iridium or some other exotic metal plated along the inside edge of the outer hull. But that seemed both too complicated and too petty for someone with Cameron's reputation and resources. Besides which, it didn't even start to explain the increasingly obsessive Patth interest in us.

Earlier I had also taken advantage of Tera's and Shawn's preoccupation with the computer to do a quiet check of their cabins, but both searches came up empty. Neither of them had a cache of hidden weapons, secret Patth code books, or instruction manuals on how to sabotage a starship. On the other hand, I found nothing in Tera's cabin to confirm that she was a member of any of those first-name-only religious sects, either. Perhaps she was just the cautious type who didn't like giving her full name to strangers.

Overall, crew morale didn't fare very well during that leg of the trip. Everett's private reservations about going to a criminal hellhole like Morsh Pon didn't stay private very long, and starting about two hours into the trip I had him, Shawn, and Tera all campaigning for me to find someplace else for our next fueling stop. Nicabar and Chort didn't join in the chorus, but in Nicabar's case I had the distinct feeling he was wondering if I'd chosen Morsh Pon deliberately to make sure he and Tera couldn't find anyone more trustworthy to replace me.

In short, it was a frustrating, aggravating three and a

half days for all of us. And with Morsh Pon waiting, I wasn't expecting it to get any better at the far end.

It was late afternoon and early evening across the main Morsh Pon colony area when we arrived over the planet, with the sunset line probably an hour past the Blue District that was our destination. We were the only ship incoming, though I spotted a couple of other freighters on their way out, all of them running IDs that were probably as phony as ours. I gave the control center our destination port, got a rectangle assignment, and eased the *Icarus* down into the darkness.

The others were all waiting in the wraparound by the time I'd secured the ship, called for a fueling team, and made my way aft. The entryway hatch was unopened; by common consent, apparently, they'd all decided I should get the honor of being first in line for any stray shots that might be flying around out there. Leaving my plasmic in its holster—Nicabar aside, none of the others knew about the weapon, and I didn't feel the need to enlighten them—I keyed the hatch and waited tautly as it swung ponderously open. This particular spaceport didn't have any of the nice concave landing cradles we'd had at our last couple of stops, with the result that I was looking out over the landscape from a vantage point ten meters up.

I'd never actually been on Morsh Pon before, but I couldn't imagine the view was any better up here than it would be at ground level. Even in the admittedly bad street light, the tavernos, flophouse brothels, and other assorted dives that crowded into the spaces between the various landing-pad clusters looked dingy and unfriendly. Most of the buildings had darkened windows and doorways, adding their individual bits to the overall gloom. Across the strip of buildings facing us was an empty pad cluster, looking rather like a bald spot amid the uneven rows of buildings encircling it. A few stars were visible in the darkening sky, but even they seemed subdued, as if they didn't really want to look down at the Blue District, either.

"Interesting," Ixil murmured from beside me. "Where is everyone?"

I frowned, looking at the scene with new eyes. He was right. I'd already noted the dark buildings and empty landing-pad cluster directly in front of me; now, leaning partially out of the entryway, I could see that *none* of the nearest landing clusters was occupied. In the distance I could see what might have been the curved hulls of a pair of ships, and a couple hundred meters off to my right I could see a single taverno with its doorway lights on. But that was it. Virtually no ships, virtually no open businesses, no vehicles except for the fueler I could see heading our way along an access road, and no pedestrians at all. It was as if we'd landed in a ghost town.

"Hey, Everett, I thought you said this place was crawling with murderers and pirates," Shawn said accusingly. "So where are they?"

"I don't know," Everett muttered behind me. "Something's wrong. Something's *very* wrong."

"Did Landing Control say anything when you checked in?" Nicabar asked. "Disease, plague, quarantine—anything?"

"Not a word," I said, studying the single lit taverno I could see. We were too far away for me to read the nameplate, but knowing Uncle Arthur I was willing to bet it was the Baker's Dozen, the place he'd named in our last conversation. "Maybe they can tell us something in there," I suggested, pointing to it. "Anyone want to join me for a little stroll?"

"Not me," Everett said firmly. "If there's some disease out there, I don't want to catch it."

"Landing Control's legally required to alert incoming ships about medical dangers," I reminded him.

"And this is Morsh Pon, where they use laws for

place mats," Everett countered firmly. "Thanks, but I'll stay here."

"Me, too," Shawn seconded.

"I'll go with you," Tera said. "I need to get out of this ship for a while."

"Count me in, too," Nicabar added.

"Sure," I said, completely unsurprised by this one. Neither Tera nor Nicabar would be nearly as concerned about possible germs as they would be that I might sneak off and do something they wouldn't approve of. "Chort? Ixil?"

"I will come," Chort said. "Perhaps the taverno will have a bottle of *kompri* for sale."

"They might," I said, wondering what *kompri* was. Some Craean drink, probably. "What about you, Ixil?"

"I want to get the fuelers started first," he said. "I'll try to join you later."

"Okay," I said, pretending to believe him as I swung around and started down the ladder. He most certainly would not be joining us; he would be staying here and watching Everett and Shawn like an iguana-faced hawk. "We won't be long."

It was an eerie walk down the deserted access walkway, our footsteps sounding unnaturally loud in the silence. I looked into each doorway and alley as we passed it, half expecting to see dark men or aliens waiting in the darkness to ambush us. But the doorways were just as deserted as the rest of the place.

We reached the taverno without incident, to find it was indeed the Baker's Dozen. The others close behind me, I pulled open the door and looked inside.

The place was quite large, a bit on the dark side, but otherwise surprisingly homey, with heavy wooden tables and chairs, a traditional Earth-style wooden bar running the length of the left-hand wall, and even a sunken fireplace, currently unlit, in the center of the room. It was also severely underpopulated. There was a group of a dozen scruffy-looking aliens gathered around three of the tables near the bar, a pirate gang if ever I'd seen one; a pair of young human females sitting together at a table near the right-hand wall; and three robed and hooded figures with faces hidden hunched over a table in the far back corner. And that was it. Behind the bar, a furry-faced Ulkomaal was leaning on the countertop gazing morosely at the dead fireplace. He looked up as I walked into the room, his bony eyebrow crest turning a faint purple with surprise. "So that *was* another ship I heard," he said, straightening up. "Welcome, patronae, welcome."

"Thanks," I said, glancing around at the other customers. The pirates had looked up as we entered, but after a quick assessment had turned back to their drinks. The two women were still eyeing us; the robed threesome in the back hadn't even bothered to turn around. Maybe they were already too drunk to care, though the collection of empty glasses traditionally associated with sleeping drunks wasn't in evidence. On the other hand, I could see that none of the tables had menu selectors, which meant the barkeep also doubled as a waiter, and from the looks of things he certainly wasn't too busy to keep the place tidy. "You still serving?"

He sighed. "For what good it does," he said. "Everyone else has already fled."

"Fled from what?" Tera asked from behind me.

The barkeep sighed again. "The Balthee," he said in a tone that managed to be both angry and resigned at the same time. "We received a report late this afternoon that they were on their way for another spraymarker raid."

"A what?" Tera asked.

"It is an example of Balthee guilt-by-association law," Chort spoke up as I led them to a table near the door and away from the other patrons. I took the chair that put my back to the wall, where I could watch the entrance and also keep the rest of the customers at least within peripheral vision. Nicabar chose the chair to my left, which would put the pirates in his direct line of sight, while Tera took the seat to my right, where she couldn't see much of anything except the door and me. If the two of them had been deliberately planning to corral me, they couldn't have done a better job of it. "Consorting with known criminals is itself a crime under Balthee law," Chort continued, easing himself delicately into the remaining chair.

"You are very knowledgeable," the barkeep complimented him. "Knowing Morsh Pon's reputation—which is wholly unjustified, I assure you—they periodically come and spray a molecularly bonded dye over all ships on our landing pads. Any such marked ship that enters a Balthee-run spaceport is immediately impounded and searched and its crew held for questioning."

"I can see why your clientele wouldn't want that," I agreed, nodding toward the pirate gang at their tables. "They not get the message?"

"Their captain tells me they do not fear the Balthee," he said, lowering his voice as he glanced in their direction. "However, another crew member confided that they plan to have all their hull plates replaced soon anyway."

He gestured to the other two occupied tables. "As to the females, they are employees of one of the guesthouses, Shick Place. And, when the word came, the gentlebeings in back were already too inebriated to try to leave."

He straightened up and cocked his head at me. "And what is *your* story?"

I frowned up at him. "What do you mean?"

"You are here," he said, waving a hand at us. "Yet there is word of an impending raid."

"Which we obviously didn't know about, did we?" I said.

"Were no other ships leaving as you arrived?" the

barkeep countered. "Some must still have been on their way out. Did no one transmit a warning to you?"

"Yes, there were other ships leaving," I said, putting some impatience into my voice even as a quiet warning bell went off in my ear. I'd never been on Morsh Pon before; but the criminal hangouts I *had* had occasion to visit had not been known for overly inquisitive waiters. This kind of interrogation was way out of character, even given that the barkeep was probably bored out of his skull. "And no, none of them bothered to give us a warning. Why do you think this is any of your business?"

"Don't mind him," a soprano voice came from my side.

I turned. One of the two women at the far table had gotten to her feet and was coming toward us. She was medium height and slender, and her step was just a bit unsteady. I wondered briefly if she could be Uncle Arthur's information courier, but the skintight outfit she was wearing couldn't have concealed a spare poker chip. At least, I thought incongruously, that also meant we didn't have to worry about her being an assassin. "I'm sorry?" I said.

"I said don't mind him," she repeated, flipping her hand toward the Ulkomaal in the more or less universal gesture of contemptuous dismissal, the dim room light glinting momentarily off the large gaudy rings she was wearing. Now that she was facing us, I could see she was wearing the display scarf of a bar girl knotted around her neck, the particular tartan pattern advertising what services she offered and the charge for them. I wondered distantly whether Tera would know about such things; I rather hoped she didn't. "Nurptric the Nosy, they call him," the woman continued. "Mind if I sit down?"

"Business slow?" Tera asked, her voice frosty. Apparently, she knew all about the scarf.

The woman gave her a smile that was a good eighty

percent smirk. "Yours too?" she asked sweetly, snagging a chair from the next table and hauling it over. With a hip she deftly shoved Tera over, to Tera's obvious consternation, and planted her chair squarely between the two of us. "I'm just being sociable, you being strangers here and all," she added, dropping into the seat and swiveling to put her face to me and her back to Tera. "Any law against that?"

"Not too many laws against anything here," Tera countered pointedly. "Obviously."

"And like you say, business is slow," the woman added, wiggling her hips and shoulders to carve a bit more room for herself. "I'm sure not going to get any decent conversation out of anyone else in here. My name's Jennifer. How about buying me a drink?"

"How about you going somewhere else?" Tera said, starting to sound angry. "This is a private conversation."

"Noisy, isn't she?" Jennifer commented, an amused smile playing around her lips. "Unfriendly, too. You come here often?"

Tera half rose to her feet, sank reluctantly back into her seat as Chort put a gentle hand on her arm. "I'm afraid we're pretty much broke, Jennifer," I said diplomatically. "We've got barely enough money for the fuel we need. Nothing left over for incidentals."

She eyed me speculatively. "Gee, that's too bad," she said, looking over at the Ulkomaal still hovering expectantly behind Chort. "Give me a small vodkaline, Nurp."

His eyebrow crest turned a brief magenta, but he nevertheless nodded. "Of course. And for the rest of you?"

"Have you *kompri,* by any chance?" Chort asked.

"No, nothing like that," Nurptric said. "We have no Craean drinks."

"We might have some back at Shick Place," Jennifer volunteered. "We cater to all sorts of vices there," she added, giving Chort a sly smile. "It's not far away if you want to go see."

Chort looked at me uncertainly. "If we have the time—?"

"No," Nicabar said flatly, his tone leaving no room for argument. "As soon as the ship's fueled, we're out of here."

"He's right," I seconded. I didn't especially like the thought of spending any more time out in the gloom than I had to, and I certainly wasn't going to let any of the group go wandering off on their own. "We'll take three caff colas and a distilled water," I added to the barkeep.

His eyebrow crest went a little mottled, either a sign of resignation or possibly contempt for such miserliness. "Yes, patronae," he said and turned back to his bar, muttering under his breath as he went.

"Three colas and a water, huh?" Jennifer said, shaking her head. "You really *are* the big spenders."

"As he said, we're short on cash," Tera said firmly. "So you might as well stop wasting your time."

Jennifer shrugged. "Fine. You know, though, there's an easy way to make some fast money."

She leaned in toward the middle of the table, beckoning us in conspiratorially. "There's a ship out there somewhere—no one knows where," she said, dropping her voice to a murmur. "You find it, and it's worth a hundred thousand commarks to you. Cash money."

A matched set of Kalixiri ferrets with cold feet began running up and down my back. "Really," I said, trying to keep my voice neutral. "How come it's worth that much? And who to?"

"I don't know why they want it," she said, half turning and snagging a folded piece of paper from the next table over that had apparently been left behind during the earlier mass exodus. "But it's all right here," she said, handing it to me.

I unfolded it. To my complete lack of surprise, it was

the same flyer James Fulbright had waved in my face back on Dorscind's World.

With two unpleasant differences. First, as Jennifer had said, the reward had been jumped from the original five thousand to a hundred thousand. And second, instead of my old Mercantile Authority photo, there was a much more up-to-date sketch. An extremely good sketch.

"Sounds like a con to me," I commented offhandedly as I folded the paper again and dropped it on the table in front of me, my skin crawling beneath the fake scars on my cheek. So that was why the Patth agent on Dorscind's World had surrendered without even token resistance. Letting me get off the planet had been less important in his eyes than making sure he stayed alive to take back a proper description to his masters. Suddenly my disguise didn't seem quite so comforting and impenetrable anymore. "So why show it to us?" I asked.

She waved a hand around. "You can see how it is," she said, her eyes and voice starting to drift toward the seductive. "I'm stuck down here. But you're not. You might run into this *Icarus* out there."

Chort made a strange sound in the back of his throat. "What ship did you say? The *Icarus*?"

"I guess no one knows what it looks like," she said, ignoring him, her eyes still on me and growing ever more seductive. "But they say that guy on the flyer is aboard it. You might spot the ship; you might spot him."

"And then?" I prompted.

She leaned close to me. "Then you could call me here," she said, breathing the words straight into my face now. The perfume mixed with the alcohol on her breath was definitely from the lower end of the price spectrum. "I know who to get the word to, and who to collect the bounty from."

"You say they just want the ship?" Tera spoke up.

She had picked up the flyer now and was looking at it, and in the admittedly inadequate light I thought her face had gone a little pale.

"They want the ship and crew both," Jennifer said, still gazing at me. "What, can't you read?"

"What for?" Tera persisted, handing the flyer off to Nicabar. "What do they want them for?"

Reluctantly, Jennifer leaned back again and looked at Tera over her shoulder. "I don't know," she growled, clearly annoyed at the interruption in her sales pitch. "And I don't care, either. The point is that there's money to be made, and we could be the ones who make it."

"And how would you propose we split it?" I asked.

She smiled at me again. The seductress role was apparently all she knew how to play. "All I want is passage back to Earth and a couple thousand to help me get set up there," she breathed, leaning toward me again. "That's all—you'd get all the rest. Just for one little StarrComm call. I'd even pay you back for the call."

"Why do we need you at all?" Nicabar put in, looking up from the flyer. "Why can't we just call this number ourselves?"

"Because I know how to get you an extra fifty thousand," the woman said, breathing her words into my face again. "Private money. Revenge money. See those three in the back?"

I turned my head. The three robed figures were still hunched over their table; but as we all looked that direction, as if on cue, one of them stirred, rolling his shoulders to the sides as if adjusting them in his sleep, then falling silent and still again. But the movement had been enough to drop his hood partially back, revealing his face.

It was another of the Lumpy Clan.

From my left, from Nicabar's direction, came a faint but sharp intake of air. I turned to look at him, but by the time I got there he had his usual stolid expression back in place.

But the stifled gasp alone was very enlightening. Clearly, somewhere along the line, Nicabar had run into these lads before.

"They passed the word that they were putting another fifty thousand into the pot," Jennifer continued. Like Chort's reaction earlier to the name of the hunted ship, she'd apparently also missed Nicabar's reaction to the Lumpies. Either she was drunker than I'd thought, or else she was putting so much effort into her attempted seduction of me that she didn't have any attention to spare for anyone else. "I hear the guy on the flyer smoked a couple of their pals."

"Not a very friendly thing to do," I said, peering with some difficulty into her face, not because she was unpleasant to look at but because she'd once again moved to a position bare centimeters away from me. Maybe she was counting on her perfume to seal this deal for her.

Inside my jacket, my phone vibrated. "Excuse me," I said, half turning away from her and digging into my pocket, glad for an excuse to break away from that gaze, even temporarily.

It was, as I'd expected, Ixil. "Everything all right?" he asked.

"Just fine," I told him as Nurptric returned to our table with our drinks. "We found out why everyone else is gone."

"Good," he said. "Whatever the reason, they're coming back."

"It seems—" I broke off. "What?"

"I'm reading fifteen ships on landing-approach vectors," he said. "At least five of them are heading for our spaceport."

I looked up at the Ulkomaal. "Nurptric, do the Balthee ever actually land to pick up prisoners?"

He seemed shocked. "Of course not. They wouldn't dare—this is Ulko sovereign territory."

"Then you're right, they're coming back," I confirmed to Ixil, trying to keep the sudden tension out of my voice. A whole crowd of returning pirates, smugglers, and cutthroats; and probably every one of them with a Patth sketch of me folded neatly in his pocket. Just what we needed. "What's the fueling status?"

"About half-done," he said. "We should be topped off by the time the first wave arrives. I presume we'd like to be buttoned down and ready to fly by then?"

"If not sooner," I told him. Whatever Uncle Arthur had cooked up for us, he'd better hit the road with it, and fast. "We're on our way."

I clicked off and returned the phone to my pocket. "Trouble?" Jennifer asked.

"Just the opposite," I assured her, lifting my glass to my lips but not drinking any of it. The barkeep might have recognized me and slipped in something special, and I didn't want to find out about it the hard way. If I hadn't been a raving paranoid before, I reflected, this trip would very likely do the trick. "Our ship's almost fueled up, and it looks like we can be out of here before the rest of your clientele start tying up all the perimeter grav beams."

Her face fell, just a bit. All that effort, and now we were about to leave without letting her finish her presentation. "Think about my offer, okay?" she said, a note of pleading in her voice. "There could be extra benefits, too, not just the money."

"Oh?" I said, resisting the temptation to look suggestively up and down her tight-fitting outfit. It would have been a cheap shot, and I imagined she got enough of that from the Baker's Dozen's usual denizens. "Such as?"

Cheap shots, apparently, were Jennifer's stock-in-trade. Putting her right hand behind my head, the corners of her ring catching momentarily on my hair, she pulled me the last thirty centimeters still separating us and kissed me.

There was nothing tentative or perfunctory about it, either. It was a full-mouth, full-pressure lip dock, with all the desperate strength of someone facing her absolute last chance. I thought about how she'd spoken of being stuck here, of how she'd asked for passage to Earth for putting us onto the Patth hunt, and for the first time since we'd met I actually felt a little sorry for her. Of all of us at that table, I could empathize most strongly with the feeling of being caught inside an ever-shrinking box.

And then the tip of her tongue pushed between my lips; and abruptly, my twinge of sympathy vanished in a sudden flush of surprise and cautious excitement.

It seemed like a long time before the pressures fore and aft slackened off and she pulled away, though it was probably no more than a few seconds. As her head moved out of my line of sight, I saw that Tera was looking at me with a cast-granite expression on her face. Irreverently, I found myself wondering how many other expressions of surprise, outrage, or disgust she'd gone through while I wasn't looking. Even a scoundrel as low-class as I was shouldn't act that way in the presence of a lady.

"Just remember, there's a lot more where that came from," Jennifer said, using her seductive voice again as she rose leisurely to her feet. Clearly, she was feeling very pleased with herself. "If you spot the *Icarus,* call the Morsh Pon StarrComm exchange and leave a message for Jennifer at Shick Place." With one last smile all around, plus a smirk for Tera, she sauntered away.

The others were all looking at me, varying degrees of expectation on their faces. "Well, don't just sit there," I said. To my perhaps hypersensitive ears my voice sounded a little slurred. "Drink up, and let's get out of here."

They did so without comment. I let my own cola sit

where it was, keeping a surreptitious eye on Jennifer as I sorted out the proper number of small-denomination coins. She returned to her table and spoke briefly with her friend there; but as the four of us stood up she left that table and wandered off again, this time heading in the general direction of the three Lumpies. "Let's go," I told the others, putting a hand on Tera's back to encourage her forward, a friendly gesture I instantly abandoned at the glare she flashed me.

We headed to the door; and as I ushered the others through, I took one final look behind us. The pirates were looking back at us, with the universal suspicious expressions of men permanently on the run. Nurptric the barkeep was busily puttering around the bar, his eyebrow crest fairly glowing with the eager anticipation of customers on their way in. Jennifer's friend had a small mirror out and was checking her makeup, with much the same air of anticipation.

And Jennifer herself was at the back table leaning over one of the Lumpies, speaking solicitously to him as if trying to wake him up, her ring again catching the light as she patted him soothingly on the back of his neck. Her eyes caught mine; and though she didn't smile, I knew we understood each other.

The trip back was very quiet. After what had happened back at the taverno, no one seemed interested in talking to me, and I certainly wasn't going to start any conversations myself.

We reached the *Icarus* to find Ixil in the process of paying off the fuelers. I ordered everyone to their stations, then waited in the wraparound until Ixil was finished so that I could personally retract the ladder and seal the hatch. Heading up the now deserted mid-deck corridor to the bridge, I sealed the door behind me and sat down in the command chair.

And only then, with no one around to see, I pulled from its resting place between my gum and cheek the poker-chip-sized object that Jennifer had transferred from her mouth to mine during our kiss. Unscrewing the top, I carefully extracted the folded microprint document nestled inside, and the six small borandis tablets that had been packed tightly together beneath it.

Uncle Arthur had come through.

The document, annoyingly but not surprisingly, was written in Kalixiri.

"I hate it when he does that," I sighed, handing the reader over to Ixil and flopping onto my back on my bunk. "Here, you do it. I'm not up to deciphering Kalixiri right now."

"Certainly," Ixil said, resettling himself comfortably against the door of my cabin and showing the good sense not to lecture me yet again as to why Uncle Arthur did things this way. Kalixiri was probably one of the least-known languages in the Spiral, which made for automatic security if the wrong person happened across one of his missives, though it was surprisingly easy for non-Kalixiri to learn. Furthermore, the way the alphabet was laid out, the words themselves were generally much shorter than the English equivalents, which meant he could cram in more text per square centimeter.

And from what I'd seen of this one, he had those square centimeters very well crammed indeed.

"We start with Almont Nicabar," Ixil said. "We have a photo. Slightly out-of-date . . . but yes, it does appear to be him. Certificate in starship drive and unofficial training in mechanics—the dates and details are here; you'll want to look them over later. Ten years in the EarthGuard Marines, just as he said, achieving rank of master sergeant . . . Interesting. Had you ever heard of an attempt six years ago by EarthGuard to get hold of a Patth Talariac Drive?"

"I hadn't until Uncle Arthur mentioned it," I told

him, wondering why the mention of six years sounded familiar. "Was Nicabar involved with that?"

"I would say so," Ixil said dryly. "He was on the commando team that penetrated the Patthaaunutth Star Transport Industries plant on Oigren."

I turned my head to look at him. "You're kidding. *Our* Almont Nicabar?"

"So it says," Ixil assured me. "Furthermore, from the listed dates, it appears he resigned from the service barely three months after the mission's failure."

A funny sensation began to dig into my stomach. That was when I remembered six years being mentioned: Nicabar had said that was how long ago he'd resigned from the Marines. "Is there any mention of why the mission failed?"

Ixil gave me an odd look. "As a matter of fact, there's a note that suggests inside information might have been leaked to the Patth. Are you seeing a connection?"

"Could be," I said grimly. "Three months is just the right length for a private confidential court-martial."

"You sure?"

"Trust me," I assured him. "I went through one, remember? One other thing. I told you about seeing three more of the Lumpy Clan back in that taverno. What I didn't tell you was that Nicabar reacted rather strongly when we got our first glimpse of one of them. Strongly for Nicabar, anyway."

For a moment Ixil digested that in silence. "Still, there must not have been a real case against him, or he wouldn't have been allowed to resign and leave gracefully."

"But there must have been enough of one for them to hold him for court-martial in the first place," I pointed out.

"Unless there was no court-martial involved," Ixil also pointed out. "It might have just been three months of general debriefing."

"And he then picked up and left a promising ten-year career just for the hell of it?" I shrugged. "Well, maybe. Still, bad feelings might explain why he jumped his last ship just because they were mask-shilling for the Patth. Is there anything else?"

"Various details of his life," Ixil said, scanning down the text. "Nothing all that interesting, though again you'll want to look them over when you're up to deciphering Kalixiri again. Mostly public and official-record material—Uncle Arthur must not have had time to have anyone dig deeper than that."

"I'm sure he'll have the really juicy details later," I said. Uncle Arthur's knack for getting his hands on supposedly confidential information was legendary. "The trick will be how we get hold of it. Who's next?"

"Hayden Everett," he said. "He was indeed a professional throw-boxer for two years, leaving the ring twenty-two years ago."

"Was he any good?"

Ixil shrugged. "His win/loss record would say no. Still, he *did* last two years on the circuit, so he must at least have had stamina."

"Or was just a glutton for punishment," I said. "I wonder if the circuit back then went into Patth space."

"I don't know," Ixil said. "However, you might be interested in knowing that his last fight was a contested loss to Donson DiHammer. That name sound familiar?"

"It certainly does," I said, frowning. Twenty years ago DiHammer had been at the epicenter of one of the biggest scandals ever to hit organized throw-boxing. "He was wholly owned and operated by one of the partners in the Tr'darmish Spiracia shipping conglomerate, wasn't he?"

"You have a good memory," Ixil confirmed. "We have the highlights listed here. Plus the interesting fact that Tr'darmish Spiracia was one of the first companies to go bankrupt when the Talariac came onto the scene."

"Interesting," I murmured. "You sure it wasn't just a case of bad management or overextension?"

"Not sure at all," Ixil said. "Spiracia's directors certainly had a reputation for corporate edge-walking. Don't forget, too, that the Talariac didn't even appear until a good six years after that fight and four years after the DiHammer scandal broke. *If* Everett was partially owned by the Patth, and *if* they took his defeat that personally, it would imply a long grudge on their part."

"As grudges go, six years wouldn't even be a regional record," I told him. "Another question to put on our next wish list for Uncle Arthur. Who's next?"

"Chort," Ixil said, peering at the reader. "Full name . . . never mind, it's unpronounceable. He's been in the spacewalking business only four years, which puts him barely into journeyman status. That might explain why he was available for Cameron to hire on Meima."

"Not to me it doesn't," I said. "Crooea are still the cream of the spacewalking crop; and just because Chort hasn't got twenty years' experience is no reason why he should have been free in the middle of nowhere like that."

"Have you asked him about that?"

"Not yet," I said. "Come to think of it, I never got around to getting Tera's story, either. I'll have to remedy that soon. Anything else on him?"

"No indication of any direct ties between him and the Patth, if that's what you mean." Ixil frowned suddenly. "Hmm. Interesting. Did you know that the Craean economy has been expanding at an annual rate of nearly sixteen percent over the past twelve years?"

"No, I didn't," I said. Considering the Spiral average, that kind of sustained growth was practically unheard-of. "Does it say what it was pre-Talariac?"

"Yes," he said after a brief search. "Between one and two percent. And that was in their better years."

I shook my head. "The stuff Uncle Arthur comes up with. Does he include an explanation for this remarkable economic boom?"

"Apparently, the Crooea grow and export a considerable range of perishable food delicacies that can't handle normal preservation methods," Ixil said. "The greater speed of the Talariac has vastly increased their potential market."

I grimaced. "Which puts them right at the top of the list of governments ripe for Patth pressure."

"Yes," Ixil said. "Fortunately, I doubt they know a Craea is aboard the *Icarus*."

"Unless they've gotten to Cameron and made him talk," I said. "He's presumably the only one who knows the whole crew list."

Ixil frowned again. "I thought your current theory was that Cameron was in a shallow grave somewhere back on Meima."

"I have no current theories," I told him sourly. "All I have are useless, outdated ones that couldn't hold glue with both hands."

Ixil didn't say there, there, but from the expression on his face he might just as well have. "Next on the list is Geoff Shawn," he said instead. "For someone only twenty-three years old, he's compiled a remarkable record: a long string of academic awards and honors, plus an almost equally long list of legal troubles."

"Serious ones?"

"Not particularly. Traffic citations, semivandalistic pranks, some petty theft of university electronics property—that sort of thing."

I grunted. "Typical hotshot student genius. Brilliant and knows it, and figures none of the usual rules apply to him. Does it mention anything about his jaunt out to Ephis?"

"Not a word," Ixil said. "Of course, he did say no one knew about that, didn't he?"

"That's what he implied," I agreed doubtfully. "But the more I think about it, the more I wonder if he and his buddies could really have pulled it off without at least being noticed."

Ixil pondered that a moment. "In which case," he said slowly, "it would raise the question of whether his borandis dependence is really a medical matter at all."

"It would indeed," I agreed. "Of course, Everett *did* confirm that was the diagnosis. But then, Everett apparently also didn't recognize the symptoms of either the drug dependency or the Cole's disease until Shawn really started getting twitchy. Is there anything there about Everett's medical training?"

Ixil adjusted the document in the reader. "Looks like just the basic Mercantile course and certification."

"How long ago?"

"Two years."

"Which leaves a twenty-year gap between his throw-boxing and medical careers," I said. "What was he doing to fill the idle workday hours?"

"A variety of different jobs," Ixil said, scanning down the text. "Let me see. He did five years of throw-boxing instruction, two as a judge/referee, and six as a casino security officer. Then there was one year each as bartender on a liner, mechanics' apprentice, and tour packager/guide on the throw-boxing circuit. After that he went in for his medical certificate."

"By my count, that leaves us two years short."

"That's taken up by the instruction regimens for the various career changes," Ixil explained. "One to eight months each."

"I wonder what he wants to be when he grows up," I murmured. Though to be fair, it didn't sound a whole lot worse than my own employment résumé. "All right, back to Shawn. Anything in there that might suggest he'd dabbled with any other drugs besides borandis?"

"Nothing," Ixil said. "Though nothing that would preclude it, either. Something else for our wish list?"

"Right," I agreed, making yet another mental note. "Okay. That just leaves Tera."

"Tera," Ixil echoed, peering at the reader. "We start with a negative: Preliminary checks of appropriate religious-group listings fail to find anyone by that name with the description you gave. After that . . ."

He paused, his face going suddenly rigid. "Jordan," he said, his voice studiously conversational, "would you say that Uncle Arthur has a tendency toward the dramatic?"

"Is moss slimy?" I countered, feeling the hairs tingling on the back of my neck as I swung my legs over the side of my cot and sat up. "How dramatic is he being this time?"

Wordlessly, he handed me the reader. I took it, glanced at the indistinct photo that might or might not have been our Tera, and with a feeling of nameless but impending doom plowed my way into the final section of the Kalixiri text.

It was as if I'd been slapped across the face with a wet rag. I read it twice, sure I must have gotten it wrong. But I hadn't. "Where's Tera now?" I asked, looking up at Ixil.

"Probably in her cabin," he said. "She's off-duty, and she hasn't shown much tendency to sit around the dayroom."

"Let's go find her," I said, making sure my plasmic was riding snugly in its holster.

I got up and headed for the door. Ixil was faster, hopping up from his place on the floor and blocking my way. "Are you sure this is a good idea?" he asked.

"Not really," I said. "But I want to find out for sure, and I want to find out now. Confronting her straight-out seems to me the best way to do it."

"Yes, but she'll want to know how we found out," he warned. "That could be awkward."

"It won't," I said, shaking my head. "She already knows we run cargoes for Antoniewicz, and she knows he's got his slimy fingers into everything. We can lay this at his feet, no problem."

He still didn't look convinced, but he nevertheless stepped aside. I tapped the release pad, confirmed there was no one loitering outside in the corridor, and headed for the aft ladder. Ixil stayed behind long enough to collect his ferrets from the floor, then followed.

We reached the top deck without seeing anyone; clearly, the *Icarus*'s antisocial atmosphere was still unsullied by anything resembling genuine camaraderie. Tera's door was closed. Bracing myself, I tapped the release pad; and as the door slid open I dodged inside.

From my previous clandestine visit to Tera's room I knew she used the lower of the three bunks, and that supposed knowledge nearly got me killed. Even as I aimed my charge toward the lower bunk, I belatedly saw in the light filtering in from the corridor that that particular bunk was in fact empty. My eyes tracked upward, caught sight of the body and sudden movement on the top bunk—clearly, she alternated bunks, probably for exactly this purpose.

I altered course in mid-charge, nearly wrenching my back in the process, reaching for her mouth to keep her from screaming. There was a faint glint of something metallic in her hand, and I shifted the direction of my hands toward the object as she tried to bring it around to bear on me. I won by a thin-sliced fraction of a second, and with a twist of my wrist wrenched it out of her hand. With my other hand I reached again for her mouth; but even as I could see her taking a deep breath Ixil's left hand closed almost delicately across it, his right taking up a supporting position behind her head.

"It's all right, Tera," I assured her quickly. "We just want to talk."

She ignored me, grabbing Ixil's hand and trying to pry it away—considering Kalixiri musculature, a complete waste of effort. From the movements of her head I guessed she was also trying to bite him, another waste of effort. Behind us, the door slid shut, plunging the silent struggle into darkness. "Really, that's all we want," I said, stepping across the darkened room and switching on the light. "We thought it would be better if what we had to say was kept quiet from the others for the moment."

Tera grunted something unintelligible but undoubtedly quite rude from behind Ixil's hand, her eyes doing their best to skewer me. "Nice to see you're armed, too," I added, looking at the gun I'd taken from her. It was a short-barreled shotgun-style pepperbox pistol, capable of making a considerable mess of an assailant at the close range inherent in shipboard combat without the danger of accidentally rupturing the hull in the process. My earlier search of her room hadn't turned it up; clearly, she made a habit of carrying it around with her. "Of course, this thing's loud enough to have brought the whole ship down on us. Good thing you didn't get a chance to fire. If Ixil takes his hand away, will you promise not to make a fuss until you hear what we have to say?"

Her eyes flicked to her gun in my hand. Reluctantly, I thought, she nodded. "Good," I said, nodding to Ixil.

He pulled his hands away slowly, ready to put them back again if she reneged on her promise. "What do you want?" she said in a low voice. There was a fair degree of tension in her face, I saw, but whatever panic there might have been had already disappeared.

"Like I said, to talk," I told her. "We want to find out what you know about this ship, Tera." I lifted my eyebrows. "Or should I call you Elaina?"

The corner of her mouth twitched. Not much, but

enough to show I'd hit the bull's-eye. Uncle Arthur had indeed come through. "Elaina?" she asked cautiously.

"Elaina," I said. "Elaina Tera Cameron. Daughter of Arno Cameron. The man who put all of us aboard this ship."

CHAPTER

12

For the space of a dozen heartbeats I thought she was going to try to play out the masquerade. She lay there on her bunk, propped up on one elbow, and stared at me, a dozen expressions flicking across her face. And then, the one hand I could see tightened into a fist, and I knew she'd given up. "What gave me away?" she asked calmly.

"It wasn't anything you said or did," I assured her. "Though now in retrospect I can see hints that you were more than you seemed. That nicely fortuitous timing when you first came to the bridge, for instance, making sure that I didn't just pocket the money your father had left for us and stroll casually off the ship. No, we simply picked up some additional information which included the interesting note that Cameron's daughter hadn't been seen for a while. Our informant was kind enough to include a photo that was just barely adequate."

"I see," she said. "Where exactly did this information come from?"

"You know how we're connected," I said, my voice heavy with significance. "Just leave it at that."

She seemed to measure me with her eyes. "All right," she said. "So. Now what?"

"Now what is that you tell us what the hell this is all about," I said. "Starting with where your father is."

"He's back on Meima, of course," she said. "You ought to know—you took off without him."

I shook my head. "Sorry, but that won't wash. The whole planet was looking to hang a murder charge on him, and there aren't a hell of a lot of places there where a human could hide."

"Which means he was already aboard when you left," Ixil added. "I presume he was the one Jordan chased briefly around the 'tweenhull area?"

Tera grimaced. So did I, feeling like a complete fool. All the way up from the lower deck knowing she was Cameron's daughter, and that part had never even occurred to me. "So he's the one who tapped into my intercom," I said. "And who tried to kill Ixil with the cutting torch."

"Dad wasn't trying to hurt him," Tera snapped, her face flushing. "Not Ixil or anyone else." She transferred her glare to Ixil. "He *thought* you'd be professional enough to check the torch before you tried lighting it."

"I'd already done so," he said calmly. "Under the circumstances, I should have known to check it again."

"I'm sorry," she growled, her expression one of anger mixed with guilt. "For whatever it's worth, he felt very bad about you getting hurt."

Ixil inclined his head. "I accept his apology."

"Accept it in person, why don't you," I put in. "Elaina, we need to talk to your father right away."

"Tera," she corrected me. "And Dad's not here. He got off at Potosi."

I threw a glance at Ixil. The biggest Patth shipping facility in the entire region; and *that* was where Cameron had chosen to jump ship? "Why?" I asked.

"I don't know," she said. "He didn't say anything about it to me beforehand. All I know is that when we all got back after looking for Shawn, he and his things were gone."

Ixil rumbled in his throat. "You'll forgive me if I say that makes no sense whatsoever."

"You can search the ship yourselves if you want," she countered tartly. "I tell you, he's not here."

"Let's go back to the beginning," I interrupted them, not about to let this degenerate into a reality-versus-logic argument if I could help it. "Let's start with how you got to Meima and why you're aboard the *Icarus* under this semiassumed identity."

Tera looked back and forth between us, a wary look on her face. "Why should I tell either of you anything?" she demanded. "You've already admitted your souls are owned by a crime boss. Why should I trust you?"

"Because you have to trust someone," I told her, putting on my quietly earnest face and gunning it for all it was worth. "And as far as this ship and crew are concerned, we're it. Did you know the Patth are hunting for us?"

She swallowed. "Yes. There were hints even before we left Meima, and Dad heard you talking about it in your cabin."

"All right," I said. "Then remember back to Potosi, where one of our fellow crewers called in a tip that nearly got us impounded by the Najiki Customs agents."

"How do you know it was one of us?" she asked.

"Because no one except the seven of us knew we were running under the name *Sleeping Beauty* at the time," I said. "If I hadn't gotten us out of that when I did, the *Icarus* would inevitably have wound up in Patth hands. That ought to prove I'm on your side."

"And which *is* my side?"

"The side of getting the *Icarus* and its cargo to Earth

intact," I told her. "I could have turned you in on Dor-scind's World, too. In fact, I risked getting shot in order not to."

I waved a hand at Ixil. "And as for Ixil here, some-one aboard—and I presume it's all the same person—is apparently trying to scare him off the ship. While the rest of you were out searching for Shawn on Potosi, he left the makings for poison gas inside the door of Ixil's cabin. And then, for good measure, smashed the release pad to keep everyone else out."

Tera stared at me. "No. I don't believe it."

I shrugged. "You can ask Everett. He was there when we found the stuff."

"The point is that someone's been operating behind the scenes," Ixil said. "But apparently, so have you and your father, for whatever reasons of your own."

"And the only way we're going to figure out who this other person is," I concluded, "is for you to tell us which were Cameron and Daughter Productions and which weren't." No doubt about it, I decided, Ixil and I could be dazzling in our logic when we wanted to be. "So: back to the beginning. How did you end up aboard the *Icarus*?"

If Tera was dazzled, she was hiding it well. But if she wasn't totally convinced, she was nevertheless con-vinced enough. "Dad was funding an archaeological dig on Meima," she said, pulling off the blanket and swinging her legs over the side of the bunk. She was fully dressed, I noted, the sort of thing that someone who's expecting trouble automatically does. She hadn't needed our arguments to know there was trouble aboard. "About three months ago they sent word that they'd found something big, something that could con-ceivably change the course of history."

"Archaeologists do get a bit dramatic sometimes," I murmured. "Especially at funding time."

"In this instance they may have understated the case," Tera said, dropping onto the deck and sitting down on the middle bunk. "Dad heard their description, and decided we needed to get it back to Earth as quickly and secretly as possible. It took him a month to make the necessary preparations, after which he flew a tech team in with the *Icarus* packed in pieces in shipping crates. They assembled the ship underground, the only place they could do it where they wouldn't be seen. A week ago Dad and I flew into Meima ourselves to oversee the final stages. He came in on his private ship, the *Mensana*, while I took a commercial liner under a false ID."

"Why?" Ixil asked. "Why did you come in by liner, I mean?"

"I was the ace up his sleeve," she said, a tight smile touching her lips briefly before vanishing again. "Or so he said. None of the others were to know I was there—as he pointed out, you can't leak information you don't have. My job was to keep an eye on the Ihmisit authorities and try to get us a heads up if anyone started showing undue interest in our activities."

"Having a starship suddenly appear out in the middle of nowhere would probably do that," I said.

"It wasn't supposed to happen that way," Tera said, glaring at me. "Give us a *little* credit. Dad had another team building a copy of the *Icarus* at one of his heavy construction plants on Rachna. The idea was for the copy to fly in, creating a nice official presence and data trail along the way, and get all legally inspected at the Meima port. Then it would fly out to the dig, we'd make a switch, and fly the original out. By the time anyone stumbled across the copy hidden in the cavern, we figured we'd be on Earth."

"What went wrong?" Ixil asked.

Tera grimaced. "Two of those bumpy aliens that slut Jennifer was trying to wake up at the Morsh Pon taverno sneaked into the dig somehow," she said bitterly. "They got Dr. Chou before they could be stopped. It was horrible—I wasn't there, but Dad said their weapons burned him alive."

"Yes, I've seen them in action," I said, feeling my own stomach turning with the memory. "It is definitely not pretty."

Her forehead creased. "That's right; she said you'd killed a couple of them, didn't she?"

"In self-defense only, I assure you," I told her, wondering what her reaction would be if I told her that far from trying to wake the Lumpies up, Jennifer had instead been dabbing them with soporific from an injector ring to make sure their blissful sleep lasted until well after the *Icarus* was off the planet. "I hope you did something similar with your batch."

She shivered. "We killed them, yes," she said quietly. "Like you, in self-defense."

"But you knew they would have friends?" Ixil prompted.

"Yes." Visibly, Tera shook the thoughts of death away from her. "We—they, rather—knew they had to get the *Icarus* out right away. So they mixed up a concoction that would scramble the spaceport sensors, blew the roof off the cavern, and Dad and the *Mensana*'s pilot sneaked the ship up and off the planet."

"Why turn around and come back?" I asked. "Why didn't they put everyone aboard while they could and head straight out?"

"Because not everyone was ready to go," she sighed. "There were several key people out of the immediate area, and we didn't want to leave without them. We also knew that after the explosion the Ihmisits would come to investigate, and we thought having the whole group still there would alleviate any suspicions they might have about the explosion."

She shook her head. "We never expected the official reaction to be so intense."

"That's because the Patth were already involved," I said, nodding heavily. "Only there was no way you could know that. The Lumpies seem to be their hired muscle of choice."

"I guess so," she said. "Anyway, the Ihmisits descended on the dig like a pack of jackals, found Dr. Chou and the two alien bodies, and arrested everyone in sight. One of the techs managed to slip out of the noose long enough to get to town and warn Dad, but he was then picked up an hour later. They got Dad's pilot, too, and the rest of those who'd been off the dig site."

"Did the Ihmisits know your father was on Meima?" Ixil asked.

"Not at first," she said. "I'm sure that's what saved him. By the time they backtracked the pilot to his ship, he'd already hired all the crewers he needed. Luckily, the computer the group had been using for their analysis—the Worthram T-66 down there—was one of the few computer systems I actually knew how to operate, so he decided I would come aboard as the computer tech."

"Were you involved with the rest of the hiring?" I asked.

She shook her head. "He wanted me completely out of it. He still thought of me as his ace, and he didn't want to risk us even being seen in the same taverno together."

"Too bad," Ixil said. "It might have been useful to compare everyone's recruiting story with an independent source."

"I can't help you there," Tera said. "Anyway, after everything was set he went to ground somewhere for the night, and in the morning headed for the ship."

"How did he get in?" I asked. "I checked the time lock he'd set on the hatch, and it hadn't been opened."

"There's a secondary hatch on the top of the engine section," she said. "Just aft of the smaller sphere. He climbed up a collapsible ladder set into the starboard side and went in, taking the ladder in with him. It and the hatch both are hidden behind all that tangle of pipes and cables back there."

So that was what the twin lines of latch grooves I'd seen on the engineering hull were for: anchor points for the ladder. "And since the guidance tags he'd given out would bring all of us to the ship from the port side, he figured that even if one of us got there before he was all the way inside he'd still be all right."

"You being the single question mark," she said. "I spotted you waiting at the south gate, ready to go charging in as soon as they opened up. Dad was going in the west gate, but the south gate was slightly closer, and I was afraid you'd get there ahead of him."

"Hence, you called in an anonymous tip," I said sourly. "And pegged it to your father, knowing that that was something they'd take seriously enough to pull me in for."

"Basically," she said. "I gave it a few minutes, then called in the second tip to discredit the first and spring you."

"Brilliant," I said. "Really brilliant. I don't suppose it occurred to you that attaching my name to Cameron's right at the beginning meant they would now have two faces to circulate instead of just one? And me with no idea anyone was even looking for me?"

"I'm sorry," she said, dropping her eyes. "Again, all I can say is that I didn't know how involved the Patth were. If I had . . ."

She eyed me, some of her latent suspicion drifting up to the surface again. "Frankly, I don't know what I'd have done. I didn't know then if I could trust you. I still don't."

I thought about reprising our logical argument on that point, decided that if it hadn't worked the first time a second rendition was unlikely to make the difference. "We'll just have to work on that, I guess," I said instead, handing her gun back to her. "Still, it looks like the Patth were playing things a little too close to their chests, too. Port Director Aymi-Mastr, for one, was clearly out of the loop of what was really going on, or she'd never have let me go so easily."

"Or let the ship lift," Ixil added.

"Right," I said. "Okay; so much for background. Let's move on to the suspicious-activities list. I assume now that you were the one who turned on the grav generator during that first spacewalk and dumped Chort down the side of the ship. I'd told him to check the engine section for hull ridges, and you were afraid he'd spot that extra hatch."

"Yes," she said, another twinge of guilt crossing her face. "It's camouflaged, but up close it's pretty easy to spot."

"And Jones's death?"

"No," she said emphatically. "Neither Dad nor I had anything to do with that."

"So we can chalk that one up to our Mr. X," I said. "As we can, I presume, the anonymous smuggling tip to Najiki Customs?"

"That wasn't me, either," Tera said. "You think I would *want* to draw official attention to us in the middle of a Patth spaceport?"

"Just making sure," I said. "And we've already established that your father was the one playing with cutting torches and intercoms. And circuit breakers, I presume?"

"That one was me, actually," she said. "He'd gotten out of the 'tweenhull area and was warning me that he might have been spotted when the intercom went dead. I was up in my cabin, and on a hunch I checked the breaker box. When I couldn't get the one to reset, I guessed what you were up to. There wasn't enough time to fix the short circuit, so I just pulled all the breakers and hid them."

"It was clever," I conceded. "Annoying, but clever. I presume it was your computer-room intercom I'd gimmicked?"

She nodded. "The access panel we'd improvised in the wall wasn't quite square, and sometimes I had to bang it into place. That was what you heard the time you came charging in on me."

"I also heard it from sick bay once when I was talking to Shawn there," I remembered. "He'd heard it a few times, too. There's another job to pin on Mr. X, by the way: loosening Shawn's straps or whatever he did that let the kid get away."

"You think that was deliberate?" Tera asked, frowning.

"Of course it was," I said. "Our Mr. X couldn't very well poke around Ixil's room with his toolbox and junior poisoner's kit while the rest of you were still aboard—too much risk someone would catch him at it. But I'd told you all to stay put, so he had to come up with a good reason to get you outside."

Ixil cleared his throat delicately. "I'm afraid you both may be missing the more important point here," he said. "Bear in mind that while everyone was conveniently off the ship, Arno Cameron vanished. Not necessarily of his own volition."

I looked at Tera, saw her face pale. "But how could they have done it?" she breathed. "How could they have even known he was there?"

"The same way I figured it out, maybe," I said, the ominous implications of a Cameron kidnapping tumbling over each other like leaves in a brisk autumn wind. "Or else he heard one of those clunks and discovered you two talking together."

"Perhaps that was the true purpose for the customs inquiry, in fact," Ixil said. "To delay the moment when his disappearance would be discovered. And to ensure we left Potosi afterward as quickly as we could, so that by the time anyone *did* notice we'd be long gone from the scene."

"But why would they take all his things with him?" Tera persisted. Clearly, this wasn't a scenario she was at all willing to accept. "He had a full camping setup: food and water packs, a roll-up mattress, even one of those little catalytic waste handlers."

"Where did he get all that?" I asked.

"I bought most of it for him during our stopover on Xathru," she said. "He'd planned to come out after the first stop, but after Jones's death we decided he should stay hidden a while longer."

"Ah," I said, remembering now all the bags she'd brought aboard at Xathru, and how annoyed she'd been that I'd cut her shopping spree short.

"But why would anyone bother to take all of it along?" she asked again.

"Perhaps they wanted to eliminate any evidence that he was ever here," Ixil said. "Their contact would have told them that your father had kept his presence aboard a secret. At this point it would be basically your word against theirs."

"If it ever even came to that," I added. "They may have something else planned for you down the line."

She tried glaring at me again, but her heart wasn't in it. "You're a real comfort to have around, McKell," she growled. "Both of you."

"Yes, well, we haven't exactly gotten what we signed up for, either," I countered. "What *I* want to know is why this ship is still flying. We've been half a grab away from them at least twice now. Why haven't they simply picked us up?"

She sighed. "I don't know."

"Perhaps it would help," Ixil suggested, "if we knew what exactly this mysterious cargo is."

For a long minute Tera remained silent, her eyes flicking between our faces, clearly trying to decide just how far she was willing to trust us. Or perhaps just trying to come up with a convincing lie. "All right," she said at last. "The *Icarus* isn't carrying any cargo. The *Icarus is* the cargo."

She waved a hand around her. "This is what the

team uncovered on Meima: two spheres, connected together, the larger one empty except for its radial gravity generator, the smaller one crammed with alien electronics."

"How alien?" Ixil asked.

"Very alien," she said grimly. "It was like nothing they'd ever seen before, with markings and notations that were also totally unknown. We still don't know whether it predates the Spiral civilizations, or is simply from outside known territory. That's why that old Worthram T-66 is aboard—it was the one the archaeologists already had hooked up to study the small sphere, and when they built the *Icarus* they just basically assembled the computer room around it."

"So that's where the spare gravity inside the outer hull came from," I said. "I'd been planning to ask you how and why you'd set that up."

"We had nothing to do with it," Tera said. "And we have no idea what it's for. All we know is that it runs about eighty-five percent Earth standard, and is completely self-adjusting, which is why it isn't fazed by the *Icarus*'s own gravity generator."

She smiled wanly. "I understand it worked the same way on Meima. Even while it was sitting there in a full planetary gravitational field, you could still walk all the way around inside the sphere without falling off."

"Must have been quite an experience," I murmured.

"Half of them loved it; the other half couldn't stand it," she said. "Anyway, that's why they built the inner hull so far away from the outer one—all the metal seems to inhibit the sphere's gravity field somehow, but if you put the two hulls any closer together you get a terrible disorientation at the edges where the two grav fields intersect."

"And *that's* what the Patth are all hot and bothered over?" I asked. "The chance to get their hands on a new-style grav generator? Hardly seems worth committing murder for."

She shook her head. "I'm not sure the Patth even know about the grav generator," she said; and there was something in her voice that sent a shiver up my back. "I said the team couldn't decipher the markings on anything in the two spheres. But the grav generator wasn't the only thing still working. A lot of the electronics in the small sphere were on what appeared to be some kind of standby, and they were able to take a lot of readings. Waveform analyses, pattern operations—that sort of thing."

She took a deep breath. "They're not sure," she said quietly. "There's a lot they still don't understand. Most of it, actually. But from what they could decipher of the patterns and power levels and even the geometric shapes of some of the components . . . well, they think this whole thing could be a stardrive."

I looked at Ixil. "What kind of stardrive?" I asked carefully.

"A fast one," she said. "A very fast one. From the readings, they think it could be as much as twenty times faster than the Patth Talariac."

"And *that*," Ixil said softly, "*is* worth committing murder over."

CHAPTER

13

We left Tera to get back to her sleep, or at least what sleep she would be able to manage after that immensely cheering conversation, and reconvened our private council of war on the *Icarus*'s bridge. Shawn, who'd been on duty, had voiced no objection at all to being relieved, heading off toward his cabin and bunk with a sort of dragging step that suggested he still wasn't fully recovered from his recent bout with Cole's disease. Or from straight borandis addiction, as the case might be.

But while the bridge provided all the privacy we could want, or at least all we were likely to get on the *Icarus*, it didn't offer anything in the way of either inspiration or answers.

"Hard though this may be to believe," I commented to Ixil as I watched his ferrets climb nose first down his legs and scamper off to their corridor and bulkhead sentry duties, "I think this whole thing is more confused now than it was before we talked to Tera."

"I don't see how," Ixil said. "Instead of having a

mysterious murderer/saboteur aboard the *Icarus,* we now only have a mysterious murderer."

"Oh, *that's* a great help," I said sarcastically.

"And we've also eliminated Tera as a suspect," he continued, ignoring the sarcasm. "Which leaves us only Chort, Nicabar, Shawn, and Everett. That should count for something."

"Only if everything she told us was true," I cautioned him. "Don't forget that photo Uncle Arthur sent was not exactly definitive. She could simply be a very accomplished liar with a gift for improvisation."

"Really," he said, his polite voice edging as close to sarcasm as Kalixiri ever got. "And does the large sphere's gravitational field come under the liar talent or the improvisational talent?"

"Fine, then," I growled, giving up. "Tera's as pure as the driven snow. Just bear in mind that even if she is who she says she is, her goals here may not coincide completely with ours."

"Granted," he said. "So where does the extra confusion come in?"

"It comes in the same place Cameron went out," I said. "With all due respect, I don't think much of your kidnapping theory. If they knew enough to get in here and snatch him, why didn't they grab the *Icarus* while they were at it?"

"Maybe they don't know its actual significance," Ixil said. "Maybe they still think the prize is in the cargo hold and didn't think they had time to get to it right then."

"Then why let us leave the planet?" I countered. "Anyway, they *have* to have at least an idea of what it is they're chasing. You don't offer hundred-grand finder's fees completely on speculation."

"That doesn't necessarily follow," he said. "Maybe all they know is that the *Icarus* is carrying something Cameron desperately wants to get to Earth, which they want to take a look at simply on general principles.

Perhaps that was what the anonymous gem-smuggling tip was all about, to give them an excuse to get into the cargo hold."

I ran that one a couple of times around in my mind. It was not, I decided, as ridiculous as it seemed at first blush. "If so, they've got terrible coordination problems," I pointed out. "The Najik let us go without even blinking an eye."

"So did Director Aymi-Mastr on Meima," Ixil said. "I don't think the Patth have quite made up their minds just how public they're willing to make their involvement with this."

"It's certainly public enough at the top levels," I reminded him darkly. "Half the governments in this region have already been threatened with sanctions if they don't find and deliver us."

"True, but that's not the same thing as working directly with local administrators and customs agents," he pointed out. "Top-level governmental officials can usually be trusted not to leak that kind of information, especially when it's something that might cause economic panic among their people."

I scowled at my displays. "So where does that leave us?"

He shrugged. "At least we're not as much in the dark as most of the people looking for us," he said. "Whatever the Patth themselves know or don't know, they most certainly haven't given the details to any of their searchers. If they knew what we were actually sitting on here, there wouldn't be a government in the Spiral who would give us up to them."

"I suppose I should be grateful for small favors," I said, trying to think of how exactly all this knowledge gave us an advantage. Offhand, I couldn't see any. "And that brings up another point. We might want to consider making ourselves a list of governments we'd be willing to surrender the *Icarus* to as a last resort, just to keep the Patth from getting it."

"We could," he said doubtfully. "The problem is finding someone who'd be less of a threat than the Patth themselves."

I cocked an eyebrow. "You *are* joking."

"Not at all," he said, his face deadly serious. "As far as we know, the Patth have no real military other than their own defense forces."

"No, they subcontract the muscle jobs out to the Lumpies," I said sourly.

"Perhaps," Ixil said. "My point is that the Patth would use the *Icarus* stardrive to cement their stranglehold on civilian shipping. Someone else might instead put it to military uses."

I chewed a corner of my lip. A faster stardrive certainly wouldn't help in space-normal combat, and of course there was no combat possible in hyperspace. It would make it easier to ferry troops, matériel, and warships around, but that wouldn't be that much of an advantage in the small brushfire conflicts that still flared up now and then. Unless we got into another of the huge regional wars that we all hoped were safely in the Spiral's past, the *Icarus* stardrive wouldn't gain an aggressor very much.

But then, maybe something like the *Icarus* stardrive was just the edge a potential aggressor was waiting for. Not a particularly pleasant thought.

"We still ought to make ourselves a surrender list," I said, getting up from the command chair and crossing to the plotting table. "Maybe try for a consortium of governments, just so no one's got a strict monopoly."

"Particularly a consortium that would allow the ship's crew to live," Ixil said. "Preferably in something less confining than a small lonely cell somewhere."

"That one's at the top of my wish list, too," I assured him, keying the table on.

"It's always nice to have a common goal. Where exactly are we headed at the moment?"

"I don't know," I said, peering at the possibilities as

they came up. "We're currently heading for Utheno, on the grounds that having a legitimate exit record from Potosi would make it easier to get in and out of another Najiki Archipelago world."

"Utheno is only, what, seventy-five hours away?"

"Seventy-three," I said. "And since that's only about half the *Icarus*'s range, I also thought a stop there might throw off anyone who might be tracking our movements."

I waved at the table. "But now I'm starting to wonder if it would be better to not get within any single government's grasp more than once."

"Perhaps," Ixil said slowly. "Still, at this point, I'm not sure it really matters. The Patth have surely alerted everyone along our vector, and whether or not we've crossed paths with any particular government agency is probably more or less irrelevant."

"Do you think we should get off this vector, then?" I suggested. "Veer off to the side, circle around, and try to sneak up on Earth from behind?"

"No." He was definite. "The Patth aren't going to be fooled that easily—they'll have the word out anywhere the *Icarus* can get to. All that would do is increase the number of fueling stops we would have to make, which is where we're most vulnerable, and give the Patth more time to learn what exactly the *Icarus* looks like."

"And if they really do have Cameron, to get a complete crew list, too," I agreed glumly. "All right; Utheno it is."

"Utheno it is," Ixil agreed, snapping his fingers to recall his ferrets. "I'm going back to my cabin to get some sleep," he continued as they bounded up his legs and clawed their way to his shoulders. "I'd like to finish healing before we hit Utheno."

"Watch yourself," I warned. "Our murderer may not content himself with leaving his next batch of poison gas unmixed."

"I'll have Pix and Pax on alert," he assured me. "And there are a couple of door-guard tricks I know. You just watch yourself."

"What, me?" I said, snorting. "The only one we know can fly this monster? I'm the safest person aboard."

"Let's hope our murderer remembers that," Ixil said pointedly, standing up and heading for the door. "And doesn't have too inflated an opinion of his own piloting skills. I'll talk to you later."

He left, leaving the door locked open behind him. I confirmed the vector and timing to Utheno, then shut down the plotting table and returned to my command chair. And tried to think.

Our talk with Tera had been good. It had been enlightening and, assuming always that everything she had told us was true, very useful as well.

The problem was that it had also swept away the whole fragile toothpick-house I'd worked so painstakingly to put together since Jones's murder. Before, I'd had a puzzle where the pieces didn't seem to fit together. Now, suddenly, not only had she swept away the pieces, she'd swept away the damn puzzle, too. The attacks on Jones and Chort, the sabotage to the cutting torch, the anonymous tips to the various customs and port authorities—every time lightning had struck I had carefully added the details to the rest of the mix, making sure to include the locations of all the possible suspects during that time. And while I didn't kid myself that I'd sorted it out into a neat package, at least I'd been getting a handle on it all.

Now, suddenly, everything had changed. Half the sabotage had been done by Tera and her father, a character I hadn't even known was on this particular stage of our little drama, and for reasons far less malevolent than their results would have suggested. And with that confession, my careful checklist of who had been where when went straight out the airlock. In fact, about all I

THE ICARUS HUNT 269

had left to explain was the gem-smuggling tip to the Najik on Potosi and the poison-gas components and smashed release pad on Ixil's room.

And, of course, Jones's murder.

And the damnable part of it was that those were precisely the incidents that no one had any possible alibi for. Anyone aboard could have sabotaged Jones's rebreather prior to his accompanying Chort on his spacewalk; and everyone was out on their own during the time Ixil's room was tampered with.

Everyone. Including Tera.

Because Ixil's opinions to the contrary, I still hadn't eliminated her as a suspect. Far from it. The photo Uncle Arthur had sent wasn't nearly definitive enough for me to accept her claimed identity, and it was for sure that if the real Elaina Tera Cameron was running around the Spiral somewhere else we'd never hear about it here on the *Icarus*. True, she'd known about the hull's alien grav generator; but if she was actually one of the archaeologists or techs, she would have also known about that. Uncle Arthur had said the Ihmisits had rounded up the whole group, but without knowing his source for that information I was forced to consider it incomplete if not downright suspect. As to the rest of her story, I hadn't actually seen Cameron aboard the *Icarus*, and I sure couldn't confirm that he was the one I'd chased leisurely around the 'tweenhull area.

And I couldn't help noticing the interesting timing of the Patth infiltrating the Meima dig with a couple of Lumpies just when the *Icarus* was ready to fly. It could be coincidence, or something in their own external intelligence had caught the roving Patth eye; but it could also be that they'd had an agent inside the dig itself. We had only Tera's word that she wasn't that agent.

But then, we had only everyone else's word for who they were, too. Tera had said Cameron had kept her presence on Meima close to the vest. Maybe he'd done the same with someone else as well, shielding this agent's presence even from his own daughter. It was the sort of double-blind stunt a man like Cameron might well have pulled; as Tera herself had said, you couldn't tell what you didn't know. Perhaps it was that second string to Cameron's bow who had been suborned by the Patth, or had simply decided he was tired of a tech's salary and that this was his big chance to retire in comfort.

And if that was true, it might finally explain why we were still free. Either our traitor hadn't turned us in to the Patth yet because he was waiting for the price to go up, or else because he suspected another of Cameron's people was aboard and didn't want to show his hand until he'd figured out who it was.

So why was Jones murdered?

Had he known something damaging to the murderer? Or, conversely, had the murderer been afraid he might learn something that he, the murderer, couldn't afford for anyone else to know? It had to be something that a ship's mechanic might learn through his normal duties, or else the follow-up attack on Ixil didn't make any sense.

Unless the poison-gas threat had been just a smoke screen. Maybe all Mr. X had wanted to do was get rid of Jones, and had pulled the cyanide threat on Ixil to make it look like he had a grudge against anyone who tried to fill the mechanic post on the *Icarus*. After all, Ixil hadn't even come close to dying on that one.

I scowled some more at my displays. This was getting me nowhere except dizzy. What could a perfect stranger like Jones—a perfect stranger to the rest of the *Icarus*'s crew, anyway—possibly know that would be worth killing him over? Perhaps the fact that, despite his claims about his mechanical skills, Nicabar didn't actually know one end of a wrench from another? But why would even an egregious bending of the truth be worth murder? Besides, Uncle Arthur's profile on Nicabar had shown that he did have those skills. Was it something about Chort, then? Or Everett, or Shawn?

A rumbling in my stomach intruded on my thoughts, an audible reminder that it had been a long time since my last meal. Giving the displays one last check, I got up and headed back to the dayroom just aft of the bridge. The ship could look after itself long enough for me to put together a quick sandwich, and maybe a liter or two of coffee would help me think. Though from the evidence to date, I doubted it.

I had assembled a sandwich from the rather unimaginative selection of ship's stores, and was pouring coffee into a spill-proof mug, when I caught the sound of a light footstep outside the door. I turned, and to my complete lack of surprise found Chort framed in the doorway. "Excuse me, Captain McKell," he said in his whistly voice. "I did not mean to intrude."

"No intrusion at all," I assured him, waving him in. "The dayroom's common property, you know. Come in, come in."

"Thank you," he said, moving somewhat hesitantly into the room. "I know that the dayroom is usually a common area. But here it does not seem to be so."

"The *Icarus* is an unusual ship," I reminded him, picking up my plate and mug and settling down at the table. So far on this trip I hadn't really had the chance to talk with Chort, and this seemed the ideal opportunity to do so. "And we're flying under very unusual conditions," I added. "Our crew doesn't have the usual cohesion of people who've traveled a lot together." I eyed him speculatively. "Though maybe that doesn't mean all that much to you. You haven't been at this sort of thing very long, have you?"

His feathery scales fluttered slightly. "Is it so very obvious?"

I shrugged. "Maybe a little," I said. "I wouldn't worry about it, though. You're a Craea; and somehow you people have space travel in your blood."

"Perhaps." His beak clicked softly twice, the first time I'd heard him make that sound. "Or perhaps that is merely a myth."

"If it is, there are an awful lot of people who've swallowed it," I told him, taking a bite of my sandwich. "There's a terrific demand out there for Craean spacewalkers."

"Perhaps the demand is justifiable," he said, eyeing me closely. "But perhaps it is not. Tell me, what did Ship Master Borodin tell you about this mission?"

"What do you mean?" I asked, frowning. *Mission,* he'd said. Not *trip* or *voyage. Mission.* "I was hired to fly the *Icarus* from Meima to Earth. Why, did he tell you something else?"

"Not something else, exactly," he said, those pure white eyes still studying me with a discomfiting intensity. "But he said there was something more involved here."

He stopped. "Go on," I encouraged him, taking another bite of sandwich so as not to look too eager.

He gave it another couple of heartbeats before he finally went on. "Twelve others were trying to hire me at the Craean employment site on Meima," he said. "Ship Master Borodin drew me aside and told me that while he could not pay as much as the others were offering, he could instead offer me a chance to do something for my people that would never be forgotten."

"Really," I said, fighting to keep my voice casual as I took another bite to hide the sudden shiver running through me. Idiot that I was, not until that moment had Tera's revelation of the *Icarus*'s true nature made even the slightest connection in my mind with the data Uncle Arthur had sent regarding the boom the Craean economy had been enjoying since the Talariac had hit the space lanes. "What else did he say?"

Faced with a nonhuman audience, I'd apparently

overplayed my casual act. "You don't believe me," Chort said, starting for the door. "I'm sorry to have bothered you."

"No, no—please," I said, gathering my feet beneath me, ready to jump out of my chair if I needed to in order to stop him. Suddenly there were a whole new raft of possibilities opening up here, possibilities I very much wanted to explore. "I didn't mean it that way. Of course I believe you. Did he say anything more?"

He stood there another moment, then slowly retraced his steps. "You do not understand," he said. "You humans. You greatly dislike the Patth—I hear you talking. But you do not understand."

"Help me understand, then," I invited, gesturing at the seat across the table from me. "Why shouldn't we dislike the Patth?"

He hesitated again, then slowly sat down in the indicated seat. "You spoke of space travel being in Craean blood," he said. "Perhaps in some ways it is. We love free fall, and thrive in space habitats. We have five in our home system; did you know that?"

I nodded. "I hear they're beautiful inside. I wish your government allowed non-Crooea to visit them."

"They are indeed beautiful," he said, the white eyes unfocusing oddly. "And it is in such places, or on our homeworld itself, that most Crooea would prefer to live if that was possible."

His eyes came back to focus on my face. "But such is not the case. We have nothing in the fields of science or technology that can compete with the products of Earth or Basni or J'kayrr. Yet we must continue to create wealth if we are to have the benefits of that technology, or if we are to build more space habitats for our people."

"You have your food exports," I reminded him. "I understand they're very much sought after."

"But they can travel only a limited distance before

spoiling," he said. "In the face of such a dilemma, what can the Crooea do?"

I sighed. I saw where he was headed now, all right. "They hire themselves out across the Spiral, of course," I said. "Tell me, how much of your pay goes directly to the Craean government?"

His beak snapped hard. "Seven-tenths," he said.

A seventy percent tax bracket. Indentured servitude, with the twist that the servitude was to their own government and people. "I've never heard anything about this before," I said. "Why have you kept it such a secret?"

His feathers fluffed briefly. "Why would we tell it?" he countered. "It is not something we are proud of. To sell ourselves into service to aliens is not a pleasant thing."

"Though it's really no different from what the rest of us do," I pointed out. "None of us are selling ourselves, exactly, just hiring our services and our expertise out to others. It's what's called a job."

"It was never the Craean way," he said firmly. "But it is our way now."

He cocked his head to one side, a quick gesture that was very birdlike. "But even now that way may be changing. The Patth merchants have given us the chance to sell our foodstuffs in more markets than ever before. In only a few short decades, perhaps we will have the resources necessary for the habitats we yet wish to build. When that happens, we will once again be able to withdraw back to our homes, and our families, and our kind."

I shook my head. "We'll miss you," I said. I meant it, too, even as I winced at how utterly banal the words sounded. "Why are you telling me this?"

He laid his delicate hands on the table, rubbing the fingertips gently together. "Once, it was thought that only our future freedom depended on the Patth and

THE ICARUS HUNT   275

their stardrive," he said, dropping his gaze to his hands. "But now, many fear that our very lives are solidly in their hands. In the cycles since Talariac began service, more and more of our resources have been devoted to the growing of foodstuffs for export. If the Patth should suddenly refuse to carry them, our economy could collapse in a single sunrise."

I felt a hard knot form in the center of my stomach. I had warned Ixil that the Crooea might be susceptible to Patth pressure; but I hadn't realized just how big the economic stick the Patth were threatening them with was. "I think I understand the situation," I said. "What is it you want from me?"

He seemed to draw himself up. "I want you to not aggravate the Patth."

I suppressed a grimace. Lord knew the last thing I wanted to do was upset the Patth; the Patth *or* their lumpy friends with the handheld crematoria. Unfortunately, as far as that crowd was concerned, even my continued breathing probably constituted aggravation at this point. "What makes you think I would want to do something like that?" I hedged.

"You dislike the Patth," he said again. "And it is the Patth who are seeking you and this ship."

The hard knot in the center of my stomach tightened a couple more turns. "Who told you that?"

His feathers fluttered. "No one told me. The beings whom the young human female pointed out to us at the Baker's Dozen taverno were members of a Patth client race."

"How do you know?"

"It is common knowledge among the Crooea," he said, sounding surprised that I even needed to ask. "All Patth merchant starships carry Craean spacewalkers. The Iykams also always travel with them as guardians and protectors. Unlike the Patth, they are crude and not very polite."

"As well as sometimes violent," I added, nodding.

At least the Lumpy Clan had a name now. Uncle Arthur would be pleased about that. "Still, just because the Iykams are mad at me doesn't mean the Patth themselves are involved."

The feathers fluttered again, this time fluffing out from his body. "Do not lie to me, Captain," he said quietly. "The Iykams do not act without Patth permission. They do not move through these areas of space without Patth presence and guidance."

"I'm not lying to you, Chort," I assured him quickly, a creepy feeling running through me. If he was right, that meant the two Iykams I'd killed on Xathru must have had a Patth overseer somewhere in the vicinity. A Patth who had just missed capturing the *Icarus* right off the blocks.

And running the logic in reverse, it also implied that the three Patth Cameron and I had seen in that Meima taverno had probably had a couple of Iykams lurking in the shadows somewhere. Something to remember if I ever spotted another Patth out in the open.

"Perhaps it was not a direct lie," Chort said. "But you are nonetheless attempting to distract me, to lure me away from the truth." He cocked his head again. "What is the truth, Captain?"

"You're right, Chort," I said with a sigh, gazing hard at his face and wishing like hell I knew how to decipher that alien expression. "The Patth do indeed want this ship. They think something aboard could be a threat to the economic empire they've carved out over the past fifteen years."

"Is that true?"

I shook my head. "I don't know. It's possible."

For a long minute he sat rigidly, his head bowed toward the table, his fingertips pressed tightly together. That one I knew: a Craean posture of deep thought. I stayed as motionless as he was, afraid that any movement on my part might break the spell, letting the silence stretch out and wishing even harder I could read Craean expressions. Nicabar had threatened to jump ship if he learned we were carrying contraband. Would Chort make the same threat—or worse, actually carry it out—now that he knew we were in serious danger of bringing Patth anger down on the Crooea?

With a suddenness that startled me, Chort looked back up at me. "This threat to the Patth," he said. "Could it be of benefit to the Crooea?"

"If it actually is the threat the Patth think it is—and that's the part I'm not sure of—then the answer is yes."

"*Would* it be of benefit to the Crooea?"

I hesitated. "I don't know," I had to admit. "If it were up to me, you would certainly be one of those to benefit, given your help on this trip. But I can't even begin to make a promise like that."

"Ship Master Borodin implied that would be the case," he reminded me. "Is he not trustworthy?"

"Oh, he's trustworthy enough," I assured him. "But we don't know where he is right now, and the decision may be taken out of his hands. Especially if someone else gets hold of the *Icarus* before we can deliver it to Earth."

He seemed to consider that. "And if we are able to deliver it to Earth?"

"Again, I can't make any promises," I said, feeling sweat breaking out on my forehead. With the perceived future of his entire race hanging in the balance, Chort was clearly figuring the odds and weighing his options.

Unfortunately, there were only three options I could see for him to choose from: jump ship, help us fly the *Icarus* to Earth, or betray us to the Patth the first chance he got in the hopes of buying economic security for his people. Only short-term security, of course—in the long run the Patth were no more grateful than any other species. But balanced against their demonstrated ability for long-term animosity, even a short-term gain was probably the most logical way to go. In Chort's place, it was probably the way I would take.

And if he did . . .

I was suddenly and uncomfortably aware of the weight of my plasmic against my rib cage. We couldn't afford to have Chort jump ship. Period. Whether he planned to turn us in or simply hoped to vanish into the sunset before the Patth found us, we couldn't have him running loose with what he knew about the *Icarus* and its crew. We would have to keep him aboard, locked up or tied up if necessary, until this macabre little hide-and-seek game was over.

Abruptly, Chort turned his head toward the back of the dayroom and the hull that lay beyond it. "There is another hull ridge forming," he said. "You had best stop the ship."

I hadn't heard or felt anything, but I didn't doubt his judgment. I was on my feet even before he finished talking, and was out the dayroom door and halfway to the bridge before it even occurred to me that I hadn't doubted his judgment. I was on the bridge and reaching for the red KILL button when the characteristic screech echoed in from the hull.

It was only much later, after the ridge had been repaired and we were on our way again, that I realized he hadn't come back to finish our conversation.

Or, rather, we *had* finished the conversation, and I simply hadn't known it. Just as I didn't know now which way he had decided to jump on the three choices set out in front of him.

For a while I thought about calling him on the intercom, or even confronting him about it in his cabin. But on further reflection I decided against doing either. I still couldn't offer him any of the assurances he obviously wanted, and without any such promise there was nothing more I could say to induce him to stick with the *Icarus*. Pressing him further would accomplish nothing except to make both of us feel uncomfortable at the effort.

Anyway, we were less than three days out from Utheno. Sometime within the first hour after landfall, it would be easy enough to figure out which way he'd jumped.

CHAPTER

14

I didn't find out within the first hour after landfall on
Utheno. I didn't find out for the simple reason that we
never made landfall on Utheno. Though I didn't know
it then, it was going to be a long time before we made
landfall anywhere.

My first hint of trouble should have been the cacophony of radio transmissions that lit up the offi-
cial-frequencies section of my comm board as the
hyperspace cutter array sliced the *Icarus* back into
space-normal. I couldn't read any of it through the
encryption, of course, but the sheer volume of mes-
sages should have told me something big was happening.

At the same time the comm board was lighting up
with chatter, the visual displays were also listing out a
horrendous tangle of ship traffic wrapped around the
planet in a hundred different holding orbits. A recorded message on the main inbound-information
channel apologized for the delay, cited a pair of colli-
sions and a ground-station sensor failure as the cause

of the backup, and promised to speed things up as quickly as possible.

And in an uncharacteristic burst of credulity, I believed them. Given that official confusion was made to order for us, I keyed in the orbit slot I was given and headed in.

"Crowded," of course, was a relative term when applied to planetary holding orbits. Our designated slot was a good fifty kilometers from anything else, with the only two ships at even that distance being a Najiki freighter fifty kilometers to port and a bulky Tleka cargo hauler the same distance to starboard. More from habit than anything else, I keyed for mid-range magnification and had a good look at both ships.

And it was as I was looking at the Tleka cargo hauler that the warning bells belatedly started going off in the back of my head.

I keyed the intercom for the engine room. "Revs, what's status on the stardrive?"

"Down and green," he said. "Why?"

"Get it up and green," I told him shortly. "Fast."

There was just the barest hesitation. "Startup procedure begun," he said. "What's the trouble?"

"We're being directed into a slot fifty klicks from a Tleka cargo hauler," I told him, still studying that display. "I can't be certain, but it looks to me like there's something lurking around the side of the hauler where I can't see it."

"As in a Najiki Customs cruiser?"

"Or something even bigger," I agreed tightly.

"So why head in at all?" he asked. "Turn around and get us out of here."

"And let them know we know they're there?" I countered. "*And* that we've got guilty consciences to boot?"

"You're right," he conceded reluctantly. "So we act innocent?"

"As the driven snow," I said. "At least until you've

got the stardrive up and running. Let's just hope they can't pull any of the telltales with their own sensor readings."

"These thrusters are pretty noisy, and across a big chunk of the spectrum," he pointed out. "That ought to mask the stardrive, at least at a fifty-klick distance. Okay; I read thirteen more minutes to full green. I'll see if I can shave a couple of minutes off that."

"Good. Do it."

I took my time bringing us in the rest of the way, managing to eat up nearly five of Nicabar's thirteen minutes before we finally settled into our designated slot. I kept two of my displays trained on our companions to either side, wondering which of them would make the first move.

The Najiki freighter took that honor. Even as I ran thrust to the forward maneuvering vents to kill some of our momentum, I saw a large side hatch slide open, and three dark gray starfighters appeared. They paused a moment as if getting their bearings, then grouped into formation and headed straight for us.

I keyed the intercom for all-ship. "This is McKell," I announced. "Everyone get strapped down and find something to hang on to. We've got unfriendly company. Revs?"

"Still at least six minutes to go," he reported. "Probably closer to seven. How long till they get here?"

"Depends on how much of a hurry they're in," I told him, watching the fighters closely, hoping even now that it was a false alarm, that they were actually interested in someone else entirely. But they were still coming, and showed no sign that they might suddenly veer off somewhere else. "Keep those thrusters running hot—they get even a hint that we're firing up the stardrive and they'll be all over us."

The words were barely out of my mouth when the Najik made it official. "Freighter *Icarus,* this is Utheno Military Command," a calm Najiki voice came over the comm speaker. "You are ordered to shut down your thrusters and prepare to be boarded."

"The thruster noise must be hurting their ears," Nicabar said mildly. "What now?"

"We ignore them," I told him. "That came in broadcast, not narrow beam, and our ID says we're the *Stewed Brunswick*. It may be they're still not sure about us and are trying to spark a guilty reaction. Anyway, we don't dare shut down the thrusters now."

"You're going to risk drawing fire," he warned.

"Not yet," I said, shifting my attention from the incoming starfighters back to the Tleka cargo hauler. It was a classic, time-tested maneuver: a group of grassbeaters in front noisily and ostentatiously driving the quarry back into the waiting arms of the hunter lurking silently in the bushes. In the bushes, or behind a Tleka cargo hauler, as the case might be.

Except that in this case the hunter was no longer hiding. He was there in full view, his port-side weapons array just coming up around the cargo hauler's dorsal spine: a Najiki pocket destroyer, its zebra-camo striping giving it an almost-delicate look. As warships went, I suppose, it wasn't much to brag about; from where we currently stood, it looked about the size of Paris.

"Watch for them to target ion beams," Ixil's voice warned from behind me.

"Thank you," I said, trying not to sound too sarcastic as I threw a quick glance over my shoulder. He was striding in through the doorway, gazing at my displays, his expression as glacially stolid as ever. The ferrets dug in on his shoulders were betraying all that surface calm, though, twitching to beat the band. "You have anything else in the way of insightful advice to offer?" I added.

"I meant as opposed to lasers or disabler missiles," he said, stepping to the plotting table. "If they're acting on their own against suspected smugglers they won't be as careful to minimize damage as they will if they're doing this at the behest of the Patth."

I was about to inform him that they'd already identified us as the *Icarus* when they helpfully made the point for me. "Freighter *Icarus,* this is your final warning," the Najiki voice announced firmly. "Shut down your thrusters or we will open fire."

And that one, unfortunately, *had* come in tight beam, for our ears and no one else's. Which meant they knew who we were, and all hopeful thoughts of fishing expeditions were gone.

As was anything to be gained by playing innocent. "Hang on," I warned Ixil, bracing myself and throwing power to the thrusters, keying the exhaust to the forward maneuvering vents. Our forward speed dropped precipitously; and with it went our orbital stability. Even as we dropped back behind the incoming fighters, we also began to fall toward the planetary surface five thousand kilometers beneath us.

Unfortunately, "precipitously" was also a sadly relative term. With a fighter or even the enhanced thrust/mass ratio I'd built into the *Stormy Banks,* such a maneuver might have caught our opponents at least partly by surprise. But with the flying cement bag that was the *Icarus,* we didn't behave so much like a leaping jaguar as we did a hippo jumping backward from a dead stop in deep mud. I could picture the Najik in the fighters and destroyer watching our elephantine escape attempt and laughing themselves silly.

They could laugh all they liked. Their logical assumption—at least, what I hoped was their logical assumption—would be that we hadn't started activating our stardrive until they'd sprung their trap, from which assumption they would further assume they still had ten to twelve minutes in which to short-circuit that activation and gather us serenely into the hunter's waiting arms. What they hopefully hadn't tumbled to yet was that we were in fact less than four minutes from escape. All I had to do was keep them off us for those four minutes, and we would be home free.

All in all, though, that was a very big *if*. Especially since the Najik in charge of this operation was apparently not the type to dawdle simply because he had a little time to kill. The starfighters were swinging to match my maneuver even before I'd completed it; and as they closed up ranks again faint green lines erupted from the ion-beam ports beneath their noses and tracked toward us.

I threw power to the *Icarus*'s port-side vents, giving us a sideways yaw, hoping to keep the hyperspace cutter array at our bow out of the ion beams. But we turned every bit as ponderously as we braked; and even as I swore helplessly under my breath the beams converged on the cutter array.

And that was that. Clenching my left hand into a fist, I continued the useless maneuvering, waiting for the buildup of localized charge and the subsequent crack of a high-voltage spark that would scramble the array's electronics and make all of Nicabar's minute-shaving so much wasted effort.

The beams momentarily drifted off target as I dropped us farther into Utheno's gravity well, converged again as the Najiki gunners reestablished their aim. Any minute now and the spark would come; and after this much charge buildup it was likely to be a memorable one. Distantly, I wondered if it might even be strong enough to jump some of the current across the fail-safes and fry my bridge controls in the bargain.

And then I frowned, a brand-new set of warning bells going off in the back of my head. There was something wrong here, something ominously wrong. I knew how ion beams worked—I'd been on the receiving end of them more times than I cared to remember—and these were taking *way* too long to show their teeth. I keyed the hull-monitor cameras toward the bow and focused in on the cutter array.

And felt the breath catch in my throat. The ion beams were converging on the *Icarus*, all right, just as the sensor display showed. But in the last meter or so before they reached the array, something completely unexpected was happening. Instead of maintaining their nice clean collimation, the beams were defocusing madly, the ions scattering wildly to hell and gone. Which meant that instead of building up the sort of localized charge that would create a devastating spark, all they were doing was dumping ions into the hull plates, where the charge could cheerfully build up without doing much of anything at all.

"It's the hull," Ixil said suddenly, his voice sounding as awestruck as I felt. "The radial gravitational field in the hull."

And then, of course, it all clicked into place. Chort's spacewalks had shown that the alien gravitational field inside the main hull was too weak to be felt outside the ship, but apparently the effect was strong enough to disrupt a beam of subatomic particles. Either that, or it was something else in the field generator that was flummoxing them.

And suddenly we had a chance again. Lunging to my control board, I keyed for more yaw. "McKell?" Nicabar called over the intercom. "What are you doing?"

"The fighters' ion beams aren't catching the cutter array," I called back, shifting my attention over to the destroyer. It was no longer waiting patiently for us to be driven into its arms, but was burning space in our direction, its own ion beam blazing away even though it was still well out of range. "I suspect the destroyer's beam won't affect it, either; but it almost certainly *will* be able to punch through the engineering hull and scramble your systems back there. So I'm turning the *Icarus* to put the main hull between you and them."

"Which will then leave the engine section open to the fighters," Ixil murmured from the plotting table. "And they're closer than the destroyer."

"But their beams are also weaker than the destroyer's," I reminded him. "There's an even chance the heavier metal back there will protect us from them. Anyway, we don't have a lot of choices right now. Revs, where's the countdown?"

"One minute twenty," he said. "At the rate that destroyer's closing, it's going to be close."

"Yes," I murmured, slowing our spin as the *Icarus*'s aft end turned to the incoming fighters, feeling sweat breaking out on my forehead. The fighters probably didn't have the kind of sensor magnification that would let them see just how peculiarly their ion beams were behaving. The destroyer, unfortunately, just as probably did. Sooner or later, the commander would get around to taking a close look at our cutter array and realize that it wasn't just poor aim on his gunners' part that was saving us. If he did, or even if he didn't, at some point he would open up with heavier weaponry rather than risk letting us get away.

Unless someone gave him a reason why that might be a bad idea.

I keyed to the frequency the Najiki orders had come in on. "Najiki Task Force, this is the *Icarus*," I announced. "I'd be careful with those ion beams if I were you. We have a lot of sensitive electronics aboard, and I'll make you a small wager the Patth will be extremely unhappy if you damage any of them."

"Freighter *Icarus*, this is Utheno Military Command," the Najiki voice came back. It didn't sound nearly so calm now as it had earlier. "This is your final warning. You will shut down your thrusters or we will shut them down for you."

"Of course, I'm sure it's occurred to you that anything the Patth are this anxious to get hold of will be equally valuable to anyone else who possesses it," I went on as if he hadn't spoken. "The Najiki Archipelago, for instance. Your superiors might want to think long and hard about that before you just turn us over to them."

"Freighter *Icarus,* you will shut down your thrusters," the voice came back. A being with a one-track mind, obviously, and not one to be drawn into a discussion of political matters outside his control.

On the other hand, he hadn't opened up with his lasers yet, either. If he held off another forty seconds, I decided as I keyed off the comm, I could call this one a victory. "Revs?"

"Still on track," he reported. "I'm getting small sparks from the starfighters' ion beams, but so far they're confined to the peripheral equipment. What in hell's name is keeping the destroyer off the cutter array?"

"I'll tell you later," I said, one eye on the dark stardrive section of my control board and the other on my displays. I was still pulling evasive maneuvers, if that was the right term for the graceless wallowing that was all the *Icarus* was capable of; but if the destroyer was showing a new caution toward us, the same could not be said of the fighters. They had increased their speed and split up their formation, still playing their ion beams across the engine section but clearly intent on bypassing that area, driving up along the hull from the rear, and converging on the cutter array from three different directions.

And while they might give their ion beams one last chance once they got there, they wouldn't waste much more time with them before switching over to their lasers and what at that range would be an almost-trivial surgical-quality operation. "Revs?" I barked.

"Thirty seconds," he called.

"We don't have thirty seconds," I snapped back. The fighters were sweeping past the engine section now, keeping close to the hull in case we had some recessed weaponry nodes hidden among the maneuvering vents. "We've got maybe ten."

"Can't do it," he insisted. "Try to stall them off."

I clenched my teeth. "Then hang on."

And jamming my hands across the whole line of control keys, I sent the thruster exhaust blasting out the entire group of maneuvering vents at once.

The *Icarus* jerked like a horse trying to dash madly off in all directions. But even with that, our reaction wasn't anywhere near as dramatic as that of the three fighters. Caught directly in the multiple blasts of super-heated gas, they wobbled outward, their nice neat pacing vectors thrown completely off target. Then they were out of the gusts, their own maneuvering vents blowing steam as they fought to correct from the outward boosts they'd just been given. I slapped all the vents back off except for the main starboard ones, sending the *Icarus* into another of its slow-motion turns. One of the fighters' tail fins scraped against our hull as he wasn't quite able to get out of the way in time, and all of them were forced to again correct their vectors. I caught the muted reflection from one of the fighters as the armorplate irised away from its forward laser cluster.

And then, with a similarly muted but far more welcome flicker of light, the stardrive section of my control board lit up. "Up and green," Nicabar shouted.

I didn't answer; my fingers were already jabbing at the activation switches and the preprogrammed course code I'd laid in. There was a noise from the comm—the Najiki commander, no doubt, saying something extremely rude—and then the cutter array did its electronic magic, and the stars vanished from around us.

"Well done," Ixil murmured.

He'd spoken too soon. I was just starting to breathe again when the deck under me lurched violently. "Revs?" I snapped.

"Spark damage," he called back. "Half the calibrations have been scrambled. We have to shut down."

"Do it," I said, keying off the controls from my end.

The stars reemerged, only this time with no planet or nearby sun anywhere in sight. I gave the area a quick scan, but it was pure reflex: Our brief flight had put us in the center of nowhere, light-years from anywhere. For the moment, at least, we were completely safe from any outside trouble.

"Okay, we're closed down," Nicabar reported a minute later.

"Damage?"

"Doesn't look like anything major," he said. "A few popped circuit breakers, probably a tube or two that'll need replacing, but I know we've got spares. And of course, a lot of recalibrating will have to be done. Time-consuming but relatively straightforward."

"Ixil can help with that," I told him, closing the rest of my board down to standby. No point leaving it active; we weren't going anywhere for a while.

"That can wait," Nicabar said. "You said you'd tell me later how we were shrugging off those ion beams. Well, it's later."

I grimaced. But he was right. It was time I clued the rest of them in on just what it was we were sitting on here. "It is indeed," I acknowledged, keying the intercom for all-ship. "Everyone, get your stuff shut down and then assemble in the dayroom. I've got a little story to tell you."

They sat in silence, looking slightly sandbagged for the most part, while I gave them the whole thing.

Most of it, anyway. I left out Tera's true identity and inside-person status, and the fact that Cameron—Alexander Borodin, rather—had been a secret passenger for the first part of our trip. I also glossed over the part Tera had played in the various incidents that had had me tied up in mental knots for most of that time. The latter part didn't take much glossing, actually, given that Ixil and I were the only ones who'd known about most of them anyway.

I also left Jones's death out of the picture, leaving it as an implied accident. Confronting a group of suspects with the knowledge that one of them is a killer might be an effective way to spark a guilty reaction, but at the moment my foremost interest was getting the *Icarus* to Earth, and for that I needed full cooperation from all of them. Time enough to sort out Jones's murder if and when we made it that far.

While the rest were busy looking flabbergasted, Tera was equally busy glaring at me in menacing silence, from which I gathered she thought I should have cleared this grand revelation with her before I let everyone else in on the big secret. I could sympathize with that attitude; but if I *had* consulted her she would probably have forbidden me to do so. Then I would have had to go directly against her wishes, which would have left her madder at me than she was already.

To say they were stunned would have been an understatement. To say they were suspicious and unbelieving, however, would have been right on the money. "You must think we're idiots, McKell," Shawn snorted when I'd finished. "Mysterious alien technology? Oh, come *on*."

"And with the whole of the Patth race panting down our necks to get at it," Everett added, shaking his head. "Really, McKell, you should have had time to come up with something better than this one."

"I expected this reaction," I said, looking over at Ixil. "You have the necessary?"

Silently, he produced the connector tool he'd brought from the mechanics room. Just as silently, he crossed to the back of the dayroom and removed one of the inner hull plates.

One by one, they went down into the 'tweenhull area to experience the alien gravitational field for themselves. Some took longer than others; but by the time they came up they were all convinced.

They were also, to a man, scared right down to their socks.

"This is crazy," Everett said, hunched over a tall whiskey sour. Alcoholic drinks of one sort or another had somehow been the beverage of choice for each of them as he came out of the 'tweenhull area. "Crazy. This is a job for professionals, not a bunch of loose spacers picked off the Meima streets."

"Believe me, I'd like nothing better than to have a squad of EarthGuard Marines on this instead of us," I agreed wholeheartedly. "But they're not here. We are."

"I presume you realize that if the Patth get their hands on us we're dead," Nicabar pointed out darkly, peering into his own drink. "Not a chance in the world they'd let us go. Not with what we know about this ship."

"And what *do* we know about it?" Shawn countered, his fingertips tapping nervously on the table. "Seriously, what do we know? McKell says he thinks it's an alien stardrive. So what makes *him* the big expert?"

"No, he may be right," Chort said before I could reply. "Early Craean stardrives used a very similar dual-sphere design, with an open resonance chamber as one of them. Though much smaller, of course."

"Yeah, but did they work?" Shawn asked. "*I* never heard of any design like that."

"Which means it can't possibly have been of any use," Tera murmured. "Not if *you* never heard of it."

Shawn turned a glare toward her. "Double-sphere designs work just fine," Nicabar put in, the firm authority in his tone cutting short any further argument. "The only reason they're not used is that the Möbius-strip arrangement is more stable."

"Terrific," Shawn said with a sniff. "An unstable stardrive. Just what we need. Just what the Spiral needs."

"It's not unstable that way," Nicabar insisted, starting to sound annoyed. "The theory shows that oscillations can form in the upper harmonics under high-stress conditions, that's all."

Shawn snorted. "Sure, but if—"

"Look, if you two want to discuss stardrive theory, go do it on your own time," Tera cut him off acidly. "What *I* want to know is how we're going to get through this gauntlet and to Earth."

"Why Earth?" Shawn demanded. Clearly, he was intent on alienating everybody aboard today. I wondered uneasily if we were getting low on his medicine again. "Just because the majority of us are human?"

"Speaking as one who is not," Ixil interjected calmly, "I would say that Borodin's ownership of the device should adequately define our final destination and cargo disposition."

"What ownership?" Shawn countered. "He dug it out of a desert on someone else's planet. What gives him any more rights than the Ihmisits who already live there?"

"Basic Commonwealth law regarding salvage and extraindigenous archaeological recovery, that's what," Tera told him stiffly. "The guidelines clearly put Borodin and his people in possession. That one's not even arguable."

"Well, well," Shawn sneered. "And when did *you* become our resident legal authority?"

"We're drifting from the point," I spoke up quickly. I had no doubt Tera could quote him the relevant laws line for line, and I had no intention of letting Shawn goad her into a display of such unreasonable expertise. "Tera's right about Borodin's claim," I went on. "But at the same time she's wrong about the functionality of this stardrive—"

"This alleged stardrive," Shawn insisted.

"This *alleged* stardrive," I corrected, "being none of our concern. In point of fact, this hunk of metal may be all that stands between us getting to Earth or winding up in the bottom of a very deep Patth pit somewhere."

For a couple of heartbeats they all just stared at me. Everett got it first, as I could tell by the distance his jaw dropped toward the floor. "You aren't saying—you're not suggesting—?"

"I think it's our best chance," I said. "The Patth know perfectly well how fast the *Icarus* can travel—it's not like stardrive speed ranges are any secret. They also don't want any more people than necessary knowing about this little hunt of theirs, which means they're probably timing their bribes and governmental pressurings to hit the systems just ahead of where we're flying at any given time."

"I see where you're going," Nicabar said, rubbing his chin thoughtfully. "If we can get ahead of that wave front, we might have a chance of landing and refueling before anyone in the area even knows what a hot ticket we are."

"Right," I said. "We may still run into a random Patth advance scout or two, but that'll be a whole lot easier to deal with than taking on an entire customs and military establishment."

"What about the underworld characters they've been bribing?" Everett asked. "Even if the Patth themselves aren't talking, they're bound to be spreading the word about us."

"True, but remember that they're only giving out half the story to that bunch," I said. "The Spiral's underworld is looking for me, and doesn't know anything about the *Icarus* itself. The *Icarus*'s name won't do them any good, since we're coming into each port under a different ID."

"Unless they also find out its shape," Shawn muttered. "We *are* just a little distinctive, you know."

"And we know the Najik have already made the connection," Nicabar added. "What's to keep them from spreading the word back to the Patth and across the rest of the Spiral?"

"The same thing that's keeping the Patth from doing so," I told him. "Namely, the desire to play this whole game as close to the vest as possible. For the Patth, the reasons are obvious; for the Najik, it'll be the hope of putting the choke collar on us themselves, thus guaranteeing themselves the full range of whatever goodies the Patth are offering."

"The basic flaw in motivation by bribery," Tera said. Her tone was neutral, but I thought I could detect a little grudging respect for my reasoning in her voice. Or maybe it was just resignation. "All your supposed allies spend as much time jockeying for position among the rest of the group as they do on the hunt itself."

"It's about all we've got going for us," I said. "That, plus the stardrive itself. *If* we can get it up and running."

Everett shook his head. "It's still crazy," he said. "What do any of us know about alien technology?"

"Not a lot," I conceded. "On the other hand, we're not exactly starting from zero, either. Tera tells me she's found what seems to be a full set of the expedition's reports in the computer."

"You're kidding," Everett said, blinking. "They put all their files aboard, too?"

"Why not?" Nicabar said. "They want to get the data to Earth, too. Why not take all of it together?"

Shawn snorted. "Ever heard of putting all your eggs in one basket?"

"Actually, I suspect it's more a case of having had all the eggs together in the first place," I told him. "I think the reason our computer is so badly suited for starship operation is that it was never intended or programmed for that purpose in the first place. It was probably the expedition's regular working computer, which was already hooked up to the alien electronics in the smaller sphere. They just left it where it was when they constructed the *Icarus* around it."

"Maybe," Shawn said. "Assuming all of this isn't just some hallucinatory wishful thinking, how exactly do you suggest we proceed? If Chort is right, where we're sitting right now is supposed to be a resonance chamber."

"Yes," I agreed. "And obviously, if it's going to resonate, it's going to have to be empty. Mostly empty, anyway."

"Resonance means *completely* empty, McKell," Shawn growled. "Any first-level physics student can tell you that. Were you thinking we could cram the whole ship into the wraparound?"

"It does not have to be completely empty," Chort said, his feathers fluffing. "In this application, the resonance effect only requires the central area."

"He's right," Nicabar seconded.

"For that matter, the presence of the interior gravitational field argues that the designers weren't expecting the whole thing to be empty," I added. "The field's clearly there to clear out the center and move everything to the edge, where it'll be out of the way."

"Unless the gravity is part of the resonance mechanism," Tera said.

"There's nothing like that in the theory," Nicabar said. "At least, not that I remember."

"Nor I," Chort said.

Shawn waved a hand. "Fine. I stand corrected."

"So what's the plan?" Nicabar asked. "Disassemble the interior corridors and bulkheads and stack everything along the inner edge?"

"Basically," I said. "Except that I don't think we have either the space or the need to keep *everything*. The interior wall and hull material should come apart into a collection of mostly one-meter-square plates, which we can dump outside through the main hatch. Ditto for some of the other unnecessary stuff."

"And what if it *isn't* a stardrive?" Shawn asked. "How do we get everything back in again?"

"We don't," I said. "That's why we only toss stuff we know we can do without."

"And what if it doesn't work?" he persisted. "We'll have lost a lot of time and won't be any better off than when we started."

"But we won't be any worse off, either," Nicabar reminded him.

"And if we *can* get it working, think of what it'll mean for all of us," Everett added thoughtfully.

Shawn sniffed. "Borodin will do great. Us, we'll be lucky to get the lousy two grand he promised us."

"We'll get it," I promised. "That, plus the bonus he mentioned in his note."

Shawn snorted. "Yeah. Right."

"Actually, we may be able to do even better than that," Everett said. "It all depends on who ends up shoveling out the money."

"I thought we'd already decided the *Icarus* belongs to Borodin," Tera said. The menace in her voice was subtle, probably too subtle for the others to notice. But I heard it, and I was sure Ixil did, too.

"We did," Everett assured her, throwing a look at Nicabar. "Mostly. I'm just suggesting that we've already earned a lot more than the two thousand he promised us on Meima."

"Fair compensation for services rendered," Shawn put in. "See? I can talk legalese, too. Here's another great legal term for you: extortion."

"And what's the 'or else'?" she countered. "Every demand has to have the threat of an 'or else' along with it. Who are you planning to offer the *Icarus* to if Borodin doesn't feel especially extortable that day? The Patth?"

"Let me just mention that anyone who wants to deal with those slime is going to have to go through me to do it," Nicabar put in.

"The Patth are hardly the only players in this game," Everett reminded him. "Potential players, anyway. If Borodin won't play ball there are a lot of other people we could sell it to."

"Maybe even the Crooea," Shawn said, throwing a sly grin at Chort. "You'd like that, wouldn't you, Chort?"

Chort's feathers ruffled, and he delivered some no doubt innocuous-sounding reply. But I wasn't listening. Suddenly, Everett's comment had sent the pieces falling into place with such loud clicks it was a wonder the rest of them couldn't hear them. Suddenly, the inconsistencies and random illogic of the *Icarus*'s entire voyage were making sense. Suddenly, small bits of data and casually odd comments were connecting together with the ease of children's playing blocks.

Suddenly, I knew why Jones had been murdered. Not who had done it, not yet. But I knew why.

"McKell?"

I blinked, dragging myself out of the depths of my introspection. Nicabar was gazing at me, a speculative look on his face. "Sorry," I apologized. "Mind wandered for a minute. What did you say?"

"I asked if that was it for the meeting," he repeated. "We've got a lot of work ahead of us."

"That's it from me," I said. That was it for right now, anyway, I amended privately. The next time I held court like this it would be to expose a murderer. "Unless anyone else has something to add?"

Chort half lifted a hand. "I have a thought," he said, almost apologetically. "Though I hesitate to mention it, as it will mean even more work for us all."

"We're facing a ton of work as it is," Ixil said. "Another half ton on top of it will hardly be noticed. Please; speak."

"As Electronics Specialist Shawn pointed out earlier, the *Icarus* has a most distinctive configuration," Chort said, still sounding a little uncertain. "And our experience at Utheno has shown that that configuration is now known. My suggestion is that we attempt to alter it."

"Straightforward enough," I said. "How do you suggest we do that?"

"The main body of the *Icarus* consists of two spheres," he said, drawing the shape in the air with his fingers. "My thought is that we could use the cast-off interior plates to build a cylindrical sheath running between them at their widest points. From the outside, the main body will then appear to be a tapered cylinder with rounded ends instead of two joined spheres."

"With just the nose cone and engine sections sticking out on either side," I said, a tingle of cautious excitement running through me as I looked over at Ixil. "Possible?"

"I don't see why not," he said. His voice was its usual calm, but the ferrets were twitching again. "At least in theory. We've got the equipment to spot-weld the plates to the spheres, and the plates themselves can be connected together with the same fasteners that are holding them together now."

"I thought the cutting torch was dead," Shawn reminded him.

"We also have an arc-welding torch," Ixil told him. "It's still functional."

"What about supports?" Nicabar asked. "You're not going to have any structural strength to speak of here."

"We could add some braces in from beneath," Ixil said. "Assuming the welding rods hold out, we ought to have enough material."

"And assuming we don't run out of power to run the welder," Tera said. "How are we on fuel, McKell?"

"We've got more than enough to drive the generators as long as we'll need," I assured her. "*My* question is how long Shawn's medicine is going to last."

There was a moment of uncomfortable silence. Apparently, that aspect hadn't yet occurred to them. "Yes, that *is* rather a limiting factor," Everett conceded. "I'd say we have no more than eight or nine days left on this supply. And that's if we stretch it out."

"Doesn't give us much time," Tera said. "Especially since we also have to get to a port once all this conversion work is finished."

"True." I looked at Shawn. "What do you think? Can you handle a week on low doses?"

He snorted. "I'll handle a week on no doses if I have to," he said bitterly. "You probably don't know it, but the Patth had some major harvesting operations on Ephis, and were furious when the Commonwealth closed them down by interdicting the place. I don't think I'd get any sympathy from them if they grabbed us. And no borandis, either."

"Though they would probably consider that you had done them a small service," Chort said quietly. "You, at least, they could allow to die naturally."

Tera shivered. "And on *that* note, I vote we get going on this."

"Seconded," I agreed, standing up. "Ixil, let's go break out the tools."

CHAPTER

15

It was one thing, I discovered, to suggest disassembling an entire starship from the inside out. It was another thing entirely to actually set about doing it.

Still, it was quickly apparent that the very nature of the *Icarus*'s odd design was going to work in our favor. On a normal starship all the bulkheads and decks were solidly riveted or welded together, with most of the various sections cast or molded to the specific fit required. Our bulkheads and decks, in contrast, were fastened together with the same connectors Cameron's people had used on the inner-hull plates, which made disassembly a fast and simple process. Furthermore, all the interior framing had been created from the same meter-square plates: a single thickness for the inner hull and most of the walls, double or triple thickness for the decks and supporting bulkheads. In one of my rare moments alone with Tera I asked about that, and she confirmed my guess that Cameron's techs had designed it that way on purpose. Shaped or molded bulkhead sections might have raised eyebrows with Meima's customs inspectors, but simple meter-square building plates wouldn't even rate a yawn.

Ixil's inventory included only three of the connector tools, but since there was also a great deal of hauling to be done the limited number worked out just fine. Cameron, bless him, had used high-strength but low-weight metal composites, which meant that even Shawn and Chort could lug the plates to the wraparound with relative ease. We rotated jobs every twenty minutes or so, with an eye toward not fatiguing any one set of muscles. As Ixil suggested at one point, there was likely to be more than enough muscle fatigue to go around.

For the first six hours we concentrated on simple disassembly, starting with the nonsupporting walls and moving on to bulkheads, shifting the plates into the wraparound and stacking them by the hatch. At that point, I decided we had enough material to start with Chort's exterior modification plan. We still had two shipboard suits—the third had been left behind on Xathru when we'd filed Jones's death report—and of course Chort had his own suit as well. Putting Tera and Nicabar into the smaller and larger sizes, respectively, I sent them out with Chort, the welder, and two connector tools and crossed my fingers.

It worked out better than even my best level of cautious hope. Chort, it turned out, was quite competent with the welder, at least as skilled as Ixil if not a shade more so. The proper positioning of the plates was another worry I'd had; Tera solved that one by the three of them assembling an entire longitudinal section and working it into place between the two spheres before Chort did any welding. With two of the connector tools now outside, the four of us inside shifted jobs again from mass disassembly to the more delicate task of moving the gear from the now nonexistent rooms to new quarters against the inside of the hull. The large sphere's gravitational level of .85 gee made the tasks of lifting and carrying marginally easier while still avoiding the missteps and inertial problems of low-gee environments.

The days settled into a steady if slightly frantic routine. Chort spent every waking hour outside, clearly loving it, except for the brief periods when he had to come in to have his rebreather recharged. Those of us who could fit into the remaining suits—which was everyone except Everett—took our turns outside with him, most of us not nearly as enthusiastic about the wide-open spaces as Chort was. The rest of our time was divided between more disassembly, shifting the necessary equipment to the inner hull and tossing the rest, or collapsing on our transplanted bunks in the near coma that had taken the place of normal sleep.

With the verbal sniping and general lack of sociability that had marked the trip up to this point I had braced myself for the escalation in overall tension that all this unscheduled exercise was bound to create. Once again—and this one was *really* to my surprise—it didn't happen. There was the occasional snapped word or under-the-breath curse, but for the most part I found my fellow travelers suddenly behaving far more like a seasoned crew than a random collection of semihostile strangers.

In retrospect, I suppose, I shouldn't have been so surprised by the sudden transformation. Before the Najiki near miss at Utheno we'd been little more than interstellar truck drivers, doing a dull job for low pay, with nothing in particular to look forward to after it was done, and with only the vague threat of a possible hijacking to make it even marginally interesting. Now, suddenly, we were on the cusp of history, with the chance to make a name for ourselves and at the same time stick it hard to the Patth and their hated economic empire. We had the chance for immortality—and, even more importantly, for possibly serious riches—and that simultaneous group grab for the brass ring was drawing us firmly together.

Of course, lurking behind the chance to make history was the darker knowledge that if the Patth caught up with us even our own personal histories would pretty well be over. That was undoubtedly part of the cooperation, too.

But whatever the reason, the progress the first four days was nothing short of remarkable. So much so that midway through the fifth day I pulled Everett and Ixil off the work crews and sent them aft to the engine room to start recalibrating the equipment that the Najiki ion attack had scrambled. Then, with Chort, Nicabar, and Shawn working outside, I took Tera over to her computer and settled in for a crash course in Alien Stardrive 101.

The class didn't take nearly as long as I'd hoped it would.

"That's it?" I asked as the last page of data scrolled to the top of the computer display. "That's all they found?"

"Be thankful we have even this much," she countered tartly. But there were worry lines creasing her forehead, too. Perhaps, like me, she was starting to realize just how much of a long shot this whole scheme really was. "The idea wasn't to sit there on Meima until they had the whole thing figured out to five decimals, you know. The minute they realized what they had, they shot that message off to Dad. This isn't much more than the five weeks it took to get the *Icarus* parts shipped in and put together."

"I suppose," I conceded, scowling at the meter-square opening into the sphere, a disguised access panel that Tera had luckily known how to open. "And they never got more than a couple of meters inside?"

"No," she said. "They were afraid of crossing circuits or damaging something else along the way. You can see for yourself what a maze of conduits and loose wires it is in there."

I stretched flat along the hull beside the hole and

shined a light in. She was right: It was a jungle in there. "Reminds me of the engine room," I said, playing the light around some more. It looked like there were panels of glowing lights on what little I could see of the wall through the wiring. "I wonder if it was planned that way or if all the cable ties just fell apart over the years. You said there was another access from the other side of the sphere?"

"Yes, behind the secondary breaker panel in the engine room," she said. "They put hinges on the breaker panel so that it swings right out."

"Has it got a better view than this one?"

"Not really." She gestured toward the access hole. "They tried sending in probes, but the umbilicals kept getting caught on the wiring and Dr. Chou was afraid they'd tear something trying to get them loose. They had one self-guided probe that got in a little farther, but something confused its sensors and it froze up completely."

"Well, we're not going to get anywhere without a complete idea of what's in there," I said.

"I hope you're not suggesting one of us go inside," she said darkly. "If the probes couldn't make it through, you certainly won't."

"I like to think I'm a bit more competent at working my way through tangled wiring than someone tugging blindly on a probe control," I told her. "As it happens, though, I was thinking of starting with someone slightly smaller."

She frowned. "Who?"

I nodded in the direction of the engine room. "Go get Ixil," I said, "and I'll show you."

Ixil wasn't any more enthusiastic about my idea than Tera was. "I don't know, Jordan," he said, stroking Pax's head uneasily as he crouched on his left forearm and hand. "Every design of stardrive I've ever heard of has had a half-dozen high-voltage sites and shock capacitors associated with it. If Pax touches one of those, it'll kill him."

"He goes through power conduits all the time," I reminded him. "How does he avoid insulation breaks and short circuits there?"

"He knows what to look for with our stuff," Ixil said. "This is an unknown alien design, with an entirely different set of cues. For that matter, even the lower-voltage lines may have lost their insulation over the years. You and I are big enough to survive a minor shock like that. Pax isn't."

"I know," I said. "And I wish there were another way. But there isn't. We have to see what's in there; and Pix and Pax are the only eyes we've got."

"Except ours," Ixil said. "Why don't I go instead?"

"No," Tera said, a fraction of a second before I could get the word out myself. "Not a chance."

"But I could see what's there," he persisted. "There are cues I know how to read that Pax hasn't got the basic intelligence to pick up on. If I go just a little way in, far enough to see past the initial tangle, I could brief him on whatever I find and *then* let him go in. It would give him a better chance."

Tera shook her head. "I'm sorry, Ixil, but I can't let you do that. Dad was absolutely adamant that no one go inside until we got all the power sources and cables mapped out, for that very reason. It's Pix or Pax or no one at all."

Ixil lowered his eyes to the ferret, his mouth tight. "All right," he said with a resigned sigh. "What exactly do you want him to do?"

"We need to find a path through to the center of the sphere," I said. "Chort and Nicabar are a little fuzzy on the details of this exotic double-sphere design of theirs, but they both agree there should be a large resonance crystal somewhere in the center, probably with a control panel either wrapped around it or somewhere nearby. If they're right, and if we can either scope out the controls—or, better yet, connect it through to a control system out here—we may be able to activate it."

"If it's even still functional after all this time," Ixil muttered, putting Pax up on his shoulder.

"Well, *something's* drawing and using power in there," I reminded him. "Though where it's getting it from I haven't the foggiest idea. Warn him to watch where he puts his feet and nose, and to take his time. We're not in any special hurry here."

Ixil nodded, and for a moment he just stood there silently, communing with the outriders. Then, taking a deep breath, he picked Pax up off his shoulder and set him down beside the opening. For a moment the ferret sniffed at the edge, his little nose wrinkling as if he didn't care for the smell of age in there. Then, with what sounded almost like a reassuring squeak, he scrabbled over the edge and disappeared.

Ixil was kneeling at the edge in an instant, plucking the light from my hand and playing it inside. "Doesn't seem to be any gravity in there," he said, leaning his face into the opening. "He's working his way along the wires the way he does in zero gee."

I looked at Tera. "I don't know," she said. "Though if the purpose of the grav field out here is to make sure the center of the resonance cavity stays clear, there really wouldn't be any need for one in the smaller sphere."

Ixil grunted, and for another few minutes we stood or crouched there in silence. Then, hunching his shoulders, Ixil straightened up again. "He's gone," he said, handing the light back to me. "Disappeared behind something that looked like a multicable coupler."

"He'll be fine," Tera said quietly, laying a hand soothingly on his arm. "He does this sort of thing all the time, remember?"

Ixil grunted, clearly not in the mood to be soothed. "I'd better get back to the engine room—there's still a lot of recalibration to be done, and Everett doesn't know how to do most of the calculations on his own. You'll call me when he comes back?"

"Yes," I assured him. "Actually, Tera, you might want to go back there with him and open the other access hole, the one you said was behind the breaker panel. If Pax gets disoriented, it would be handy for him to have a second way out."

"Good idea," she said. "Come on, Ixil."

They climbed up the slight curve—it still made me vaguely dizzy to watch people walking around the hull in here—and disappeared through the open pressure door into the zero gee of the wraparound. With a sigh, I lay down on the hull again and shined my light into the opening. Pax was gone, all right, though I imagined I could hear occasional scratching sounds as he maneuvered his way through the maze. Leaning partially over the hole, I stuck my head carefully in and played the light slowly around the inner surface.

I was halfway around in my sweep when I saw the gap.

I was still lying there studying it two minutes later when Tera returned. "He's really not happy about this, is he?" she commented as she sat down cross-legged beside me. "He claims they're not pets, but I think he really—"

"Did Chou and his people take photos of what they could see from this opening?" I interrupted her.

She took a half second to switch gears. "I think so," she said. "At least some. I hadn't pulled them up before because—"

"Pull them up now," I ordered, trying to keep my sudden apprehension out of my voice. "Find me one that shows a gray trapezoid about half a meter across with about two dozen wires coming off gold connectors along its edges."

She was already at the computer, fingers playing across the keys. "What is it?" she asked tightly.

"Just find me the picture," I said tersely, getting up and stepping to her side.

Dr. Chou's people, it turned out, had taken a lot of pictures. It took Tera nearly a minute to find the specific area I was looking for.

And when she did, my apprehension turned to full-blown certainty.

"Tera, you told me your dad left the ship at Potosi," I said. "How do you know? Did he leave a note?"

She shook her head, her neck twisted to look up at me. "No, nothing like that," she said, a note of uncertain dread in her voice as she picked up on my own mood. "I told you: He and his things were gone, and I couldn't find him anywhere on the ship."

"Right," I nodded. "Except that you didn't think to look inside the small sphere here, did you?"

Her eyes widened, her throat muscles suddenly tense. "Oh, no," she breathed. "He's not—oh, God."

"No, no, I can't see him," I hastened to assure her. "There's no—I mean—"

"No body?"

"No body," I confirmed. At least not one I could see, I carefully refrained from saying. "What there is by that trapezoid is a gap in the wiring. A big gap, as if someone maneuvered his way through the thicket, creating a hole as he went."

"It couldn't have been Pax?" she asked, her voice going even darker.

"It's man-sized," I told her gently. "Look, maybe he's just lying low in there."

She shook her head, a short, choppy movement. "No, we've been doing work here by the access panel off and on for the past couple of days. He'd have heard my voice and come out." She swallowed. "If he could."

I looked back over at the hole, coming to the inevitable decision. "I'm going in," I announced, taking a step that direction.

A step was all I got. Like a rattlesnake her hand

darted out and grabbed my arm. "No!" she snapped, holding on with a strength that surprised me. "No! If he's dead, it means something in there killed him. We can't risk you, too."

"What, all this concern for a soul-dead smuggler?" I retorted. It wasn't a nice thing to say, but at the moment I wasn't feeling particularly nice. "Maybe he's not dead in there—you ever think of that? Maybe he's injured, or unconscious, or paralyzed. Maybe he can't get to the opening, or can't even call out to you."

"If he went in while we were on Potosi, he's been in there eleven days," she said. Her voice sounded empty, but her grip on my arm hadn't slackened a bit. "Any injury serious enough to prevent him from getting out on his own would have killed him long before now."

"Unless he just got the injury," I shot back. I wasn't ready to give in, either. "Maybe he got thrown around while I was dodging the ion beams off Utheno. He could still be alive."

She took a deep breath. "We'll wait for Pax to come out."

"We'll wait half an hour," I countered.

"One hour."

I started to protest, took another look at her face, and gave it up. "One hour," I agreed.

She nodded, and for a long moment she stared down at the access hole. Then, reluctantly, she keyed off the computer photo we'd been looking at and sat down on the deck. "Tell me about yourself, McKell," she said.

I shrugged, sitting down on the deck beside her. "There's not very much to tell."

"Of course there is," she said quietly. "You had hopes and plans and dreams once. Maybe you still do. What would you be doing now if you weren't smuggling?"

"Who knows?" I said. She didn't care about my hopes and dreams, of course. I knew that. She was just casting around looking for some mindless chatter, something to distract herself from the mental image of her father floating dead in there. "Once, I thought I might have a career in EarthGuard. That ended when I told a superior officer exactly what I thought of him."

"In public, I take it?"

"It was public enough to earn me a court-martial," I conceded. "Then I thought I might have a career in customs. I must have been a little too good at it, because someone framed me for taking bribes. Then I tried working for a shipping firm, only I lost my temper again and slugged one of the partners."

"Strange," she murmured. "I wouldn't have taken you for the terminally self-destructive type."

"Don't worry," I assured her. "I'm only self-destructive where potentially promising careers are concerned. When it comes to personal survival, I'm not nearly so incompetent."

"Maybe the problem is you're afraid of success," she suggested. "I've seen it often enough in other people."

"That's not a particularly original diagnosis," I said. "Others of my acquaintance have suggested that from time to time. Of course, for the immediate future my options for success of any sort are likely to be seriously limited."

"Until about midway into the next century, I believe you said."

"About that."

She was silent a moment. "What if I offered to buy you out of your indenture to that smuggling boss?"

I frowned at her. There was no humor in her face that I could detect. "Excuse me?"

"What if I offered to buy out your indenture?" she repeated. "I asked you that once, if you recall. You rather snidely countered by asking if I had a half million in spare change on me."

I felt my face warm. "I didn't know who you were then."

"But now you do," she said. "And you also know—or you ought to if you don't—that I have considerably more than a half-million commarks to play with."

A not-entirely-pleasant tingle ran through me. "And you're suggesting that bailing me out of my own pig-headed mismanagement would be worth that much to you?" I asked, hearing a hint of harshness in my voice.

"Why not?" she asked. "I can certainly afford it."

"I'm sure you can," I said. This was *not* safe territory to be walking on. "The Cameron Group probably spends half a million a year just on memo slips. Which, if I may say so, is a hell of a better investment than I would be for you."

"Who said anything about you being an investment?" she asked.

"Process of elimination," I said. "I don't qualify as a recognized charity, and I'm too old to adopt."

Somewhere along in here I'd expected her to take offense. But either she was too busy worrying about her father to notice my ungrateful attitude, or she had a higher annoyance threshold than I'd thought. "Perhaps it's a reward for bringing the *Icarus* safely home," she said. "Payment for services rendered."

"Better wait until it's sitting safely on the ground before you go off the edge with offers of payment," I warned. "Unless, of course, you think I'm likely to weaken before we get to Earth and figure this is the best way to lock in my loyalty."

"Or else I just want to give you a new chance," she said, still inexplicably unruffled. "You don't belong with smugglers and criminals. You're not the type."

It was worse than I'd thought. Now she was sensing nobility and honor and decency in me. I had to nip this in the bud, and fast, before there was trouble I couldn't talk my way out of. "Not to be insulting or anything," I said, "but the high-society life you grew up with is not exactly the sort of background you need for judging people in my line of work. I could tell you about a man with a choirboy face and manner who could order one of his thugs to rip your heart out and watch him do it without batting an eye."

"You seem awfully vehement about this," she commented.

"I don't want you to get hurt dabbling in things you don't understand, that's all," I muttered. "More than that, I don't want *me* to get hurt. Stick with corporate mergers or archaeological digs or whatever it is you do for your father, Elaina Tera Cameron. You'll live longer that way."

I frowned, an odd connection suddenly slapping me in the face. "Elaina Tera Cameron," I repeated. "E.T.C. As in et cetera?"

She smiled wanly. "Very good," she complimented me. "Yes, it was my father's little joke. I was the fourth of the three children they'd planned on. But the first three were boys, and Mom had always wanted a girl. And Mom generally got what she set her mind on."

"Hence, the et cetera?"

"She didn't even notice for four years," Tera said. "Not until I started learning to write and was putting my initials everywhere."

"I'll bet she was really pleased with your father."

"Actually, she was mostly just annoyed that she'd missed the joke. Especially since Dad was famous for that sort of wordplay."

"Nothing like that with your brothers' initials?"

She shrugged. "If there was, it was something so obscure none of us ever figured it out. Dad certainly never let on about any jokes hidden there."

"Sounds like him," I said. "He's always had a reputation for playing his cards all the way inside his vest."

"Only when it was necessary," Tera insisted. "And he never hid them from his family and close friends." She looked past me at the access hole. "Which just makes this all the stranger. Why would he go in there without telling me? Especially after forbidding anyone else to do so?"

"Maybe he was afraid I would come into the 'tween-hull area after him again," I suggested.

"But why didn't he tell me?" she persisted. "There was a day and a half between that incident and our landing on Potosi. If he thought he needed to hide out from you, there was plenty of time for us to talk it over."

"Unless he thought I might drop in on him unexpectedly," I said. "Remember, there was nowhere else on the ship he could hide."

"Of course there was," she said. "The Number Two cabin on the top deck, the one Jones used before he died. After Ixil took the release pad off to put on his own door, it would have been a perfect place for him to hide. We were planning to move him in there while we were on Potosi."

"With access in and out through the inner hull?" I asked, feeling my face warm and hoping it didn't show. Once again, an angle I'd missed completely. Though to be fair, by the time I knew we even had a stowaway he was already gone.

"If he needed to move around, yes," she said. "We couldn't very well take the chance of letting one of the others see him, could we? We had some of the hull connectors gimmicked so that he could get quickly in and out."

"Ah," I said, feeling even more like Nobel prize material. I'd been through that whole 'tweenhull area from starboard to port, and it had never even occurred to me to check for loose or missing inner-hull connectors. "But he never took up residence there?"

She shook her head. "We were planning to move him in while you were out hunting for Shawn's medicine. But then Shawn escaped, and we all had to go out and look for him. Then with the trouble we had with customs, I didn't get a chance to look for Dad until we were long gone from there."

"Is that why you were in the mechanics room when Everett found you?" I asked. "You were actually there to pick up a connector tool?"

She smiled tightly. "You *are* sharp, aren't you?" she commented. "Yes, that's exactly why I was there. When Everett charged in on me I thought we'd been found out, but he just told me Shawn was gone and charged back out again without asking any questions about what I was doing there."

She shrugged. "Then, of course, after you asked and I'd spun you the computer story, I had to take the computer apart and pretend there was a genuine glitch somewhere. Just as well I did, I suppose, given all the sand that had gotten in. That was as big a surprise to me as it was to anyone else."

There was a faint and distant-sounding noise like metal scratching on metal, and I looked hopefully back at the access hole. But there was no sign of Pax. Probably one of the group outside had banged the hull or something. "Maybe one of the others *did* see him," I suggested slowly. "That might account for his deciding he needed somewhere else to hide."

"But then why hasn't that person said something?" Tera pointed out. "I mean, after that note he left you about how he wouldn't be coming along, don't you think seeing him aboard would have been worth at least a passing comment?"

"It should have," I agreed. "Unless that someone had a reason for keeping it secret. Maybe your father caught him doing something that—oh, *damn*."

Tera got it at the same time I did. "The poison you found in Ixil's room," she breathed. "Of course. Dad was going down the corridor for some reason and spotted him setting that up."

Abruptly, her eyes widened. "Oh, my God. Mc-

Kell—maybe he *didn't* go in there voluntarily. Maybe he was . . . put there."

I got to my feet. "I'm going in," I told her, snagging my flashlight and stuffing it securely into my belt. "There should be a couple of medkits over with the sick-bay stuff. Go get me one."

She set off across the curved surface at a fast run, her footsteps echoing eerily through the mostly empty space. I headed off in nearly the opposite direction, across the broken landscape that was what was left of the *Icarus*'s inner hull, toward the two piles of equipment from the mechanics and electronics shops. Sorting through the piles, I picked out a tool belt, an electronic-field detector, a couple of rolls of insulator tape, and a handful of small tools.

Tera was already waiting by the computer by the time I started back. "Here's the medkit," she said as I came up to her, holding out a large belt pack. "I put in a bottle of water and some emergency ration bars, too."

"Thanks," I said, resisting the urge to remind her that wrapping me in unnecessary bulk would only make my trip through the sphere more difficult than it was promising to be already. But she was only trying to help, and I couldn't see how a single water bottle was likely to be the deciding factor one way or the other. I strapped the pack around my waist where it wouldn't block access to my tools, and settled everything in place. "All right," I said as casually as I could manage. "I'll see you later."

"Good luck," she said quietly.

I threw her a frown, wondering if I was imagining the concern I heard in her voice. But then I realized that the fear wasn't for me, or at least not primarily for me. It was for her father.

Turning away from her, I lay down on the floor beside the access hole. Taking a deep breath, I got a grip on the edge and pulled myself in.

CHAPTER

16

The first leg of the trip was uneventful enough. There was plenty of light coming in behind me, the zero gee made precision movement reasonably easy, and I had a mostly clear path up to the gap I'd pointed out to Tera. I held the electronic-field sensor at arm's length in front of me the whole way like a mystical talisman, keeping a close eye on its readings and pausing to check out the source of anything that made its indicators so much as twitch.

There was current flowing in here, all right, plenty of it. Fortunately for purposes of navigation, the strongest sources seemed to be the handful of panels spaced irregularly along the inner surface. From the limited view I'd had from the access hole the nature of the panels had been a mystery; up close and direct, the situation wasn't much clearer. They might have been readout displays, giving ever-changing equipment-status reports in a strange and incomprehensible alien script. Unfortunately, they could just as easily have been ever-changing mood lights there for the edification of whoever it was the mindless electronics thought was on duty in here. All in all, I decided, I should probably stick with flying starships and leave the more esoteric alien evaluations alone.

After a few minutes I reached the gap, only to discover that my earlier interpretation of its significance was not nearly as clear-cut as I'd thought. It turned out, in fact, to be far from certain that the opening was proof of a human-sized body having gone through that direction at all. Partly it was a matter of that particular region being clearer than the surrounding area; partly it was a trick of perspective that had made the spot seem more open than it really was.

And it *wasn't* particularly open. There were at least a dozen wires crisscrossing the gap a half meter farther in, which I hadn't been able to see from my previous vantage point. If Cameron had come this way, he'd done a good job of smoothing out his footprints behind him.

Which further meant that it was suddenly far from certain that Cameron had ever come in here at all, let alone that he was floating unconscious or dead somewhere inside.

For a minute I played my light through the gap into the darkness beyond, watching the glints as the beam reflected off bits of alien metal or plastic or ceramic, wondering what I should do now. If Cameron wasn't in here, then continuing on would be not only unnecessary but probably dangerous as well.

Of course, if Cameron wasn't in here, then we were back to the sticky question of where in blazes he'd gotten to. If he'd left the *Icarus* at Potosi, voluntarily or otherwise, then he was likely in worse trouble than if he were in here. In fact, as I thought about it, I realized his abduction on Potosi might explain why the Najik had identified the *Icarus* so quickly at Utheno. Though that could equally be the Potosi customs report catching up with us.

On the other hand, whether Cameron was in here or not, we still had to figure out how the stardrive worked if we were going to pussyfoot our way out of the Patth net. Still, it would definitely be the better part of valor for me carefully to back out of here at this point and postpone any other plans until Pax came back with his report.

And then, even as I gave the light one last sweep around, I heard a soft, distant sound. Unlike the noise I'd heard while talking with Tera, though, this one was very familiar. It was the screech of a startled Kalixiri ferret, the kind of verbal reaction that usually went quickly up the tonal scale and then just as quickly back down again.

Only this one didn't. It went halfway up the scale, then abruptly cut off.

And with the sudden silence ringing in my ears, I stared into the darkness, feeling sweat beading up on my forehead and neck. There hadn't been even the whisper of a trailing edge to that call; no whimper, no gasp, no sigh. None of the sounds that should have come from the last escaping bit of air in Pax's lungs as he collapsed into sleep or unconsciousness.

Which meant he hadn't collapsed into sleep or unconsciousness. He was dead.

And something in here had killed him.

I looked back toward the access hole, the movement of my head sending droplets of sweat flying off my face to drift their way to oblivion among the maze of circuitry. If Tera had heard that abbreviated death cry, she would be sticking her head into view any second now to demand an explanation. But the seconds ticked by, and there was no Tera, and I realized with decidedly mixed feelings that I alone knew what had just happened.

Which meant that the decision of what to do next was also mine alone. Probably just as well. Wiping the surface layer of sweat off my forehead with my left sleeve, I eased the blocking wires out of the way and headed cautiously in.

I'd told Ixil and Tera that we weren't in any particular hurry here. With Pax's screech echoing through my memory, I was even less inclined to take unnecessary chances. I kept it slow and careful, checking every wire and conduit in my path, both visually and with my field sensor, before getting anywhere near it. Before moving it aside I also made sure to trace along it as best I could through the tangle, trying to see where it intersected the wall or other components and making sure it had enough slack for me to safely push it aside without straining anything. If it didn't have that slack, if it even looked marginal, I changed course and found another route.

It took me nearly an hour to work my way through that first three and a half meters; and I was just beginning to wonder if I was going to be able to do the whole ten meters to the center in one try when I eased through a gap in a fish-net-style mesh and abruptly found myself in open space.

I held on to the mesh with one hand, balancing myself parallel to it in the zero gee, and played my light around. The space wasn't quite as empty, I could see now, as it had looked in that first glance. A dozen different cable loops that had worked their way through the holes in the mesh were bobbing gently around the edges, looking like some exotic form of seaweed drifting in a calm current. Half a dozen of the lighted displays I'd seen against the walls were also at the edge of the open area, fastened by wires through the mesh and facing inward toward the center; from one of them a slender, articulated black-and-silver-banded extension arm stretched right to the point six and a half meters away from me where the center of the sphere should be. All the display lights were red, giving the area an eerie, blood-tinged look. I moved my light around the room again, steeling myself for what would probably be the very unpleasant sight of a dead ferret. But there was no sign of his body. Apparently, he hadn't made it through the wire maze before he died.

And then, abruptly, I caught my breath, swinging my light back toward the center again. So intent was I on looking for Pax's body that it had only now occurred to me that there should have been something else in here: the resonance crystal and control board that Nicabar and Chort said a stardrive like this was supposed to come equipped with.

Unfortunately, this one wasn't.

Carefully, I ran my light over every square centimeter of the place, a tight knot twisting like a case-hardened drill bit into my stomach. I'd pinned a lot on Tera's assumption that the *Icarus* concealed an alien stardrive, but not until that moment did I realize just how much pinning I had actually done. If we couldn't get this thing to jump us past the Patth net, then we'd had it, pure and simple. I remembered Shawn's question on that point, and how glibly I'd brushed him off with the suggestion that we would be no worse off if Cameron's archaeologists had been wrong.

But I'd been the one who'd been wrong. All the work we'd done had indeed been for nothing, just as Shawn had warned. Worse, my brilliant scheme had cost us precious time, a loss I realized now we were going to sorely regret. Not only had the Patth been given the opportunity to consolidate and perhaps reconfigure their hunt for us, but the lost days had let Shawn's medical condition deteriorate to the point where there were probably no more than three or four planets we could reach in time to get him the borandis he would soon be needing. And to top it off, if the Patth had guessed we had had to go to ground for repairs or recalibration after the Utheno attack, then they would be concentrating everything they had on this region. The region that, sooner or later, we were going to have to pop up into.

On the other hand, if this electrician's nightmare *wasn't* a stardrive, what the hell would the Patth want with it anyway? A possibly reassuring thought; but not, I realized immediately, nearly as reassuring as it might have been. The *Icarus* could still be the massive alien stardrive Cameron's people suspected, only with the vital crystal either removed or crumbled into dust. That would put us in the depressing position of having something that was totally useless to us, yet was still worth killing us to get.

Unless . . .

I played the light around again. If it *was* merely a matter of finding the right kind of crystal, that was the kind of miracle we still had an outside chance of pulling off. I doubted such a rock would be an off-the-shelf item these days, but if I could get a message to Uncle Arthur, he might be able to dig one up from somewhere and get it to us.

I let go of the mesh, hovering in midair as I wiped some more sweat from my face. And as I did so, I suddenly heard a sound like two pieces of metal scratching together. The same sound, I realized, that I'd heard while sitting out in the big sphere with Tera.

Only this time it was coming from somewhere nearby.

I swung my light around, hoping to catch a glimpse of moving machinery. But the sound had stopped before I could get the light more than a fraction of the way around, despite the fact that I'd whipped my arm fast enough to send the rest of my body into a slow tumble. Cursing under my breath, I reached back out for the mesh.

My fingers closed on thin air. The mesh was out of my reach.

I tried again, swinging my body awkwardly over as I tried to get enough extension, frowning at the complete illogic of the situation. I'd been motionless relative to the mesh when I'd started; and no matter how much I'd twisted and turned, my center of mass should have remained that same distance away from it. That was basic level-one physics.

Yet there the mesh was, sitting a good five centimeters outside my best reach. I knew I hadn't bumped the mesh, which might have given me the necessary push, and any air current strong enough to account for this much movement ought to have been whistling in my ears, which it wasn't. Muttering a curse, I reached to my tool pouch for the longest probe I had with me. The patented McKell luck was running true to form, gumming up my life with complications I didn't need, didn't want, and most certainly didn't have time to deal with. I got a good grip on the end of the probe and stretched it out to the mesh.

It didn't reach.

I stared at the gap between mesh and probe, a bad taste suddenly tingling against my tongue. I was moving away from the mesh, all right. Slowly and subtly, but now that I was looking for it I could definitely see the mesh receding. And the only way I could be moving like this was if the small sphere had suddenly developed a gravitational field like its big brother beside it.

I looked around again, paying special attention to the loops of cable hanging through to my side of the mesh. No, the field wasn't exactly like that of its big brother, I corrected myself. It was, instead, an exact inverse of it. Instead of pulling everything toward the outer wall, this one was pushing everything toward the center. I tried to think how it could be pulling that one off, but my mind wasn't up to it.

Besides, I had more urgent things to think about at the moment. If the field was focused toward the center of the sphere—and that was certainly how it looked from the way the hanging cables were now pointed inward—then once I hit the zero mark I would be pretty well stuck there. Any direction I turned I would be looking uphill; and with absolutely nothing available to kick or push off against, I would be as solidly pinned as a mosquito in a spiderweb.

I picked another curse out of my repertoire, a heavy-duty one this time, as I swung my light around looking for inspiration. There were the hanging cables, of course, now resembling Spanish moss more than they did floating seaweed. But without knowing what any of them were for I would have to be pretty desperate before I'd risk damage to either the *Icarus* or myself by tugging at them. Besides which, a second look showed that I wasn't going to get anywhere within grabbing range of any of them.

Still, once I'd choked down the panic reaction and forced myself to think rationally, I realized that I was hardly in dire straits. Tera knew I was in here, and once I failed to emerge it would only be a matter of time before Ixil or one of the others ventured in to find out what had happened to me. A rope belayed outside and carefully threaded in through the tangle of wires, and I could pull myself to the mesh and ultimately to safety. Tera's insistence that I bring food and water in here might turn out to have been a good idea after all.

I seemed to be drifting faster now, though it was difficult to tell for sure. A sudden yellow glow appeared from the corner of my eye, and I turned to see that one of the flat displays that had been showing the same red symbols as all the others had suddenly changed to a grid pattern of yellow-and-black squares. Even as I studied it another of the displays also changed, this one to squares of orange and black. For a minute I glanced between them, trying to see if there was any pattern in the layout of their colored squares. But if there was it was too subtle for me to pick out.

I was about two meters from the center, still drifting at a leisurely pace, when it suddenly occurred to me that if I kept on this same course I was going to run directly into the articulated arm angling across my path.

I played my light over the arm, feeling a fresh batch of sweat leaching onto my face as I did so. I'd already noted that the arm was composed of an alternating series of black-and-silver bands; what I hadn't noticed until then was that at the very tip of the arm the color scheme changed to about twenty centimeters of a disturbingly luminescent gray. My field sensor wasn't picking up anything from it yet, but I was still too far away for any current less than a couple hundred volts to register. The arm didn't look like any of the power cables I'd had to sneak through on my way in, but considering the alien origin of this place that didn't give me much comfort.

What *was* clear, and of no comfort whatsoever, was that even if the arm suddenly came to life with enough power to light up New Cleveland, there was still no way in space for me to miss running into it. About all I could think of to do was to try to get a careful grip on it as I approached and use it as a fulcrum to swing the bulk of my body around it instead of hitting it full force.

The problem with that idea was that if it didn't have the structural strength necessary to handle that kind of sudden stress, the gray end was probably going to break off in my hand. On the other hand, if it was that weak and I *didn't* grab it, it would probably break anyway as I slammed into it.

And as my train of thought reached that depressingly no-win conclusion, I was there. Clenching my teeth, feeling rather like someone trying to sneak up and grab a sleeping pit viper, I reached out with my right hand and got a careful grip on the arm.

Too careful. The material was far more slippery than it looked, and before I knew it my hand was sliding straight down the striped section toward the gray end. I squeezed harder, simultaneously trying to swing my body around as I'd originally planned. But my lack of purchase on the arm meant I had no leverage at all, and

I found myself instead sliding along the arm in a sort of low-gravity version of a fireman and his pole.

It was hardly the way I'd planned things, but at least the arm was clearly stronger than my worst-case scenario had anticipated. Even with my full weight pressing on it via my one-handed grip, it was showing no sign of breaking or even bending. Maybe even strong enough that I'd be able to use it to climb back out to the mesh.

Assuming, of course, I could figure out how to get a solid grip on the damn thing. Swinging my body partially around, I got my other hand in place and grabbed as hard as I dared.

The two-handed grip helped some, but not enough. I was still sliding serenely down the arm, now almost to the gray section at the end. If I couldn't stop myself, I knew, my momentum would cause me to overshoot the end of the arm and go straight through the sphere's center. Hardly a catastrophe, since there was nothing over there for me to crash into, but it would cost me more of our increasingly precious minutes while I waited for the gravitational field to slow me to a stop and bring me back to the center again.

And then I was to the gray section of the arm. Clenching my teeth, knowing this was my last chance to stop myself with a modicum of dignity, I squeezed it hard.

It was as if I'd grabbed hold of a live hundred-volt wire. Suddenly my whole body was tingling, the hairs on my neck and arms standing straight up, my clenched teeth trying to vibrate against each other. And on top of all of it was the chagrin that after all of my exaggerated caution and borderline paranoia, I'd finally hit a live wire. What made it even worse was that I'd even hit it entirely on purpose.

And yet, at the same time, the small part of my mind that hadn't gone into instant panic mode was noticing that if this *was* an electric shock it was like none I'd ever experienced before. There was no pain, for one thing, and none of the subtle promises of future pain, either. In addition, the tingling was running uniformly through my entire body, not simply along my arms and chest as a normal current ought to flow. There was a distant sound like the awful ripping thunder crack from a too-close lightning strike, and everything went black.

It didn't stay black long. Almost before the darkness had a chance to register, the lights came back on again. Not the harsh, sharp-edged beam of my flashlight, but a softer, much more muted glow. For a second I wondered if I had blacked out, but both the darkness and the light had come without any of the normal cues and sensations of a loss and regaining of consciousness.

It was at about that point in my slow-motion cogitation that I suddenly noticed the striped arm with the booby-trapped end was gone. So was the tangle of wiring and geometric monitor shapes I'd been facing across the small sphere.

So, for that matter, was the small sphere.

Belatedly, I focused my eyes straight ahead of me on the now familiar curving gray hull. So I *had* blacked out in there, at least long enough for the jolt to kick me out here to the center of the *Icarus*'s big resonance sphere. I winced as I thought of all the stuff I must have torn through on my way out—I was probably lucky I hadn't been electrocuted for real.

Though if I'd wrecked enough of the alien electronics to render the stardrive inoperable I would probably soon wish I *had* been crisped. Twisting around in the catlike, half-swimming movements of standard zero-gee maneuvering technique, I worked myself around toward the access hole, wondering why Tera wasn't screaming her head off at me.

The reason was very simple. Tera wasn't there.

Neither was the tool kit I'd left beside the opening. Neither was the ship's computer that had been more or less permanently mounted there. Neither, for that matter, were the stacks of meter-square panels, the piles of mechanical equipment, or the consolidated bits of personal effects.

I was in the large sphere, all right. Problem was, I wasn't in the *Icarus*.

A familiar sense of falling permeated my confusion: The sphere's gravitational field had taken hold and was pulling me gently down toward the inner surface. Too slowly, or so it seemed, considering the .85-gee pull we had on the *Icarus*. I had just about decided that this sphere's field was set lower when I got within a meter of the surface and the field abruptly increased dramatically. I barely got my knees prepared for the impact before I was down, hitting the metal with a dull thud. Clearly, the gravitational field was a lot more radially variable than I'd realized, though how they were managing that trick I couldn't even begin to guess.

And then, as the echo of my landing faded away, I heard another sound. Faint, distant, but extremely familiar. A sort of thoughtful squeak, coming from the direction of the access hole leading into the smaller sphere.

It sounded like Pax.

I had my plasmic in my hand before I'd taken two steps toward the small sphere. Pure reflex on my part, of course—Lord knew I had no idea what I was going to do with it. I certainly couldn't shoot or even threaten to shoot whoever or whatever I found in there. Not if I ever wanted to find out what the hell was going on here.

I did the last three meters to the access hole in a low crouch, listening as hard as I could with the noise of my heart thudding in my ears. I could hear faint ferret snufflings now from inside; more to the immediate point, I could also hear the subtle sounds of something else moving around in there with him. And if I didn't dare open fire indiscriminately, there was no guarantee that whatever was in there would have any such qualms itself. Dropping flat on the deck, I inched my way the last half meter and cautiously looked in.

At first glance the interior of the small sphere seemed to be nothing at all like the setup I'd seen back on the *Icarus*. A second, closer look showed that at least most of the apparent difference was due to the fact that all the couple of meters' worth of loose wiring I'd waded through in the *Icarus*'s sphere was here neatly packed against the inner surface, held in place by a tighter version of the netting I'd had to maneuver through there. The same type of displays were scattered around various spots on the netting, their multicolored lights providing the glow I'd seen out in the larger sphere. The black-and-silver-striped arm I'd played alien water slide with was also there, stretching its slightly angled way from the mesh to the center.

In some ways having all the wiring squeezed together this way made it look even more tangled than it had when it was spread out over a larger volume. It certainly made the whole spectacle more colorful, which was probably why it took me another couple of seconds before I noticed the movement a little way to my right. It was Pax, all right, looking hale and hearty and perfectly at home as he strolled across the netting toward me, sniffing curiously at everything in sight.

"Hello, McKell," a voice called out, the unexpectedness of it making me jump. "You certainly took your time getting here."

I looked in the direction of the voice. A quarter of the way around the sphere, almost hidden in the glare from one of the sets of displays, a figure was sitting on the netting. Gazing up at one of the other displays, he was scribbling madly on a notepad balanced across his knee.

It was Arno Cameron.

CHAPTER
17

It was a situation that called for a brilliant comment, a witty rejoinder, or complete silence. Not feeling either brilliant or witty at the moment, I kept my mouth shut, put away my plasmic, and concentrated instead on negotiating what I suspected would be a fairly tricky transition between the two spheres.

It turned out not to be nearly as difficult as I'd expected. This small sphere, unlike the one I'd had to burrow my way through on the *Icarus,* had its gravitational field pointed toward the surface rather than the center, so that aside from a little disorientation as I crawled around the edge of the access hole there was really nothing to it.

Between the maneuvering itself and a short face-licking attack from a Kalixiri ferret clearly relieved to see someone familiar, I managed to buy myself nearly a minute of recovery time before I had to try speaking. "So," I said, getting carefully to my feet on the netting and looking across at Cameron. The word was supposed to sound casual and debonair, as if I did this sort of thing all the time. Instead, it came out like the croak of a teenager facing down the parents of his very first date. So much for the efficacy of all that stalling.

But Cameron merely smiled as he turned off his notepad and laid it on the netting beside him. "I screamed and cried for half an hour after *I* got here," he said. "If that helps your dignity any."

"Thanks, but my dignity is expendable," I told him. This time the words came out much better. "Right now I'm more concerned with life, liberty, and the pursuit of greedy Patth and their vindictive buddies."

I glanced around. "And frankly, anything that scares Arno Cameron that much is something I really hesitate to tangle with."

"Don't worry, it's not as bad as I first thought." His eyebrows lifted slightly. "So you know who I am. What else do you know?"

I shrugged. "I know our alleged computer specialist Tera is your daughter Elaina Tera Cameron," I said. "Is it safe to walk on this stuff?"

"Perfectly safe," he assured me. "I'd avoid stepping on the displays, but everything else is as solid as the commark."

"The wires won't break or come loose?" I asked, dubiously eyeing the multicolored tangle beneath my feet.

"I've had a lot of time to examine them," he said. "Trust me, they're every bit as solid as the ones on the *Icarus*."

"Ah," I said, taking a cautious step toward him. "So in other words, all that exaggerated care I took getting through the *Icarus* sphere was a waste of effort?"

"If you want to look at it that way," he said with a shrug. "Personally, I've never found any effort to be completely wasted."

"Sure," I said noncommittally. The cables and conduits made little squooshing sounds as I walked over them, but aside from that it all felt firm enough. Still, there was no point in taking chances, and I kept it slow and careful. The gravity, I estimated, was about the same .85 gee as we had in the *Icarus*'s large sphere.

"So Elaina told you who she was," he commented as I picked my way toward him. "I'm a little surprised by that. I was very clear she was to keep her identity secret."

"It was a bit more complicated than that," I said, passing over the details. "Just to save time, I also know how you smuggled the *Icarus* onto Meima, both in its original disassembled form and then the orbital loop you did to bring it out of hiding and over to the spaceport. I know the Patth are becoming very insistent about getting their little paws on it."

I looked around the sphere. "And I *used* to know *why* they wanted it. Apparently, I was wrong."

Cameron exhaled noisily. "As were we all, my boy. Tell me, do you have any idea where we are right now?"

"Inside another of your alien artifacts, obviously," I said. "Which means that instead of a simple little stardrive, what your people dug up was actually the Holy Grail of the Einstein-Bashermain Unified Field Theory."

"An interesting but succinct way of putting it," Cameron said. "Yes, we are in fact sitting inside the physical proof that all those exotic wormhole and teleportation theories are more than just mathematical constructs. There's going to be a considerable amount of both gloating and backpedaling in the halls of academia when word of this gets out."

"Assuming word of it ever *does* get out," I said darkly. I had reached him now, and gave him a quick and hopefully unobtrusive once-over as I sat down gingerly on the mass of wiring in front of him. His face was drawn and pale, his cheeks and chin peppered with an impressive collection of beard stubble. He hadn't yet stood up; I wondered if he was perhaps too weak to do so. "If the Patth were willing to bribe, suborn, and kill for a stardrive that might or might not compete with theirs, imagine what they would do to get hold of a real working stargate."

"The Patth or anyone else, for that matter," he said with a grimace. "Which makes it all the more urgent that we get the *Icarus* to Earth before anyone else *does* find out what it is."

I cleared my throat. "Yes, well, I can immediately see a problem or two with that. Do you happen to have any idea how far we are from the *Icarus*?"

"All I know is that it's a considerable distance," he said, gesturing toward the large sphere. "There are a handful of small viewports out in the receiver chamber—they're unobtrusive, but I found the controls to open them. I've spent a good part of the past two days searching for a constellation—any constellation—that I can recognize. There's not a single one I can find, not even in distorted form."

"And I can assume you're not just talking Earth constellations?" I asked, just for the record.

The smile this time was very brittle. "I've been from one end of the Spiral to the other, McKell," he said. "I say again: Nothing was recognizable."

I felt a lump form in my throat. "Terrific," I murmured. "I hope like hell we're not poaching on someone else's territory."

"That could be unpleasant," he agreed. "Still, I've been here eleven days, and no one but you and your little pet here has shown up."

He frowned suddenly. "It *has* been eleven days since we landed on Potosi, hasn't it? Time rather blends together here."

"Yes, eleven's about right," I confirmed. "I take it this little side trip wasn't part of your scheme?"

He snorted. "Why, did you think it might be?"

"Considering all the rest of the finagling you and your daughter have done on this trip, I thought it worth asking," I said pointedly. "So how exactly *did* you wind up falling down the rabbit hole?"

He grimaced. "I slipped into the *Icarus*'s transmission chamber a little while before we left Potosi," he said. "Right after my encounter with the would-be murderer. I worked through the wiring—"

"Wait a second," I interrupted, the back of my neck tingling. "What do you mean, would-be murderer?"

"The man who was apparently planning to poison one of your crewers," he said. "Cabin Seven, down on the lower deck. Didn't you know?"

Ixil's cabin. "We knew something strange had happened there," I told him grimly. "But we haven't been able to make sense out of it. How about filling in the blanks?"

He shrugged. "There's not much I can tell you," he said. "Elaina told me everyone was leaving to look for a runaway crewer—Shawn, I think she said, the one with the medical condition. I had already decided to temporarily relocate to the small sphere, so I waited until the ship was quiet and headed to the lower deck to pick up some extra food supplies."

"How did you get out of the 'tweenhull area?" I asked. "Through Cabin Two, Jones's old cabin?"

"That's right," he said. "Elaina told you about that, too, I see. I take it that was you who chased me around the 'tweenhull area?"

"That's right," I confirmed.

"I thought so. At any rate, after you nearly caught me, I realized the 'tweenhull area wasn't a safe hiding place. I also didn't think it safe to stay permanently in Jones's cabin, which was why I'd decided to move into the small sphere. But when I reached the lower deck, I found that all the overhead lights had been turned off and there was a man with a small finger-light working on the cabin door."

"Could you see who it was?" I asked, feeling my

heartbeat pick up. At last, I was going to have a name to connect with Jones's murder.

The anticipation was premature. "Sorry," Cameron said, shaking his head. "The finger-light was set very low, and he was nothing more than a shadowy shape crouching by the doorway. From what little reflected backlight I was getting on his face, though, he didn't look familiar. Possibly someone from the port area who'd sneaked aboard while everyone was gone."

I clenched my teeth in frustration. "Unfortunately, the hatch was locked when they all left the ship," I said. "Which means one of the crew had to have come back to let him in."

"Ah." He peered closely at me. "Jones's murderer, you think?"

"I think having both a murderer and the accomplice of an entirely different murderer aboard a ship the size of the *Icarus* would be pushing coincidence a bit far," I said sourly. "All right, fine, so our murderer has friends. Who doesn't? What happened next?"

"He obviously thought the ship was deserted, because he was so engrossed in his work that I was nearly to him before he even realized I was there," Cameron said. "He'd gotten a big wrench wedged into the doorway to hold it open. Oh, I didn't mention that part. The door was only opening partway—"

"Yes, I know," I interrupted him. "I was the one who gimmicked it that way."

"Ah." He gave me an odd look, then shrugged. "At any rate, he turned just as I got within about two steps of him. I frankly didn't think I would make it the rest of the way, but he froze just long enough before straightening up and grabbing for the wrench. Fortunately for me, it was jammed in fairly tightly and he didn't have good leverage reaching over his shoulder that way, which meant I was able to step in close and get in the first punch. Edge-hand blow to the side of his neck."

I glanced down at his arms. Still well muscled, but to my perhaps hypercritical eye they looked thinner than they had when I'd seen him on Meima. "I gather it worked," I said.

"Rather to my amazement, it did," he said. "Especially since his light was dazzling my eyes at the time, which limited my ability to pick my target. I made sure to hit him again a couple of times on his way down, just to make sure. Again fortunately for me, he hit the deck and stayed there."

"It's so gratifying when they do that," I agreed. "Do you think you'd recognize him if you saw him again?"

"I doubt it," he said. "I really didn't get a good look at him. Besides, I imagine it's a moot point by now. He surely hightailed it off the ship as soon as he woke up. Unless you and the *Icarus* have suddenly picked up a new passenger, that is."

"No, no new passengers," I confirmed.

He spread his hands. "So that's that," he said. "You have to admit it's a big Spiral for a single man to lose himself in."

"I once thought it was a big Spiral for a single starship to lose itself in," I countered. "I don't think so anymore. So then what did you do?"

"After he was unconscious, I spotted the bottles he'd been working with on the floor and looked them over," he said. "Any doubts I'd had about hitting him vanished at that point; they turned out to be the ingredients for a cyanide-gas bomb.

"I knew I didn't have much time before he either awoke or all of you came trooping back aboard the ship, and I didn't have anything I could tie him up with, so I decided all I could do would be to thwart this particular scheme and call it a draw. The cabin door was still wedged open, so I resealed the bottles and put them as far inside as I could reach and then pulled the wrench out and let the door slam shut. Then, just to make sure he didn't have time to try anything else, I pulled the opening mechanism's control chip and added it to the pile and smashed what was left."

"Leaving a very thorny mystery in your wake," I said. "We were going nuts trying to figure out what happened there."

"I'm sorry," he said. "All I can say is that it wasn't my intent to be so mysterious. My plan was to hide out just for a day or two, until you'd had a chance to thoroughly search the 'tweenhull area and confirm there wasn't anyone in residence there. At that point I expected you to conclude that it had been one of the crew you'd chased around, give up your search for stowaways, and I could come back out. Then I'd be able to tell Elaina the whole story, and she would have found a way to warn you about future incursions into the ship from outside."

He shook his head, his throat tightening visibly. "Only it didn't quite work out that way. I made it through that tangled mess of a decompressed-wiring zone and found myself in a nice clear space. But then gravity came on, pulling me in toward the middle. I grabbed that striped arm to try to slow myself down, hit what I now realize was the triggering mechanism in the end, and here I am."

"A long way from nowhere," I said heavily, studying his slightly sunken cheeks. "Not to mention out of delivery range of the nearest grocery store. I'm a little surprised you haven't starved to death."

"My meals have been a bit sparse lately," he conceded. "I wasn't planning on being here very long, though of course I made sure to leave myself a wide margin for error. Not quite this wide, though. That's not a water bottle you have there with your pack, is it?"

I'd completely forgotten about the water bottle and food bars I was carrying. "Sure is," I said, feeling a twinge of admittedly selfish reluctance as I handed it over to him. This wasn't going to last even one person very long, let alone two of us. "Your daughter must be psychic," I added as he uncapped the bottle and drank deeply. "I was only planning a quick look into the small sphere, but she still made me take a survival pack along."

There was a moment of silence as he drank. I looked around the sphere again, this time spotting his camper's mattress and catalytic waste handler half-hidden in the glare of one of the display boards.

"Bless her heart," he said when he finally came up for air. I noticed with another twinge that the bottle was now only two-thirds full. "Fortunately for us, we're not going to need it."

I frowned. "What do you mean?"

"I mean we're going home," he said. He raised the bottle and had another drink, a shorter one this time. "Just as soon as we can gather my things together."

"Really," I said, my tone studiously neutral. I'd never heard of anyone going insane between eye blinks, which implied that he must have gone round the bend before I even got here. "Tell me how."

"No, my mind hasn't snapped, McKell," he assured me as he lifted an arm and pointed off to my right. "Look over there."

I followed the direction of his finger and found myself looking at one of the alien displays, this one marked with yellow-and-black squares. "All right. What is it?"

"It's the destination setting," he said. "Destination being defined as the particular stargate you'll be traveling to if you slide down the centering arm and hit the trigger. Now; do you see the display to its left?"

"Such as it is," I said. The second display was an identical array of squares, except that all of them were black.

"That one gives the identification code for the stargate you just left," he said. "Unfortunately, whether by design or malfunction, it only stays lit for a few minutes after transport before going blank again. That's why I couldn't get back by myself; by the time I realized the significance of that particular display, it had long since gone black. However—"

"Wait a minute," I said, frowning. "How do you know all this? Tera told me the Meima archaeologists didn't get very far in their analysis of the thing."

He shrugged. "Well, I *have* been here eleven days, you know," he reminded me. "I couldn't just sit around and do nothing. And though you probably didn't know it, I was once a Trem'sky Scholar in Alien Studies. I did quite a fair bit of archaeology and alien translation back in my youth."

It was a speech clearly and carefully designed to impress and lull the gullible. But I wasn't in the mood to be impressed, and lulling was completely out of the question. "That's baloney, and you know it," I said bluntly. "You had one course in archaeology and three in alien language, all of which focused on known species and didn't have a thing to do with interpreting unknown scripts. And that Trem'sky Scholarship was an honorary title Kaplanin University gave you after you donated fifty million commarks to them for a new archaeological research center."

His face had gone rigid. "You're very well informed," he said softly. "One might wonder how. And why."

"The *how* is that I have friends with good memories," I said. "The *why* is just as simple: I like to know who it is I'm working for. I certainly won't find that out by taking what *you* say at face value."

He eyed me speculatively. "You can see for yourself why I've been secretive about myself and my agenda," he said, waving a hand around him. "What's *your* excuse?"

"I like my life," I told him. "Not my current circumstances, necessarily, but the basic idea of continued existence."

"And what *are* your current circumstances?"

"Somewhat messy," I said. "But we're getting away from the point. How do you know so much about the stargate?"

We locked gazes for another few seconds. Then his eyes drifted away from mine, as if he was too tired to keep up his end of the nonverbal battle. "Elaina doesn't know this," he said, "but the archaeologists had already cracked much of the alien script before my people and I arrived on Meima to build the *Icarus*. With that hurdle crossed, we were able to gain considerable knowledge of the inner workings of the artifact."

His lips puckered. "Though we still thought that what we had was a new stardrive, with the destination and incoming displays having to do with navigation."

"So where is all this knowledge?" I asked. "I presume you're not going to try to tell me you memorized it."

His expression had gone all speculative again. "Why do you need to know?"

"In case something happens to you," I explained patiently. "I don't know whether you know it, but you're the very last of the Mohicans now—the rest of your group has been rounded up and are in Ihmisit hands. Possibly Patth hands by now, actually; I haven't kept up-to-date on developments. If they get you, too, that'll be it as far as the good guys are concerned."

"And if you know where the data is, you might be tempted to trade it for that life you want so much to keep," he pointed out. "I think it might be safer if I kept that little secret to myself for the time being."

I snorted. "Standing tall and stalwart against the invading hordes might be good melodrama, but it makes lousy real-world policy," I told him flatly. "Face it, Cameron, you're in a dangerous and completely untenable position here, and you're going to have to bite the bullet and trust someone. At the moment, that's me."

Again his eyes drifted away. "I suppose you're right," he said with a sigh. "All right. The data is stored in code in a file on my notepad here. If something happens to me, either Elaina or my executive assistant Stann Avery will be able to locate and decode it."

"Got it," I said. It wasn't the entire truth, I knew—he'd given in much too easily for that. But it was probably at least a partial truth, and for the moment I could live with that. "All right, then. I'll send you in some more food and water when I get back to the *Icarus*. Is your little toilet system working okay?"

"Wait a minute," he said, his face suddenly gone taut. "What do you mean, when *you* get back? We can both go—no one has to stay here to operate the device."

I shook my head. "Sorry, but I'm afraid you can't show your face yet. I didn't tell you: We've disassembled most of the ship's interior. Makes it a lot safer for the return trip, but it also means there's no place left where you could have been hiding. You suddenly pop up now and someone's going to start putting the pieces together."

"What about the smaller sphere?" he asked, his voice taking on an edge of panicked insistence. "I could have been hiding in the smaller sphere."

"Besides which, you're the one who holds the key to this bombshell," I continued, gesturing at his notepad. "Don't forget, we've got a murderer aboard the *Icarus*. The farther you and your notepad stay away from him, the better."

He wasn't happy about it—that much was evident from the play of emotions across his face. But he could see the logic in what I was saying, and a few extra days of isolation didn't stack up all that badly against the possibility of being knifed in the back. Slowly, reluctantly, he gathered control of himself and nodded.

"You're right," he said with a sigh. "All right, I'll stay. Any idea how long I'll have to be here?"

"Until we find a safe place to put down," I said. "Don't worry, I'll let you know."

"You'd better," he warned with a game attempt at a smile. "The view in here doesn't really have all that much to recommend it."

"You can start naming the constellations," I suggested, getting to my feet. "So. How do I work this thing?"

He gestured to the articulated arm angling its way toward the center of the sphere twenty meters above us. "Once I've set the destination panel, I expect all you'll need to do is work your way along the arm to the trigger section at the end," he said. "Basically the same as you did on the *Icarus*."

Except that on the *Icarus* the gravitational field had been pointing the other way. It looked like I was in for a long climb. "Right," I said. "Don't worry if it takes me a couple of hours to get the supplies to you. There isn't a lot of privacy in the ship right now, and I don't want anyone to catch me putting a survival pack together. Someone might jump to the wrong conclusion."

"Or even the right one?" he suggested.

I nodded. "Especially the right one."

A ghost of something flicked across his face. "You'll let my daughter know I'm all right, won't you? We've hardly spoken since the trip began—there just haven't been any safe opportunities—but I know she's worried about me."

"And vice versa?" I suggested.

His lips compressed. "Very much vice versa," he agreed quietly. "I'd appreciate it if you'd watch over her for me."

"I will," I promised. "You can count on it."

For a moment he studied my face, as if trying one last time to see if I was indeed someone in whom he could place this kind of trust. I met his eyes stolidly, not flinching away from the probe, exuding all the sincerity I could muster. And after a couple of heartbeats he nodded. "All right," he said with a sigh. "You'd best be on your way, then."

I nodded and gave a whistle. Pax emerged from a mass of wiring he'd been nosing through and bounded enthusiastically over to me. I managed to catch him before he could start with equal enthusiasm up my leg and settled him into a cradling carry in the crook of my elbow. "I'll let you know when you can come out," I told him, crossing the sphere to where the arm was anchored. "I'll either come myself or send in one of the ferrets."

"Understood," he said. "Good luck."

"You, too," I said. Reaching up with my free hand, I wrapped my legs around it and started awkwardly to climb.

The awkwardness didn't last long. I'd barely started my climb when I felt myself rapidly going weightless. For about five seconds I hung there in zero gee, and then the gravity began again, only this time pointed the opposite direction, toward the center of the sphere. I quickly turned myself around, noticing that Cameron was still glued, albeit openmouthed, to the inner surface. I don't know why finding a two-tier artificial gravity in our unknown aliens' bag of tricks should have surprised me, but it did. The level of the pull stayed about where it had been aboard the *Icarus*, keeping me moving inward without giving me the feeling of uncontrolled falling. I looked over—up, rather—at Cameron once as Pax and I slid down toward the center, wondering if he'd noticed that I'd somehow never gotten around to agreeing to his request that I tell Tera he was here.

Because there was no way I was going to let her in on what the *Icarus* really was. No way in hell; for the simple reason that that would require me letting her know that *I* knew what it really was. As a possibly advanced stardrive that might or might not still function, the *Icarus* had a value that was potentially high but still nebulous. As a stargate with proven capabilities, that value had suddenly solidified to an astronomical level.

And I had no intention of letting Tera come to the realization that the *Icarus*'s asking price was now light-years beyond the paltry half-million debt that held me enslaved to Brother John and the Antoniewicz organization. Enough to buy me out of that contract, guarantee me immunity from prosecution for every illegal act I'd ever committed, and set me up for a lifetime of luxury on top of it.

I had reached the trigger. I took one last look at Cameron, who didn't know any of what his daughter had learned about me. But as I squeezed the trigger, and the tingling and blackness closed in around me, I wondered oddly if he might possibly have guessed the truth.

CHAPTER
18

The trip back to the *Icarus* probably took no longer than the trip out from it had. I say *probably* because it definitely seemed longer. Partly that was due to the fact that I was expecting it, with the accompanying sense of slightly cringing anticipation, and partly because this time I had a Kalixiri ferret cradled in my arm, whose main reaction to the tingling sensation was to attempt to dig his claws into whatever patches of skin were within easy reach.

Mostly, though, it was due to the uncomfortable awareness that a single miscalculation on Cameron's part would leave me in very serious trouble indeed. Because if Cameron *had* guessed that I was not precisely what he thought he'd hired back at that Meima taverno, and if he'd decided he didn't want someone like me aboard his ship anymore, then a small mistake on the encoding panel would be the absolute simplest way of getting rid of me for good.

But Pax's claws didn't get to anything that wouldn't heal by itself, and Cameron hadn't made any mistakes, deliberate or otherwise. There below me were the stacks of interior wall panels awaiting the attention of Chort and his welding team outside, the other stacks of equipment and paraphernalia, and the archaic computer humming beside the gaping access panel.

The relatively minuscule part of my mind that hadn't been worried about me ending up in the wrong stargate at the wrong end of the universe had occupied itself with the question of how I was going to explain my sudden appearance to Tera without giving away the true nature of her father's discovery. But to my mild surprise Tera was nowhere to be seen, either at the access panel or half-hidden in the shadows thrown by the sections of inner hull that we'd left in place because of the wiring conduits fastened to their undersides. For a moment I wondered uneasily if she might have taken it upon herself to crawl into the small sphere after me, but as I began the by-now-familiar downward drift toward the surface I realized she had more likely simply gone around to the access panel in the engineering section to see if I was coming out there.

For a change, Lady Luck seemed to be smiling on me. Then again, maybe the fickle wench was just lulling me into a false sense of security while she reached for a rock.

I had made it to the surface, ready this time for the sudden surge in gravitational strength in that final meter, and was picking my way through the obstacle course toward the access panel when the hatchway to the wraparound opened. Tera, undoubtedly, come to ask questions I had no intention of answering.

But to my mild surprise it wasn't Tera who came crawling out of the zero gee of the wraparound toward me. It was, instead, Chort, still vacsuited but with his helmet hanging from the neck connector and bouncing gently against his shoulder blades. "Captain McKell," he puffed as he caught sight of me. "Good—I had hoped to find you here."

I resisted the impulse to ask where else he thought I might have gotten to. It would have been unnecessarily sarcastic, and given my experiences of the past hour, would have been rather disingenuous as well. "Is there a problem?" I asked instead as I set Pax down.

"We have to leave this place," he said, pulling himself the rest of the way into the sphere and standing up. "As soon as possible."

I frowned. "Are you finished with the cowling already?"

He twitched his head. "No, not entirely," he said. "But there will be no finishing. Electronics Specialist Shawn is ill."

I grimaced. In the excitement of my trip to nowhere and back I'd almost forgotten about this constraint on our little operation. "How bad is he?"

"You will see for yourself soon," Chort said, his voice noticeably more whistly than usual. "Drive Specialist Nicabar will be bringing him inside as soon as his seizure is ended."

I felt the hairs on the back of my neck tingling unpleasantly. Seizures? That was a new one on me. "Does Revs need help?"

Another twitch of the head. "He assured me he can manage on his own. But we will need to obtain more medicine as soon as possible."

"Understood," I said, stepping over to the computer and tapping the intercom to the engine room. "Ixil?"

"There you are," Tera's voice came back almost instantly. "Where have you *been*?"

"Where do you think I've been?" I retorted. "Inside that damn puzzle box disentangling Ixil's damn ferret from all that damn wiring. Why, wasn't I moving fast enough for you? Put Ixil on."

She didn't reply, and I could imagine her floundering with surprise at my uncharacteristic harshness. I felt a twinge of guilt, but at the moment hurt feelings were low on my priority list. "Yes, Jordan?" Ixil's voice came calmly.

"Shawn's having some kind of seizure," I told him. "Revs will be bringing him in as soon as it's over. Start kicking the thrusters and stardrive back to life, and send Everett and Tera over to this side before we have to seal down the wraparound again."

"Understood," he said. "They're on their way."

"Good," I said. "Oh, and I've got Pax. He's safe and sound." A thought occurred to me—"I'll bring him back around to you in a minute."

I keyed off before he could ask why I would waste time bringing a safe and sound ferret around to him now instead of concentrating on the navigational part of our upcoming trip. "What shall I do?" Chort asked.

"Go get the treatment table ready for him," I said, pointing across toward the pile of sick-bay equipment. "Then stand by to assist Everett. I've got to get Pax back to Ixil in case he needs him."

The excuse, lame though it was, was unnecessary. Chort probably didn't even hear it as he took off at a quick jog across the sphere. I headed in the opposite direction, toward my personal kit and the food supplies that had been stored near my cabin and were now conveniently piled nearby. I'd promised Cameron some supplies, and this could very well be my last clear chance for a while to get them to him.

I'd just finished filling my bag with food bars and water bottles when Everett and Tera emerged from the wraparound. Everett made a beeline for Chort and the medical setup; Tera, not surprisingly, made an equally straight beeline for me.

I met her halfway. "Well?" she asked in a low and anxious voice, her expression that of someone braced for the worst.

I shook my head. "He's not in there," I said. "Not alive, not dead, not injured."

The anxiety in her face eased, but only fractionally. "Then where *is* he?" she asked.

"I don't know," I told her, a statement that was technically correct, though misleading as hell. "Maybe he got off at Potosi after all."

She turned her eyes away from me. "He wouldn't have left the *Icarus*," she said quietly. "Not voluntarily."

I thought about that one. Another technically correct statement, though she didn't know it. "Perhaps," I said. "I wouldn't give up hope, though. If anyone can find a place to hide where the Patth can't find him, it'll be your father."

She took a careful breath. "I hope so."

"I know so," I said, turning my eyes away from her in turn. The quiet pain on her face was tugging hard at my conscience, making me want to tell her that he was all right.

But with a heroic effort I resisted the temptation. If I even let myself start dropping hints as to the true situation here, I would go from comforter to suspect in nothing flat. Neither of us could afford that. "Look, I'd love to chat some more," I said instead. "But I have to get this stuff to Ixil before Nicabar needs to turn the wraparound into an airlock again."

"Sure," she said automatically, her thoughts clearly still with her father.

Which for the immediate moment was all to the good. If I could get out of her sight before she thought to ask what I had in my bag, it would mean one less thing I would have to lie to her about. Whistling for Pax, who was rooting around the food stores, I headed out into the wraparound.

Ixil was drifting around the cramped space of the engine section like a massive cloud, checking and double-checking monitors and indicators as he eased the thrusters and stardrive back to life. "I'm glad to see you're all right," he said, dropping his eyes to Pax as I gave the ferret a nudge that sent him floating through the air in Ixil's direction, squeaking happily as his claws scrabbled through the air in search of a pawhold. "Both of you," he added as Pax reached him and clawed his way up the tunic to his accustomed place on Ixil's shoulder. "Any problems?"

"Hang on to your teeth," I advised, crossing toward the access panel into the small sphere, which Tera had thoughtfully left open for me. "I'll make you a small wager you're not going to believe the ride Pax and I had."

The tangle of wiring on this side of the sphere was as bad as the matching set on the other side had been. Now, though, after Cameron's assurances that the stuff was stronger than it looked, I was far less concerned that an accidental bump might irrevocably damage something. Accordingly, I plowed my way inside, pushing the wires and conduits aside with relatively reckless abandon, and as a result took only five minutes to reach the mesh instead of the hour it had taken me going in from the opposite side.

Hovering just inside the mesh, I pulled out a pad and scribbled a quick note to Cameron, warning him again not to budge from his private hermitage until one of the ferrets or I came for him. I stuffed the note into the pack, and with careful aim sent the whole bundle dropping gently toward the end of the control arm. At the last minute it occurred to me that perhaps having the pack bump into the end wouldn't be enough, that it might require an actual grip of some sort to trigger the mechanism. If so, I would have to figure out a way to retrieve the bag and send it back down with Pix strapped somehow to it. At that point I would also have to figure out how to explain the ferret's disappearance to the rest of the crew, because the last thing I could afford would be for Pix to suddenly appear in the center of the large sphere with the whole bunch of us in there with him.

But evidently a grip was not required. The bag slid down the arm to the end, and without any fuss whatsoever it vanished. There was a faint, brief breeze as air rushed into the hole where it had been, and that was that.

I worked my way out back to the rim—another five-minute trip—and climbed out into the engine section. Ixil was strapped into the control chair now, both ferrets on his shoulders, a look on his face that I'd never seen before. "So," I said conversationally as I swung the hinged breaker panel closed again over the access hole. "What do you think?"

With an obvious effort he focused on me. "It's unbelievable," he said quietly. "Absolutely unbelievable."

"Isn't it though," I agreed. "But it's real."

Absently, Ixil reached up to rub Pax's head. "We can't let the others know about this," he said. "The Patth would be willing to topple whole governments if they really knew what it was they were chasing."

"Yes, I've already worked through the logic," I assured him. "Including the fact that we can't tell Tera, either."

The ferrets did one of their unison twitches. "Because we work for Brother John?"

"And because turning the *Icarus* over to him would more than buy our way clear of the whole organization," I said. "She doesn't trust us as it is—she'd spot-weld our butts to the hull if she knew the bargaining chip we held here."

"Yes." Ixil was silent a moment. "Which unfortunately loops us back to the question of our immediate future."

I grimaced. "I don't think we have any choice," I said. "Unless we want to sit out here and watch Shawn die, we have to go get him some more borandis."

"I wonder," Ixil said thoughtfully. "We have only his word that he even has the disease, you know. As I recall, Everett was unable to either confirm or deny it.

What if he's faking all this, with these seizures his way of pulling us out of hiding before we're ready?"

"In that case, we're back to the question of why he didn't betray us earlier and save everyone a lot of trouble," I reminded him.

"I suppose." He eyed me closely. "You wouldn't be holding out on me, would you?"

"Holding out how?" I asked.

"Oh, I don't know," he said with a shrug. "Actually considering offering the *Icarus* to Brother John without consulting me first, for example."

"Don't be silly," I said, putting some huff into my voice. "Though you have to admit that would be one way to keep it safe."

" 'Safe' being an extremely relative term."

"True," I conceded. "Still, Brother John could probably give even the Patth a pretty good run for their money."

"And of course, turning such a plum over to him would give us a giant step up in the Antoniewicz organization," he continued. "Don't pretend that hadn't already occurred to you, either."

"Occurred, pondered, and dismissed," I assured him. "I have plenty of faults, but ambition on that scale isn't one of them." I cocked an eyebrow at him. "Unless *you'd* like to take a shot at it."

"What, be the first nonhuman in Antoniewicz's direct line of command?" he asked dryly. "Thanks, but I think I'll pass."

I waved a hand. "Up to you. By the way, do you happen to know if Nicabar's gotten Shawn back inside the ship yet?"

"Yes, they came in while you were inside the small sphere," he said. "Tera will let us know when the wraparound's been repressurized." He cocked his head to the side. "She seemed rather annoyed you'd gotten yourself trapped on this side of the wraparound when you had work to do over there."

"Actually, there's very little work left to do," I said with a shrug. "I already know where we're heading."

"And that is?"

I cleared my throat. "I thought we'd try the Grand Feast of Plorins on Palmary."

The ferrets twitched again, quite impressively this time. "You *are* joking," Ixil said. "The Grand Feast of *Plorins*?"

"Can you think of a better place to hide than square in the middle of a wall-to-wall crowd of people?" I asked reasonably.

"With half the thieves, lifters, and cons for two hundred light-years working that same crowd?" he countered. "*And,* as a consequence, half the badgemen for the same two hundred light-years there to keep an eye on them? And both groups busy looking for us?"

"Of course it's crazy," I agreed. "That's why no one will be expecting it."

He shook his head. But at least the ferrets had settled down again. He must be getting used to the idea. " 'Crazy' isn't nearly strong enough a word," he said with a sigh. "But under the circumstances I suppose it's as good a plan as any."

"That's the spirit," I said approvingly. "Besides, they'll be watching every port within a thousand light-years of Utheno anyway. The bigger the clog of space traffic we sneak in under, the better the chances they'll miss us completely."

He gave me one of his repertoire of sour looks. "And the more confusion and panic we can stir up if they don't?"

I shrugged. "Something like that."

The intercom clicked. "McKell?" Tera's voice came. "Wraparound's ready again. You feel like getting your butt in here and finding us a place to land?"

"Yes, dear," I murmured.

"What was that?"

"I said I'll be right there," I said. "And tell Revs to

get back here and give Ixil a hand with the startup procedure."

Palmary was one of those semi-independent colony worlds that, while relatively newly settled, still somehow managed to seem like it had been there forever. Part of that was the fact that, unlike most colonies, there was no dominant species controlling most of the local real estate. The Trinkians had found the world about twenty years ago and started its development, but within a few years they'd been joined by Wanch settlers, Porpyfian miners, and k'Tra foresters. Someone on some news service had touted the place, commenting favorably on its egalitarian flavor, and within a few years more the planet was starting to seem almost crowded.

The Grand Feast of Plorins was something the k'Tra had brought with them, and the rest of the egalitarians on the planet had grabbed on to the idea with both hands. Depending on who you talked to, the Grand Feast was either a deeply meaningful manifestation of esoteric historic and cultural significance, or else the greatest excuse to party the Spiral had ever known. I assumed the truth was probably somewhere in the middle, where truth has a tendency to lurk anyway, but I was certainly willing to concede the point that millions of beings who had not the slightest interest in k'Tra history or culture nevertheless descended enthusiastically on the planet every year for a three-week bash.

The Grand Feast was sometimes compared to the annual Mardi Gras celebrations that still took place in various places on Earth and its colonies. Mardi Gras invariably lost.

I had used the hull cameras to take a quick look at the changes that had been made to the ship before we ever took to hyperspace again. Chort was right: The disguise was far from perfect. On the other hand, he and his helpers had gotten enough of the plates in place to markedly change both our visual and radar signatures, which was hopefully all we would need to get to the ground without tripping alarms from the underworld to the Patth and back again.

Once we were on the ground, of course, it would be a different story. Someone who wandered in close for a good look would easily be able to see through the gaps to the distinctive joined spheres beneath. But I had a couple of ideas for dealing with that one; and anyway, getting to the ground was the first order of business.

After the near disaster at Utheno the situation at Palmary was decidedly anticlimactic. The official start of the Grand Feast was still three days away, but the hard-core party types were already clogging the space lanes as they headed in to scope out the best celebration spots or just get a head start on the festivities. With our new silhouette, plus yet another of Ixil's fake IDs identifying us as the *Sherman's Blunder,* we sailed straight through the prelanding formalities. A harried-sounding controller directed me to a landing rectangle at the Bangrot Spaceport, a name that didn't even show up on my supposedly comprehensive listing, and instructed us to have a good time.

The reason for the lack of a listing was apparent as soon as I got within visual range of the coordinates I'd been given. The Bangrot Spaceport was nothing more than a large open area stretching across the southern ends of the twin cities Drobney and k'Barch, an area that looked to me like a former condemned building development. Apparently, the Grand Feast had grown so large they were now having to park spaceships on every reasonably sized vacant lot they could find.

And the official celebration didn't even start for three more days. Give this whole thing a few years, and they might as well declare it a permanent party and be done with it.

One might have assumed that the Bangrot Expansion Spaceport would be only sparsely settled, with the bulk of the space still waiting for the arrival of the latecomers. But one would have been wrong. The place was crowded with ships, already crammed in practically nose to tail, with the narrow spaces between them crawling with activity. As far as this party was concerned, we *were* the latecomers.

I was also a little worried about what would happen to the definitions of "up" and "down" inside the *Icarus* as we went deeper into the Palmary gravity field. Tera had told us that on Meima the alien gravity generator in the large sphere had been able to cancel out all other gravitational effects, but that was before Cameron's techs had gotten in and started messing around. If it failed to overcome Palmary's gravitational attraction I was going to suddenly find myself lying on my back in my seat as I tried to pilot the ship to the ground. Or worse, our jury-rigged seating system might fail completely and I would find myself, my seat, and possibly my entire control board falling to the bottom of the sphere some twenty meters below.

That particular set of fears proved groundless. With the removal of the metal baffling that had been created by the inner hull, walls, and corridors, the alien generator had come back to full strength, and I didn't feel so much as a flicker of change in the gravity as I eased the *Icarus* down onto the undersized plot of ground we'd been assigned.

"Now what?" Tera called to me from across the sphere, her voice echoing through the open space as I keyed the ship's systems back to standby.

"I go scare us up some borandis," I said, craning my neck to look up at her, watching the top of her head as she got up from her seat at the computer and walked toward the wraparound.

"What about the rest of us?" Shawn called up from a quarter of the way around the sphere, at the natural bottom point of the ship. I'd stationed everyone else except Nicabar down there on the theory that there was no point in letting *everyone* fall to their deaths if the alien gravity failed. "I suppose we're all going to sit around here like we did before and just wait for you? Twiddling our thumbs or whatever?"

"You're welcome to twiddle whatever you want," I told him, walking down the curve toward them, "since you and Everett are staying in here where he can try to keep you quiet until I get back with the medicine."

I pointed at Chort and Tera, the latter approaching the group from the other side. "*You* two and Nicabar, on the other hand, aren't going to have time to twiddle much of anything. I want the three of you to collect all the emergency lights we've got and start stringing them just inside the gaps in the shroud out there, with the lights shining outward. All nice and decorative for the Grand Feast, and with any luck the glare will keep everyone from seeing past them to the linked spheres underneath."

"Maybe we could also get hold of some colored transparent sheeting to cover them with," Tera suggested. "They'd look even more festive that way."

"Probably would," I agreed. "But I don't know how well they've got this temporary spaceport equipped. I don't want anyone wandering too far afield hunting for anything that's not really vital."

"They've got tram systems leading from the port into each of the two city centers," Nicabar put in from the wraparound, apparently having arrived in time to hear this last exchange. "I spotted them on the monitors while you were putting us down. If they had time to set those up, they've surely got an outfitters' shop or two in place. I can go check—it won't take me long."

"Forget it," Shawn growled before I could answer. "He never lets anyone go anywhere except him, remember? Just him."

"Shawn," Everett said warningly, putting a massive hand on the kid's shoulder.

"Don't 'Shawn' me," Shawn snapped, angrily shrugging off the hand. "I'm not a child, you know."

"If you want to make a quick check, go ahead," I told Nicabar. "Just watch yourself, and be back in half an hour to help Tera and Chort with the lights."

"I will," Nicabar promised. "Don't worry—it's a zoo out there. I won't even be noticed." Turning, he disappeared back down the wraparound.

"What about him?" Tera asked, nodding toward Ixil, who was standing slightly off to the side keeping out of the conversation.

"He'll be in overall charge here," I told her, ignoring the glare Shawn was giving me, this particular bile probably a result of me proving him wrong by letting Nicabar go. Even at his best Shawn hated being proved wrong, and in the middle of borandis withdrawal he was a long way from his best. "He'll also be using Pix and Pax to keep an eye on things outside the ship."

"How do you plan to get it this time?" Tera asked. "The borandis, I mean."

I focused on her face. She was gazing evenly back at me, her expression not giving anything away.

But then, the fact that she didn't want her expression giving anything away spoke volumes all by itself. "Why, you feeling squeamish?" I countered. "I'll do whatever I have to. Leave it at that."

"Fine," she said, not taking offense. At least no visible offense. "I just want to remind you that we can't afford for you to get into any trouble. If you don't make it back, we don't lift."

"I'll make it back," I assured her, brushing past her and heading up toward the wraparound. "Don't worry about me," I added over my shoulder. "You just concentrate on getting those lights up and running."

The transition between the different gravity vectors

of the sphere and the wraparound was as always a bit tricky to navigate, but I managed it without any serious loss of balance or dignity. Nicabar had already opened the hatchway and lowered the ladder the ten meters to the ground; checking to make sure my plasmic was riding loose in its holster, I stepped to the top of the ladder and looked down.

Nicabar had been right: It was indeed a zoo out there. The close packing of the parked ships was funneling the prospective merrymakers down the relatively narrow lanes between them, lanes they were further having to share with fueling trucks, the occasional token customs vehicle, and about a million little two-man runaround cars that were obviously intended to alleviate the pedestrian congestion but were only succeeding in making it worse.

All of which boiled down to about as ideal a situation as I could have asked for. Even if the Patth and their lumpy Iykami allies were out there looking for us, the sheer volume of people they would have to sift through ought to make this as quick and clean as possible. Getting my bearings toward the nearest spur of the tram lines Nicabar had mentioned, I headed down the ladder and elbowed my way into the river of pedestrians.

My first thought had been to try to corral one of the cars for myself. But there weren't any unused ones in sight, so I set off on foot. Which was just as well, I quickly realized, as I saw how easily the cars were getting snarled up in the traffic flow. The tram spur wasn't that far away, and I could use the exercise. And the time to do some hard thinking.

But not about how I was going to acquire Shawn's borandis. Despite my somewhat melodramatic pronouncement to Tera about doing whatever I had to, that part was actually going to be the least of my worries. With borandis a perfectly legal substance for at least a dozen of the species jostling against me, every pharmacy on the planet would have the stuff in stock, with few if any questions asked. No, the immediate and burning question right now was the same one that had been gnawing at me for quite a while: how to get the *Icarus* to Earth ahead of the Patth.

Along with the subsidiary question of whether that was even the smart thing for me to do.

Because lurking in the back of my mind was my most recent conversation with Ixil, and his half-joking question of whether I would be offering the *Icarus* to Brother John instead. Then, I'd assured him I had no intention of doing so; now, though, I wasn't nearly so sure it wasn't the best solution we had. It would keep the stargate in human hands—bloody hands, certainly, but human nevertheless—as well as giving me the kind of career boost someone in my position could usually only dream of. I might even get to meet the elusive Mr. Antoniewicz, which would put me in exalted company indeed.

Cameron wouldn't be pleased by such a move, of course. Neither would Tera; and if Tera wasn't happy, Nicabar probably wouldn't be happy, either. The two of them seemed to have become quite chummy since that confrontation on the bridge regarding my shadier business associations. Still, at this point, other people's happiness or lack thereof wasn't particularly high on my priority list. We'd covered barely a fifth of the distance from Meima to Earth, and already we'd had far too many close calls than I cared to think about. The others, believing that the *Icarus* was a superfast alien stardrive, undoubtedly still had their hopes pinned on using it to beat out the Patth net; Ixil and I, on the other hand, knew that hope was nonexistent.

On almost every level I could think of, the idea made sense. And Cameron and Tera would surely get over their pique eventually. Still, I reluctantly concluded, I wasn't quite ready to make such a decision. Not yet. Maybe once we were off Palmary.

The tram line, for all its obviously quick assembly, was still more comfortable and professional than transports I'd used on a lot of supposedly more advanced worlds. I arrived at the platform to find a pair of trams already waiting, one each heading in to the cities of Drobney and k'Barch. I picked the k'Barch one, reasoning that the place with a k'Tra name would probably have a more frenetic celebration level, and hence more cover for a man on the run.

Most of my fellow travelers had apparently come to a similar conclusion, though undoubtedly with different motivations. I let the traffic flow carry me in through the doors and to a standing point midway down one of the cars, jammed between a group of sweaty Narchners and a group of clean but equally aromatic Saffi.

We headed out. I had enough of a view out one of the side windows to see that Nicabar's assumption had been correct: Not only was there a good-sized outfitters' store at the junction of the two tram lines, but also a collection of restaurants, tavernos, and gawk-shops. Even StarrComm had gotten into the act, setting up a prefab satellite station so that spacers who felt the need to get in touch with the outside universe wouldn't have to go to wherever their main building was in the twin-city area. Once again, I raised my estimate of how much money this Grand Feast must pour into the Palmary economy.

We rumbled our way to the end of the line, which from the look of things was relatively close to the middle of k'Barch and perilously near the epicenter of the upcoming celebrations. The earlier flow through the tram doors reversed itself, and a few chaotic minutes later I was maneuvering my way down a sidewalk that was only marginally less crowded than the inside of the tram had been. About a block ahead, I could see the rustling display flag of a pharmacy, and I concentrated on making my way toward it.

I had reached the shop and was working my way sideways through the crowd toward the door, when something exploded against the back of my neck, plunging me into darkness.

CHAPTER
19

I came to slowly, drifting back toward consciousness in gradual and tortured stages. There was a vague sensation of discomfort, which first coalesced into an overall chill and stiffness before zeroing in on a throbbing somewhere in the back of my head. There was something wrong with my arms, though I couldn't figure out exactly what. There was light somewhere, too, though as vague and undefined as the discomfort had originally been, and the distant thought occurred to me that if I turned my head maybe I could figure out where it was coming from. It took some time and effort to remember how that could be done, but finally I had it doped out. Feeling rather pleased with my accomplishment, I turned my head a little to the side.

And instantly came fully awake as a flare of pain burned through the back of my skull. Someone, apparently, was doing his best to rip my head off my spine with his bare hands. Clenching my teeth, I waited until the pain had mostly subsided; then, keeping my head as motionless as possible, I eased open my eyes.

I was sitting in a plain wooden armchair, unpadded, my head lolled forward with my chin resting on my chest. What was wrong with my arms was quickly apparent: both wrists were handcuffed to the chair arms on which they were resting. Experimentally, I shifted my right foot a bit and found that they hadn't bothered to lock my feet in place as they had my arms. In the background I could hear the faint sounds of distant music; closer at hand, somewhere just in front of me, I could also hear the sounds of quiet alien conversation. Slowly, mindful of the trip-hammer waiting to resume work on the back of my skull, I carefully raised my head to look.

And immediately wished I hadn't. I was in a medium-sized room, plain and largely unfurnished, with a single light in the ceiling and a single closed door maybe four meters directly ahead of me. Seated behind a low wooden table midway between the door and me, my partially disassembled phone on the tabletop in front of them, were two more members of the lumpy Iykami Clan.

At the moment, though, they weren't paying any attention to the phone, nor to any of the rest of my pocket equipment that had been unceremoniously dumped out onto the table. My efforts at stealthy wakefulness to the contrary, they were looking straight at me.

And not, as near as I could tell from those alien faces, with particularly friendly expressions. They were more the sort of expressions worn by people who have orders to keep a prisoner alive and mostly well, but who are at the same time secretly longing for said prisoner to make trouble and thus provide them with an excuse to beat the living daylights out of him.

Cooperative type that I was, it seemed a shame to disappoint them.

I came up on my feet, hunched forward for balance as I gripped the arms to hold the chair more or less in place against my back and rear. Their secret hopes notwithstanding, a sudden and clearly suicidal attack on my part was probably the last thing they were actually expecting; and the shock had just enough time to register on their faces as I took two quick steps forward and swung 180 degrees around, taking care not to let my chair get hung up on the edge of their table. With all the strength I could muster, I heaved myself and the chair as hard as I could squarely on top of them.

They saw it coming, of course. But seated with their legs under the table, there wasn't a single thing they could do about it. We all went down together in a confused and thunderous crash of splintering wood and alien curses. Still handcuffed to the chair, my movements were severely limited, but even so I was in a far better fighting position than my opponents. Flailing back and forth, hammering them with the chair and keeping them pinned beneath me, I lashed out with my feet, throwing kick after kick to head and torso and anything else I could reach. After what seemed like forever through the haze of pain from my head, they stopped moving. I gave them each another couple of kicks, just in case they were faking, then collapsed in a panting heap amid the carnage.

I didn't stay collapsed long, though. It had been a serious gamble on my part, taking them on just after waking up, but I hadn't had much choice in the matter. Two-to-one odds were as good as I was likely to get; and if I'd waited for them to call whoever was in charge with the news that the sacrificial Voodoo doll was awake and ready to have pins stuck in him, I'd never have left the room alive.

An unhappy ending that could still very easily happen. The brief fight had been anything but quiet, and the music I could hear in the distance meant that there was at least *someone* else in the immediate vicinity. My chair had suffered some damage in the fight, but enough of it had survived to keep me pinioned. Rolling around awkwardly, keeping an ear cocked for the inevitable reaction, I started checking my unconscious jailers for the keys to my handcuffs.

They were wearing the same sort of neo-Greek tunics as the two who'd jumped me on Xathru, and it didn't take long to find out that the limited pocket space that came with the outfits included no handcuff keys. One had a belt pouch, similarly bereft of keys. Neither was carrying a weapon.

But a couple of meters away on the floor where it had fallen at the table's collapse was my phone.

My imprisoning chair had gotten itself caught in a slight hollow formed by the bodies of the two Iykams, but a little rocking broke me free. I rolled up onto my knees, got to my feet, and picked my way through the debris to the phone. At this range I could see the Iykams hadn't gotten any further in their disassembly of the device than merely pulling the back off, though why they'd even done that I didn't know. Perhaps they were hoping to tease a latent phone number or two out of the memory that they could use.

If so, they were out of luck. That was the phone I'd taken from James Fulbright on Dorscind's World, and there were no incriminating numbers connected with me anywhere in there, latent or otherwise.

Still, I was glad they'd kept the phone around long enough to try, since it had now put communication with the outside world in my hands. Easing onto my side on the floor within reach of the phone, I rolled the device onto its back. I was still in big trouble, but a quick call to Ixil would at least alert the others that the Patth were here and on the hunt. With one final glance at the door, I keyed it on and reached an outstretched finger toward the keypad.

And paused.

There was something too easy about this. Something *far* too easy. Where were the alert reinforcements rushing in to save the day? Why were these two Iykams fiddling with my phone instead of someone in a properly equipped workroom? For that matter, why only two guards in the first place?

I keyed off the phone and turned it over again, angling it so that I could get a really good look at the exposed circuitry. And this time, knowing what to look for, it wasn't hard to spot.

My clever little playmates had wired a repeater chip into the transmitter line, on the upstream side of the encryption sticker. I couldn't read the fine print on the chip, but it almost didn't matter. With the simpler Mark VI chip they would be able to eavesdrop on any conversation I might have. With the more advanced Mark IX version and a properly equipped phone elsewhere in the city they'd not only be able to listen in but could also triangulate through the local phone system to get the location of the other end of the conversation. I'd been wrong about the Voodoo pins; they intended to get hold of the *Icarus* the easy way.

I was willing to help out guards who wanted me to make trouble, but my cooperation with the enemy only went so far. Rolling back up to my knees, I left the phone where it was and headed toward where my plasmic lay next to my ID folder.

I was just leaning down to pick it up when the door slammed open.

I dropped the rest of the way to the floor, my outstretched hand snatching up the weapon as I hit the ground hard enough to reignite the blazing pain in my head. Ignoring the red haze that had suddenly dropped in front of my eyes, I swiveled both my body and the plasmic to face the door.

It was, I had to admit, an impressive sight. Four Iykams stood in a semicircle just inside the doorway, each holding one of those nasty coronal-discharge weapons, their alert motionlessness giving them the appearance of transplanted gargoyles. Behind them, I could see a couple more of the ugly beasts outside the door, undoubtedly waiting eagerly for their chance at me.

And standing right in the middle of the doorway between the two groups was a gray-robed Patth.

"Don't bother with the weapon, Mr. McKell," he said. His voice was typical Patth, managing to mix sincere, contemptuous, and smarmy into a sound that was as distinctive in its own way as Chort's Craean whistling. "You don't seriously believe we would leave you a functional weapon, do you?"

"After that rather heavy-handed trick you tried with my phone, not really," I agreed. It was hard to aim properly with my gun hand cuffed to a chair arm, but insofar as I was able I pointed the plasmic squarely at the center of his torso. "At least, not on purpose. You ever hear of a three-pop?"

There was a slight but noticeable rustling among the gargoyles. "I don't think so," the Patth said, adding a bit more amusement into the smarmy part of his vocal mix. "But I'm sure you're dying to tell me."

"An appropriate choice of words," I said approvingly. "A three-pop is a high-power capacitor wired internally into a plasmic's fire circuit, kept charged by the main power pack but otherwise independent of it. It holds enough juice for two to four shots." I squinted consideringly. "That means you and up to three of your toadies will die if any of you comes any closer. If you'd like to point out your least favorites among them, I'll see what I can do to oblige you."

The four front Iykams had stopped looking like friendly little gargoyles. All four corona guns were up and aimed, held in taut-looking grips at the full extension of taut-looking arms. But for once I had the advantage, and they all knew it. Lying there four meters away from them, I was right on the edge of their kill zones, while they were well inside mine. Add to that the point that they couldn't afford to kill me—and the equally important point that none of them was especially eager to get killed, either—and we had the makings here of a good old-fashioned standoff.

And for a minute it looked as if I might actually get away with it. Very little of the Patth's face was visible in the shadow of that hood, but what I could see seemed to be in the throes of serious indecision as he weighed the merits of risking his personal skin against the reality that the *Icarus* still had a long way to go before we were home free. This was no professional bounty hunter, or even a standard flunky used to obeying orders without the luxury of being able to factor personal preference into the equation. Odds were this was a reasonably senior Patth citizen, pressed by necessity and desperation into this hunt for us.

But even as he hesitated a new voice from the outer room joined the discussion. Another Patth voice, just as smarmy as the first, but carrying with it the unmistakable weight of authority. "Nonsense," he said. "He's bluffing. Enig, tell your fools to go get the weapon. We don't have time for this."

The Patth in the doorway grunted something and two of the Iykams stepped reluctantly forward, their corona guns rigidly pointed at me. I let them get within two steps, just in case someone decided to have second thoughts, then let my plasmic settle harmlessly to the floor. "You're right," I acknowledged. "I'm bluffing."

"Bring him in here," the second voice ordered. There was no gloating in the tone that I could detect, nor any relief either. He'd made a decision, had issued an order and had it obeyed, and was not surprised by either the obedience or the fact that his decision had turned out to be right. Clearly, we had suddenly jumped a whole bunch of rungs upward on the Patth social ladder.

The Iykams hauled me to my feet and half pulled, half dragged me into the other room. This one was much nicer, nearly three times the size of my original cell and furnished better, with a couple of chairs and lamps scattered around. Near the wall to my left was a desk with a handful of monitors arranged along its front edge, and the other Patth seated behind it. The room was also swarming with Iykams, but you couldn't have everything.

"Not bad," I said, looking around as they led me to another plain wooden armchair that had been placed in front of the desk. Again, there seemed to be only one door leading out of the place, directly across the room from the door to my cell. Framed in the ceiling overhead was what at first glance looked like a skylight, but which on second glance proved to be only a standard light fixture designed to look that way. There were a couple of ventilation vents at ceiling and floor level, with decorative crosshatched gratings that looked flimsy enough to tear right off the wall. But through the holes in those same gratings I could see that the ductwork beyond was far too narrow for even someone as thin as Chort to fit through. A quick count of the Iykams came up with a total of eight. "Not bad at all," I added as my guards unfastened my handcuffs from the broken chair, shoved me down into the new one, and secured my wrists to the arms again. This time, I took particular note of which of them pocketed the keys. "If you kept your prisoners in a place like this instead of that converted stockroom back there you'd probably get better cooperation."

There was no comment from the other side of the desk. I finished my survey of the room in a leisurely fashion, then finally turned my full attention to the other Patth.

If anything, my earlier hunch about his status had fallen short of the mark. Instead of the usual unadorned gray worn in public by most Patth, his robe was instead gray with dark burnt-orange slash marks set into the sleeves and edge of the hood. This was one of the Patth elite diplomatic corps, possibly even the

Palmary ambassador himself. "I'm impressed," I said. "May I ask whom I have the honor of addressing?"

He regarded me another moment before answering. "You may call me Nask, Mr. McKell. You have been a most troubling person, indeed."

"Thank you," I said, inclining my head slightly, ignoring the fresh swell of pain the motion induced. "You seem to think the game is over."

"What makes you say that?" he asked calmly. "It is, of course, but what makes you phrase it that way?"

"Your so-called name," I said. " 'Nask' is one of the Patth words for 'victor.' "

"Interesting," he said. "We were right about you. You're not just a simple merchant pilot."

"That's right, I'm not," I told him. "I'm an employee of a very powerful and dangerous man. A figure who, I daresay, could cause immense trouble for even the Patth economic empire."

"Let us guess whom you refer to," the other Patth, Enig, put in. He had moved through the circle of glowering Iykams to a spot behind Nask, where he now stood at respectful attention. He didn't sound particularly smarmy at the moment, probably rather miffed that my bluff with the plasmic had made him look silly in front of his superior.

And now, in the better light in here, I could also see the telltale glitter of starship-pilot implants around his eyes. His deference was more proof, if I'd needed it, that Nask was a very high-ranking Patth indeed. "Would this powerful and dangerous man by any chance be Johnston Scotto Ryland?" Enig went on.

"You *are* well informed," I said, trying to hide the sudden sinking sensation in my stomach. If they knew about my connection with Brother John, and weren't worried about it, they must know something I didn't. "I imagine you also know what crossing a man like that means."

"We do," Nask said. "But you're sadly mistaken if

you think there is any crossing involved. Once your connection with Mr. Ryland became known, we contacted his organization. Would you care to hear his response, delivered to the Patthaaunutth Director General approximately six hours ago?"

The sinking sensation sank a little deeper. "Sure, go ahead."

Nask reached forward and keyed one of the displays. "Quote: 'Jordan McKell not known to this organization.' Unquote. Succinctly put, wouldn't you say?"

"Very," I agreed with a sigh. The heat had been turned up, and Brother John had responded by throwing me to the wolves. Typical. "So where does that leave us?"

"It leaves us in position to bargain," Nask said. "And without any external entanglements."

I frowned. "Excuse me?"

"You heard me correctly," he assured me. "You have the *Icarus*. I want it. It's that simple."

"Really," I said, trying in vain to read that half-shadowed face. Coming from a human, such an implied offer would carry the strong implication that the bargainer was offering to cut his superior completely out of the picture. But Nask was a Patth. Surely that couldn't be what he meant. Could it? "Would you care to elaborate as to what specific entanglements you hope to avoid?"

He waved a hand. "The usual ones. Legal questions, the Commonwealth Uniform Code, human governmental interference. All the various stumbling blocks that impede the progress and prosperity of reasonable beings."

"And does that list include other governmental interference?" I asked.

"It includes all governments that impede progress," he said. "Naturally, governments that instead enhance progress would be welcome."

"Ah," I said, nodding. In other words, he was proposing the three of us make a deal, which Nask and Enig would then turn around and sell to the Patth government for, no doubt, a tidy profit. I could presumably make a more personalized deal with Nask than I could with the Patth Director General, Nask and Enig would both move a few rungs up the ladder for their efforts, and the Patth as a whole would get the *Icarus*.

I looked around at the Iykams. And, of course, if Nask's generosity didn't prove sufficiently tempting, his hatchetbeings could take me apart piece by piece without any official Patth governmental involvement, should it ever come to that. "Let's hear your offer," I said, looking back at Nask.

He shrugged, a gesture the Patth had picked up from us. Somehow, it made him look less human than the other way around. "Let's hear your request," he countered. "We're prepared to be quite generous."

"Suppose my price includes more than just cash?" I asked, wishing desperately I had some idea how long I'd been unconscious. At some point, I knew, Ixil would conclude I'd been taken and would find a way to get the *Icarus* off Palmary without me. If I could stall that long, at least the others would be safe. "What if it includes the lives and freedom of my crew as well?"

"Their lives can certainly be included in any deal," Nask said. "Their freedom . . . well, that may be a bit more difficult to arrange."

"How much more difficult?"

He shrugged again. "They would need to remain guests of the Patthaaunutth Director General for a time. In quite pleasant surroundings, I assure you. Eventually, they would certainly be released."

"I'm sure they would be counting the days," I said. "And how long would you anticipate this luxury vacation would last?"

His eyes seemed to probe mine. "Until such time as the alien device you carry could be made operational or else proved nonfunctional. Your assistance, or lack of it, could certainly affect the length of that study."

"Only if I knew anything about it," I said, wondering how much he knew about the artifact. Or rather, how much he *thought* he knew about it. "It's completely sealed up."

"The unsealing will be the least of our difficulties," Nask said dryly. "So: the lives and eventual freedom of your traveling companions. What else?"

"Well, there'd have to be money, of course," I said. "Lots of it." I lifted my eyebrows to him. "Unfortunately, money's not much use if you aren't able to spend it. And I'll hardly be able to spend it if I'm locked away, will I?"

He made an unfamiliar gesture with his fingertips. "If you're worried about retribution from your companions, we can arrange that you be housed separately."

"You misunderstand," I said. "I'm saying that I walk. Immediately. You can lock up the others from now till doomsday as far as I'm concerned. But I get my money and walk."

He shook his head. "I'm sorry, but I'm certain the Director General would never agree to that. We can't allow even a hint of this find to leak out to the rest of the Spiral."

"What about Cameron himself?" I countered. "He knows about the *Icarus,* and last I heard he was still at large."

"Your information is out-of-date," Enig spoke up. "Arno Cameron was apprehended on Meima two days ago. He is being held at our compound there."

"Ah," I said. So much for Brother John's support; now, so much for Patth honesty, too. Big surprise on both counts.

"Still, I can assure you that during the time you're detained you'll have accommodations and treatment suitable for Steye'tylian royalty," Nask went on, his voice low and earnest and utterly trustworthy. Even the normal smarminess level had been muted for the occasion. "And afterward, you will be a friend to the Patthaaunutth for the rest of your life."

"Something to strive for, all right," I said with only a trace of sarcasm. The glow on his face, I noticed, had changed subtly. Had one of the displays facing him altered? "But suppose the device turns out to be useless? How much of a friend will I be then?"

"When the Patthaaunutth promise friendship, that promise is always fulfilled," he said. "Your goodwill and assistance will be counted toward that end, no matter what the final result."

"I see," I said, the hairs on my neck rising. Suddenly Nask's words and tone had gone mechanical, his full attention riveted to the displays. Something was happening out there, something even more important than sweet-talking me out of the *Icarus*. "Suppose I can find a way to guarantee my silence in some other way—"

"You must choose quickly," Nask interrupted me. "Tell me where the *Icarus* is, or the decision will be snatched from your hands."

"What are you talking about?" I demanded, the sinking sensation back in my stomach. "How could—"

I broke off at the sound of clinking from the door to my right. The sound of a lock being keyed. "He is here," Nask said with a forlorn-sounding wheeze I'd never heard a Patth make before. "The glory and profit now pass to the Director General."

The door swung open. I turned to look—

And felt my breath catch like fire in my throat. Two figures were striding into the room, looking as if they owned the place and were about to raise the rent. One was another robed Patth, the by-now-familiar starship-pilot implants twinkling around his eyes.

The other was Revs Nicabar.

CHAPTER

20

It was, on stunned reflection, about the last sight I would have expected to see. The last person in the Spiral I would have thought would be striding with such casual arrogance into a Patth den. I opened my mouth to say something—anything—but he beat me to the punch. "I see you've got him," he said to Nask. "About time."

"Yes, I have," Nask said, considerably less taken aback by Nicabar's appearance than I was. "And you are . . . ?" he added as Nicabar crossed the room toward him.

"What do you mean, who am I?" Nicabar countered scornfully. "Weren't you watching when Brosh held my ID up to the monitor?"

"Only the Director General's seal was clear," Nask said. "Not the number or rank designation."

With a supremely restrained sigh, Nicabar pulled an ID folder out of his inner pocket and dropped it on the desk. "Fine. Help yourself."

Nask did. For nearly half a minute he studied the

folder, while the rest of us sat or stood where we were in silence. Nicabar sent his gaze around the room, pausing briefly and measuringly on each of the Iykams in turn, sent me a brief and totally impassive glance, then looked back at Nask.

Finally, almost reluctantly I thought, the Patth closed the folder and laid it back down on the table in front of him. "Satisfied?" Nicabar asked.

"Quite satisfied, Expediter," Nask said, his voice almost sullen.

"Good," Nicabar said, holding out his hand. "Then you can return the favor. Brosh tells me you're the ambassador to Palmary. Unless you want to try telling me this is an embassy annex, I'd like to see some proof of that."

"Of course this isn't the embassy," Nask said stiffly, reaching into his robe and pulling out his own ID folder. "I chose this place precisely because I didn't want the encounter taking place on official Patthaaunutth soil."

"So where exactly are we?" I asked.

Nask glanced at me but didn't answer. Nicabar, studying Nask's ID, didn't even bother to look at me. I looked around at the Iykams, but none of them seemed interested in talking to me, either. After a moment, Nicabar closed Nask's ID and dropped it onto the desk beside his own. "Fine," he said. "Any progress so far?"

"We have him," Nask said, gesturing toward me. "That's a start." He cleared his throat. "You'll forgive me if I find myself surprised by your unexpected arrival, Expediter. I was not informed of your presence on Palmary."

"You'll be even more surprised when I tell you the name of the ship I came in on," Nicabar said dryly. "A little independent freighter by the name of *Icarus*."

It was as if all three Patth had simultaneously grabbed hold of the same high-voltage wire. "What?"

Enig said, the sound coming out more as a gasp than a legitimate word. "The *Icarus*?"

"What, don't you read your own government's hotsheets?" Nicabar sniffed. "My picture ought to be plastered all over the embassy identifying me as one of the *Icarus*'s crewers."

"There have been no such pictures," Nask said. "We have only now begun to piece together the profile of the *Icarus*'s crew from sifting through the various reports, and there are no pictures or sketches as yet."

Nicabar grunted. "Sloppy."

"We are doing the best we can with what we have," Nask insisted, his voice still civil but clearly showing some strain. "It was mere blind luck that one of Enig's defenders spotted McKell heading for that pharmacy and was able to see through his disguise."

"*Enig*'s defenders?" Nicabar echoed, looking over at Enig.

"Yes," Nask said. "Enig and Brosh are the pilot and copilot of the freighter *Considerate*."

"*Civilians?*" Nicabar demanded, his eyes blazing. "You brought *civilians* into this?"

"I had no choice," Nask snapped back. "I couldn't involve my staff for the same reason I didn't take McKell to the embassy. Besides, Brosh and Enig are no longer precisely civilians. Their ship happens to be the only Patthaaunutth vessel currently on the planet, and once we have the *Icarus* we'll need someone who can fly it back to Aauth. I've therefore commandeered both of them into official service."

"I see," Nicabar said, glancing at me. "You know where the ship is, then?"

"Not yet," Nask had to admit. "I was just beginning negotiations when you arrived." He sent me a rather disgusted look. "Now, I presume, the question is moot."

"Not quite," Nicabar said. "The rest of the crew

know he's missing and are on the alert. We have to be careful or we'll risk damaging the artifact."

"That would just be too bad, wouldn't it," I murmured.

Nicabar regarded me as if I were something he'd found on the bottom of his shoe. "Who are all of these?" he asked, waving at the assembled Iykams. "More merchant-ship conscripts?"

"They're my ship's personal defenders, Expediter," Brosh said, bristling noticeably at what he obviously took to be a slight. "They're more than equal to whatever task you require of them."

"I suppose we'll find that out, won't we?" Nicabar said, leaving the desk and moving through the gathered Iykams, looking at each in turn with the piercing glance of military inspection officers everywhere. "Do I also assume you have cloaks of invisibility for all of them?"

"What?" Brosh asked, clearly startled. "Cloaks of *what*?"

"That's the only way they're going to get close enough to the *Icarus* to use these," Nicabar said, lifting the nearest Iykam's gun hand and tapping the corona weapon.

"Yes, I see," Nask said with a nod. "A good point. Brosh, do any of the defenders standing guard outside have plasmics with them?"

"Some of them, yes," Brosh said, glaring from under his hood at Nicabar. Apparently, he wasn't used to dealing with top-ranking Patth agents. He certainly didn't seem to care much for their style. "I'll call them and ask."

"No—no phones," Nicabar said as Brosh reached beneath his robe. "We don't want anything going through the phone system that could be backtracked later. You three"—he jabbed a finger at a clump of Iykams—"go to the others and collect all their plasmics from them."

"Wait a minute," Brosh protested, pointing at me. "You can't just send them away. What about him?"

"What, it takes more than five of your highly competent defenders to guard a single manacled prisoner?" Nicabar countered scornfully.

"He has a point, Expediter," Nask put in. "McKell is a highly dangerous human, and has slipped out of several other traps. Enig can go check on the weapons."

"I don't want you three going outside this room any more than you have to," Nicabar said in a voice of strained patience. "You shouldn't even *be* in this part of town, let alone wandering around loose."

"It's the Grand Feast," Nask pointed out tartly. "All races mix freely together for that. But if you insist." He nodded to the three Iykams Nicabar had marked out. "Carry out your orders."

"And make sure you bring back one for me," Nicabar added as the three headed to the door.

"You're not armed, Expediter?" Nask asked as the Iykams left the room, closing the door behind them.

"You know I'm not," Nicabar said. "I presume you were watching as Enig and his defenders checked me for weapons outside."

"My question was more along the lines of why you didn't have a weapon at all," Nask said. "I was under the impression Expediters were routinely armed."

"Most Expediters don't have to live aboard a ship the size of the *Icarus* with people like McKell poking their noses into everything," Nicabar reminded him. "He'd have fingered me long ago if I'd brought a gun aboard."

"You had us fooled, all right," I growled, trying not to sound too bitter. "Especially that little speech you made back in the engine room. That was a nice touch."

He lifted his eyebrows mockingly. "I don't know why," he said. "I thought I made it pretty clear that I thought the Patthaaunutth were being unfairly picked on just because they happened to be more technically innovative than the rest of us. You must not have been listening very well."

"I guess not," I murmured, a sudden surge of adrenaline jolting through my system. I *had* been listening to that conversation; had been listening with everything I had. And that was *not* in any way what Nicabar had said or implied.

Which either meant he was playing a completely pointless game with me . . . or else there was something else entirely going on here.

And then, even as Nicabar turned contemptuously away from me and back to Nask, I heard the most beautiful sound I'd ever heard in my life. A soft sound, hardly audible, certainly not at all melodic. But a sound nevertheless that three minutes ago I would have sworn I would never hear again.

The soft sneeze of a Kalixiri ferret.

I would have been surprised if any of the others noticed it. Certainly they gave no sign that they had. Nicabar was conversing in a low but intense tone with Nask, probably discussing plans for the upcoming raid on the *Icarus,* and all the Iykams in my field of view were still glowering at me with the same unfriendly expressions that their companions had worn in the back room just before I'd dropped a chair on them. Slowly, making it look like I was checking them out in turn, I moved my head just enough to see the lower of the room's air vents.

And there he was, barely visible in the shadows behind the vent's crosshatched grating: Pix or Pax, I couldn't tell which, his head turned to the side as if he was grooming himself or gnawing at an itch. Just as slowly, I turned back to the desk again, not wanting my interest in that part of the room to spark any unwelcome curiosity.

Nicabar was looking sideways at me, still talking to Nask. I dropped one eyelid a millimeter and got an equally microscopic nod in return from him before he seemed to notice his ID still lying on the desk and returned it to his pocket. Not his ID, rather, but the one I'd taken off the Patth agent on Dorscind's World after my old buddy James Fulbright's attempt to cash in on the reward. Clearly, my original estimation of Thompson as little more than a glorified Patth accountant had been seriously off target.

"I suppose you're wondering what we've got planned," Nicabar spoke up into my thoughts.

"Oh, no, don't tell me," I said, remembering to put the same bitterness into my voice that I'd been feeling two minutes earlier. "I just love surprises."

"I'd be a little less flippant if I were you," Nicabar said reprovingly. "Whether the rest of the *Icarus* crew lives or needlessly dies is going to depend entirely on you. In fact, I'd go so far as to say that—what the *hell*?" He jumped away from the desk toward the wall, just as Nask let out a yelp of his own.

And for good reason. The air vents, upper and lower both, were suddenly spewing a dense, pale yellow smoke. "We're on fire!" Enig gasped.

"You three get out of here!" Nicabar snapped. He'd reached the area of the lower vent now, his head and torso disappearing as he bent down into the smoke. "You—defenders—get that top vent sealed!"

Two of the five Iykams were already scrambling against the wall, straining to reach the upper vent's sealing lever. From Nicabar and the lower vent came a teeth-grinding screech of torn metal; and then abruptly he was standing upright again out of the cloud of smoke, a cloud that seemed already to be starting to dissipate.

And in his hand was Fulbright's Kochran-Uzi three-millimeter semiautomatic.

His first two shots took out two of the Iykams still standing guard over me. The third guard nearly got his own weapon up and aimed in time, but lost the last chance he would ever have as I leaned sideways and kicked his gun arm out of line. I swiveled back around as Nicabar systematically took out the rest of the guards, heaving myself up with the chair on my back again, and hurled myself across the desk at Nask.

The Patth threw his own chair backward as he saw me coming, making one last futile grab for something in the drawer he'd opened as he got out of my way. But the desk was higher than the table in the back room had been, and with the additional barrier of the monitors along its edge I only made it about halfway across before I ran out of momentum. Nask, belatedly seeing that his reflexive dodge had been unnecessary, killed his own backward momentum and dived out of his chair toward the open drawer.

"Don't," a familiar voice warned from the doorway.

Nask froze, his head twisting to look in that direction, his hand still outstretched toward the drawer. I looked, too, trying to ignore the fresh red haze my sudden bit of exercise had sent swimming across my vision. Ixil stood in the doorway, the plasmic in his hand pointed squarely at Nask, his wide shoulders and settled-looking stance blocking any hope of escape for the two Patth pilots standing rigidly in shock in front of him.

"I see," Nask said. I looked back to find he had straightened up again, his hand fallen empty at his side.

"It's like a class reunion in here," I said, my voice sounding distant in my ears through the trip-hammer that had apparently finished its lunch break and started up work again on the back of my head. "I hope someone thought to bring some painkillers along."

"We did better than that," Ixil assured me, motioning Brosh and Enig back toward Nask and closing the door behind him. "We've got Everett waiting outside."

"Everett?" I echoed. "I told him to stay with Shawn."

"Tera and Chort are with Shawn," Nicabar told me.

He was at my side now, examining the handcuffs. "It occurred to us that you might need medical attention more urgently than he did."

"I don't, but I might have," I admitted, nodding toward one of the guards lying dead on the floor. "That one. Keys in his belt pouch. How did you find me, anyway?"

"We never really lost you," Nicabar said, dropping to one knee and digging into the pouch. "Tera wanted to know just where you were going to go on your errand."

I looked at Nask, who was standing stiffly glowering at us. "Don't worry about giving anything away," I told Nicabar. "They *were* staking out pharmacists, after all. Like he said, they're putting together the pieces."

"And we already have most of them," Nask said quietly. "Sooner or later we *will* get you."

He drew himself up. "And when we do, you will wish you had bargained here and now. You will wish it very much."

"I'll make you a small wager that we don't," I offered. But the words were automatic, and ninety percent bluster besides. For at least the foreseeable future, the smart money was definitely still on the Patth. "So what, after I left she called and had you tail me?" I asked, turning back to Nicabar.

"Actually, we'd already set it up," Nicabar said. He found the keys and set to work on my cuffs. "After the Iykams jumped you, I followed your party back here and then called Ixil. He brought the chemicals I needed, and while I mixed up the smoke bombs and time fuses he sent his ferrets in to reconnoiter. They came back, and we rigged them with harnesses to drag the bombs and gun inside."

The last cuff came loose. "You certainly had me going," I said, massaging my wrists. So that was what the ferret in the vent had been doing: chewing through his harness straps so that he wouldn't have to be sitting on top of the smoke bomb when it went off. "How exactly does the rest of the plan go?"

Nicabar nodded at the three Patth. "We cuff our friends together and get out of here."

"Good plan," I said. "There's only one problem. This ship of theirs, the *Considerate*. It must be pretty good-sized, or Nask wouldn't have thought they'd be able to handle the *Icarus*. If they get loose before we make it off-planet, they might take it into their heads to try and intercept us."

"A good point," Nicabar admitted. "Well . . . if you want, I'll deal with it."

"Be warned," Nask said. Suddenly every trace of smarminess was gone from his voice, leaving nothing but simmering threat in its place. "The murder of a Patthaaunutth citizen is punishable by the most severe consequences imaginable."

"And how would they know who'd done it?" Nicabar scoffed.

"There are ways," Nask said, still in that same tone. "There are always ways."

"Doesn't matter," I said before Nicabar could reply. "We can't shoot down unarmed civilians in cold blood anyway."

"Then what do we do?" Nicabar demanded. "Just leave them here like this?"

"We leave them here," Ixil said, stepping forward and handing me his gun. "But not precisely like this. Jordan, if you'd be so kind as to watch them; and Revs, I'd appreciate it if you'd get that upper vent open so that Pix can get out."

"What are you going to do?" I asked, keeping one eye on the three Patth and the other on Ixil. He had retrieved one of the corona guns and was fiddling with a pair of control settings.

"This will be an experiment," Ixil said. "I found this setting when I was examining the weapons you brought from your encounter on Xathru. It's quite low-power—far too low, in fact, to possibly serve as a credible weapon."

"What's it for, then?" Nicabar asked, grunting as he tore the grating from the upper vent. Pix was more than ready, diving out of the opening almost before the grating was all the way off. Hitting the floor, he dodged around the Iykams' bodies and scampered up Ixil's leg.

"I expect it's used for torture," Ixil said, squinting at the dials. "Something to cause pain without the risk of physical damage."

"What an efficient idea," I muttered, gazing hard at Nask. He said nothing, his eyes riveted on the weapon in Ixil's hand. "No reason you should have to carry both a gun *and* a set of thumbscrews, too."

"Indeed," Ixil said. Finishing his adjustments, he headed toward Brosh.

"Just a moment," Brosh said, taking a hasty step back. "I'm a simple starship pilot, from a civilian merchant ship. I have nothing to do with decisions or policies of that sort."

"I realize that," Ixil said, reaching out his free hand and taking one of Brosh's arms in an unbreakable grip. "And for that reason I sincerely hope this doesn't hurt too much."

And pressing the corona gun against Brosh's left cheekbone, he pulled the trigger.

There wasn't any flash—the current flow was far too low to produce a spark. But from the effect on Brosh Ixil might have just put a thousand volts across his face. He gasped sharply, his head jerking back with such violence that my own head injuries throbbed in sympathetic pain. Ixil didn't give him a chance to recover his balance, but simply leaned forward and delivered a second jolt to the other cheekbone. Brosh gasped again, a sound that seemed to be on the edge of panic or hysteria. "Just one more," Ixil soothed him, and delivered a third shock to his forehead just above his eyes.

Abruptly, Nask snarled something in the Patth language. About a step behind me, he'd suddenly figured out what Ixil was doing. "You *sacundian* alien *frouzht*—"

"—and then we move on to the hands," Ixil said, ignoring both Nask's curses and Brosh's yelps and delivering a quick jolt to the backs of each of the pilot's hands. "And that," he added, letting go of Brosh's arm so quickly that the other nearly toppled over backward, "is that."

"Yes, indeed," I agreed. "And with all that lovely implanted circuitry now scrambled or fried, the *Considerate* is without a chief pilot."

"And will be also without its backup pilot in a moment," Ixil agreed, moving to where Enig was cringing.

Enig demonstrated himself capable of more dignity and self-control than his superior, leaving Nask's continuing stream of invective unpunctuated by gasps or moans. "*Now* it should be safe to secure them to the desk," Ixil said, tossing the weapon distastefully across the room and taking his plasmic back from me. "Revs, if you'll do the honors?"

A minute later, the three Patth were trussed like a matched set of Thanksgiving turkeys. They maintained a stoic silence throughout the operation, even Nask apparently having run out of things to call us. But the ambassador stared at Ixil the whole time, and there was something about the very deadness of his expression that sent a chill up my back.

"Looks good," I said after Nicabar had finished, giving his handiwork a quick examination. Not that I didn't trust him to do a proper job, but it was too late in the day to be taking unnecessary chances. "I presume one of you knows the best way out?"

"Straight through the club," Ixil said. He snapped his fingers and Pax abandoned his examination of one of the dead Iykams and scurried toward him. "Did you know you were in the back rooms of a night-to-dawn club, by the way?"

"No, but I should have guessed from the music I was hearing," I said as Pax climbed up and took his accustomed place on Ixil's other shoulder. It occurred to me that I hadn't actually heard the band for some time now; straining my ears, I discovered I still couldn't hear it. Either Nicabar's gunshots had affected my hearing, or else the club had suddenly gone silent. An ominous possibility, that one. "Let's go."

I headed for the door, scooping up one of the corona guns along the way just to have some kind of weapon in my hand. Nicabar and Ixil moved into support positions on either side of me, Nicabar easing the door open for a cautious look as Ixil kept an eye on our three Patth friends. "All clear," Nicabar murmured. He started out—

"Kalix."

I turned around. Nask was still staring at Ixil, the look of death still smoldering in his eyes. "For what you did here you will pay dearly," the ambassador said quietly. "You, and all your species with you. Remember this night as you watch your people starve to death."

For a moment Ixil looked back at him, his own face expressionless, and I wondered uneasily if he was having second thoughts about the side he'd chosen. If Nask wasn't just blowing off steam—and if he could persuade the Patth Director General to back him up— the Patth certainly had it within their economic power to make life miserable for the Kalixiri.

"Ixil?" Nicabar prompted quietly.

His voice seemed to break the spell. "Yes," Ixil said, turning back. "Go ahead. I'll take the rear."

Seconds later, the three of us were moving along a well-lit but deserted corridor. There was still no music; nor, as we moved along, could I hear any sounds at all other than our own. "What did you do, scare away all the patrons when you came in?" I murmured.

"Something like that," Nicabar murmured back.

"I hope you scared away the Iykams, too," I said. "Nask implied he had a whole troop of them guarding the building."

"He did," Ixil said grimly. "Everett and I dealt rather more permanently with them while the Patth were distracted with you and Nicabar."

"And where *is* Everett?"

"On guard in the main club area," Ixil said. "It's right up here on the right."

We rounded a corner, to find ourselves at the edge of a garishly decorated wiggle floor, its flickerlights still playing to its departed clientele, a scattering of spilled drinks and a couple of lost scarves adding color to the floor itself. Beyond the wiggle floor, surrounding it on all three sides other than the one we were on, were the drinking and conversation areas, consisting of a collection of close-packed tables. Most of them sported abandoned bottles and glasses, with the disarrayed chairs around them evidence of just how rapidly the club's clientele had departed. The arrangement of lights had put most of the conversation area into deep shadow, a fact I didn't care much for at all.

Especially given that there was no sign of Everett. On guard or otherwise.

Nicabar had made the same observation. "So where is he?" he murmured.

"I don't know," Ixil said as we hugged the corner. "Maybe he went outside for some reason."

Or maybe the Patth or Iykams had spirited him away, I didn't bother to add. If so, the evening was still a long way from being over. "Where's the door?" I asked.

"There's an emergency exit behind that cluster of orange lights in the corner," Nicabar answered.

"It opens onto an alleyway just off one of the major streets."

"Let's hope he's out there," I said. "After you."

Silently, Nicabar headed off, angling across the wiggle floor toward the orange lights he'd pointed out. We were about two-thirds of the way across the wiggle floor, pinned like moths in the glow from the flicker-lights, when I caught a glimpse of movement from behind the mass of darkened tables to our left. "Watch it!" I snapped, jabbing a finger that direction.

But my warning was too late. There was the muted flash of a plasma-bolt ignition, and with a gasped curse Nicabar dropped to one knee, his gun firing spasmodically toward the area where the shot had originated.

"Damn," I snarled, jumping to his side and pulling him flat onto the floor as Ixil's plasmic opened up from behind me, laying down a spray of cover fire.

"Shoulder," Nicabar bit out from between clenched teeth, his voice almost inaudible over the rapid-fire hiss of Ixil's plasma fire and the louder three-millimeter rounds from his own gun. "Not too bad. Can you see him?"

I couldn't, though I could make out vague movements back in the shadows as our unseen assailant apparently repositioned himself for his next shot. But without a weapon that could reach that far it didn't much matter whether I could see him or not. Instead, I darted to the edge of the wiggle floor, grabbed the nearest table, and half shoved, half threw it to where Nicabar was firing.

And then, even as the table skidded with a horrendous screech into a position where he could use it for cover, there was another plasmic flash from just to the right of our attacker's direction, this one accompanied by a startlingly forlorn sort of squeak. "I got him," a hoarse voice croaked. "Come on—I got him!"

"Stay here," Ixil ordered quietly, pushing me unceremoniously into the cover of the table beside Nicabar.

Before I could do more than flail around for balance he heaved himself up from his prone position on the floor and was gone, charging in a broken run across the open area with a speed and agility that were surprising in a being of his size and bulk. Pix and Pax had already made it across the floor, and I caught a glimpse of them as they disappeared among the maze of tables and chairs on that side. I held my breath, watching Ixil run, waiting in helpless agony for the shot that would take him down.

But that killing shot didn't come; and then he was there, ducking down and using the tables for maximum cover as he headed in.

Abruptly he stopped. I held my breath again—

"Come on," he called, waving toward us as he holstered his plasmic. "It's Everett. He's hurt."

I felt like saying who isn't, but with an effort I managed to restrain myself. Helping each other, with the added incentive of not knowing whether another attacker might be lurking in the shadows somewhere, Nicabar and I made it across the wiggle floor in record time.

It was indeed Everett, lying beside a tangle of chair legs, and he was indeed hurt. A single plasmic burn, a pretty severe one, in his left thigh just above the knee. "I must have been looking the wrong way at the wrong time," he explained, managing a wan smile as Ixil carefully tore the charred pant leg away from the wound. "Sorry."

"Don't worry about it," I said, taking his plasmic from him and making a quick but careful survey of the area. If there were more attackers lying in wait, they were being awfully quiet about it. "None of the rest of us are exactly in mint condition at the moment, either. Where's the chap who was shooting at us?"

"He's over there somewhere," he said, nodding to the side.

"I see him," I said, stepping over to a misshapen

bundle on one of the chairs a couple of tables away from Everett's position. The bundle turned out to be another of the ubiquitous Iykams, this one lying draped across the seat with a plasmic still hanging loosely from his hand. Cause of death was obvious: a close-range plasmic burn in his back. "Nice shooting."

"Thanks," Everett said, the word cut off by a hissing intake of breath as Ixil finished with the charred cloth. "I'm sorry I didn't get him sooner—I've been drifting in and out of consciousness. I didn't even know he was there until he took that shot at you. How bad is that burn, Revs?"

"Hurts like hell, but I don't think there's any serious damage," Nicabar said. He was on one knee beside Everett, rummaging around in the medical pack lying on the floor beside him. "So how come they left you here alive after they shot you?"

"I don't know," Everett confessed. "I'm just glad they did."

"Ditto," I said. "Can you walk?"

"Do I have a choice?" Everett countered. He dug into the med pack, pushing Nicabar's hands impatiently out of the way, and came up with a couple of burn pads. "I presume you know how to apply one of these," he said to Nicabar as he handed him one of the pads.

"I've had more practice than I care to remember," Nicabar grunted, pulling the charred shirt material away from his shoulder with stoic disregard for the pain.

"What about you, McKell?" Everett went on as he opened his own pad and arranged it carefully over his burn. "I seem to remember you being the one we were charging in to rescue in the first place."

"I'm all right," I assured him. "I could use a pain-killer for my head, but they hadn't started on the really rough stuff yet. Aside from Ixil, I think I'm probably in the best shape of all of us."

"I wouldn't tempt fate that way if I were you," Nicabar warned. "Everett?"

"I'm ready," Everett said, wincing once as he pressed the edges of the pad firmly into place against his leg. "Though I may need some help until the anesthetic takes effect."

I sighed. We were, without a doubt, just exactly the right men to be challenging the giant octopus of Patth economic domination. Humanity was counting on us, and humanity was in trouble. "Tell me some more good news," I said sourly.

"As a matter of fact, I can," he said, digging out a bottle of painkillers and tossing it to me. "I've found us a safe haven. A temporary one, at least."

I frowned at him. "What are you talking about?"

"I got in touch with a friend of mine on my way over from the ship," he said, dropping his voice. "Called him on that StarrComm station by the tram lines. He's a retired doctor, one of my instructors when I went through med training. He's running a private ski and ice-climbing place now on a quiet little resort world about five days away, complete with a small but full-service landing area. Fuel supply, landing-pad repulsors, perimeter lift-assist grav beams—the works."

"He'll be used to private yachts there," Nicabar pointed out doubtfully. "Can he handle a ship the size of the *Icarus*?"

"I spelled out the dimensions and he says he can," Everett said. "And it's off-season there right now, which means the place is deserted."

"Other towns?" Ixil asked.

"Nearest is two hundred kilometers away," Everett said. "We'll have time to finish the camouflage work on the ship and give all these burns some healing time." He lowered his voice still further. "We might even be able to get the stardrive working."

"Sounds too good to be true," I said. "What's the catch?"

"No catch," Everett said. "He has no idea who or what we are—I told him you were a group of investors interested in buying into resorts like his and pouring expansion money into the more successful ones. He won't even be there—he's heading out in two days on an equipment-buying trip. We'll have the whole place to ourselves."

I looked at Ixil and lifted my eyebrows questioningly. He shrugged slightly in reply, his expression mirroring my own thoughts. Even if this turned out to be a trap, given that the Patth were already breathing down our necks we didn't have a lot to lose. At least with a trap set the Patth and Iykams might not be so quick to flail around with blunt objects, a restraint that would not only give my head a chance to heal but would also automatically raise our chances of slipping or fighting our way out of it. "All right," I said. "We'll try it. Where is this place?"

Everett hesitated, glancing around the darkened room. "I don't know," he said. "Out here in the open—you know."

"I want to know now," I told him, moving close and putting my ear to his lips. "Just whisper it."

He sighed, his breath unpleasantly warm on my cheek. "It's on Beyscrim," he whispered. "The northwest section of the Highlandia continent."

"Got it," I said, getting a grip under his arm. He was right; even whispering it in here was risky. But I needed to know, and I needed to know before we got back to the ship. "Okay. *Now* we can go."

CHAPTER

21

After all the firepower that had been expended inside the club, I'd half expected to find a wall of local police surrounding the place as we slipped out the emergency exit and down the alley onto the crowded k'Barch streets. But to my mild surprise not a single badgeman was visible anywhere among the colorfully dressed celebrants. Either they just hadn't made it to the scene yet because of the crowds or because they were tied up with other more pressing business, or else a little good-natured gunplay wasn't remarkable enough during the Grand Feast to warrant official attention.

Especially without the club's ownership making any complaints; and it was for sure that Ambassador Nask wouldn't have risked losing Patth control of the *Icarus* by calling the local authorities in.

Which was just as well, considering how much trouble we had making our escape even without governmental interference. Now that it was full night, the crowds filling the streets were at least twice as dense as they'd been when I'd first arrived, and it seemed like every third step one of us managed to get jostled or bumped in a tender spot by some boisterous or flat-out drunk reveler. Even the high-quality painkillers and anesthetic pads Cameron had stocked the *Icarus* with could only do so much, and by the end of the second block I was about ready to haul out my plasmic and start shooting us a clear path.

Adding to the physical torture of pushing through the morass was the tension of wondering if and when the Patth would be able to regroup for another stab at us. Even in a multispecies gathering like this Ixil and his ferrets stood out, drawing far more attention than any of us liked. But like the badgemen, the Patth and their Iykami minions failed to materialize. Either we'd already taken out the bulk of their force, or else Nask had decided to concentrate whatever he had left on the various spaceport entrances instead of trying to comb the entire city. I could only hope that the informally thrown-together Bangrot Spaceport wouldn't have made it onto his map.

It turned out that the night-to-dawn club wasn't too far from the pharmacy where the Iykams had jumped me, which was itself not very far from the tram station where I'd first gotten off. But from the unfamiliar terrain we quickly passed into, it was clear that Ixil was leading us in a different direction entirely. I understood the tactical reasoning behind the plan: The nearest station would naturally be where the Patth would concentrate any observers they might be able to pull together. But at the same time, I found myself privately grousing at having to put up with more of this than I absolutely had to.

But we made it through the crowds, and my head didn't fall off along the way, and finally I saw the undulating sign of a tram station ahead of us. "Wait here," Ixil said, steering the three of us into the mouth of another alleyway. "I'll go check for unwelcome company."

THE ICARUS HUNT   397

"Right," I said, helping him ease Everett to the ground. "The k'Tra might have monitor cameras in there, too."

"I'll take care of them," he promised. Two steps later, he was lost to sight among the teeming multitudes.

"What was all that about monitors?" Everett asked, rubbing his leg at the edge of the burn pad.

"Monitor cameras can be used by people other than those who set them up," I told him. "It could be the Patth aren't bothering to look for us out here because they've already tapped into the k'Tra citywide monitor system."

"A fact Ixil seemed to pick up on right away," Nicabar said. He was leaning against the opposite wall from me, regarding me with a thoughtful expression. "Has he had any military experience, McKell?"

I shrugged. "We started flying the *Stormy Banks* together about six years ago," I told him. "I can't recall him ever mentioning military service in any of that time."

"Interesting," Nicabar said. He had closed his eyes, and I saw now that what I'd taken to be thoughtfulness was merely a deep fatigue. "In some ways he thinks like a military man."

"Probably my influence," I said. "I had five years in EarthGuard back in my twenties."

"Yes, Tera told me a little about your career," Nicabar said, opening his eyes briefly, then closing them again. "Anyway, I hope you realize what a good partner you've got there."

I didn't straighten up, or inhale sharply, or do any of the other things that traditionally accompany a moment of blinding epiphany. But with Nicabar's words, the last of the stubborn pieces finally fell into place. I knew now who had murdered Jones, had tried to murder Ixil, and had been working at cross-purposes to us ever since the *Icarus* lifted off Meima.

And perhaps even more important, I knew why.

I was still working out all the ramifications when Ixil reappeared in the alleyway. "All clear," he said, offering Everett a hand. "I can see the lights of an incoming tram headed our direction."

"Good," I said, helping him get Everett to his feet. "You three get going. I'll meet you back at the ship."

They looked at me as if I'd just sprouted a second head. "What are you talking about?" Nicabar demanded.

"I'm talking about finishing the job I came here to do," I said. "I never had a chance to get Shawn's borandis. Speaking of which, Nask has all my cash."

"I'll go get the borandis," Ixil volunteered. "You head back with the others."

I shook my head. "They're walking wounded, Ixil," I reminded him. "You're the only able-bodied person we've got this side of the ship. They need you to help them get back safely."

"But what about you?" Everett objected. "It's not exactly safe for you to wander around alone, you know."

"He's right," Nicabar agreed. "Ixil, you help Everett back. I'll go with McKell."

"Ixil might need your help, too," I said. "Everett could still go into delayed shock and have to be carried. For that matter, Revs, *you* could go into shock, and there's no way in hell *I* could lug you back by myself." I craned my neck. "And if you don't get moving, you're going to miss this tram."

"But—" Nicabar began.

"Save your breath," Ixil advised, settling Everett's arm in place over his shoulder, Pix and Pax scrabbling around for new positions out of the way. "It's no use arguing with him when he's made up his mind this way."

"And what if the Iykams find him?" Nicabar growled.

"The Iykams are dead or scattered," I said. "Personally, I'm more worried about what'll happen if the Patth stumble onto the ship and none of you are there to defend it. Or do you really think Tera and Chort can hold off a concerted attack by themselves?"

"I suppose he's right," Everett said reluctantly.

"Of course I'm right," I said. "Give me one hour after you get to the ship for me to catch up with you. If I'm not back, Ixil, you'd better try lifting off. Head for Everett's hiding place, and I'll try to catch up with you. And let me have some money, will you?"

"Here," Ixil said, pulling out his wallet and handing it to me, his eyes steady on my face. "There should be enough there."

"Thanks," I said as I took it. There was a lot he wanted to say, I could tell, but didn't dare do so in front of the others. "Now get going."

Ixil nodded. "Be careful."

"Trust me," I promised.

They headed out, varying degrees of unhappiness mirrored in their faces and postures. I leafed through the wallet—three hundred commarks; more than enough—making sure to give them a good head start. Then, diving into the crowd, I followed after them. Partly it was simple caution on my part, a desire to be in backup position in case the Iykams *hadn't* all been killed or scattered. Mainly, though, I wanted to make sure all three actually got on that tram and stayed there. What I was about to do next I couldn't afford to let even a hint leak out about.

And so I stood half-concealed behind a group of Skanks and watched as they got aboard. I hung around until the tram pulled out; then, standing on tiptoe to study the flapping display flags, I headed for the nearest pharmacy.

I had anticipated having no trouble picking up borandis in the middle of the Grand Feast, and no trouble was exactly what I got. Ten minutes after entering, I was out on the street again, two hundred commarks' worth of borandis safely tucked away in my inner pocket. With any luck that would be far more than we would actually need, but it would look suspicious if I'd only brought enough to get us to Everett's Beyscrim hideout. I made my way back to the station and hid in the crowd until the next tram arrived.

Not surprisingly, the tram was quite uncrowded; with the revels in full swing the majority of the traffic was headed into the cities and not vice versa. The sparse occupancy meant I was more conspicuous than I might otherwise have been, but it also meant I got a seat all to myself, plus a few minutes of badly needed rest. All in all, I decided it was a fair trade.

The ride was uneventful. I saw no Patth, no Iykams, and no sign that I was being either watched or followed. And after what seemed like far too short a trip the doors opened onto the Bangrot Spaceport platform.

It was going to be another long hike back to the *Icarus*, unless opportunity and diminished crowd density enabled me to take one of the little runaround cars instead. But whichever, ride or walk, it was going to be postponed a little while longer. Instead of turning right and making for the *Icarus*, I turned left and headed to the StarrComm building.

The receptionist at Uncle Arthur's left me on hold for several minutes, which was a bad sign all by itself. It meant they were having to wake him up, and Uncle Arthur roused from his beauty sleep was never even remotely at his best. Add to that the news I was about to give him, and this was likely to be one of our less pleasant conversations.

My first look at him, when the display finally cleared, was the first indication that my assessment of the situation had been ominously off target. Uncle Arthur was not garbed in sleep shirt and hastily thrown-on robe, his hair tousled into a multidirectional halo. He was instead immaculately groomed, every hair in place, and dressed in the sort of upscale finery I hadn't seen him wear in years.

Which meant that instead of hauling him out of bed, I'd instead interrupted a meeting with those higher up in the food chain than he was, out in those murky waters he'd spent so much of his life swimming in. I tried to decide whether that was better or worse than waking him up, but my throbbing head wasn't up to the task.

And then I took my first look at his face, and felt an icy cold begin to seep into my heart. It was a graveyard face, the look of a man who's been backed into a corner by his enemies with nowhere else to go and no more tricks left to use. The look of a chess master down to his king and one pawn, with the painful knowledge that that pawn is about to be sacrificed.

"Jordan," he said, his voice studiously neutral. "We were just talking about you. What's the situation?"

"Mine's not so hot," I said. "How's yours?"

"Not very good, I'm afraid," he conceded. "Where are you now?"

"In the middle of the Grand Feast celebration on Palmary," I told him. "And hoping to get the hell out as fast as we can."

"I take it you had some trouble?"

"You might say that," I agreed tartly. "The Patth caught up with me and let their Iykami underlings play a brief drum solo on my head. My crew was able to spring me, but two of them took plasmic burns on the way out. I know you don't like getting overtly involved with my life, but we need some backup. And we need it now."

His expression, if anything, went a little more neutral. "Do you have a destination in mind after you leave there?"

"One of the crew has a friend on Beyscrim with an isolated lodge he's not using," I said, feeling the cold dread settling a little more deeply into me. He hadn't responded to my call for reinforcements; and now the mention of Beyscrim should have had him busily punching his off-screen computer keys for data. But he wasn't. "It's supposed to be a five-day flight from here, which I figure should put it within reach of at least some of your people."

"Yes, it would," he agreed heavily. "Jordan . . . I'm afraid there won't be any backup."

I stared at him. "May I ask why not?"

"To be blunt, because Earth has caved," he said, his voice suddenly bitter. "Not fifteen minutes ago Geneva issued a formal notice that no public, governmental, or private organizations or persons with citizenship ties to Earth or Earth-allied worlds are to offer information, personnel, matériel, or any other assistance to the outlaw starship flying under the name *Icarus*."

His lip twitched. "You were also specifically mentioned in the order, Jordan. Along with Ixil and two or three others of your crew for whom they have names."

"This is nonsense," I said, my voice sounding unreal through the noise of my suddenly pounding heart. Uncle Arthur had been my absolute last chance. "They can't do that. The stakes here—"

"The stakes are precisely what they're thinking about," he said with a grimace. "I didn't tell you the other part. Approximately ten minutes before Geneva issued their order the Patth issued one of their own. The entire Kalixiri populace has been declared anathema."

I stared at him, Nask's parting-shot curse against Ixil and his people echoing through my mind. "That was fast," I said. "It wasn't even an hour ago that the Patth ambassador made that threat."

"Yes," Uncle Arthur said. "Whatever you did to irritate them, it would seem the Patth have suddenly decided to stop playing games."

I exhaled loudly. "I liked it better when they were skulking around not telling anyone who or what they really wanted. Has Geneva forgotten that Arno Cameron's involved here?"

He shrugged. "I presume not. If Cameron himself were there I'm sure he'd be pulling strings and cashing out favors all over the city. But as far as I know he's still missing, and those kinds of strings don't pull themselves." His eyes narrowed slightly. "Unless *you* know where he is."

"If I did, I certainly wouldn't tell *you*," I countered sourly. "At least not in the hearing of whoever the high-nosed flacks are back there who are listening in."

He glanced down at his clothing. "I suppose this outfit *is* something of a giveaway, isn't it?" he conceded. "Yes, Geneva was thoughtful enough to send a pair of representatives to deliver to me a personal copy of their edict. However, they are not, in fact, listening in on us."

"I suppose I should be thankful for small favors," I grumbled. "So much for our private little arrangement."

"So much for it, indeed," he agreed. "I'm somewhat surprised the authorities hadn't forgotten about me after all this time."

"A pity they hadn't," I said, probing carefully at the lump on the back of my head. It felt about the size of a prize-winning grapefruit. "All right, so you've been ordered not to deal with me, along with everyone else in the Spiral with ten toes and red blood. What exactly does that mean?"

He sighed. "I'm afraid it means exactly what it says. I can't have anything whatsoever to do with you."

I snorted. "Oh, come *on*. Since when have you worried about what anyone says you can or can't do? Especially anyone in Geneva?"

He shook his head. "You still don't understand, Jordan. This isn't some strategic or political decision on the part of reasoned statesmen. This is the panic reaction of people who are terrified of what the Patth might do to us if any human in the Spiral—*any* human—is seen to be assisting you."

"That's ridiculous," I insisted. "The Patth are bluffing—they have to be. Human-owned and -associated shipping must make up four to six percent of Patth cargoes. They can't afford to lose all that with the stroke of a pen."

"They did it with the Kalixiri," he reminded me. "And yes, I know the Kalixiri total is minuscule compared to ours. But no one in Geneva is ready to call that bluff." He hesitated. "And to be quite honest, I'm not convinced it *is* a bluff. Not when you consider that the Patth economic future could hinge on what the *Icarus* contains."

For perhaps half a minute neither of us spoke. Uncle Arthur broke the silence first. "What about Ryland or Antoniewicz?" he asked. "I doubt Geneva has been able to deliver to *them* a personal copy of the edict."

"They didn't have to," I said, frowning as a sudden thought struck me. "The Patth ambassador told me Brother John had already disavowed any connection between us."

"Too bad," he murmured. "No matter what you think of Antoniewicz, his group might have had the resources to help you out."

"Oddly enough, Tera made a similar suggestion," I said, thinking furiously as yet another layer of the Jones murder peeled away, onionlike, in my mind. "Though unlike you, she didn't care for the idea of turning the *Icarus* over to criminals."

"I can't say I care for it myself," Uncle Arthur admitted. "But if it comes to a choice of Antoniewicz or the Patth having the *Icarus* . . ." He shook his head.

I took a deep breath. This was it. All the pieces were finally in place, and it was time to make my pitch. "What if you could have it all?" I asked. "The *Icarus,* and everything else? Everything you've always wanted. How far would you go to get it?"

For a long moment he didn't speak, his pale blue eyes gazing at me in that way that always made me feel like he was trying to drill his way down through the various layers of my psyche to my soul. "You're serious," he said at last. It wasn't a question.

"Deadly serious," I agreed. "I can do it. Bear in mind, too, that if we don't do something, we *will* lose the *Icarus*. Either to the Patth or—"

"All right, you've sold me," he cut me off. "What do you need?"

And for the next ten minutes, in great detail, I told him.

There were, predictably, none of the little runabout cars available as I left the StarrComm building, which meant another long walk. Mindful of the hour's grace time I'd given Ixil before he was to try his hand at piloting the *Icarus,* I hurried as quickly as my throbbing head and the need to remain reasonably inconspicuous would permit.

None of the others was visible outside the ship as I finally dragged myself into view of it. But then, I wasn't really expecting to see anyone, not with Ixil and Nicabar in charge of arranging guard duty. It wasn't until I was nearly to the foot of the ladder that I spotted Pix crouched in the shadow of one of the ship's landing skids, staying clear of the press of spacers wandering around even at this hour. I whistled, and he bounded away from his spot and scampered over to me. I managed to catch him before he could try his tree-climbing act with my shin and scritched him briefly behind his ears. "Ixil?" I called quietly.

"Here," a voice answered from above and to my left. I looked up, just as Ixil appeared from behind the festively glowing lights that had been set up as per my orders in the gaps of our camouflaging cowling. "Any trouble?"

"None," I said, watching as he eased his way through one of the larger gaps and dropped to the ground. "You?"

He shook his head. "It's been very quiet," he said, waving somewhere behind me. I turned to look, saw Chort detach himself from a parked fueler and head toward us. "You like the job Chort and Tera did with the lights?"

"Very nice," I agreed, looking up at the lights again. "Nice little sniper's position you found up there, too."

"Chort's idea, actually," Ixil said as he took Pix back from me and set him on his shoulder. "He was up there on guard when Nicabar and Everett and I got back. Since Kalixiri are slightly more conspicuous than Crooea, I took it over and set him up in the more visible spot over at that fueler."

"Sounds reasonable," I said. "How's Shawn doing?"

"Bad, but not critical. At least this time he didn't get loose. Tera made sure he was securely strapped down before she set up her own guard position just inside the hatchway." He peered up. "She should still be there, in fact—neither Everett nor Nicabar was in any shape to take over from her. Be sure to announce yourself before you step inside the wraparound; I get the feeling she's still a little nervous."

"I know exactly how she feels," I said dryly as Chort came up beside us. "You all right, Chort?"

"Quite well, Captain McKell, thank you," he whistled, peering closely at me. "I understand you have not had such fair fortune, however."

"I've been worse," I assured him. "Looks like Ixil will be on engine-room duty for lift; I'd like you to stay back there with him in case he needs assistance. We *did* get fueled, didn't we?"

"Loaded and topped off and paid for," Ixil assured me. "Easily enough to get where we're going."

"Good," I said, putting one foot on the bottom rung

of the ladder and taking one last look around. There were no Patth or Iykams anywhere to be seen. Nor, for that matter, were there any police or customs officials visible, either. But then, now that the last onion layer had been peeled away, that didn't especially surprise me. "Let's do it."

CHAPTER
22

The five-day trip to Beyscrim was the longest jump at one stretch that we'd tried yet with the *Icarus*. We paid the price for such daring, too, to the tune of three hull ridges and a pair of hairline cracks. Each required from two to six hours of outside work; together, they added nearly a full day to our travel time.

The most frustrating part, at least to some of the more impatient members of the crew, was that it was no longer clear whether such repair work was even necessary, given what we now knew about the true nature of the *Icarus*. The cracks and ridges were only in the outer-hull plating that Cameron's people had layered over the artifact sphere, and there was no indication that the alien metal beneath was being affected in the slightest by the hyperspace pressure it was being subjected to. There were several lively discussions about that, in fact, most of them occurring while Chort and Ixil were busy outside with the latest repair job. But the arguments presented were for the most part completely moot. I voted to continue stopping for repairs, whether they were necessary or not, and no one else got a vote.

It wasn't simply caution, though, or even a lack of faith in the *Icarus*'s original designers. Despite Everett's assurance that his doctor friend was above reproach, we were heading into a largely unknown situation on a completely unknown world. With three of us qualifying as walking wounded—four if you counted Shawn's medical problems—I figured the more recovery time we had along the way, the better.

Still, I had to admit that our first pass by Beyscrim showed the place to be pretty much as advertised. The planet boasted just five public spaceports, none of them up to even Meima's casual standards, with the coordinates Everett's friend had supplied reading halfway up a mountain and very literally in the middle of nowhere. The automated landing system guided us in to a group of five pads about three hundred meters west and slightly downslope from the mansion-sized lodge itself, the pad cluster edged in turn on its downslope side by an extensive range of bushy blue-green trees. I chose the pad closest to the trees, setting us down parallel to them and as close to their outstretched branches as I could manage, remembering first to rotate the ship so that the hatchway was on the open, non-tree side facing the lodge.

Tera questioned my choice of placement, pointing out that resting so close to the edge of an artificially built-up landing area was an invitation to disaster should the *Icarus*'s weight cause the edge to collapse. Everett was equally critical of my landing site, except that his argument was that I'd chosen the pad farthest from the lodge, thereby putting us an extra hundred meters from the comforts we all hoped were waiting for us up there. I pointed out to Tera that the idea was for the trees to provide us at least a little bit of visual cover from any aircraft that happened to pass overhead; to Everett, I rather ungraciously suggested that if after several days of rest the walk was still too much for him, he was welcome to stay aboard while the rest of us checked the place out.

That was exactly what he did, though he phrased it more along the lines of standing guard over the ship than of anything so childish as a fit of sulking or pique. I accepted his offer, pretended also to accept his rationale for it, and together the rest of us trooped on up through the cool afternoon air to the lodge.

I'd noted on the way in that the lodge was good-sized, but I hadn't realized just how extensive the place actually was. Besides the main rectangular section running parallel to the landing area, there was also a full wing extending back from the middle toward the mountain itself, giving the building an overall T-shape. How I'd missed that back wing I didn't know, except to assume that the rough-cut slate roofing had blended so well into the rocky slope beyond that I hadn't realized it was part of the lodge. Beyscrim, I decided, must be a fantastically popular place at the height of the tourist season.

The size of the lodge also meant that the six of us— or seven, whenever Everett deigned to join us—would have the chance to get seriously lost from each other. After the forced intimacy we'd created by ripping out the *Icarus*'s decks and cabins, the thought of a little personal privacy was something the whole crew was definitely champing at the bit for. I thought about keeping us all together at least long enough to check out the public areas of the lodge for signs of recent occupancy, but when I offered the suggestion Tera made it clear that she wasn't interested in anyone else's company for a couple of hours at least. Snagging the key for one of the guest rooms—old-fashioned permanent keys were apparently part of the rustic atmosphere of the place—she headed off to get some sleep on a real bed. Shawn and Nicabar took her cue and picked out rooms of their own, while Chort headed instead to the kitchen area to see what sort of food might be available. Giving up, I sent Ixil with him and then headed back outside onto the lodge's wide front portico.

It had been late afternoon when we'd landed, and from what the nav listing had said about Beyscrim's rotation period I had assumed we would have another two to three hours of daylight left. But I had failed to take into account the effects of the mountain range to the west that rose dramatically behind the *Icarus* and its shading trees. Already the sun was dipping behind the taller peaks, and I could see now that it would be dusk in probably half an hour.

Still, half an hour of sun and fresh air was better than nothing. Snagging one of the sturdy lounge chairs lined up along the portico's back wall, I pulled it to the front edge and sat down.

Everett had evidently been thinking along the same lines I had, at least as far as the fresh air was concerned. From where I sat I could make out his figure in the wraparound just behind the open hatchway, gazing back in my direction. I thought about waving to him, but concluded after a minute that the lack of any such gesture on his part probably meant he was still not feeling all that sociable, at least not toward me. So I just settled more comfortably into my chair, aware of Everett's presence but not acknowledging it any more than he was acknowledging mine.

We sat there, wrapped in our own little worlds, as the sun vanished and the western sky faded from sunlight into a multicolored glow into dusk. Ixil came by once to tell me that Chort had located a cache of stored food and was busy preparing dinner for us all, then disappeared back inside to assist him. I stayed where I was a few minutes more, watching the sky and mountains as the dusk darkened to full night and a scattering of brilliant stars appeared. Everett, I presumed, was

similarly watching the lodge and the mountains rising
behind it. Or possibly he was just watching me.

It had been full night for about twenty minutes
when the dropping air temperature finally began to
penetrate my jacket and I decided enough was enough.
Picking my way carefully downslope, with only the
decorative lights of the portico to illuminate the path, I
made my way back to the *Icarus*.

I found Everett stretched out on his cot in the main
sphere, leafing through the ship's pharmaceutical listing, his injured leg propped up on one of the medical
kits. "The wraparound get too boring for you?" I
asked as I made my way toward him.

"It got too chilly," he said. "What's happening out
there?"

"Absolutely nothing," I said. "Oh, except that dinner is going to be ready soon. Thought you might want
to join us."

"What are we having?" he asked.

"No idea," I admitted. "However, Chort's in charge
of preparation, so I expect it'll at least be palatable."

"Probably," Everett said, wincing slightly as he
shifted his leg. "Unfortunately, I don't know if I'm up
to the walk."

"Really," I said, frowning, as I squatted down beside him. "I didn't realize it was bothering you that
badly or I wouldn't have jumped on you earlier.
Sorry."

He waved the apology away. "Don't worry about it.
You were right—it *should* be mostly healed by now.
Maybe it's the cold and lower air pressure up here
that's bothering it."

"Then the lodge and a real bed are exactly what you
need," I said briskly, straightening up and reaching
down to him. "Come on—I'll give you a hand."

"No, that's all right," he said. "Let me just rest it a
while longer, and I'll come up later."

"You're going to join us for dinner, Everett," I said

firmly. "This is the first decent meal we'll have had since I don't know when, and you and your leg aren't going to miss out on it."

"Look, I appreciate the thought. But—"

"Besides, we have to have a serious talk about what we're going to do after we leave here," I said. "And that's going to concern all of us. So, bottom line: Either you let me help you up to the lodge, or I'm going to send Nicabar and Ixil to carry you. Your choice."

"You win," he said, putting down the listing and smiling wryly. "They wound up mostly carrying me back to the *Icarus* on Palmary, and I'm not in any hurry to repeat the experience."

We made our way around the curve of the hull and into the wraparound. Everett's leg didn't seem to be giving him all that much trouble that I could see, but I nevertheless kept a hand ready to assist if it should suddenly go weak on him. I turned on the entryway floodlights for better lighting and preceded him down the ladder. He reached the ground safely, and we headed toward the lodge.

A gentle breeze had started up since I'd entered the *Icarus*, stirring up the cold mountain air and making it feel that much colder, and Everett's leg reacted by stiffening up even more. It took us over ten minutes to cross the four hundred meters to the lodge, and by the time we made it up the steps to the portico he had given his pride a vacation and was leaning heavily on my arm. "Sorry about this," he puffed as I steered us to the main door. "I guess I should have let Ixil carry me after all."

"Not a problem," I assured him. "You'll be better once we get you out of all this cold night . . . damn."

"What?" he asked.

"The lights," I said, turning around to look behind us. Sure enough, the *Icarus* was beautifully bathed in the backwash from the floodlights. "I wasn't even thinking. Too used to always leaving them on in port, I guess."

"You going to go back and turn them off?" Everett asked.

"Unless we want to advertise our presence to anyone who happens to pass by," I said, getting the door open and helping him limp over the threshold. The delicate aromas coming from the kitchen area made my stomach growl. "Go on in—the dining area's off to the left, around that corner and through a sort of rectangular archway. I'll be back in a minute."

"Better grab a flashlight for the way back," he warned as I headed back across the portico. "That ground's pretty uneven in places."

"I will," I called back over my shoulder. "Assuming I can remember where we stashed them. Make sure Chort saves me some of whatever that is, all right?"

"Sure," he called. "Well, probably."

Between the portico lights behind me and the floodlights in front of me I had no problem traversing the terrain this time around. I climbed up the ladder and shut off the floodlights, then headed forward into the main sphere.

Contrary to what I'd implied to Everett, I knew exactly where the flashlights were, and it was the work of ten seconds to unearth one from the pile of machine-shop equipment. But now that I was finally alone in the ship there were other more urgent matters that needed to be attended to, and the excuse of hunting for a flashlight should give me the time I needed.

I tackled the helm and nav systems first, my familiarity with them permitting me to finish the job in probably two minutes. Tera's computer was next on my list, another relatively quick and easy job given how much time I'd spent around it lately. After that, making sure to stay well back in the wraparound as I slipped past the open hatchway, I headed back into the engine section.

Even with full lighting the maze of cables and conduits back there was a pain to get through. With only a flashlight, and one that had been adjusted to its lowest setting yet, such a safari was downright dangerous. But I made it through to the control station without garroting myself, and five minutes later I was done.

The hidden access to the inner sphere was sitting wide-open, just as I'd instructed Ixil to leave it. I shined my light briefly inside, but there was nothing to be seen except the usual tangle of wiring. I looped a few turns of conduit over the hinged breaker panel, just to make sure no one thoughtlessly closed it, then left the engine section, making sure that the door to the wraparound was also locked open.

I left my flashlight off as I slipped out of the hatchway and climbed down the ladder. Everett or someone else might be looking in this direction, and I still had one last task to perform before I could head back up for dinner. Careful of my footing, I circled the aft end of the ship and made my way around to the ship's starboard side.

With the tree branches towering over me blocking out the starlight, this side of the ship was even darker than the port side had been. Even so, it wasn't difficult to locate the set of latch grooves I'd spotted on my first inspection of the ship back at Meima, the grooves I'd later learned Cameron had anchored a collapsible ladder into for his backdoor entrance into the ship that morning. Probing carefully with my little finger, I felt in one of the two bottom grooves for the piece of guidance tag I'd wadded up and put inside.

The folded piece of plastic was no longer wedged halfway down the opening as I'd left it. Instead, it had been jammed all the way to the bottom of the groove. A quick check of the other groove showed the other half of the tag had likewise been crammed into the bottom.

Feeling my way along the side of the ship, I circled

around the drive thrusters and worked my way back to the base of the ladder. Then, and only then, did I turn on my flashlight and head up to the lodge.

Everett was not, as I'd expected, waiting for me in the expansive foyer where I'd left him. He had instead found his way to the dining room and seated himself at the far end of one of the rustic hewn-wood tables. Shawn, Tera, and Nicabar had reappeared from their rooms and were in the process of choosing seats of their own at the table, with Chort and Ixil just lugging in a large steaming stewpot containing whatever it was I'd smelled earlier. Four seats were still empty: one on each side of Everett at the far end, one beside Shawn, the fourth at the end of the table closest to me, the seat facing away from the entrance archway. Choosing that one, leaving Chort and Ixil to fight over the other three chairs, I sat down.

Dinner was a curious affair, full of odd contrasts. The couple of hours of privacy had done small but noticeable wonders for the civility level among the group, particularly for Tera and Shawn, who mentioned that they'd spent their time catching up on badly needed sleep. The fact that the quiet surroundings lent themselves to a sense of security was also undoubtedly a calming factor.

At the same time, though, there was an underlying tension permeating the whole event, a tension that showed up in a hundred little ways, from the slightly stilted conversation and long uncomfortable silences to the way everyone's eyes periodically and suddenly darted to the archway behind me as if expecting the entire population of the Patth homeworld Aauth to suddenly come charging in on us. Tera seemed the worst in this respect, though Shawn's natural twitchiness brought him in a close second. By a sort of unspoken mutual consent we avoided the topic of the rest of our trip, and our chances of actually getting to Earth with the whole Spiral breathing down our necks.

I gave it half an hour, until the stew was gone and the conversation had again lagged and they were starting to make the small but unmistakable signs of getting ready to take their leave. Then, clearing my throat, I lifted my left hand for attention. "I know you're all tired and anxious to start settling down for the night," I said. "But there are one or two matters we still need to deal with."

Their expressions could hardly be considered hostile, but there certainly was no particular enthusiasm I could detect. "Can't it wait until morning?" Everett asked from the far end of the table. "My leg's starting to hurt again, and I'd like to go somewhere where I can prop it up."

"This will only take a few minutes," I assured him. "And no, it really can't wait."

"Of course not," Shawn muttered under his breath. "Not when McKell thinks it's important."

"First of all," I said, nodding toward Chort and then Ixil, "we need to thank Chort and Ixil for the excellent dinner we've just eaten. Especially Chort, who I understand did most of the preparation."

There was a somewhat disjointed chorus of nods and thank-yous, accompanied by the gentle scraping of chair legs on the floor as Shawn and Nicabar pushed their seats back in preparation for getting up. "Anything else?" Everett asked, half standing.

"Actually, yes," I said, lifting my right hand above the level of the table to reveal the plasmic I was holding. "If you'll all sit back down again and put your hands on the table," I said into the suddenly shocked silence, "there's a murderer I'd like you to meet."

CHAPTER

23

For a half-dozen heartbeats they stood or sat in utter silence like carved marble statues, every eye staring either at my face or else the gun in my hand. I didn't move or speak either, giving them as much time as they needed to catch up with the bombshell I'd just dropped in their laps.

Everett recovered first, easing back down onto his chair as if there were a row of eggs waiting there and he didn't want to break any of them. As if that were a signal, Shawn and Nicabar just as carefully unfroze and hitched their own chairs back to the table. The three men and Ixil already had their hands on the table as instructed; I sent a querying look at Chort and Tera and they reluctantly followed suit.

"Thank you," I said, leaning back in my chair but keeping my plasmic ready. "We have had, from the very beginning of this trip, a number of unexplained and, at least on the surface, inexplicable events dogging our heels. We had the ship's gravity go on unexpectedly while Chort was working on that first hull ridge, which could presumably have seriously injured or even killed him if he'd hit something wrong on his way down. We had the malfunction with the cutting torch that gave Ixil some bad burns and would probably have killed *him* if Nicabar and I hadn't been able to shut it off in time. We also had a combination of potentially lethal chemicals put inside Ixil's cabin and the cabin door release smashed while he was recovering from those burns.

"There are others, but I mention these particular three first because it turns out they're the most easily and innocently explained. It seems that Tera was the one who turned on the gravity during the spacewalk in order to keep Chort from discovering a secret about the ship that she didn't want revealed."

All eyes, which had been locked on me, now turned as if pulled by a set of invisible puppet strings to Tera. "That *she* didn't want revealed?" Nicabar asked.

"Specifically, a secondary hatchway on the top of the engine section," I said. "A hatch her father had used to sneak into the ship that morning on Meima."

"Wait a minute," Shawn said, sounding bewildered. "Tera is . . . she's *Borodin's* daughter?"

"Exactly," I said, nodding approvingly and trying to ignore the aghast look on Tera's face. "Except that the man who called himself Alexander Borodin was in fact a rather better-known industrialist by the name of Arno Cameron."

There was the sound of jaws dropping all around the table. "Arno *Cameron*?" Everett all but gasped. "Oh, my God."

"I wondered about that," Nicabar murmured. "Someone had to have had tremendous resources to put a ship like the *Icarus* together in the first place."

"And if there's one thing Cameron's got, it's tremendous resources," I agreed. "It also turns out that Cameron was the one who sabotaged the cutting torch, though Ixil getting burned was an accident. He'd eavesdropped on Ixil and me as we discussed cutting a hole into the cargo area, and for obvious reasons didn't want us to do that. Gimmicking the torch was the only way he could come up with to stop us in the limited time he had to work with."

"Borodin—I mean, Cameron—was aboard the *Icarus* with us?" Shawn asked. "Where was he hiding?"

"He must have been in the gap between the inner and outer hulls," Nicabar said. "It was the perfect hiding place. None of us even knew there was that much space in there until we started taking the ship apart."

"That's exactly it," I confirmed. "He surfaced once or twice to touch base with Tera, or to check our course heading on the computer-room repeater displays. But mostly he just lay low."

"So where is he now?" Everett asked. "I trust you're not going to try to tell us he's still hidden aboard somewhere?"

"I'd be very surprised to find that he was," I said. "Getting back to the main point, it turns out Cameron was the one responsible for those lethal chemicals being in Ixil's cabin in the first place."

"You're wrong," Tera snapped, her eyes blazing. "I already told you Dad didn't want to hurt him or anyone else."

"I didn't say he did," I said mildly. "Actually, his part in all that was to save Ixil's life. But I'll come back to that.

"So as I said, some of these incidents can be explained away," I continued, letting my gaze sweep around the table. "But not all of them, unfortunately. Which brings us to the murder—the deliberate murder—of our first mechanic, Jaeger Jones."

"Murder?" Chort said, his voice almost too whistly in his agitation for me to understand. "I thought it was an accident."

"It wasn't," I told him. "But the murderer hoped

most of us would think it was. All of us, in fact, except one person."

"But that's ridiculous," Everett snorted. "Why would the Patth want to kill Jones?"

"I never said the Patth had anything to do with it," I said. "But since you bring it up, that very question is what had me stymied for so long. You remember Shawn's disease-crazed escape on Potosi, and the Najiki Customs officials who nearly impounded the ship? That was our murderer's handiwork, too."

"What do you mean, his handiwork?" Tera asked. "I thought Shawn broke free on his own."

"No, he had help, though he probably doesn't remember it," I said. "The murderer needed Shawn to run away so that everyone would scatter to search for him and he'd be free to make a couple of private vid calls. The stumbling point here is that our killer seemed hell-bent on stopping the *Icarus,* no matter what he had to do. Yet at every place where he might have turned us over to the Patth, he didn't do it."

"Sounds like you're describing a schizophrenic," Everett murmured.

"Or a plain, flat-out psycho," Shawn added, glancing furtively around the table. "Someone who kills just for the fun of it."

"Actually, there's nothing unbalanced about him at all," I assured them. "But all right; let's assume for a minute that he *is* a nutcase. Let me then throw out another question, one that helped me start thinking in the right direction. Here we have Arno Cameron, creator of an enormous financial and industrial empire, wandering through the hot spots of Meima looking for a crew to get this vitally important piece of hardware back to Earth. Question: Given that Cameron's success must have been at least partially based on being an excellent judge of character, how in the world did he *not* catch on to the fact that one of the people he was hiring was a schizophrenic, psychotic potential murderer?"

For a minute all I saw in their faces was confusion, either at the question itself or because they were puzzling over the answer to it. All their faces, that is, except Tera's. In that instant I saw in her suddenly wide eyes that the pieces were finally starting to fall into place. "The answer, of course," I continued, not waiting for the class to respond, "is that he didn't sense any such problem because one of you is *not* the man he hired for your particular slot on the ship."

Chort found his voice first. "That is incredible," he said, the whistling under only slightly better control. "How would anyone have known the *Icarus* was valuable enough to do such a thing?"

"And once he knew it, why didn't he just go to the Patth and turn us in?" Shawn added. "This makes less sense than the psycho nutcase theory."

"Not really," I said. "The answers, in order, are that he had no idea at all that there *was* anything special about the *Icarus*. And he didn't turn the ship in to the Patth because his purpose in coming aboard was something else entirely."

I nodded to Everett. "Everett was the one who finally pushed me onto the right track," I said. "It was back when you all learned what the *Icarus* was carrying, and he pointed out that Borodin and the Patth weren't the only possible players in this game. I suddenly realized that he was right; and furthermore realized who the other player was."

"Who?" Tera demanded.

I lifted a hand. "Me."

There was a short silence. "I don't get it," Shawn said. "What are you talking about?"

"I'm talking about me, and about the people I work for," I told him. "And about the fact that the murderer came aboard the *Icarus* for the sole purpose of delivering me a message. A lesson in obedience."

My gun had been waving almost idly around the table, the hand gripping it making small gestures as I spoke. Now, in a single smooth motion, I brought it to point rock-steady at the center of the large torso looming up over the far end of the table from me. "You can tell him, Everett," I said quietly, "that I got the message."

Another silence descended on the room, this one as thick and dark as tar paste. "I don't know what the hell you're talking about," Everett said at last, his voice husky and as dark as the silence had been.

"I'm talking about a crime boss named Johnston Scotto Ryland," I said. "A man who thought I needed to be taught a lesson about strict obedience to one's orders and one's master."

"Wait a minute, wait a minute," Shawn said, sounding bewildered. "You've lost me completely. How did a crime boss get into this?"

"Because he's a crime boss who's holding a half million of McKell's debt," Nicabar said, his eyes studying me with an intensity I didn't much care for. "McKell's been smuggling for him for the past few years."

"You're a *smuggler*?" Shawn demanded, staring accusingly at me. "So that's how you got the borandis so easily. I should have guessed that a big simon-pure hotshot like you—"

"Put a baffle on it, Shawn," Nicabar cut him off. "So what did you do to earn this lesson, McKell?"

"Ixil and I had a cargo of his bound for Xathru," I said. "We were running a little ahead of schedule, so I diverted us briefly to Meima."

"Why?" Tera asked.

"I'll get to that later," I said. "Ryland has informers everywhere, even on a backwater world like Meima. I think Ryland was already having suspicions about my loyalty, so when one of his snitches reported I'd landed there instead of Xathru he apparently concluded I was getting ready to jump ship or double-cross him or some such thing. Regardless, he decided I needed a lesson on why that was a bad idea. Were you that informer, Everett, or just the local muscle for the territory?"

Everett didn't answer. "Well, the personnel list's not important," I said. "Either way, Ryland ordered Everett to tail me and find out what I was up to. He followed me as I wandered around Meima; and was probably right there in that taverno when Cameron came over and offered me the pilot's post aboard the *Icarus*."

"How did he know you'd been hired?" Tera asked. "Unless he was close enough to overhear, couldn't you two just have been having a chat?"

"I'm sure he wasn't that close," I said. "I was keeping a close watch, and I would have remembered anyone sitting that close. But he didn't have to hear anything. All he needed was to see Cameron give me a guidance tag to know I was taking a job with him.

"So when Cameron left, Everett decided to tail him instead of staying on me, probably hoping to find out who exactly I was dealing with. I had planned to follow Cameron myself, but I got diverted by a trio of unhappy Yavanni and lost him. He followed Cameron, watched him hire a couple more crewers; and then apparently decided to take a closer look at one of you. So he let Cameron leave, followed his latest acquisition into a nice dark alley, and clobbered him."

"And this person was who?" Tera asked.

"Whoever Cameron had hired to be ship's medic, of course," I said. "Because when Everett called to report what he'd found—which wasn't much—Ryland told him to take this person's place and follow me aboard the *Icarus*. Fortunately for us, Everett was actually qualified to handle the job. Or maybe it wasn't just luck; maybe he'd picked on the medic on purpose."

Chort whistled suddenly, a sound that hurt my ears. "I remember," he said. "He was the last to arrive. He said he had been delayed at the gate."

"Actually, he'd probably been skulking around the side of one of the other ships watching the rest of us gathering," I said. "He probably had a whole story worked out to spin for Cameron about how he'd bought the job from a buddy who'd suddenly taken ill or something."

Nicabar snorted gently. "Pretty pathetic story."

"It may have been something better." I cocked an eyebrow at Everett. "Feel free to jump in if you feel your creativity or cleverness is being maligned."

"No, no, keep going," he said evenly. "It's all nonsense, of course, but it does make for fascinating listening."

Out of the corner of my eye I caught the slight wrinkling of Nicabar's forehead. Everett didn't seem particularly worried; and if there was anyone who had a right to be worried at the moment, it was Everett.

"Whatever his story was, it turned out to be unnecessary," I continued, trying to distract Nicabar's attention away from questions about Everett's unconcerned attitude. The last thing I wanted right now was to have a former EarthGuard Marine to go all suspicious of this setup. "Cameron didn't show up, so Everett simply pretended he was the one who'd been hired in the first place."

"You know, McKell, Everett's right," Shawn growled. "This is all Grade-A speculation. You said yourself Cameron got away from you on Meima. How could you possibly know what happened?"

"It's not speculation at all," I said. "You see, I had a brief talk with Cameron after the incident with Ixil's cabin. He told me he'd tackled someone busily preparing a poison-gas mixture out in the *Icarus*'s lower corridor; but he further told me that *it wasn't anyone from the crew*. His assumption was that it was someone who'd come in from outside the ship; but if one of the crew had let a stranger in, why wasn't he there with him to help carry out this second murder? No, it's much simpler to assume that one of his original crewers was replaced right from the start."

"You said Everett came aboard to deliver a message," Tera said. "What did you mean by that?"

"In Ryland's eyes, I was flirting with treason," I said, feeling my fingers tightening on my plasmic as I stared blackly across the length of the table at Everett. "But apparently he thought I could still be redeemed, or at least could be scared back into the fold. And so in his typically crude and heavy-handed way, he ordered Everett to kill my partner."

"Your partner?" Tera gasped. "Jones was your partner?"

"No, of course not," I bit out, a flood of emotion suddenly washing over me. An innocent man had died, all because of me. "Jones was exactly as advertised: a mechanic Cameron hired off the street for the *Icarus*. And that's where Everett made the mistake that so muddied the water that it took me until now to figure it out. He was so convinced that my partner and I were both jumping ship and abandoning Ryland's contraband on Meima that he just assumed that the *Icarus*'s mechanic was my partner. Add to that Jones's natural friendliness and social ease, and it probably looked to him like we'd known each other for years.

"And so, knowing that it was traditionally the mechanic's job to assist with any spacewalks, he sabotaged the rebreather on the suit that was Jones's size and sat back to wait for the inevitable."

I gestured toward Everett with my plasmic. "But then you made a slip, a small one, which I didn't catch until a comment Revs made on Palmary jogged it back to mind. We'd gone to Xathru to turn Jones's body over to the port authorities and incidentally to pick up Ixil. While we were all out of the ship you called Ryland to report that the foul deed was done, but also told him I'd said something about bringing yet another partner aboard to fill Jones's slot. Ryland confirmed that you'd missed your intended target, but since his cargo had indeed been delivered on schedule it was all cool now and to just stay aboard and keep an eye on me."

"So where was the slip?" Shawn asked. "I don't see any slip."

"The slip came later," I said, watching Everett's face. "When you came into the ship while I was talking to Ixil in the wraparound. You took one look at him and said, 'So *this* is your partner.' There's no reason for you to have put it that way unless you'd already believed someone else was my partner."

Everett's expression didn't change, but there was just the slightest twitch of his lip. Enough to show that, despite his protests, I'd hit the mark.

Nicabar cleared his throat. "Question. If everything was so cool, why did he try to kill Ixil on Potosi?"

"Because between Xathru and Potosi the situation suddenly stopped being cool," I told him. "The first thing I did when we reached Potosi was to call Ryland to get the location of a dealer I could buy borandis from. By that time the swirl of Patth activity around the *Icarus* was starting to heat up, and Ryland was none too happy that one of his people—me—was at the center of all the attention."

"Why. didn't he just tell you to jump ship?" Shawn asked.

"Because he knew I wouldn't do it," I said. "I'd already told him that part of my cover as a poor but honest ship's pilot was to stick with the *Icarus,* and he knew better than to argue the point with me over a StarrComm link. Besides, he already had a plan that would preempt the whole decision.

"You'd all been told to stay aboard ship while I went to get the borandis. But Everett had orders to check in with Ryland, so he loosened Shawn's restraints enough that he'd be able to work his way free and escape. Then, while the rest of you were out searching, Everett headed to the StarrComm building. Maybe you even called while I was still talking to him; he was off the line a long time looking up the location of a drug dealer to steer me to.

"Anyway, Ryland told him to do two things. First, to phone in an anonymous tip to Najiki Customs that we had smuggled gemstones aboard; and second, to kill Ixil, who Everett told him was still sleeping off his burns. When customs found a dead body aboard and locked the *Icarus* down for investigation, Ryland reasoned, I would be out by default.

"Unfortunately for all his cleverness, everything went wrong from that point on. Cameron caught Everett preparing to kill Ixil, clobbered him, and put the chemical vials inside Ixil's room where Everett couldn't easily get at them again."

I looked at Tera. "Do you remember, Tera, when you cut into my phone conversation with Everett to tell us you'd found Shawn? Do you remember how he sounded?"

"He did seem a little odd," she said, her forehead wrinkled with thought. "A little blurry, as I recall."

"He was a lot blurry, actually," I said. "At the time, I assumed it was because Shawn had hit him during his escape. Now, I know it was because he hadn't yet recovered from your father's one-two punch."

"Dad keeps in pretty good shape," Tera said. "I'll bet he still can pack a wallop."

"Especially when properly inspired," I agreed. "I'll have to look up your throw-boxing record, Everett, and see if you had a history of easy knockouts or whether Cameron was just lucky. At any rate, when Everett came to, he knew he wouldn't have time to come up with a Plan B before the Najik arrived, so he hightailed it off the ship, remembering to lock the hatchway behind him the way it had been when you'd all scattered to look for Shawn.

"Sure enough, the Najik arrived in force and prepared to open the ship the hard way. And there Everett's second stroke of bad luck came in: Chort returned to the ship about the same time and decided they shouldn't go in without the captain being there. So he blocked their path; and *no* one in the Spiral goes out of their way to irritate Crooea. The Najik were probably in the process of discussing protocol with their HQ when the third and final bit of bad luck arrived."

"You?" Nicabar suggested.

"Me," I confirmed. "Ryland knew how far across the city he had sent me for the borandis, and figured the whole thing would be over and done with long before I could make it back. What he didn't know was that the sky was going to open up and rain small mammals, and that as a result I would hire a cab instead of using the more anonymous public transports the way his employees are supposed to. At any rate, I got back in time to bluff the Najik out of a real search, and we were off again."

"An amazing bit of deduction," Everett commented, shaking his head in feigned wonderment. Apparently, he still wasn't ready to give it up. "Seriously flawed, of course, but still interesting to listen to. Tell me this, then, Mr. Detective: If I was so determined to get you or Ixil, why did I risk my life to help get you away from the Patth on Palmary? To the point of even getting shot, as you may recall?"

"Oh, I recall, all right," I said with a nod. "And the reason is simple, even if the rest of the details are a little murky. You didn't hurt Ixil or me because by then you knew just how valuable the *Icarus* really was and that Ryland would definitely want to get hold of it himself. You needed a pilot to get off the planet; hence, the selfless volunteer work."

With my free hand I gestured to Nicabar. "Revs,

however, was a different and more serious matter entirely. You needed a pilot and an engine specialist to fly the *Icarus;* but with Ixil and Revs both around, you had *two* engine specialists. Under other circumstances you probably would have been happy to have the duplication; but sometime in the preparation for my rescue Revs must have let it slip that he was an ex-EarthGuard Marine. That was great for getting me out, but not so great when you looked further down the line.

"And so, when Ixil left you in the main club room as rear guard, you propped up one of the dead Iykams in a likely position behind some of the tables, picked out a spot nearby, and then shot yourself in the leg."

"He shot *himself*?" Chort whistled. "But why?"

"Two reasons," I said. "First, because he needed an excuse for why he was out of sight when Revs and Ixil brought me in from the back room. Remember, he had to shoot at Revs from concealment near where he'd set up the dead Iykam, then move a couple of tables away from there and shoot the corpse in the back if it was to look plausible. The only possible reason he could have for lying down on the job was if he'd been shot."

I shrugged. "As it happened, he wasn't as good or as lucky as he'd hoped, and was only able to wound Revs instead of killing him. Still, for putting him more or less out of action it was good enough."

I was looking directly at Everett as I spoke; and so it was that I caught the flicker of relief that crossed his face just before the quiet and all-too-familiar voice came from the archway behind me. "Very clever, Jordan," the voice said. "Very clever indeed."

I took a deep breath as the rest of the people around the table once again became stunned marble statues. "And the second reason he shot himself," I added, letting the breath out in a resigned sigh, "was that he wanted an excuse to stay aboard the *Icarus* after the rest of us came up here to the lodge. That StarrComm call he'd made, you see, wasn't to any doctor friend."

With my free hand, not turning or even looking around, I gestured to the archway behind me. "May I introduce you all to Johnston Scotto Ryland."

CHAPTER

24

"I'm impressed, Jordan, really I am," Brother John said, his voice accompanied by the sound of measured footsteps coming toward me across the wooden floor. "So that's why you were sitting on the portico all afternoon, was it? Waiting to see if I'd show up?"

"Not really," I told him. "No—don't try it," I added, shifting my aim toward Nicabar as he began to ease one hand toward the edge of the table.

"Yes, do listen to the man," Brother John agreed. "At least, if you want to live. You can put your gun down, too, Jordan, there's a good boy. So you didn't expect me to show up?"

"Not while I was watching, no," I said, laying my plasmic on the table and only then half turning to look around behind me. Brother John was standing in the archway, beaming with apparent ease in our direction, as six of the biggest and meanest-looking thugs I'd ever seen strode purposefully toward us. Their faces were without a doubt those of casual killers; the large black guns they were pointing at us made my plasmic look like a toy in comparison. "I assumed Everett was watching the cliffs behind the lodge, waiting for you to arrive."

"Don't be absurd," Brother John said. His voice was still cheerful, but there was a sudden undercurrent of menace beneath it. "You don't really think I'd have let you get here ahead of us, do you? We've been waiting in the back wing of the lodge for almost a day now. No, I think you were waiting for Everett to get tired of his vigil and come inside."

"What exactly is going on here?" Tera asked, her voice trying hard to be calm but not entirely succeeding.

"I should think that was obvious," Brother John said, his gaze still on me. "We're taking the *Icarus* and its alien stardrive off your hands."

"I'm afraid I hadn't gotten to that part yet," I said apologetically, turning back to the table. The bodyguards had reached us now, and as four of them stood watch the other two hauled Ixil and Chort to their feet and began a quick but thorough frisking. "Everett was told to lure us here with the promise of a safe haven. Mr. Ryland and his people were, we know now, waiting in hiding here in the comfort of the lodge. As soon as the rest of us were inside out of the way, the plan was to sneak out to the ship and take off, leaving us stranded."

The thugs found no weapons on Ixil or Chort, pushed them back down into their chairs, and moved on to Tera and Shawn. "I'm surprised they didn't just line us up and shoot us," Tera bit out, glaring ice-shredders at Brother John and ignoring as best she could the hands moving over her body.

"You underestimate Mr. Ryland," I told her.

"Yes, indeed," Brother John seconded. "After all, you already owe me your lives once over. It was my people on Palmary who stood guard over the spaceport during your mad rush off the planet. As well as in the control tower, I might add."

"I wondered why we got away so easily," Nicabar murmured. "The least the Patth should have done was lock down all departures."

"They tried," Brother John said, beaming some more. "Indeed they did. The pressure was applied, and the governmental authorities had given the orders. Somehow, though, the controllers were able to see through to a better and more enlightened reasoning."

"We do owe him that," I agreed. "But when I said you'd underestimated him, Tera, I was referring to something else entirely. Mr. Ryland would never think of killing us here. Not when he can make a little extra money by turning us over to the Patth."

Tera stared at me, her mouth dropping open. "Are you saying—?" She looked back at Brother John. "You *are* a slime."

"I'd warn your lady friend to be quiet, Jordan," Brother John said, a mid-November chill in his voice. "Particularly since the value of your lives has decreased markedly in the past three minutes."

"What's that supposed to mean?" Nicabar asked calmly. The thugs had relieved Tera of her pepperbox shotgun pistol; and now it was Nicabar's and my turn.

"He means he wasn't planning to sell us to the Patth just to pick up a little spare change," I explained, wincing as the searching hands ran afoul of my assortment of sore muscles and joints. "It was mainly to buy him more time to get the *Icarus* out of here and bury it somewhere. Since none of us would know what had happened to the ship, the Patth could interrogate us until June without learning anything that would do them any good."

"Nice guys," Shawn muttered, shying back as one of the thugs sent him a warning look.

"You know, Jordan, I do believe I've been guilty of underestimating you," Brother John said as one of the searchers found Nicabar's Kochran-Uzi and tucked it away. "No, no, don't sit," he added as they started to push the two of us back into our seats. "You and your alien partner are coming with me. You realize you never told me he was an alien?"

"Yes, I know," I said. "Which was why Everett was able to mistake Jones for my partner in the first place. You hadn't told him Ixil was an alien because at the time you didn't know it yourself."

"I hate aliens," Brother John said conversationally. "Almost as much as I hate alien-lovers. Everett, you might as well come with us, too. The rest of you will stay here while we decide what to do with you."

"You might want the girl, too, Mr. Ryland," Everett said, gesturing toward Tera as he got to his feet. "Mc-Kell says she's Arno Cameron's daughter."

"Really," Brother John said, and for the first time since he'd come in I saw a flicker of genuine surprise cross his face. "By all means, bring her along. After all, McKell might need extra persuasion."

"Persuasion?" Nicabar asked as the nearest thug hauled Tera back to her feet.

"Yes," Brother John said, his voice suddenly dark. "It seems our too-too-clever alien-lover did something to the *Icarus*'s control systems. Our people can't get anything to work."

"I didn't want you leaving without having a chance for this little chat," I said mildly, looking over at Everett. "Everett, tell the truth. You put up a good show here; but you really *did* kill Jones, didn't you?"

He snorted. "So for all that bluster you really didn't know for sure, huh?" he sneered. "Of course I killed him. What, you think *Chort* did it?"

"Just wanted to make sure," I murmured.

"Glad we could clear that up," Brother John said. "Dar, Kinrick; you stay here. The rest of you, come with me."

The walk back to the *Icarus* seemed a lot longer this

time. Brother John took the lead, with Everett and one of his men at his sides. Behind them, Ixil, Tera, and I were herded along by the other three, who made sure to keep us a respectful five paces behind the others in case one of us suddenly felt the urge to commit suicide by trying to jump them.

It was darker outside now. Darker and colder, and the light breeze that had been rustling the leaves earlier had picked up into something stiff and unpleasant. Which were, not coincidentally, words that also described Tera as she stalked along in bitter silence beside me, undoubtedly heaping full blame for the situation squarely on my head. To be fair, it was hardly a point of view I could disagree with.

But at the moment I didn't really care about the cold or the footing or Tera's anger or even the gun digging into my left kidney. My entire attention was on the dice I could visualize rolling across a mental table in front of my eyes. The dice had been thrown, the gamble had been made; and in a handful of minutes I would find out whether I'd won or lost.

There was a shadowy figure waiting in the open hatchway as we reached the *Icarus* and started up the ladder. Brother John went first, followed by his bodyguard and Everett, then Tera, another guard, and Ixil. The other two guards saved me for last, then sandwiched me between them as the three of us went up the ladder. Either Brother John considered me the most dangerous of the group, or else the fact that I had been the one to gimmick the ship entitled me to special handling.

Brother John had gone on ahead, but Tera and Ixil were still waiting as I reached the wraparound, together with their guards, the shadowy figure I'd seen waiting up there, and two more of his buddies. I'd thought the bodyguards Brother John had brought to the lodge were big, ugly, and well armed, but this latter group beat them hands down on all three counts. Silently, they gestured with their guns; just as silently, we walked along the wraparound to the main sphere.

The hatch to the sphere was closed. The leading thug opened it and stepped through, bobbling his balance somewhat as he passed through the gravity change. Tera and Ixil went next, negotiating the discontinuity with the grace of long practice. Holding my breath, I followed.

The sphere looked more or less the way I'd left it earlier that evening, except that the inner lights were blazing cheerfully away and that there were another eight strangers glowering at us. Four of them, stamped from the same mold as our current escort, were standing in a loose group near the bottom of the sphere; three others, working diligently at my helm and nav setup up the forward side of the hull, were apparently the pilot and engine specialists who were supposed to have had the *Icarus* well on its way by now.

But it was the eighth man who caught my full attention, the man waiting at the exact bottom of the sphere as if not trusting the alien gravity that pinned his tech people to the deck halfway up the side. He was a small man, at least compared to the four bodyguards grouped around him, well past middle age despite the signs of extensive rejuvenation therapy, wearing a dark and expensive suit and some muted and even more expensive jewelry. His face was old; his expression was impassive; and his eyes were as dead as a thousand-year-old corpse. He was a man I had never met, but I knew instantly who he was.

The rolling dice had come to a halt. And I'd won.

"You must be McKell," the man said as Brother John led us down the hull toward him, his voice as dead as his eyes.

"Yes," I acknowledged. "And you must be Mr. Antoniewicz. I'm very pleased to finally meet you."

"Are you," he said. Some people, or so the saying goes, can undress you with their eyes. Antoniewicz's look was more like stripping me straight down to the bone. "Interesting. Most of those who are brought to meet me are not at all looking forward to the experience. Many of them find themselves screaming, in fact, and don't seem able to stop."

I swallowed despite myself, all the stories and rumors of what happened to people brought before Antoniewicz flashing through my mind. "I understand that, sir," I said humbly. "But if I may be so bold, I suspect none of those others were bringing the sort of gift I have to offer you."

The corners of his lips might have turned up, but it would have taken a micrometer to measure it. The smile, if that's what it was, made his eyes look even deader. "Really. I was under the impression that the *Icarus* was now mine by simple right of possession."

"I agree," I said, passing over the fact that if I hadn't cooperatively flown the ship into his waiting arms it *wouldn't* have been in his possession. Considering the size and number of his bodyguards, comments like that were quite easy for me to stifle. "I was actually speaking of something else entirely. Or, rather, some*one* else entirely."

"Wait a minute," Everett growled, taking a step toward me. "You take credit for her and I'll cave your face in."

"Ryland?" Antoniewicz invited, gesturing at Tera.

"Everett claims she's the daughter of Arno Cameron," Brother John said. I could still hear the phony good humor in his voice, but it was curiously subdued. Most everything good, I suspected, humor included, would darken or wilt in Antoniewicz's presence. "Cameron's the man who—"

"I know who he is," Antoniewicz said. "Tell me why Everett thinks he deserves credit for her."

"I'd like to take a moment to remind everyone that I'm not anyone's carnival prize," Tera cut in, glaring at each of us in turn but saving her most withering look for me. I couldn't really blame her on that count, either; if I hadn't revealed her identity during my brilliant summing up of the case a few minutes ago, she'd be just one more anonymous prisoner back in the lodge.

I cleared my throat. "If I might explain—"

"Quiet," Antoniewicz said. He hadn't raised his voice, or changed his inflection, or even looked at me—the full force of his gaze was on Tera at the moment. And yet, my mouth clamped shut, almost of its own accord, my attempted mediation cut short as if guillotined. The sheer presence of the man, the power and evil lurking veiled beneath the surface, were almost physical qualities like his voice or face or expensive suit. For the first time, I truly understood how it was he'd been able to create such a huge and wide-ranging criminal empire.

Tera wasn't nearly as easily impressed as I was. "I don't know who exactly you are," she continued on into the silence, "but whatever it is you think I'm worth to you, you're sadly mistaken."

"No, I don't think so," Antoniewicz disagreed mildly. "Of all those who worked closely on this ship, only your father remains at large. You're the lever that will pry him out of hiding."

"If you think that, you're more of a fool than I thought," Tera scoffed, clearly not caring whether she offended him or not. Across our little circle I saw both Everett and Brother John wince, with Pix and Pax giving a little twitch as well. One simply didn't talk that way to Mr. Antoniewicz. "My father is fully aware of what this ship is worth to humanity," Tera continued. "And he has never yet let personal considerations get in the way of what needs to be done. Whatever information he has about the *Icarus,* the last thing he'll do is give it away to someone like you. Certainly not under duress."

"Not even with his daughter's life at stake?" Antoniewicz asked, his voice politely incredulous.

"No," Tera said flatly, straightening to an almost-haughty posture as pride momentarily eclipsed every evidence of fear and uncertainty. I could imagine the true royalty of old facing the peasant mobs with the same courage and disdain.

And with the same results. "Pity," Antoniewicz said, sounding almost regretful. "In that case, you're worth nothing to me at all." He looked at the man standing behind me to my right and lifted a languid hand.

And abruptly, the pressure of the gun muzzle on my back vanished as, out of the corner of my eye, I saw him bring the weapon around to point straight at Tera's face.

I don't know why I did it. Antoniewicz was bluffing, and I *knew* he was bluffing. He would never kill a potential hostage whose usefulness hadn't yet been tested, not even one who'd verbally spit in his eye the way she had. I knew it was an act, and if I'd had another fraction of a second to think about it I'd have realized that I was playing directly into his hands.

But I'd promised Cameron that I would watch over his daughter, and the reflexes just kicked in on their own. With my right hand I slapped the thug's gun off target, then spun around on my right heel to drive my right elbow into his solar plexus as I grabbed for the weapon with my left hand.

It was about as close to a complete failure as anything I'd ever tried in my life. My elbow struck an unyielding slab of body armor, my snatch for the gun missed completely as he twitched it aside out of my reach, and before I could regain my balance to try something else he'd taken a long pace backward and was looking at me with the sort of expression you might use for a particularly interesting new species of insect. About the only thing that kept it from being a

THE ICARUS HUNT 441

complete failure was that I didn't fall flat on my face in the process.

I braced myself, waiting for the inevitable flurry of shots and the searing pain that would accompany them. But once again, my reflexive thought was out of step with reality. "Interesting," Antoniewicz said, his voice cutting calmly across the sudden tension. "You were right, Ryland. He *is* something of the heroic type, isn't he?"

"And seems to have soft feelings for Ms. Cameron, besides," Brother John agreed. He was openly gloating now, I saw, though whether that was at my failure or his own cleverness I couldn't tell.

"The only feelings I have for her are ones you couldn't understand," I growled back with the ill temper of a man who's just completely humiliated himself. "Loyalty, for one. Or any of the other sympathetic emotions human beings have for each other. Of course, in your case, I use the term 'human being' in its loosest possible sense. You're a lot less human than most of the aliens I know."

The gloating vanished from Brother John's face, the handsome face turning suddenly ugly. "Listen, McKell—"

"Enough," Antoniewicz cut him off, giving me the same interesting-insect look his bodyguard had. "Whatever the details of his character flaws, it's clear now that McKell would not wish harm to come to the lady." He lifted his eyebrows slightly. "That *is* clear, is it not?"

I looked at Tera. Some of that earlier defiance was still simmering in her eyes, but the face behind them had gone noticeably pale. The aura of death and evil surrounding Antoniewicz was starting to get to her. "What's that supposed to mean?" I asked, giving bluff and bluster one last try.

I might as well have saved myself the trouble. "Don't play stupid, McKell," Antoniewicz reproved me. "It doesn't suit you. Will you release the locks you put on the *Icarus*'s systems? Or do my men take Ms. Cameron back to the engine room?"

The ship, I noticed dimly, suddenly felt very cold. "Let me offer an alternative deal," I said, my tongue feeling sluggish in my mouth. Antoniewicz was starting to get to me, too. "If you'll let Tera, Ixil, and me leave here unharmed, I'll ungimmick the ship *and* give you something that'll be far more valuable to you than all three of us put together."

"He's stalling," Brother John said contemptuously. "He hasn't got anything left to bargain with."

"On the contrary," I said. "I have Arno Cameron."

"You can tell us where he is?" Antoniewicz asked.

"I can do better than that," I said, trying hard to ignore the suddenly stricken look on Tera's face. "I can deliver him to you. Right now."

The atmosphere was suddenly electric. "What are you talking about?" Brother John demanded, looking around as if expecting Cameron to pop out of the alien hull. "Where is he?"

"He's hiding in the smaller sphere," I said, settling for the simplest explanation. Giving them the complete story would only confuse the issue. "I can go in there and get him."

"Really," Antoniewicz said, his voice suddenly cold. "Do you think us fools, McKell? My people checked every cubic centimeter of this ship before I came aboard."

"Maybe everything out here and in the engine section, but not the small sphere," I said, shaking my head. "Not visually, anyway. That place is a mess of cables and wires—they'd have been hours at it. What did they use, body-heat sensors and motion detectors?"

"And a few other specialized devices," Antoniewicz said, eyeing me speculatively. "You realize, I trust, that Cameron dead is not a bargaining chip."

"He's not dead," I assured him. "There's an area in

there that sensors can't reach. All that alien machinery, I suppose."

Antoniewicz glanced at Brother John, turned back to me. "All right," he said. "Tell me where he is. I'll send one of my men in after him."

"It's very hard to find the place," I said. "Besides, if it's anyone but me, he'll probably put up a fight. That could damage something."

"Possibly even Cameron himself," Brother John murmured.

"I'm not letting you out of my sight," Antoniewicz said in a tone that said there would be no further discussion on the matter. "Tell us where he is."

I sighed. "That's not necessary," I said reluctantly. "I told him that when it was safe to come out I'd either come personally or else send in one of Ixil's ferrets. There's an entrance in the engine room that should be open."

"Good," Antoniewicz said. He was all calm again now that he'd gotten his way. "Send him."

I looked at Ixil and nodded. He nodded back, and Pix scampered down his leg and headed up toward the wraparound. "You'd better tell whoever you have in the wraparound and engine room not to stop him," I warned.

"There's no one back there," Antoniewicz said. "I presume Cameron will be coming out the same way?"

"No, he'll come out here," I said, pointing to the covered access hole beside Tera's computer. "There's a better access panel over there."

"Open it," Antoniewicz said, flicking his eyes to one of the bodyguards. "While we wait, McKell, you can start fixing my ship."

"Yes, sir," I said. Furtively, with the feeling of someone about to rub salt into his own raw flesh, I looked over at Tera. Knowing that, however painful it was going to be, I had to see how she was taking this.

I was prepared for rage, for fear, for even borderline

hysteria. But there was none of that in her face. Not anymore. Her face was instead totally drained of emotion, as dead as Antoniewicz's eyes, the face of someone facing the end of all things with the certain knowledge that there was nothing left to be redeemed from the ashes. The strong industrialist's daughter, the proud and defiant royal personage—all of that was gone. There was nothing left but fatigue, and a young woman facing the inevitability of her own death.

"I trusted you," she said quietly.

I turned my eyes away. It hurt just exactly as bad as I'd expected it to. "I'm sorry," I said. "I did what I had to."

I estimated it would take about ten minutes for Pix to make it to the center of the sphere and trip the stargate mechanism. I took my time unlocking the seals I'd put on the *Icarus*'s helm and nav systems, with the result that nine of those minutes were gone by the time I walked back down to where Antoniewicz and the others were still waiting. "They can get started now," I told Antoniewicz, nodding up at the techs. "I locked down the computer and engine controls, too, but I can't undo that until the helm and nav have been fired up and done their self-checks."

"Then you should go up there so as to be ready for that occurrence," Antoniewicz said, gesturing up toward the computer and the two bodyguards standing watch over the now open access panel. "You've cost me far too much time as it is."

"It'll take another few minutes before I can get started," I told him. "In the meantime, I wanted to give you a warning."

His eyebrows lifted in obvious amusement. "Indeed? Something to do with you and the others, no doubt?"

"Not at all," I said. "I wanted to tell you that I've heard rumors that Geneva has folded under Patth pressure and forbidden all Earth citizens and associates to give aid to the *Icarus*."

"And you think such orders apply to *me*?" Antoniewicz said, even more amused.

"Not your core people, no," I said. "But a lot of your looser associates might get cold feet under that kind of pressure, particularly those quiet government and military contacts you've got who will now have management or senior officers looking over their shoulders. Add to that the Patth reward, which is probably doubling every six hours, and even you might have trouble moving and hiding the *Icarus*."

"I'm quite aware of the challenges involved," Antoniewicz said. "That was precisely why I came myself, bringing only those most loyal to me." He gave me another of those micrometer smiles. "That's also why I'll be taking the *Icarus* to one of my private estates when we leave here."

I glanced at Ixil. "I see," I said. "I presume you'll be dropping Ixil and Tera and me off on the way?"

He frowned, another micrometer-level expression. "Who said anything about dropping you off anywhere?"

"That was the deal," I reminded him, frowning in turn. "I would give you Cameron in exchange for Tera."

"Ah, yes," Antoniewicz said. "I forgot." He craned his neck to look at the helm. "Yodanna?" he called.

"Helm coming up now, Mr. Antoniewicz," one of the techs called back.

"What about the rest of the ship?"

"Checking now, sir, but it looks promising."

Antoniewicz looked back at me. "For such a clever man, McKell, you're amazingly stupid sometimes," he said. "Ms. Cameron is far too useful as insurance for her father's cooperation for me to release her. As for you and your alien, the two of you are far too dangerous to keep around any longer than necessary." He looked up again. "Yodanna?"

"Yes, sir," the call wafted its way back down to us.

"I've got the sequence he used. We can unlock the computer and engine systems ourselves."

Antoniewicz looked back at me. "And I would say that the moment of obsolescence has arrived sooner than expected," he said quietly. "I always offer a man the chance for final words, McKell. Have you any?"

A ripple of breeze brushed past my hair. "No last words, Mr. Antoniewicz," I said firmly, standing up straight and closing my eyes. "Go ahead and shoot."

Even with my eyes closed, it was like a strobe light had gone off in my face. A multiple strobe light, a dozen flickering bursts of light like the prophet Elijah calling fire down from heaven. I heard a gasp from somewhere beside me, a startled reflexive scream from Tera, an equally startled curse from Brother John.

And then, silence. Cautiously, wary of another round of flashes, I eased open my eyes.

Antoniewicz was standing rigidly exactly where I'd left him, his face utterly expressionless. Everett had turned completely white. Brother John's face was white, too, his expression that of a man walking through a graveyard in the dead of night.

Which was, I decided as I looked around, an extremely apt analogy. All around us, this most loyal group of Antoniewicz's bodyguards were sprawled on the deck where they'd stood, their weapons for the most part still clutched in rigid hands, the tops of their heads smoking with the nose-curling stink of burnt hair and skin and bone. Fire from heaven, indeed.

From Tera's direction came a sudden choked gasp—apparently, her vision was just now clearing up from the aftereffects of that multiple stutter of laser fire. "It's all right, Tera," I assured her quickly, crossing to her side. "Just relax. It's all over."

"But—" She broke off, looking back over her shoulder at the entrance to the wraparound.

"Not there," I told her, pointing above us. "There."

Even having known what to expect, I had to admit

the sight was something to behold. There were twelve of them grouped together in a tight knot in the center of the sphere, starting now to drift off in various directions toward the hull under the influence of the alien grav field. Their squashed-iguana faces were only partly visible through their helmet faceplates, the body-armored ferrets crouching on their broad shoulders adding a surrealistic touch of the ridiculous to the scene.

But there was nothing either surrealistic or ridiculous about the heavy military combat lasers in their hands, or in the steady professional grip with which they pointed them at Antoniewicz, Brother John, Everett, and the three techs.

"They're Royal Kalixiri commandos," I said into the stunned silence, just in case my audience was too shy to ask the question themselves. "Loaned to us by the one government in the Spiral that no longer has anything to lose by defying the Patth."

Tera was still staring up at them. "But—you said—where's my father?"

"He's safe," I told her. "The *Icarus* isn't a stardrive, you see. It's a stargate, connected to a duplicate somewhere hell and away across the galaxy. Your father accidentally triggered it and got bounced to the other end."

"The other end has Kalixiri in it?" Everett demanded, his voice distant and confused.

"Hardly," I said. "Or rather, it didn't until a couple of hours ago. The Kalixiri were waiting here when we landed, hidden down in the trees—that's the main reason I insisted on parking the ship so close in under the branches. Once it was dark, and once I'd chased Everett out and put on the hatchway floodlights so that the glare would mask their movements, they used a collapsible ladder and the latch grooves on the starboard side to climb onto the engine section, go in through that dorsal hatch, and from there into the small sphere and down the rabbit hole to where your father was waiting."

"So then . . . Pix?"

"Actually, I worked rather hard to maneuver Mr. Antoniewicz into insisting that Pix go in instead of me," I said, looking at Antoniewicz. The dead look had been replaced now by a clear and violent lust for death. My death. But then the Kalixiri were landing on the deck around him, and the commandos and armor and heavy lasers were between him and the rest of us, and he'd lost his chance forever. "When Pix went across, he took with him his visual memories of the number, weapon-status, and approximate placement of the men they'd have to take down. Popping in from nowhere, and in the last place anyone would expect an attack to come from, the whole thing was almost literally a duck shoot. The only real question was whether they'd get here before Antoniewicz decided I wasn't useful anymore and had me shot."

I looked at one of the commandos as he walked toward me, an empty spot on his shoulder showing where Pix had been sitting. Pix himself, I noted, was already settling onto Ixil's shoulder. "Speaking of being in time, Commander, what's the status of the lodge?"

"It has been taken," he said, his voice flavored with a thick regional accent. "I have only now been so informed."

"What are you talking about?" Brother John demanded. "You said—"

"Well, they didn't *all* go down the rabbit hole," I explained apologetically. "A second group was hidden somewhere in or near the lodge to take care of anyone you'd left outside the ship. Once the commander learned from Pix's memories that Nicabar and the others were being held hostage there, he knew to call in the details to the reserve troops as soon as they popped in here."

Tera looked at Brother John, then back to me. "But I thought you worked for these people," she protested. "You said you owed them a half-million commarks."

"So I did," I acknowledged. "And so I do. But you see, I was working for someone else long before Brother Johnston Scotto Ryland came out of the woodwork and smilingly mortgaged my soul. For that matter, long before I even ran up the debt that attracted him to me in the first place."

And then, finally, she got it. "You mean—?"

"Yes," I said, straightening up into an almost-forgotten military attention. I had my pride, too . . . and it had been a long time since I'd been able to say this to anyone at all. "I'm Major Jordan McKell, EarthGuard Military Intelligence, detached on Special Covert Branch duty. May I also introduce my boss: Colonel Ixil T'adee, Kalixiri Special Command for Drug Enforcement. Our job these past twelve years has been to work our way inside the Spiral's worst drug and gunrunning organizations and try to bring them down."

I turned to Antoniewicz. "And as I said before, Mr. Antoniewicz," I added quietly, "I'm very pleased to meet you. Badgemen all over the Spiral have been waiting a long time for you to come out of your hole so that you could finally be arrested. I'm honored you chose to do it for me."

CHAPTER

25

It was not exactly what you would call a cheerful group that was gathered around the table in the lodge dining room a little after dawn the next morning, but it beat to hell the atmosphere that had been there the last time around. Partly it was the smaller and more intimate nature of the assemblage, with Shawn and Chort off somewhere being debriefed, Ixil directing the group looking over the *Icarus,* and Antoniewicz and his assorted plug-uglies long gone under heavy Kalixiri guard. The fact that Cameron had had time for a shower probably helped a lot, too.

"I hope you know how close you came to getting your neck broken last time we were in here," Nicabar commented, picking carefully at the Kalixiri military delicacies the occupation troops had whipped up. It was a far cry from Chort's gourmet Craean stew, but the taste was adequate and it was certainly filling enough. "When you turned that plasmic on me I figured all that talk about Everett was just you stalling while you waited for your pals to arrive."

"You'd never have made it even halfway to my neck," I told him. "Antoniewicz's thugs would have cut you down in a heartbeat if you'd tried anything. Including going for your gun, incidentally, which is why I drew on you in the first place."

He snorted gently. "I thought I was being reasonably subtle about it."

"You were," I agreed. "But I haven't spent twelve years in Intelligence work without knowing what a surreptitious grab for a weapon looks like. Give me *some* credit."

"Personally, I give you a great deal of credit," Cameron commented around a mouthful of food. Alone of the four of us, he was already on his second helping. "You had me fooled all the way down the line, from Meima to our little chat at the other end of the starbunny trail, right up to the moment those Kalixiri commandos popped in and nearly gave me a heart attack."

"Sorry about that," I apologized. "Though I did wonder after our talk at the edge of forever whether you'd finally figured me out."

"I knew you weren't as simple as you seemed," he said, shaking his head. "But beyond that I didn't have a clue."

"You might have told him," Tera said, a touch of reflexive accusation in her voice. "He certainly wasn't going to tell anyone in *there*."

"But he would be coming out sometime," I reminded her. "And I didn't yet know what the circumstances of that homecoming were going to be."

"And it's infinitely safer in this sort of game if no one has had even a peek at your cards," Cameron said, rising to my defense. "Sir Arthur explained all of that in his message."

"What message?" Tera asked.

"A note from my boss," I explained. "Retired—sort of—General Arthur Sir Graym-Barker, former Intelligence Level Two Overseer and the Earthside director of this quiet little combined-services unit Ixil and I have been involved with all these years. The commando team brought it through the stargate with them so that your father would know what was going on."

"Unlike the rest of us," Nicabar said pointedly. "So what was that fluff you spun to Tera about having been kicked out of EarthGuard?"

"Not a single bit of fluff to it," I assured him. "The court-martial was completely and totally official. It had to be—I was trying to worm my way into the center of the Spiral's underworld, and everything in my record had to stand up to the kind of scrutiny we knew it would be getting someday. The time I spent with Customs and Rolvaag Brothers Shipping was more of the same window dressing, with the added value of giving me practical training in the sorts of things a soon-to-be smuggler needs to know. When I was finally ready, they gave me the *Stormy Banks* and instructions to pile up a mountain of debts and turned me loose."

"And that was when you met Ixil?" Nicabar asked.

"Actually, Ixil and I go back all the way to my EarthGuard days," I said. "In fact, he was the one who spotted me while trolling for prospective recruits and suggested to Uncl—I mean, Sir Arthur—that I be invited in. He spent my training years building up his own sordid background, so that when we publicly linked up we were about as sorry a pair of misfits as you could ever hope to meet."

"And you already knew this General Graym-Barker?" Tera asked, looking at her father.

"I met him about fifteen years ago, when we were developing an advanced targeting-system countermeasure for military stealthers," Cameron said. He made a face at me. "Of course, I thought he really *was* retired now or I never would have contacted him in the first place. The last thing I wanted was for the leaky bureaucratic sieve at Geneva to get hold of any of this."

"So *that's* why you were on Meima when this whole

thing started," Tera said, turning back to me. "You never did answer that question."

I nodded. "Sir Arthur told us your father was in some kind of trouble on Meima during one of my check-ins and asked us to swing over and assess the situation. I'd been wandering around the local tavernos for nearly four hours looking for him when we finally ran into each other."

I looked at Cameron. "Interestingly enough, he even said that, depending on how serious the danger you were in, I was authorized to do whatever was necessary to protect you, up to and including blowing my cover if there was no other way. Shows you just how highly you're considered up there in the corridors of power."

"I'm honored," Cameron murmured. "That's rather amusing, really, considering that I was prepared in turn to tell whoever he sent everything about the *Icarus* if there was no other way to secure his help."

"Just as well you didn't," I said. "You start showing your cards to someone and you never know if someone else is looking over your shoulder."

"As opposed to just dropping the cards faceup on the table," Nicabar commented dryly. "I thought Tera was going to have a stroke when you announced in front of everyone who she really was."

"I presume you've figured out why I did that?" I asked.

He nodded. "It took me a while, but eventually I got it."

"Well, *I* haven't," Tera said, frowning at me. "I assumed you were just tired. Or suddenly gone senile."

"Tired, yes; senile, possibly," I said. "But not on that account. Remember, I'd already checked the *Icarus* and knew the Kalixiri were aboard and the trap there was set. What I *didn't* know was what kind of contingency plan they had for anyone left behind in the lodge, whether they'd be able to move quickly enough to get you out. I made sure that Everett knew who you were so that you'd be brought back to the ship with us. You were in no danger from Antoniewicz—as he'd already explained, you were far too valuable to simply shoot out of hand. Whether or not the commandos arrived in time to save me, they would certainly be in time to save you."

There was a flicker of movement across the room, and I looked up to see Ixil step in through the wooden archway. "Ah, there you are," he said as he came toward our table. "Not sitting with your back to the door this time, I see."

"Don't be snide," I reproved him with an air of injured pride. "You know perfectly well I just didn't want my gun pointed anywhere near Brother John and his goons when they burst in on us. Any news?"

"All sorts of news," he said, pulling up a chair and sniffing appreciatively at the food. Pix and Pax weren't nearly so reticent; they bounded straight off his shoulders and headed for the serving plate. "The pilot tried to scramble the preliminary helm setting he'd been coding in, but we were able to reconstruct it. The combined force landed twenty minutes ago inside Antoniewicz's estate. They report it's been secured."

"Combined, eh?" I commented approvingly as Nicabar spooned some of the Kalixiri food onto his plate for the two ferrets. "I take it that means Sir Arthur was able to get Geneva to loosen up and send some human troops to assist."

"I believe he convinced them this operation had nothing to do with the *Icarus* and the Patth ultimatum," Ixil said. "Which is not entirely untrue."

"Not entirely at all," I agreed. "I hope they're being careful—Antoniewicz is bound to have a few booby traps set up for unexpected visitors."

"I'm sure they are." Ixil looked over at Cameron. "The other news you may be interested in is that there was a bit of confusion off Trondariok about two hours ago. A ship identified as the renegade freighter *Icarus* barely escaped from a group of three customs cruisers."

Cameron threw a startled look at Tera. "The *Icarus*? Was seen where?"

"Trondariok," Ixil repeated. "It's a Dariok colony world about ten light-years from Rachna."

For a moment Cameron still didn't get it. I watched his face, wondering idly how long it was going to take. And then, his face suddenly cleared. "Of course," he said, nodding. "Rachna. It's the duplicate *Icarus* we were building at the construction plant there. The one I was going to have flown to Meima."

"That's the one," I confirmed. "One of my other suggestions to Sir Arthur. A second Kalixiri commando team got in and commandeered it, with instructions to fly around that area for a week or so and make sure they're seen and identified."

"By then, if we're lucky," Ixil added, "the group we've got at Hinsenato will have finished making *their* copy off the blueprints the Kalixiri sent them from Rachna."

"Wait a minute," Nicabar said, his forehead wrinkled in thought. "Rachna. That's way over in the Eta Sindron region, isn't it?"

"That's right," I said.

"Well, hell, that's no good," he objected. "The Patth know we were on Palmary less than a week ago. We couldn't possibly have made it all the way to—"

He broke off, his face changing as he suddenly got it. "Oh," he said. "Right. Of course we couldn't make it with a standard stardrive. But the *Icarus* isn't supposed to be running with just a standard stardrive."

"And as far as the Patth are concerned, this little incident should solidly clinch that theory for them," I said, nodding. "So now we just have to lead them on. A couple of days after the *Icarus* disappears from the Trondariok area, it'll be spotted near Hinsenato, then somewhere else, and so on. The idea is to draw the chase far enough away from here that we'll be able to quietly move the real *Icarus* somewhere secure where we can start studying it."

"And what happens to us?" Nicabar asked. "The same gilded cage the Patth were offering?"

"For Shawn and Chort, some kind of protective custody will be required," I conceded. "At least until the *Icarus* has been tucked away someplace safe. That'll also give us some time to get their testimonies against Everett."

"So that was why you maneuvered him into admitting Jones's murder in front of all of us," Tera murmured. "So you'd have witnesses to his confession."

"Right," I said. "Just one more lever we can use against him if he decides to be stubborn about helping us dismantle Antoniewicz's organization. As for you and your father, power and influence being what it is, you're pretty much exempt from any threats Geneva can throw at you. Though I suspect Sir Arthur will strongly suggest you both stay with the project, wherever it finally gets set up."

"Don't worry on that count," Cameron said firmly. "The *Icarus* is my discovery and my property. Wild Yavanni couldn't drag me away from it now."

"Likewise," Tera seconded.

"We sort of figured you'd see things that way," I said. "And Ixil and I are accounted for, too." I turned to Nicabar. "Which just leaves you."

"What are my options?" he asked calmly.

"The Kalixiri want to toss you into the gilded cage with Shawn and Chort," I told him. "Frankly, I think that would be a waste of talent and ability.

"So here are your choices, or at least the ones I'm going to recommend to Sir Arthur. You can stay with Cameron and the research group, using your commando training and experience to help protect the project; or we can take you to meet Sir Arthur and see if he thinks you've got it in you to be a down-and-out smuggler type. We may have gotten Antoniewicz, but there are a lot of other fish in the cesspool that we'd like to see flopping around the bottom of our boat."

"I appreciate the offer," he said, looking at Cameron and Tera. "But this one's no contest. Here with the *Icarus* is where the future is going to be created. If we can figure out how that stargate works, the Spiral is going to change, almost overnight. The Spiral, hell— we'll be able to get to places in the rest of the galaxy we could never reach before."

He looked back at me. "And the one thing sure as hell is that the Patth will fight like demons every step of the way to keep us from pulling their little gold-weave rug out from under them. No, I think I'd like to stay here."

"Okay," I said, catching Ixil's eye and getting to my feet. "I'll go give Sir Arthur a call, and we'll see what we can work out. I'll let you know what he says." Nodding to Cameron and Tera, I headed across the room, leaving Ixil to the task of prying his ferrets away from their impromptu snack.

There in the archway, though, I paused and looked back. Nicabar was deep in quiet conversation with the Camerons; but as he leaned across the table it seemed to me that his eyes were lingering more on Tera than they were on her father, an attention that seemed to be reasonably mutual. And it occurred to me that after all the time the two of them had spent aboard the *Icarus,* surrounded by loathsome smugglers and potential murderers, having only each other to trust, they might have become a bit more than just shipmates. It would be interesting to drop back by the project in, say, six months and see if Cameron was now working under the protection of a future son-in-law.

Ixil was coming toward me now, Pix and Pax still munching away as they rode his shoulders. I made a mental note to offer him a small wager.

ABOUT THE AUTHOR

TIMOTHY ZAHN is one of science fiction's most popular voices, known for his ability to tell very human stories against a well-researched background of future science and technology. He won the Hugo Award for his novella *Cascade Point* and is the author of nineteen science fiction novels, including the bestselling *Star Wars* trilogy: *Heir to the Empire, Dark Force Rising,* and *The Last Command;* the novels *Conquerors' Pride, Conquerors' Heritage,* and *Conquerors' Legacy;* and three collections of short fiction. Timothy Zahn lives in Oregon.

Also from
TIMOTHY ZAHN
The #1 bestselling saga

Join Luke, Leia, Han, Chewbacca, and
all your favorite *Star Wars* characters for a
rousing romp among the stars. . . .

"Moves with a speed-of-light pace that captures the
spirit of the movie trilogy so well, you can almost hear the
John Williams sound track." —*The Providence Sunday Journal*

"Chock-full of all the good stuff you've come to expect from
a battle of good against evil." —*Daily News,* New York

___29612-4	HEIR TO THE EMPIRE	$5.99/$7.99 in Canada
___56071-9	DARK FORCE RISING	$5.99/$7.99
___56492-7	THE LAST COMMAND	$5.99/$7.99
___29804-6	SPECTER OF THE PAST	$5.99/$7.99
___57879-0	VISION OF THE FUTURE	$5.99/$8.99